J. Cooper

The Monikins

Anatiposi

J. Cooper

The Monikins

Reprint of the original, first published in 1871.

1st Edition 2023 | ISBN: 978-3-38211-415-2

Anatiposi Verlag is an imprint of Outlook Verlagsgesellschaft mbH.

Verlag (Publisher): Outlook Verlag GmbH, Zeilweg 44, 60439 Frankfurt, Deutschland
Vertretungsberechtigt (Authorized to represent): E. Roepke, Zeilweg 44, 60439 Frankfurt, Deutschland
Druck (Print): Books on Demand GmbH, In de Tarpen 42, 22848 Norderstedt, Deutschland

THE MONIKINS.

By J. FENIMORE COOPER.

"Then thou knewest her?" said the Knight

"Not I," answered the Squire; "but the person who told me the story said it was so true and certain, that if ever I should chance to tell it again, I might affirm upon oath that I had seen it with my own eyes." — SANCHO PANZA.

COMPLETE IN ONE VOLUME.

NEW EDITION.

NEW YORK:
PUBLISHED BY HURD AND HOUGHTON.
Cambridge: Riverside Press.
1871.

MONIKINS.

INTRODUCTION.

It is not improbable that some of those who read this book, may feel a wish to know in what manner I became possessed of the manuscript. Such a desire is too just and natural to be thwarted, and the tale shall be told as briefly as possible.

During the summer of 1828, while travelling among those valleys of Switzerland which lie between the two great ranges of the Alps, and in which both the Rhone and the Rhine take their rise, I had passed from the sources of the latter to those of the former river, and had reached that basin in the mountains that is so celebrated for containing the *glacier* of the Rhone, when chance gave me one of those rare moments of sublimity and solitude, which are the more precious in the other hemisphere from their infrequency. On every side the view was bounded by high and ragged mountains, their peaks glittering near the sun, while directly before me, and on a level with the eye, lay that miraculous frozen sea, out of whose drippings the Rhone starts a foaming river, to glance away to the distant Mediterranean. For the first time, during a pilgrimage of years, I felt alone with nature in Europe. Alas! the enjoyment, as all such enjoyments necessarily are amid the throngs of the old world, was short and treacherous. A party came round the angle of a rock, along the narrow bridle-path, in single files; two ladies on horseback followed by as many gentlemen on foot, and preceded by the usual guide. It was but small courtesy to rise and salute the dove-like eyes and blooming cheeks of the former, as they passed. They were English, and the gentlemen appeared to recognize me as a countryman. One of the latter stopped, and politely inquired if the passage of the Furca was obstructed by snow. He was told not, and in return for the information, said that I would find the Grimsel a little ticklish; "but," he added, smiling, "the ladies succeeded in crossing, and you will scarcely hesitate." I thought I might get over a difficulty that his fair companions had conquered. He then told me Sir Herbert Taylor was made adjutant-general, and wished me good morning.

I sat reflecting on the character, hopes, pursuits and interests of man, for an hour, concluding that the stranger was a soldier, who let some of the ordinary workings of his thoughts overflow in this brief and casual interview. To resume my solitary journey, cross the Rhone, and toil my way up the rugged side of the Grimsel, consumed two more hours, and glad was I to come in view of the little chill-looking sheet of water on its summit, which is called the Lake of the Dead. The path was filled with snow, at a most critical point, where, indeed a misplaced footstep might betray the incautious to their destruction. A large party on the other side appeared fully aware of the difficulty, for it had nalted, and was in earnest discussion with the guide, touching the practicability of passing. It was decided to attempt the enterprise. First came a female of one of the sweetest, serenest countenances I had ever seen. She, too, was English; and though she trembled, and blushed, and laughed at herself, she came on with spirit, and would have reached my side in safety, had not an unlucky stone turned beneath a foot that was much too pretty for those wild hills. I sprang forward, and was so happy as to save her from destruction. She felt the extent of the obligation, and expressed her thanks modestly but with fervor. In a minute we were joined by her husband, who grasped my hand with warm feeling, or rather with the emotion one ought to feel who had witnessed the risk he had just run of losing an angel. The lady seemed satisfied at leaving us together.

"You are an Englishman?" said the stranger.

"An American."

"An American! This is singular——will you pardon a question?—You have more than saved my life—you have probably saved my reason——will you pardon a question?——Can money serve you?"

I smiled, and told him, odd as it might appear to him, that though an American, I was a gentleman. He appeared embarrassed, and his fine face worked, until I began to pity him, for it was evident he wished to show me in some way, how much he felt he was my debtor, and yet he did not know exactly what to propose.

"We may meet again," I said, squeezing his hand.

"Will you receive my card?"

"Most willingly."

He put "Viscount Householder" into my hand, and in return I gave him my own humble appellation.

He looked from the card to me, and from me to the card, and some agreeable idea appeared to flash upon his mind.

"Shall you visit Geneva this summer?" he asked, earnestly.

"Within a month."

"Your address——"

"Hotel de l'Ecu."

"You shall hear from me.—Adieu."

We parted, he, his lovely wife and his guides descending to the Rhone, while I pursued my way to the Hospice of the Grimsel. Within the month, I received a large packet at l'Ecu. It contained a valuable diamond ring, with a request that I would wear it, as a memorial of Lady Householder, and a fairly written manuscript. The following short note explained the wishes of the writer.

"Providence brought us together for more purposes than were, at first, apparent. I have long hesitated about publishing the accompanying narrative, for in England there is a disposition to cavil at extraordinary facts, but the distance of America from my place of residence will completely save me from ridicule. The world must have the truth, and I see no better means than by resorting to your agency. All I ask is that you will have the book fairly printed, and that you will send one copy to my address, Householder-hall, Dorsetshire, England, and another to Capt. Noah Poke, Stonington, Connecticut, in your own country. My Anna prays for you, and is ever your friend. Do not forget us.

Yours, most faithfully,

HOUSEHOLDER."

I have rigidly complied with this request, and having sent the two copies according to direction, the rest of the edition is at the disposal of any one who may feel an inclination to pay for it. In return for the copy sent to Stonington, I received the following letter.

"On board the Debby and Dolly Stunnin'tun,
April 1st, 1835.

AUTHOR OF THE SPY, Esquire,

Dear Sir,—Your favour is come to hand, and found me in good health, as I hope these few lines will have the same advantage with you. I have read the book, and must say there is some truth in it, which, I suppose, is as much as befalls any book, the Bible, the Almanac, and the State Laws, excepted. I remember Sir John well, and shall gainsay nothing he testifies to, for the reason that friends should not contradict each other. I was also acquainted with the four Monikins he speaks of, though I knew them by different names. Miss Poke says she wonders if it's all true, which I wunt tell her, seeing that a little unsartainty makes a woman rational. As to my navigating without geometry, that's a matter that was'n't worth booking, for it's no cur'osity in these parts, bating a look at the compass once or twice a day, and so I take my leave of you, with offers to do any commission for you among the Sealing Islands, for which I sail to-morrow wind and weather permitting.

Yours to sarve,

NOAH POKE.

To the Author of the Spy, Esquire,
—— town, ——— County, York State.

P. S. I always told Sir John to steer clear of too much journalizing, but he did nothing but write, night and day, for a week; and as you brew, so you must bake. The wind has chopped, and we shall take our anchor this tide; so no more at present.

N. B. Sir John is a little out about my eating the monkey, which I did, four years before I fell in with him, down on the Spanish Main. It was not bad food to the taste, but it was wonderful narvous to the eye. I r'ally thought I had got hold of Miss Poke's youngest born."

THE MONIKINS

CHAPTER I.

The Author's pedigree—also, that of his Father.

THE philosopher who broaches a new theory is bound to furnish, at least, some elementary proofs of the reasonableness of his positions, and the historian who ventures to record marvels that have hitherto been hid from human knowledge, owes it to a decent regard to the opinions of others, to produce some credible testimony in favor of his veracity. I am peculiarly placed in regard to these two great essentials, having little more than its plausibility to offer in favor of my philosophy, and no other witness than myself to establish the important facts that are now about to be laid before the reading world, for the first time. In this dilemma, I fully feel the weight of responsibility under which I stand; for there are truths of so little apparent probability as to appear fictions, and fictions so like the truth that the ordinary observer is very apt to affirm that he was an eye-witness to their existence: two facts that all our historians would do well to bear in mind, since a knowledge of the circumstances might spare them the mortification of having testimony that cost a deal of trouble, discredited in the one case, and save a vast deal of painful and unnecessary labor, in the other. Thrown upon myself, therefore, for what the French call *les pièces justificatives* of my theories, as well as of my facts, I see no better way to prepare the reader to believe me, than by giving an unvarnished narrative of my descent, birth, education and life, up to the time I became a spectator of those wonderful facts it is my happiness to record, and with which it is now his to be made acquainted.

I shall begin with my descent, or pedigree, both because it is in the natural order of events, and because, in order to turn this portion of my narrative to a proper account, in the way of giving credibility to the rest of it, it may be of use in helping to trace effects to their causes.

I have generally considered myself on a level with the most ancient gentlemen of Europe, on the score of descent, few families being more clearly and directly traced into the mist of time, than that of which I am a member. My descent from my father is undeniably established by the parish register, as well as by the will of that person himself and I believe no man could more directly prove the truth of the whole career of his family, than it is in my power to show that of my ancestor up to the hour when he was found, in the second year of his age, crying with cold and hunger, in the parish of St. Giles, in the city of Westminster, and in the United Kingdom of Great Britain. An orange-woman had pity on his sufferings. She fed him with a crust, warmed him with purl, and then humanely led him to an individual with whom she was in the habit of having frequent but angry interviews—the parish officer. The case of my ancestor was so obscure as to be clear. No one could tell to whom he belonged, whence he came, or what was likely to become of him; and as the law did not admit of the starvation of children in the street, under circumstances like these, the parish officer, after making all proper efforts to induce some of the childless and benevolent of his acquaintance, to believe that an infant thus abandoned was intended as an especial boon from Providence to each of them in particular, was obliged to commit my father to the keeping of one of the regular nurses of the parish. It was fortunate for the authenticity of this pedigree, that such was the result of the orange-woman's application; for, had my worthy ancestor been subjected to the happy accidents and generous caprices of voluntary charity, it is more than probable I should be driven to throw a veil over those important years of his life that were notoriously passed in the work-house, but which, in consequence of that occurrence, are now easily authenticated by valid minutes and documentary evidence. Thus it is that there exists no void in the annals of our family, even that period which is usually remembered through gossiping and idle tales in the lives of most men, being matter of legal record in that of my progenitor, and so continued to be down to the day of his presumed majority, since he was indented to a careful master the moment the parish could with any legality, putting decency quite out of the question, get rid of him. I ought to have said, that the orange-woman, taking a hint from the sign of a butcher opposite to whose door my ancestor was found, had very cleverly given him the name of Thomas Goldencalf.

This second important transition in the affairs of my father, might be deemed a presage of his future fortunes. He was bound apprentice to a trader in fancy articles, or a shopkeeper who dealt in such objects as are usually purchased by those who do not well know what to do with their money. This trade was of immense advantage to the future prosperity of the young adventurer; for, in addition to the known fact that they who amuse are much bet ter paid than they who instruct their fellow-creatures, his situation enabled him to study those caprices of men, which, properly improved, are of themselves a mine of wealth, as well as to gain a knowledge of the important truth that the greatest events of this life are much oftener the result of impulse than of calculation.

I have it by a direct tradition, orally conveyed from the lips of my ancestor, that no one could have been more lucky than himself in the character of his master. This personage, who came, in time, to be my maternal grandfather, was one of those wary traders who encourage others in their follies, with a view to his own advantage, and the experience of fifty years had rendered him so expert in the practices of his calling, that it was seldom he struck out a new vein in his mine, without finding himself rewarded for the enterprise, by a success that was fully equal to his expectations.

"Tom," he said one day to his apprentice, when time had produced confidence and awakened sympathies between them, "thou art a lucky youth, or the parish officer would never have brought thee to my door. Thou little knowest the wealth that is in store for thee, or the treasures that are at thy command, if thou provest diligent, and in particular faithful to my interests."—My provident grandfather never missed an occasion to throw in a useful moral, notwithstanding the general character of veracity that distinguished his commerce.—"Now, what dost think, lad, may be the amount of my capital?"

My ancestor in the male line hesitated to reply, for, hitherto, his ideas had been confined to the profits; never having dared to lift his thoughts as high as that source from which he could not but see they flowed in a very ample stream; but thrown upon himself by so unexpected a question, and being quick at figures, after adding ten per cent. to the sum which he knew the last year had given as the nett avails of their joint ingenuity, he named the amount, in answer to the interrogatory.

My maternal grandfather laughed in the face of my direct lineal ancestor.

"Thou judgest, Tom," he said, when his mirth was a little abated, "by what thou thinkest is the cost of the actual stock before thine eyes, when thou should'st take into the account that which I term our *floating* capital."

Tom pondered a moment, for while he knew that his master had money in the funds, he did not account that as any portion of the available means connected with his ordinary business; and as for a floating capital, he did not well see how it could be of much account, since the disproportion between the cost and the selling prices of the different articles in which they dealt was so great, that there was no particular use in such an investment. As his master, however, rarely paid for any thing until he was in possession of returns from it that exceeded the debt some seven-fold, he began to think the old man was alluding to the advantages he obtained in the way of credit, and after a little more cogitation, he ventured to say as much.

Again my maternal grandfather indulged in a hearty fit of laughter.

"Thou art clever in thy way, Tom," he said "and I like the minuteness of thy calculations, for they show an aptitude for trade; but there is genius in our calling as well as cleverness. Come hither, boy," he added, drawing Tom to a window whence they could see the neighbors on their way to church for it was on a Sunday that my two provident progenitors indulged in this moral view of humanity as best befitted the day, "come hither, boy, and thou shalt see some small portion of that capital which thou seemest to think hid, stalking abroad by day-light, and in the open streets. Here, thou see'st the wife of our neighbor, the pastry-cook; with what an air she tosses her head and displays the bauble thou sold'st her yesterday: well, even that slattern, idle and vain, and little worthy of trust as she is, carries about with *her* a portion of my capital!"

My worthy ancestor stared, for he never knew the other to be guilty of so great an indiscretion as to trust a woman whom they both knew bought more than her husband was willing to pay for.

"She gave me a guinea, master, for that which did not cost a seven-shilling piece!"

"She did, indeed, Tom, and it was her *vanity* that urged her to it. I trade upon her folly, younker, and upon that of all mankind; now dost not see with what a capital I carry on affairs? There—there is the maid, carrying the idle hussy's pattens in the rear; I drew upon my stock in that wench's possession, no later than the last week, for half a crown!"

Tom reflected a long time on these allusions of his provident master, and although he understood them about as well as they will be understood by the owners of half the soft humid eyes and sprouting whiskers among my readers, by dint of cogitation he came at last to a practical understanding of the subject, which before he was thirty he had, to use a French term, pretty well *exploité*.

I learn by unquestionable tradition, received also from the mouths of his contemporaries, that the opinions of my ancestor underwent some material changes between the ages of ten and forty, a circumstance that has often led me to reflect that people might do well not to be too confident of their principles, during the pliable period of life, when the mind, like the tender shoot, is easily bent aside and subjected to the action of surrounding causes.

During the earlier years of the plastic age, my ancestor was observed to betray strong feelings of compassion at the sight of charity-children, nor was he ever known to pass a child, especially a boy that was still in petticoats, and who was crying with hunger in the streets, without sharing his own crust with him. Indeed, his practice on this head was said to be steady and uniform, whenever the rencontre took place after my worthy father had had his own sympathies quickened by a good dinner; a fact that may be imputed to a keener sense of the pleasure he was about to confer.

After sixteen, he was known to converse occasionally on the subject of politics, a topic, on which he came to be both expert and eloquent before twenty. His usual theme was justice and the sacred rights of man, concerning which he sometimes uttered very pretty sentiments, and such as were altogether becoming in one who was at the bottom of the great social pot that was then, as now, actively boiling, and where he was made to feel most, the heat that kept it in ebullition. I am assured that on the subject of taxation, and on that of the wrongs of America and Ireland, there were few youths in the parish who could discourse with more zeal and unction. About this time, too, he was heard shouting "Wilkes and Liberty!" in the public streets.

But, as is the case with all men of rare capacities, there was a concentration of powers in the mind of my ancestor, which soon brought all his errant sympathies, the mere exuberance of acute and overflowing feelings, into a proper and useful subjection, centering all in the one absorbing and capacious receptacle of self. I do not claim for my father any peculiar quality in this respect, for I have often observed that many of those who, (like giddy-headed horsemen that raise a great dust, and scamper as if the highway were too narrow for their eccentric courses, before they are fairly seated in the saddle, but who afterwards drive as directly at their goals as the arrow parting from the bow,) most indulge their sympathies at the commencement of their careers, are the most apt towards the close to get a proper command of their feelings, and to reduce them within the bounds of common sense and prudence. Before five-and-twenty, my father was as exemplary and as constant a devotee of Plutus, as was then to be found between Ratcliffe Highway and Bridge Street:—I name these places in particular, as all the rest of the great capital in which he was born is known to be more indifferent to the subject of money.

My ancestor was just thirty, when his master, who like himself was a bachelor, very unexpectedly, and a good deal to the scandal of the neighborhood, introduced a new inmate into his frugal abode, in the person of an infant female child. It would seem that some one had been speculating on his stock of weakness too, for this poor, little, defenceless and dependent being was thrown upon his care, like Tom himself, through the vigilance of the parish-officers. There were many good-natured jokes practised on the prosperous fancy-dealer, by the more witty of his neighbours, at this sudden turn of good fortune, and not a few ill-natured sneers were given behind his back; most of the knowing ones of the vicinity finding a stronger likeness between the little girl and all the other unmarried men of the eight or ten adjoining streets, than to the worthy housekeeper who had been selected to pay for her support. I have been much disposed to admit the opinions of these amiable observers as authority in my own pedigree, since it would be reaching the obscurity in which all ancient lines take root, a generation earlier than by allowing the presumption that little Betsey was my direct male ancestor's master's daughter; but, on reflection, I have determined to adhere to the less popular but more simple version of the affair, because it is connected with the transmission of no small part of our estate, a circumstance of itself that at once gives dignity and importance to a genealogy.

Whatever may have been the real opinion of the reputed father touching his rights to the honors of that respectable title, he soon became as strongly attached to the child, as if it really owed its existence to himself. The little girl was carefully nursed abundantly fed, and throve accordingly. She had reached her third year, when the fancy-dealer took the small-pox from his little pet, who was just recovering from the same disease, and died at the expiration of the tenth day.

This was an unlooked-for and a stunning blow to my ancestor, who was then in his thirty-fifth year and the head-shopman of the establishment, which had continued to grow with the growing follies and vanities of the age. On examining his master's will, it was found that my father, who had certainly aided materially of late in the acquisition of the money, was left the good-will of the shop, the command of all the stock at cost, and the sole executorship of the estate. He was also intrusted with the exclusive guardianship of little Betsey, to whom his master had affectionately devised every farthing of his property. An ordinary reader may be surprised that a man who had so long practised on the foibles of his species, should have so much confidence in a mere shopman, as to leave his whole estate so completely in his power; but, it must be remembered, that human ingenuity has not yet devised any means by which we can carry our personal effects into the other world; that "what cannot be cured must be endured;" that he must of necessity have confided this important trust to some fellow-creature, and that it was better to commit the keeping of his money to one, who, knowing the secret by which it had been accumulated, had less inducement to be dishonest, than one who was exposed to the temptation of covetousness, without having a knowledge of any direct and legal means of gratifying his longings. It has been conjectured, therefore, that the testator thought, by giving up his trade to a man who was as keenly alive as my ancestor to all its perfections, moral and pecuniary, he provided a sufficient protection against his falling into the sin of peculation, by so amply supplying him with simpler means of enriching himself. Besides, it is fair to presume that the long acquaintance had begotten sufficient confidence to weaken the effect of that saying which some wit has put into the mouth of a wag—"make me your executor, father; I care not to whom you leave the estate." Let all this be as it might, nothing can be more certain than that my worthy ancestor executed his trust with the scrupulous fidelity of a man whose integrity had been severely schooled in the ethics of trade. Little Betsey was properly educated for one in her condition of life; her health was as carefully watched over as if she had been the only daughter of the sovereign instead of the only daughter of a fancy-dealer; her morals were superintended by a superannuated old maid; her mind left to its original purity; her person zealously protected against the designs of greedy fortune-hunters; and, to complete the catalogue of his paternal attentions and solicitudes, my vigilant and faithful ancestor, to prevent accidents, and to counteract the chances of life, so far as it might be done by human foresight, saw that she was legally married, the day she reached her nineteenth year, to the person whom, there is every reason to think, he believed to be the most unexceptionable man of his acquaintance,—in other words, to himself. Settlements were unnecessary between parties who had so long been known to each other, and, thanks to the liberality of his late master's will in more ways than one, a long minority, and the industry of the ci-devant head-shopman, the nuptial benediction was no sooner pronounced, than our family stepped into the undisputed possession of four hundred thousand pounds. One less scrupulous on the subject of religion and the law, might not have thought it necessary to give the orphan heiress a settlement so satisfactory, at the termination of her wardship.

I was the fifth of the children who were the fruits of this union, and the only one of them all, that passed the first year of its life. My poor mother did not survive my birth, and I can only record her qualities through the medium of that great agent in the archives of the family, tradition. By all that I have heard, she must have been a meek, quiet, domestic woman; who, by temperament and attainments, was admirably qualified to second the prudent plans of my father for her welfare. If she had causes of complaint, (and that she had, there is too much reason to think, for who has ever escaped them?) they were concealed, with female fidelity, in the sacred repository of her own heart; and if truant imagination sometimes dimly drew an outline of married happiness different from the facts that stood in dull reality before her eyes, the picture was merely commented on by a sigh, and consigned to a cabinet whose key none ever touched but herself, and she seldom.

Of this subdued and unobtrusive sorrow, for I fear it sometimes reached that intensity of feeling, my excellent and indefatigable ancestor appeared to have no suspicion. He pursued his ordinary occupations with his ordinary single-minded devotion, and the last thing that would have crossed his brain was the suspicion that he had not punctiliously done his duty by his ward. Had he acted otherwise, none surely would have suffered more by his delinquency than her husband, and none would have a better right to complain. Now, as her husband never dreamt of making such an accusation, it is not at all surprising that my ancestor remained in ignorance of his wife's feelings, to the hour of his death.

It has been said that the opinions of the successor of the fancy-dealer, underwent some essential changes between the ages of ten and forty. After he had reached his twenty-second year, or, in other words, the moment he began to earn money for himself, as well as for his master, he ceased to cry "Wilken and Liberty." He was not heard to breathe a syllable concerning the obligations of society towards the weak and unfortunate, for the five years that succeeded his majority; he touched lightly on Christian duties in general, after he got to be worth fifty pounds of his own; and as for railing at human follies, it would have been rank ingratitude in one who so very unequivocally got his bread by them. About this time, his remarks on the subject of taxation, however, were singularly caustic, and well applied. He railed at the public debt, as at a public curse, and ominously predicted the dissolution of society, in consequence of the burthens and incumbrances it was hourly accumulating on the already overloaded shoulders of the trader.

The period of his marriage and of his succession to the hoardings of his former master, may be dated as the second epocha in the opinions of my ancestor From this moment his ambition expanded, his views enlarged in proportion to his means, and his contemplations on the subject of his great floating capital became more profound and philosophical. A man of my ancestor's native sagacity, whose whole soul was absorbed in the pursuit of gain, who had so long been forming his mind, by dealing as it were with the elements of human weaknesses, and who already possessed four hundred thousand pounds, was very likely to strike out for himself some higher road to eminence, than that in which he had been laboriously journeying, during the years of painful probation. The property of my mother had been chiefly invested in good bonds and mortgages; her protector, patron, benefactor, and legalized father, having an unconquerable repugnance to confiding in that soulless, conventional, nondescript body corporate, the public. The first indication that was given by my ancestor of a change of purpose in the direction of his energies, was by calling in the whole of his outstanding debts, and adopting the Napoleon plan of operations, by concentrating his forces on a particular point, in order that he might operate in masses. About this time, too, he suddenly ceased railing at taxation This change may be likened to that which occurs in the language of the ministerial journals, when they cease abusing any foreign state with whom the nation has been carrying on a war, that it is, at length, believed politic to terminate; and for much the same reason, as it was the intention of my thrifty ances tor to make an ally of a power that he had hitherto always treated as an enemy. The whole of the four hundred thousand pounds were liberally intrusted to the country, the former fancy-dealer's apprentice entering the arena of virtuous and patriotic speculation, as a bull; and, if with more caution, with at least some portion of the energy and obstinacy of the desperate animal that gives title to this class of adventurers. Success crowned his laudable efforts; gold rolled in upon him like water on the flood, buoying him up, soul and body, to that enviable height, where, as it would seem, just views can alone be taken of society in its innumerable phases. All his former views of life, which, in common with others of a similar origin and similar political sentiments, he had imbibed in early years, and which might with propriety be called near views, were now completely obscured by the sublimer and broader prospect that was spread before him.

I am afraid the truth will compel me to admit, that my ancestor was never charitable in the vulgar acceptation of the term; but then, he always maintained that his interest in his fellow-creatures was of a more elevated cast, taking a comprehensive glance at all the bearings of good and evil,—being of the sort of love which induces the parent to correct the child, that the lesson of present suffering may produce the blessings of future respectability and usefulness. Acting on these principles, he gradually grew more estranged from his species in appearance; a sacrifice that was probably exacted by the severity of his practical reproofs for their growing wickedness, and the austere policy that was necessary to enforce them. By this time, my ancestor was also thoroughly impressed with what is called the value of money; a sen nment which, I believe, gives its possessor a livelier perception than common of the dangers of the precious metals, as well as of their privileges and uses. He expatiated occasionally on the guarantees that it was necessary to give to society, for its own security; never even voted for a parish-officer, unless he were a warm substantial citizen; and began to be a subscriber to the patriotic fund, and to the other similar little moral and pecuniary buttresses of the government, whose common and commendable object was, to protect our country, our altars, and our firesides.

The death-bed of my mother has been described to me as a touching and melancholy scene. It appears that as this meek and retired woman was extricated from the coil of mortality, her intellect grew brighter, her powers of discernment stronger, and her character in every respect more elevated and commanding. Although she had said much less about our firesides and altars than her husband, I see no reason to doubt that she had ever been quite as faithful as he could be to the one, and as much devoted to the other. I shall describe the important event of her passage from this to a better world, as I have often had it repeated from the lips of one who was present, and who has had an important agency in since making me the man I am. This person was the clergyman of the parish, a pious divine, a learned man, and a gentleman in feeling as well as by extraction.

My mother, though long conscious that she was drawing near to her last great account, had steadily refused to draw her husband from his absorbing pursuits, by permitting him to be made acquainted with her situation. He knew that she was ill; very ill, as he had reason to think; but, as he not only allowed her, but even volunteered to order her all the advice and relief that money could command, (my ancestor was not a miser in the vulgar meaning of the word,) he thought that he had done al. that man could do, in a case of life and death, interests over which he professed to have no control. He saw Dr. Etherington, the rector, come and go daily, for a month, without uneasiness or apprehen sion, for he thought his discourse had a tendency to tranquillize my mother, and he had a strong affec tion for all that left him, undisturbed, to the enjoyment of the occupation in which his whole energies were now completely centered. The physician got his guinea at each visit, with scrupulous punctuality; the nurses were well received and were well satisfied, for no one interfered with their acts but the doctor; and every ordinary duty of commission was as regularly discharged by my ancestor, as if the sinking and resigned creature from whom he was about to be for ever separated, had been the spontaneous choice of his young and fresh affections.

When, therefore, a servant entered to say that Dr. Etherington desired a private interview, my worthy ancestor, who had no consciousness of having neglected any obligation that became a friend of church and state, was in no small measure surprised.

"I come, Mr. Goldencalf, on a melancholy duty," said the pious rector, entering the private cabinet to which his application had for the first time obtained his admission; "the fatal secret can no longer be concealed from you, and your wife at length consents that I shall be the instrument of revealing it."

The Doctor paused; for, on such occasions it is perhaps as well to let the party that is about to be shocked, receive a little of the blow through his own imagination; and busily enough was that of my poor father said to be exercised on this painful occasion. He grew pale, opened his eyes until they again filled the sockets into which they had gradually been sinking for twenty years, and looked a hundred questions that his tongue refused to put.

"It cannot be, Doctor," he at length querulously said, "that a woman like Betsey has got an inkling into any of the events connected with the last great secret expedition, and which have escaped my jealousy and experience!"

"I am afraid, dear sir, that Mrs. Goldencalf has obtained glimpses of the last great and secret expedition on which we must all, sooner or later, embark, that have entirely escaped your vigilance.—But of this I will speak some other time. At present it is my painful duty to inform you it is the opinion of the physician, that your excellent wife cannot outlive the day, if, indeed, she do the hour."

My father was struck with this intelligence, and for more than a minute he remained silent and without motion. Casting his eyes towards the papers on which he had lately been employed, and which contained some very important calculations connected with the next settling day, he at length resumed:

"If this be really so, Doctor, it may be well for me to go to her, since one in the situation of the poor woman may indeed have something of importance to communicate."

"It was with this object that I have now come to tell you the truth," quietly answered the divine, who knew that nothing was to be gained by contending with the besetting weakness of such a man, at such a moment.

My father bent his head in assent, and, first carefully inclosing the open papers in a secretary, he followed his companion to the bed-side of his dying wife.

CHAPTER II.

Touching myself and ten thousand pounds.

ALTHOUGH my ancestor was much too wise to refuse to look back upon his origin in a worldly point of view, he never threw his retrospective glances so far as to reach the sublime mystery of his moral existence; and while his thoughts might be said to be ever on the stretch to attain glimpses into the future, they were by far too earthly to extend beyond any other settling day than those which were regulated by the ordinances of the stock exchange. With him, to be born was but the commencement of a speculation, and to die was to determine the general balance of profit and loss. A man who had so rarely meditated on the grave changes of mortality, therefore, was consequently so much the less prepared to gaze upon the visible solemnities of a death-bed. Although he had never truly loved my mother, for love was a sentiment much too pure and elevated for one whose imagination dwelt habitually on the beauties of the stock-books, he had ever been kind to her, and of late he was even much disposed, as has already been stated, to contribute as much to her temporal comforts as comported with his pursuits and habits. On the other hand, the quiet temperament of my mother required some more exciting cause than the affections of her husband, to quicken those germs of deep, placid womanly love, that certainly lay dormant in her heart, like seed withering with the ungenial cold of winter. The last meeting of such a pair was not likely to be attended with any violent outpourings of grief.

My ancestor, notwithstanding, was deeply struck with the physical changes in the appearance of his wife.

"Thou art much emaciated, Betsey," he said, taking her hand kindly, after a long and solemn pause; "much more so than I had thought, or could have believed! Does nurse give thee comforting soups and generous nourishment?"

My mother smiled the ghastly smile of death: but waved her hand, with loathing, at his suggestion.

"All this is now too late, Mr. Goldencalf," she answered, speaking with a distinctness and an energy for which she had long been reserving her strength. "Food and raiment are no longer among my wants."

"Well, well, Betsey, one that is in want of neither food nor raiment, cannot be said to be in great suffering, after all; and I am glad that thou art so much at ease. Dr. Etherington tells me thou art far from well bodily, however, and I am come expressly to see if I can order any thing that will help to make thee more easy."

"Mr. Goldencalf, you can. My wants for this life are nearly over; a short hour, or two, will remove me beyond the world, its cares, its vanities, its——" My poor mother probably meant to add, its heartlessness or its selfishness; but she rebuked herself, and paused—"By the mercy of our blessed Redeemer, and through the benevolent agency of this excellent man," she resumed, glancing her eye upward at first with holy reverence, and then at the divine with meek gratitude, "I quit you without alarm, and were it not for one thing, I might say without care."

"And what is there to distress thee, in particular, Betsey?" asked my father, blowing his nose, and speaking with unusual tenderness; "if it be in my power to set thy heart at ease on this, or on any other point, name it, and I will give orders to have it immediately performed. Thou hast been a good pious woman, and can have little to reproach thyself with."

My mother looked earnestly and wistfully at her husband. Never before had he betrayed so strong an interest in her happiness, and had it not, alas! been too late, this glimmering of kindness might have lighted the matrimonial torch into a brighter flame than had ever yet glowed upon the past.

"Mr. Goldencalf, we have an only son——"

"We have, Betsey, and it may gladden thee to hear that the physician thinks the boy more likely to live than either of his poor brothers and sisters."

I cannot explain the holy and mysterious principle of maternal nature that caused my mother to clasp her hands, to raise her eyes to heaven, and, while a gleam flitted athwart her glassy eyes and wan cheeks, to murmur her thanks to God for the boon. She was herself hastening away to the eternal bliss of the pure of mind and the redeemed, and her imagination, quiet and simple as it was, had drawn pictures in which she and her departed babes were standing before the throne of the Most High, chanting his glory, and shining amid the stars—and yet was she now rejoicing that the last and the most cherished of all her offspring, was likely to be left exposed to the evils, the vices, nay, to the enormities, of the state of being that she herself so willingly resigned.

"It is of our boy that I wish now to speak, Mr Goldencalf," replied my mother, when her secret devotion was ended. "The child will have need of instruction and care; in short, of both mother and father."

"Betsey, thou forgettest that he will still have the latter."

"You are much wrapped up in your business, Mr. Goldencalf, and are not, in other respects, qualified to educate a boy born to the curse and to the temptations of immense riches."

My excellent ancestor looked as if he thought his dying consort had in sooth finally taken leave of her senses.

"There are public schools, Betsey; I promise thee the child shall not be forgotten: I will have him well taught, though it cost me a thousand a year!"

His wife reached forth her emaciated hand to that of my father, and pressed the latter with as much force as a dying mother could use. For a fleet moment she even appeared to have gotten rid of her latest care. But the knowledge of character that had been acquired by the hard experience of thirty years, was not to be unsettled by the gratitude of a moment.

"I wish, Mr. Goldencalf," she anxiously resumed, "to receive your solemn promise to commit the education of our boy to Dr. Etherington — you know his worth, and must have full confidence in such a man."

"Nothing would give me greater satisfaction, my dear Betsey; and if Dr. Etherington will consent to receive him, I will send Jack to his house this very evening; for, to own the truth, I am but little qualified to take charge of a child under a year old

A hundred a year, more or less, shall not spoil so good a bargain."

The divine was a gentleman, and he looked grave at this speech, though, meeting the anxious eyes of my mother, his own lost their displeasure in a glance of reassurance and pity.

"The charges of his education will be easily settled, Mr. Goldencalf"—added my mother—"but the Doctor has consented with difficulty to take the responsibility of my poor babe, and that only under two conditions."

The stock-dealer required an explanation with his eyes.

"One is, that the child shall be left solely to his own care, after he has reached his fourth year; and the other is, that you make an endowment for the support of two poor scholars, at one of the principal schools."

As my mother got out the last words, she fell back on her pillow, whence her interest in the subject had enabled her to lift her head a little, and she fairly gasped for breath, in the intensity of her anxiety to hear the answer. My ancestor contracted his brow, like one who saw it was a subject that required reflection.

"Thou dost not know perhaps, Betsey, that these endowments swallow up a great deal of money—a great deal—and often very uselessly."

"Ten thousand pounds is the sum that has been agreed upon between Mrs. Goldencalf and me," steadily remarked the Doctor, who, in my soul, I believe had hoped that his condition would be rejected, having yielded to the importunities of a dying woman, rather than to his own sense of that which might be either very desirable or very useful.

"Ten thousand pounds!"

My mother could not speak, though she succeeded in making an imploring sign of assent.

"Ten thousand pounds is a great deal of money, my dear Betsey;—a very great deal!"

The colour of my mother changed to the hue of death, and by her breathing she appeared to be in the agony.

"Well—well, Betsey," said my father a little hastily, for he was frightened at her pallid countenance and extreme distress—"have it thine own way—the money—yes, yes—it shall be given as thou wish'st—now set thy kind heart at rest."

The revulsion of feeling was too great for one whose system had been wound up to a state of excitement like that which had sustained my mother, who, an hour before, had seemed scarcely able to speak. She extended her hand towards her husband, smiled benignantly in his face, whispered the word "Thanks," and then, losing all her powers of body, sunk into the last sleep, as tranquilly as the infant drops its head on the bosom of the nurse. This was, after all, a sudden, and, in one sense, an unexpected death: all who witnessed it were struck with awe. My father gazed for a whole minute intently on the placid features of his wife, and left the room in silence. He was followed by Dr. Etherington, who accompanied him to the private apartment, where they had first met that night, neither uttering a syllable until both were seated.

"She was a good woman, Dr. Etherington!" said the widowed man, shaking his foot with agitation.

"She was a good woman, Mr. Goldencalf."

"And a good wife, Dr. Etherington."

"I have always believed her to be a good wife, sir"

"Faithful, obedient, and frugal."

"Three qualities that are of much practical use in the affairs of this world."

"I never shall marry again, sir."

The divine bowed.

"Nay, I never could find such another match!"

Again the divine inclined his head, though the assent was accompanied by a slight smile.

"Well, she has left me an heir."

"And brought something that he might inherit"—observed the Doctor, dryly.

My ancestor looked up inquiringly at his companion, but apparently most of the sarcasm was thrown away.

"I resign the child to your care, Dr. Etherington, conformably to the dying request of my beloved Betsey."

"I accept the charge, Mr. Goldencalf, conformably to my promise to the deceased; but you will remember that there was a condition coupled with that promise which must be faithfully and promptly fulfilled."

My ancestor was too much accustomed to respect the punctilios of trade, whose code admits of frauds only in certain categories, which are sufficiently explained in its conventional rules of honor; a sort of specified morality, that is bottomed more on the convenience of its votaries than on the general law of right. He respected the letter of his promise, while his soul yearned to avoid its spirit; and his wits were already actively seeking the means of doing that which he so much desired.

"I did make a promise to poor Betsey, certainly," he answered in the way of one who pondered—"and it was a promise, too, made under very solemn circumstances."

"The promises made to the dead are doubly

binding; since, by their departure to the world of spirits, it may be said they leave the performance to the exclusive superintendence of the Being who cannot lie."

My ancestor quailed; his whole frame shuddered, and his purpose was shaken.

"Poor Betsey left you as her representative in this case, however, Doctor"—he observed, after the delay of more than a minute, casting his eyes wistfully towards the divine.

"In one sense, she certainly did, sir."

"And a representative, with full powers, is legally a principal under a different name. I think this matter might be arranged to our mutual satisfaction, Dr. Etherington, and the intention of poor Betsey most completely executed; she, poor woman, knew little of business, as was best for her sex; and when women undertake affairs of magnitude, they are very apt to make awkward work of it."

"So that the intention of the deceased be completely fulfilled, you will not find me exacting, Mr. Goldencalf."

"I thought as much—I knew there could be no difficulty between two men of sense, who were met with honest views to settle a matter of this nature. The intention of poor Betsey, Doctor, was to place her child under your care, with the expectation—and I do not deny its justice—that the boy would receive more benefit from your knowledge than he possibly could from mine."

Dr. Etherington was too honest to deny thes premises, and too polite to admit them without an inclination of acknowledgment.

"As we are quite of the same mind, good sir, concerning the preliminaries," continued my ancestor, "we will enter a little nearer into the details. It appears to me to be no more than strict justice, that he who does the work should receive the reward. This is a principle in which I have been educated, Dr. Etherington; it is one in which I could wish to have my son educated; and it is one on which I hope always to practise."

Another inclination of the body conveyed the silent assent of the divine.

"Now, poor Betsey, Heaven bless her!—for she was a meek and tranquil companion, and richly deserves to be rewarded in a future state—but, poor Betsey had little knowledge of business. She fancied, that in bestowing these ten thousand pounds on a charity, she was acting well; whereas, she was in fact committing injustice. If you are to have the trouble and care of bringing up little Jack, who but you should reap the reward?"

"I shall expect, Mr. Goldencalf, that you will furnish the means to provide for the child's wants."

"Of that, sir, it is unnecessary to speak," interrupted my ancestor, both promptly and proudly. "I am a wary man, and a prudent man, and am one who knows the value of money, I trust; but I am no miser, to stint my own flesh and blood. Jack shall never want for any thing, while it is in my power to give it. I am by no means as rich, sir, as the neighbourhood supposes; but then I am no beggar. I dare say, if all my assets were fairly counted, it might be found that I am worth a plum."

"You are said to have received a much larger sum than that, with the late Mrs. Goldencalf," the divine observed, not without reproof in his voice.

"Ah, dear sir, I need not tell you what vulgar rumor is——but I shall not undermine my own credit; and we will change the subject. My object, Dr. Etherington, was merely to do justice. Poor Betsey desired that ten thousand pounds might be given to found a scholarship or two: now, what have these scholars done, or what are they likely to do, for me or mine? The case is different with you, sir; you will have trouble—much trouble, I make no doubt; and it is proper, that you should have a sufficient compensation. I was about to propose, therefore, that you should consent to receive my check for three,—or four,—or even for five thousand pounds," continued my ancestor, raising the offer as he saw the frown on the brow of the Doctor deepen. "Yes, sir, I will even say the latter sum, which possibly will not be too much for your trouble and care; and we will forget the womanish plan of poor Betsey, in relation to the two scholar ships and the charity. Five thousand pounds down, Doctor, for yourself, and the subject of the charity forgotten for ever."

When my father had thus distinctly put his proposition, he awaited its effect with the confidence of one who had long dealt with cupidity. For a novelty, his calculation failed. The face of Dr. Etherington flushed, then paled, and finally settled into a look of melancholy reprehension. He arose and paced the room for several minutes in silence; during which time his companion believed he was debating with himself on the chances of obtaining a higher bid for his consent, when he suddenly stopped and addressed my ancestor in a mild, but steady tone.

"I feel it to be a duty, Mr. Goldencalf," he said, "to admonish you of the precipice over which you hang. The love of money, which is the root of all evil, which caused Judas to betray even his Saviour and God, has taken deep root in your soul. You are no longer young, and, although still proud in your strength and prosperity, are much nearer to your great account, than you may be willing to believe. It is not an hour since you witnessed the departure of a penitent soul for the presence of her God; since you heard the dying request from her lips; and since, in such a presence and in such a scene, you gave a pledge to respect her wishes and, now, with the accursed spirit of gain upper most, you would trifle with these most sacred obliga tions, in order to keep a little worthless gold in a hand that is already full to overflowing. Fancy that the pure spirit of thy confiding and single-minded wife were present at this conversation; fancy it mourning over thy weakness and violated faith—nay, I know not that such is not the fact; for there is no reason to believe that the happy spirits are not permitted to watch near, and mourn over us, until we are released from this mass of sin and depravity in which we dwell—and, then, reflect what must be her sorrow, at hearing how soon her parting request is forgotten, how useless has been the example of her holy end, how rooted and fearful are thine own infirmities!"

My father was more rebuked by the manner than by the words of the divine. He passed his hand across his brow, as if to shut out the view of his wife's spirit; turned, drew his writing materials nearer, wrote a check for the ten thousand pounds, and handed it to the doctor with the subdued air of a corrected boy.

"Jack shall be at your disposal, good sir," he said, as the paper was delivered, "whenever it may be your pleasure to send for him."

They parted in silence; the divine too much dis pleased, and my ancestor too much grieved, to indulge in words of ceremony.

When my father found himself alone, he gazed furtively about the room, to assure himself that the rebuking spirit of his wife had not taken a shape less questionable than air, and then he mused for at least an hour, very painfully, on all the principal occurrences of the night. It is said that occupation is a certain solace for grief, and so it proved to be in the present case; for luckily my father had made up that very day his private account of the sum total of his fortune. Sitting down, therefore, to the agreeable task, he went through the simple process of substracting from it the amount for which he had just drawn, and, finding that he was still master of seven hundred and eighty-two thousand three hundred and eleven pounds odd shillings and even pence, he found a very natural consolation for the magnitude of the sum he had just given away, by comparing it with the magnitude of that which was left.

CHAPTER III.

Opinions of our author's ancestor, together with some of his own, and some of other people's.

Dr. Etherington was both a pious man and a gentleman. The second son of a baronet of ancient lineage, he had been educated in most of the opinions of his caste, and possibly he was not entirely above its prejudices; but, this much admitted, few divines were more willing to defer to the ethics and principles of the bible, than himself. His humility had, of course, a decent regard to station; his charity was judiciously regulated by the articles of faith; and his philanthropy was of the discriminating character that became a warm supporter of church and state.

In accepting the trust which he was now obliged to assume, he had yielded purely to a benevolent wish to smooth the dying pillow of my mother Acquainted with the character of her husband, he had committed a sort of pious fraud, in attaching the condition of the endowment to his consent; for, notwithstanding the becoming language of his own rebuke, the promise, and all the other little attendant circumstances of the night, it might be questioned which felt the most surprise after the draft was presented and duly honored, he who found himself in possession, or he who found himself deprived, of the sum of ten thousand pounds sterling. Still, Dr. Etherington acted with the most scrupulous integrity in the whole affair; and, although I am aware, that a writer who has so many wonders to relate, as must of necessity adorn the succeeding pages of this manuscript, should observe a guarded discretion in drawing on the credulity of his readers, truth compels me to add, that every farthing of the money was duly invested, with a single eye to the wishes of the dying Christian, who, under Providence, had been the means of bestowing so much gold on the poor and unlettered. As to the manner in which the charity was finally improved, I shall say nothing, since no inquiry, on my part, has ever enabled me to obtain such information as would justify my speaking with authority.

As for myself, I shall have little more to add touching the events of the succeeding twenty years. I was baptized, nursed, breeched, schooled, horsed, confirmed, sent to the university and graduated, much as befalls all gentlemen of the established church, in the United Kingdoms of Great Britain and Ireland, or, in other words, of the land of my ancestor. During these pregnant years, Dr. Etherington acquitted himself of a duty that, judging by a very predominant feeling of human nature, (which, singularly enough, renders us uniformly averse to being troubled with other people's affairs,) I think he must have found sufficiently vexatious, quite as well as my good mother had any right to expect. Most of my vacations were spent at his rectory; for he had first married, then become a father, next a widower, and had exchanged his town-living for one in the country, between the periods of my mother's death and that of my going to Eton; and, after I quitted Oxford, much more of my time was passed beneath his friendly roof, than beneath that of my own parent. Indeed, I saw little of the latter. He paid my bills, furnished me with pocket-money, and professed an intention to let me travel after I should reach my majority. But, satisfied with these proofs of paternal care, he appeared willing to let me pursue my own course very much in my own way.

My ancestor was an eloquent example of the truth of that political dogma which teaches the efficacy of the division of labor. No manufacturer of the head of a pin ever attained greater dexterity in his single-minded vocation, than was reached by my father in the one pursuit to which he devoted, so far as human ken could reach, both soul and body. As any sense is known to increase in acuteness by constant exercise, or any passion by indulgence, so did his ardor in favor of the great object of his affections grow with its growth, and become more manifest as an ordinary observer would be apt to think the motive of its existence at all had nearly ceased. This is a moral phenomenon that I have often had occasion to observe, and which there is some reason to think, depends on a principle of attraction that has hitherto escaped the sagacity of the philosophers, but which is as active in the immaterial, as is that of gravitation in the material world. Talents like his, so incessantly and unweariedly employed, produced the usual fruits. He grew richer hourly, and, at the time of which I speak, he was pretty generally known to the initiated, to be the warmest man who had any thing to do with the stock exchange.

I do not think that the opinions of my ancestor underwent as many material changes between the ages of fifty and seventy, as they had undergone between the ages of ten and forty. During the latter period, the tree of life usually gets deep root, its inclination is fixed, whether obtained by bending to the storms, or by drawing towards the light; and it probably yields more in fruits of its own, than it gains by tillage and manuring. Still my ancestor was not exactly the same man the day he kept his seventieth birth-day, as he had been the day he kept his fiftieth. In the first place, he was worth thrice the money at the former period, that he had been worth at the latter. Of course his moral system had undergone all the mutations that are known to be dependent on a change of this important character. Beyond a question, during the last five-and-twenty years of the life of my ancestor, his political bias, too, was in favor of exclusive privileges and exclusive benefits. I do not mean that he was an aristocrat in the vulgar acceptation. To him, feodality was a blank; he had probably never heard the word. Portcullises rose and fell, flanking towers lifted their heads, and embattled walls swept around their fabrics in vain, so far as his imagination was concerned. He cared not for the days of courts leet and courts baron; nor for the barons themselves; nor for the honors of a pedigree (why should he?—no prince in the land could more clearly trace his family into obscurity, than himself,) nor for the vanities of a court, nor for those of society; nor for aught else of the same nature, that is apt to have charms for the weak-minded, the imaginative, or the conceited. His political prepossessions showed themselves in a very different manner. Throughout the whole of the five lustres I have named, he was never heard to whisper a censure against government let its measures, or the character of its administration, be what it would. It was enough for him that it was government. Even taxation no longer excited his ire, nor aroused his eloquence. He conceived it to be necessary to order, and especially to the protection of property, a branch of political science that he had so studied, as to succeed in protecting his own estate, in a measure, against even this great ally itself. After he became worth a million, it was observed that all his opinions grew less favorable to mankind in general, and that he was much disposed to exaggerate the amount and quality of the few boons which Providence has bestowed on the poor. The report of a meeting of the whigs, generally had an effect on his appetite; a resolution that was suspected of emanating from Brookes', commonly robbed him of a dinner, and the radicals never seriously moved that he did not spend a sleepless night, and pass a large portion of the next day, in uttering words that it would be hardly moral to repeat. I may without impropriety add, however, that on such occasions, he did not spare allusions to the gallows: Sir Francis Burdett, in particular, was a target for a good deal of billingsgate; and men as upright and as respectable even as my lords Grey, Lansdowne, and Holland, were treated as if they were no better than they should be. But, on these little details it is unnecessary to dwell, for it must be a subject of common remark, that the more elevated and efined men become in their political ethics, the more they are accustomed to throw dirt upon their neighbors. I will just state, however, that most of what I have here related, has been transmitted to me by direct oral traditions, for I seldom saw my ancestor, and when we did meet, it was only to settle accounts, to eat a leg of mutton together, and to part like those who, at least, have never quarrelled.

Not so with Dr. Etherington. Habit (to say nothing of my own merits) had attached him to one who owed so much to his care, and his doors were always as open to me, as if I had been his own son.

It has been said, that most of my idle time (omitting the part mispent in the schools) was passed at the rectory.

The excellent divine had married a lovely woman, a year or two after the death of my mother, who had left him a widower, and the father of a little image of herself, before the expiration of a twelvemonth. Owing to the strength of his affections for the deceased, or for his daughter, or because he could not please himself in a second marriage as well as it had been his good fortune to do so in the first, Dr. Etherington had never spoken of forming another connexion. He appeared content to discharge his duties, as a Christian and a gentleman, without increasing them by creating any new relations with society.

Anna Etherington was of course my constant companion, during many long and delightful visits at the rectory. Three years my junior, the friendship on my part had commenced by a hundred acts of boyish kindness. Between the ages of seven and twelve, I dragged her about in a garden-chair, pushed her on the swing, and wiped her eyes and uttered words of friendly consolation, when any transient cloud obscured the sunny brightness of her childhood. From twelve to fourteen, I told her stories; astonished her with narratives of my own exploits at Eton, and caused her serene blue eyes to open in admiration, at the marvels of London. At fourteen, I began to pick up her pocket-handkerchief, hunt for her thimble, accompany her in duets and to read poetry to her, as she occupied herself with the little lady-like employments of the needle. About the age of seventeen, I began to compare cousin Anna, as I was permitted to call her, with the other young girls of my acquaintance, and the comparison was generally much in her favor. It was also about this time, that, as my admiration grew more warm and manifest, she became less confiding, and less frank: I perceived too that, for a novelty, she now had some secrets that she did not choose to communicate to me, that she was more with her governess, and less in my society than formerly, and, on one occasion (bitterly did I feel the slight) she actually recounted to her father the amusing incidents of a little birth-day fête at which she had been present, and which was given by a gentleman of the vicinity, before she even dropped a hint to me, touching the delight she had experienced on the occasion! I was, however, a good deal compensated for the slight, by her saying kindly, as she ended her playful and humorous account of the affair,—

"It would have made you laugh heartily, Jack to see the droll manner in which the servants acted their parts;" (there had been a sort of mistified masque) "more particularly the fat old butler, of whom they had made a Cupid, as Dick Griffin said, in order to show that Love becomes drowsy and dull by good eating and drinking—I *do* wish you *could* have been there, Jack."

Anna was a gentle feminine girl, with a most lovely and winning countenance, and I did inherently like to hear her pronounce the word "Jack"—it was so different from the boisterous screech of the Eton boys, or the swaggering call of my boon companions, at Oxford!

"I should have liked it excessively myself, Anna," I answered; "more particularly as you seem to have so much enjoyed the fun."

"Yes, but that *could not* be"—interrupted Miss-Mrs. Norton, the governess.—"For Sir Harry Griffin is very difficult about his associates, and you know, my dear, that Mr. Goldencalf, though a very respectable young man himself, could not expect one of the oldest Baronets of the county, to go out of his way to invite the son of a stock-jobber to be present at a fête given to his own heir."

Luckily for Miss-Mrs. Norton, Dr. Etherington had walked away, the moment his daughter ended her recital, or she might have met with a disagreeable commentary on her notions concerning the fitness of associations. Anna herself looked earnestly at her governess, and I saw a flush mantle over her sweet face, that reminded me of the ruddiness of morn. Her soft eyes then fell to the floor, and it was some time before she spoke.

The next day I was arranging some fishing-tackle under a window of the library, where my person was concealed by the shrubbery, when I heard the melodious voice of Anna wishing the rector good morning. My heart beat quicker as she approached the casement, tenderly inquiring of her parent how he had passed the night. The answers were as affectionate as the questions, and then there was a little pause.

"What is a stock-jobber, father?" suddenly resumed Anna, whom I heard rustling the leaves above my head.

"A stock-jobber, my dear, is one who buys and sells in the public funds, with a view to profit."

"And is it thought a *particularly* disgraceful employment?"

"Why, that depends on circumstances. On 'Change it seems to be well enough—among merchants and bankers, there is some odium attached to it, I believe."

"And can you say *why*, father?"

"I believe," said Dr. Etherington, laughing, "for no other reason than that it is an *uncertain* calling—one that is liable to sudden reverses—what is termed gambling—and whatever renders property insecure, is sure to obtain odium among those whose principal concern is its accumulation; those who consider the responsibility of others of essential importance to themselves."

"But is it a dishonest pursuit, father?"

"As the times go, not necessarily, my dear; though it may readily become so."

"And is it disreputable, generally, with the world?"

"That depends on circumstances, Anna. When the stock-jobber loses, he is very apt to be condemned; but I rather think his character rises in proportion to his gains. But why do you ask these singular questions, love?"

I thought I heard Anna breathe harder than usual, and it is certain that she leaned far out of the window, to pluck a rose.

"Why, Mrs. Norton said, Jack was not invited to Sir Harry Griffin's, because his father was a stock-jobber. Do you think she was right, sir?"

"Very likely, my dear," returned the divine, who I fancied was smiling at the question. "Sir Harry has the advantages of birth, and he probably did not forget that our friend Jack was not so fortunate—and, moreover, Sir Harry, while he values himself on his wealth, is not as rich as Jack's father, by a million or two—in other words, as they say on 'Change, Jack's father could buy ten of him. This motive was perhaps more likely to influence him than the first. In addition, Sir Harry is suspected of gambling himself in the funds, through the aid of agents; and a gentleman who resorts to such means to increase his fortune, is a little apt to exaggerate his social advantages, by way of a set-off to the humiliation."

"And *gentlemen* do really become stock-jobbers, father?"

"Anna, the world has undergone great changes in my time. Ancient opinions have been shaken, and governments themselves are getting to be little better than political establishments to add facilities to the accumulation of money. This is a subject, however, you cannot very well understand, nor do I pretend to be very profound in it, myself."

"But is Jack's father really so very, very rich?" asked Anna, whose thoughts had been wandering from the thread of those pursued by her father.

"He is believed to be so."

"And Jack is his heir?"

"Certainly—he has no other child; though it is not easy to say, what so singular a being may do with his money."

"I hope he will disinherit Jack!"

"You surprise me, Anna!—You, who are so mild and reasonable, to wish such a misfortune to befall our young friend, John Goldencalf!"

I gazed upward in astonishment, at this extraordinary speech of Anna, and, at the moment, I would have given all my interest in the fortune in question, to have seen her face, (most of her body was out of the window, for I heard her again rustling the bush above my head,) in order to judge of her motive by its expression; but an envious rose grew exactly in the only spot where it was possible to get a glimpse.

"Why do you wish so cruel a thing?" resumed Dr. Etherington, a little earnestly.

"Because I hate stock-jobbing, and its riches, father. Were Jack poorer, it seems to me, he would be better esteemed."

As this was uttered, the dear girl drew back, and I then perceived that I had mistaken her cheek for one of the largest and most blooming of the flowers. Dr. Etherington laughed, and I distinctly heard him kiss the blushing face of his daughter. I think I would have given up my hopes in another million, to have been the rector of Tenthpig, at that instant.

"If this be all, child," he answered, "set thy heart at rest. Jack's money will never bring him into contempt, unless through the use he may make of it. Alas! Anna, we live in an age of corruption and cupidity! Generous motives appear to be lost sight of, in the general desire of gain; and he who would manifest a disposition to a pure and disinterested philanthropy, is either distrusted as a hypocrite, or derided as a fool. The accursed revolution among our neighbors, the French, has quite unsettled opinions, and religion itself has tottered in the wild anarchy of theories, to which it has given rise. There is no worldly advantage that has been more austerely denounced by the divine writers, than riches, and yet it is fast rising to be the god of the ascendant. To say nothing of an hereafter, society is getting to be corrupted by it to the core, and even respect for birth is yielding to the mercenary feeling."

"And do you not think pride of birth, father, a mistaken prejudice, as well as pride of riches?"

"Pride of any sort, my love, cannot exactly be defended on evangelical principles; but surely some distinctions among men are necessary, even for quiet. Were the levelling principle acknowledged, the lettered and the accomplished must descend to an equality with the ignorant and vulgar, since all men cannot rise to the attainments of the former class, and the world would retrograde to barbarism. The character of a Christian gentleman is much too precious to trifle with, in order to carry out an impracticable theory."

Anna was silent. Probably she was confused between the opinions which she most liked to cherish, and the faint glimmerings of truth to which we are reduced, by the ordinary relations of life. As for the good rector himself, I had no difficulty in understanding his bias, though neither his premises nor his conclusions possessed the logical clearness that used to render his sermons so delightful, more especially when he preached about the higher qualities of the Saviour's dispensation, such as charity, love of our fellows, and, in particular, the imperative duty of humbling ourselves before God

A month after this accidental dialogue, chance made me the auditor of what passed between my ancestor and Sir Joseph Job, another celebrated dealer in the funds, in an interview that took place in the house of the former, in Cheapside. As the difference was so *patent*, as the French express it, I shall furnish the substance of what passed.

"This is a serious and a most alarming movement, Mr. Goldencalf," observed Sir Joseph, "and calls for union and cordiality among the holders of property. Should these damnable opinions get fairly abroad among the people, what would become of us?—I ask, Mr. Goldencalf, what would become of us?"

"I agree with you, Sir Joseph, it is very alarming!—frightfully alarming!"

"We shall have Agrarian laws, sir.—Your money, sir, and mine,—our hard earnings, will become the prey of political robbers, and our children will be beggared, to satisfy the envious longings of some pitiful scoundrel without a six-pence!"

"'Tis a sad state of things, Sir Joseph; and government is very culpable that it don't raise at least ten new regiments."

"The worst of it is, good Mr. Goldencalf, that there are some jack-a-napes of the aristocracy who lead the rascals on, and lend them the sanction of their names. It is a great mistake, sir, that we give so much importance to birth in this island, by which means proud beggars set unwashed blackguards in motion, and the substantial subjects are the sufferers. Property, sir, is in danger, and property is the only true basis of society."

"I am sure, Sir Joseph, I never could see the smallest use in birth."

"It is of no use, but to beget pensioners, Mr. Goldencalf.—Now, with property, it is a different thing—money is the parent of money, and by money a state becomes powerful and prosperous. But this accursed revolution among our neighbors, the French, has quite unsettled opinions, and, alas property is in perpetual danger!"

"Sorry am I to say, I feel it to be so in every nerve of my body, Sir Joseph."

"We must unite and defend ourselves Mr Goldencalf, else both you and I, men warm enough and substantial enough at present, will be in the ditch. Do you not see that we are in actual danger of a division of property?"

"God forbid!"

"Yes, sir, our sacred property is in danger!"

Here, Sir Joseph shook my father cordially by the hand, and withdrew. I find, by a memorandum among the papers of my deceased ancestor, that he paid the broker of Sir Joseph, that day month, sixty-two thousand seven hundred and twelve pounds of difference, (as bull and bear,) owing to the fact of the knight having got some secret information through a clerk in one of the offices; an advantage that enabled him, in this instance, at least, to make a better bargain than one who was generally allowed to be among the shrewdest calculators on 'Change.

My mind was of a nature to be considerably exercised, (as the pious purists express it,) by becoming the depository of sentiments so diametrically opposed to each other, as those of Dr. Etherington and those of Sir Joseph Job. On the one side, I was taught the degradation of birth; on the other, the dangers of property. Anna was usually my confidant, but on this subject I was tongue-tied, for I dared not confess that I had overheard the discourse with her father, and I was compelled to digest the contradictory doctrines by myself, in the best manner I could.

CHAPTER IV.

Showing the ups and downs, the hopes and fears, and the vagaries of love, some views of death, and an account of an inheritance.

From my twentieth to my twenty-third year, no event occurred of any great moment. The day I became of age, my father settled on me a regular allowance of a thousand a year, and I make no doubt I should have spent my time much as other young men, had it not been for the peculiarity of my birth, which I now began to see was wanting in a few of the requisites to carry me successfully through a struggle for place, with a certain portion of what is called the great world. While most were anxious to trace themselves into obscurity, there was a singular reluctance to effecting the object as clearly and as distinctly as it was in my power to do. From all which, as well as from much other testimony, I have been led to infer, that the doses of mistification which appear to be necessary to the happiness of the human race, require to be mixed with an experienced and a delicate hand. Our organs, both physically and morally, are so fearfully constituted, that they require to be protected from realities. As the physical eye has need of clouded glass, to look steadily at the sun, so it would seem the mind's eye has also need of something smoky, to look steadily at truth. But, while I avoided laying open the secret of my heart to Anna, I sought various opportunities to converse with Dr. Etherington and my father, on those points which gave me the most concern. From the first, I heard principles which went to show that society was of necessity divided into orders; that it was not only impolitic, but wicked, to weaken the barriers by which they were separated; that Heaven had its seraphs and cherubs, its archangels and angels, its saints and its merely happy, and that, by obvious induction, this world ought to have its kings, lords, and commons. The usual winding up of all the Doctor's essays, was a lamentation on the confusion in classes that was visiting England as a judgment. My ancestor, on the other hand, cared little for social classification, or for any other conservatory expedient but force.

On this topic he would talk all day, regiments and bayonets glittering in every sentence. When most eloquent on this theme, he would cry, (like Mr. Manners Sutton,) "ORDER—order!" nor can I recall a single disquisition that did not end with, "Alas, Jack, property is in danger!"

I shall not say that my mind entirely escaped confusion among these conflicting opinions, although I luckily got a glimpse of one important truth, for both the commentators cordially agreed in fearing and, of necessity, in hating the mass of their fellow-creatures. My own natural disposition was inclining to philanthropy, and, as I was unwilling to admit the truth of theories that arrayed me in open hostility against so large a portion of mankind, I soon determined to set up one of my own, which, while it avoided the faults, should include the excellencies, of both the others. It was, of course, no great affair merely to form such a resolution; but I shall have occasion to say a word hereafter, on the manner in which I attempted to carry it out in practice.

Time moved on, and Anna became each day more beautiful. I thought that she had lost some of her frankness and girlish gaiety, it is true, after the dialogue with her father; but this I attributed to the reserve and discretion that became the expanding reason and greater feeling of propriety that adorn young womanhood. With me she was always ingenuous and simple, and were I to live a thousand years, the angelic serenity of countenance with which she invariably listened to the theories of my busy brain, would not be erased from recollection.

We were talking of these things one morning quite alone. Anna heard me when I was most sedate with manifest pleasure, and she smiled mournfully when the thread of my argument was entangled by a vagary of the imagination. I felt at my heart's core what a blessing such a Mentor would be, and how fortunate would be my lot could I succeed in securing her for life. Still I did not—could not summon courage to lay bare my inmost thoughts, and to beg a boon that, in these moments of transient humility, I feared I never should be worthy to possess.

"I have even thought of marrying," I continued, so occupied with my own theories as not to weigh, with the accuracy that becomes the frankness and superior advantages which man possesses over the gentler sex, the full import of my words—"could I find one, Anna, as gentle, as good, as beautiful, and as wise as yourself, who would consent to be mine, I should not wait a minute; but, unhappily, I fear this is not likely to be my blessed lot. I am not the grandson of a Baronet, and your father expects to unite you with one who can at least show that the "bloody hand" has once been borne on his shield; and, on the other side, my father talks of nothing but millions." During the first part of this speech, the amiable girl looked kindly up at me, and with a seeming desire to soothe me; but at its close, her eyes dropped upon her work, and she remained silent. "Your father says that every man who has an interest in the state should give it pledges,"—here Anna smiled, but so covertly, that her sweet mouth scarce betrayed the impulse—"and that none others can ever control it to advantage. I have thought of asking my father to buy a borough and a baronetcy, for with the first, and the influence that his money gives, he need not long wish for the last; but I never open my lips on any matter of the sort, that he does not answer—'Fol lol der rol, Jack, with your knighthoods and social order and bishoprics and boroughs—property is in danger!—loans and regiments, if thou wilt,—give us more order—'ORDER—order'—bayonets are what we want, boy, and good wholesome taxes. to accustom the nation to contribute to its own wants, and to maintain its credit. Why, youngster if the interest on the debt were to remain unpaid twenty-four hours, your body corporate, as you call it, would die a natural death; and what would then become of your knights-barro-knights—and barren enough some of them are getting to be, by their wastefulness and extravagance. Get thee married, Jack, and settle prudently. There is neighbor Silverpenny has an only daughter of a suitable age; and a good hussy is she, in the bargain. The only daughter of Oliver Silverpenny will be a suitable wife for the only son of Thomas Goldencalf; though I give thee notice, boy, that thou wilt be cut off with a competency; so keep thy head clear of extravagant castle-building, learn economy in season, and, above all, make no debts.'" Anna laughed as I humorously imitated the well-known intonations of Mr. Speaker Sutton, but a cloud darkened her bright features when I concluded.

"Yesterday I mentioned the subject to your father," I resumed, "and he thought with me, that the idea of the borough and the baronetcy was a good one. 'You would be the *second* of your line, Jack,' he said, 'and that is always better than being the first; for there is no security for a man's being a good member of society, like that of his having presented to his eyes the examples of those who have gone before him, and who have been distinguished by their services, or their virtues. If your father would consent to come into parliament and sustain government at this critical moment his origin would be overlooked, and you would have pride in looking back on his acts. As it is, I fear his whole soul is occupied with the unworthy and debasing passion of mere gain. Money is a necessary auxiliary to rank, and without rank there can be no order, and without order no liberty; but when the love of money gets to occupy the place of respect for descent and past actions, a community loses the very sentiment on which all its noble exploits are bottomed.' So, you see, dear Anna, that our parents hold very different opinions on a very grave question, and between natural affection and acquired veneration, I scarcely know which to receive. If I could find one, sweet, and wise, and beautiful as thou, and who could pity me, I would marry to-morrow, and cast all the future on the happiness that is to be found with such a companion."

As usual, Anna heard me in silence. That she did not, however, view matrimony with exactly the same eyes as myself, was clearly proved the very next day, for young Sir Harry Griffin (the father was dead) offered in form, and was very decidedly refused.

Although I was always happy at the rectory, I could not help feeling, rather than seeing, that, as the French express it, I occupied a false position in society. Known to be the expectant of great wealth, it was not easy to be overlooked altogether in a country whose government is based on a representation of property, and in which boroughs are openly in market; and yet they who had obtained the accidental advantage of having their fortunes made by their grandfathers, were constantly convincing me that mine, vast as it was thought to be, was made by my father. Ten thousand times did I wish (as it has since been expressed by the great captain of the age,) that I had been my own grandson; for, notwithstanding the probability that he who is nearest to the founder of a fortune, is the most likely to share the largest in its accumulations, as he who is nearest in descent to the progenitor who has illustrated his race, is the most likely to feel the influence of his character, I was not long in perceiving that in highly refined and intellectual communities, the public sentiment, as it is connected with the respect and influence that are the meed of both, directly refutes the inferences of all reasonable conjectures on the subject. I was out of my place, uneasy, ashamed, proud, and resentful;—in short, I occupied a *false position*,—and, unluckily, one from which I saw no plausible retreat, except by falling back on Lombard Street, or by cutting my throat. Anna, alone,—kind, gentle, serene-eyed Anna, entered into all my joys, sympathized in my mortifications, and appeared to view me as I was; neither dazzled by my wealth, nor repelled by my origin. The day she refused young Sir Harry Griffin, I could have kneeled at her feet, and called her blessed!

It is said that no moral disease is ever benefited by its study. I was a living proof of the truth of the opinion, that brooding over one's wrongs or infirmities seldom does much more than aggravate the evil. I greatly fear it is in the nature of man to depreciate the advantages he actually enjoys, and to exaggerate those which are denied him. Fifty times, during the six months that succeeded the repulse of the young baronet, did I resolve to take heart, and to throw myself at the feet of Anna, and as often was I deterred by the apprehension that I had nothing to render me worthy of one so excellent, and especially of one who was the granddaughter of the seventh English baronet. I do not pretend to explain the connexion between cause and effect, for I am neither physician nor metaphysician; but the tumult of spirits that resulted from so many doubts, hopes, fears, resolutions and breakings of resolutions, began to affect my health, and I was just about to yield to the advice of my friends (among whom Anna was the most earnest and the most sorrowful,) to travel, when an unexpected call to attend the death-bed of my ancestor was received. I tore myself from the rectory, and hurried up to town, with the diligence and assiduity of an only son and heir, summoned on an occasion so solemn.

I found my ancestor still in the possession of his senses, though given over by the physicians; a circumstance that proved a degree of disinterestedness and singleness of purpose on their part, that was scarcely to be expected towards a patient who it was commonly believed was worth more than a million. My reception by the servants, and by the two or three friends who had assembled on this melancholy occasion, too, was sympathizing, warm, and of a character to show their solicitude and forethought.

My reception by the sick man was less marked. The total abstraction of his faculties in the one great pursuit of his life; a certain sternness of purpose, which is apt to get the ascendant with those who are resolute to gain, and which usually communicates itself to the manners; and an absence of those kinder ties that are developed by the exercise of the more familiar charities of our existence, had opened a breach between us, that was not to be filled by the simple unaided fact of natural affinity I say of natural affinity, for, notwithstanding the doubts that cast their shadows on that branch of my genealogical tree by which I was connected with my maternal grandfather, the title of the King to his crown is not more apparent, than was my direct lineal descent from my father. I always believed him to be my ancestor de jure, as well as de facto, and could fain have loved him and honoured him as such, had my natural yearnings been met with more lively bowels of sympathy on his side.

Notwithstanding the long and unnatural estrangement that had thus existed between the father and son, the meeting, on the present occasion, however, was not entirely without some manifestations of feeling.

"Thou art come at last, Jack," said my ancestor. "I was afraid, boy, thou might'st be too late."

The difficult breathing, haggard countenance, and broken utterance of my father, struck me with awe. This was the first death-bed by which I had ever stood; and the admonishing picture of time passing into eternity, was indelibly stamped on my memory. It was not only a death-bed scene, but it was a family death-bed scene. I know not how it was, but I thought my ancestor looked more like the Goldencalfs than I had ever seen him look before.

"Thou hast come at last, Jack," he repeated, "and I'm glad of it. Thou art the only being in whom I have now any concern. It might have been better, perhaps, had I lived more with my kind—— but thou wilt be the gainer. Ah! Jack, we are but miserable mortals, after all!—To be called away so suddenly, and so young!"

My ancestor had seen his seventy-fifth birth-day; but, unhappily, he had not settled all his accounts with the world, although he had given the physi cian his last fee, and sent the parson away with a donation to the poor of the parish, that would make even a beggar merry for a whole life.

"Thou art come at last, Jack!—Well, my loss will be thy gain, boy! Send the nurse from the room."

I did as commanded, and we were left to ourselves.

"Take this key," handing me one from beneath his pillow, "and open the upper draw of my secretary. Bring me the packet which is addressed to thyself."

I silently obeyed; when my ancestor, first gazing at it with a sadness that I cannot well describe—for it was neither worldly, nor quite of an ethereal character, but a singular and fearful compound of both,—put the papers into my hand, relinquishing his hold slowly and with reluctance.

"Thou wilt wait till I am out of thy sight, Jack?"

A tear burst from out its source, and fell upon the emaciated hand of my father. He looked at me wistfully, and I felt a slight pressure that denoted affection.

"It might have been better, Jack, had we known more of each other. But Providence made me fatherless, and I have lived childless by my own folly. Thy mother was a saint, I believe; but I fear I learned it too late. Well, a blessing often comes at the eleventh hour!"

As my ancestor now manifested a desire not to be disturbed, I called the nurse, and quitted the room, retiring to my own modest chamber, where the packet, a large bundle of papers sealed and directed to myself in the handwriting of the dying man, was carefully secured under a good lock. I did not meet my father again, but once, under circumstances which admitted of intelligible communion. From the time of our first interview he gradually grew worse, his reason tottered, and, like the sinful cardinal of Shakspeare, "he died and gave no sign."

Three days after my arrival, however, I was left alone with him, and he suddenly revived from a state approaching to stupor. It was the only time, since the first interview, in which he had seemed even to know me.

"Thou art come at last!" he said, in a tone that was already sepulchral—"Canst tell me, boy, why they had golden rods to measure the city?"—his nurse had been reading to him a chapter of the Revelations, which had been selected by himself—"Thou seest, lad, the wall itself was of jasper, and the city was of pure gold—I shall not need money in my new habitation—ha! it will not be wanted there!—I am not crazed, Jack—would I had loved gold less and my kind more.—The city itself is of pure gold, and the walls of jasper—precious abode!—ha! Jack, thou hearest, boy—I am happy—too happy, Jack!—gold—gold!"

The final words were uttered with a shout. They were the last that ever came from the lips of Thomas Goldencalf. The noise brought in the attendants, who found him dead. I ordered the room to be cleared, as soon as the melancholy truth was fairly established, and remained several minutes alone with the body. The countenance was set in death. The eyes, still open, had that revolting glare of frenzied delight with which the spirit had departed, and the whole face presented the dread picture of a hopeless end. I knelt, and, though a Protestant, prayed fervently for the soul of the deceased. I then took my leave of the first and the last of all my ancestors.

To this scene succeeded the usual period of outward sorrow, the interment, and the betrayal of the expectations of the survivors. I observed that the house was much frequented by many who rarely or never had crossed its threshold during the life of its late owner. There was much cornering, much talking in an under-tone, and looking at me, that I did not understand, and gradually the number of regular visiters increased, until it amounted to about twenty. Among them were the parson of the parish, the trustees of several notorious charities, three attorneys, four or five well-known dealers of the stock-exchange, foremost among whom was Sir Joseph Job, and three of the professionally benevolent, or of those whose sole occupation appears to be that of quickening the latent charities of their neighbors.

The day after my ancestor was finally removed from our sight, the house was more than usually crowded. The secret conferences increased both in earnestness and in frequency, and finally I was summoned to meet these ill-timed guests in the room which had been the sanctum sanctorum of the late owner of the dwelling. As I entered among twenty strange faces, wondering why I, who had hitherto passed through life so little heeded, should be so unseasonably importuned, Sir Joseph Job presented himself as the spokesman of the party.

"We have sent for you, Mr. Goldencalf," the knight commenced, decently wiping his eyes, "because we think that respect for our late much-esteemed, most excellent, and very respectable friend requires that we no longer neglect his final pleasure, but that we should at once proceed to open his will, in order that we may take prompt measures for its execution. It would have been more regular had we done this before he was in terred, for we cannot have foreseen his pleasure concerning his venerable remains; but it is fully my determination to have every thing done as he has ordered, even though we may be compelled to disinter the body."

I am habitually quiescent, and possibly credulous, but nature has not denied me a proper spirit. What Sir Joseph Job, or any one but myself, had to do with the will of my ancestor, did not strike me at first sight; and I took care to express as much, in terms it was not easy to misunderstand.

"The only child, and, indeed, the only known relative of the deceased," I said, "I do not well see, gentlemen, how this subject should interest, in this lively manner, so many strangers!"

"Very spirited and proper, no doubt, sir," returned Sir Joseph, smiling; "but you ought to know, young gentleman, that if there are such things as heirs, there are also such things as executors!"

This I did know already, and I had also somewhere imbibed an opinion that the latter was commonly the most lucrative situation.

"Have you any reason to suppose, Sir Joseph Job, that my late father has selected you to fulfil this trust?"

"That will be better known in the end, young gentleman. Your late father is known to have died rich; very rich—not that he has left as much by half a million as vulgar report will have it—but what I should term comfortably off; and it is unreasonable to suppose that a man of his great caution and prudence should suffer his money to go to the heir-at-law, that heir being a youth only in his twenty-third year, ignorant of business, not over-gifted with experience, and having the propensities of all of his years in this ill-behaving and extravagant age, without certain trusts and provisions, which will leave his hard earnings, for some time to come, under the care of men who, like himself, know the full value of money."

"No, never!—'tis quite impossible—'tis more than impossible!" exclaimed the by-standers, all shaking their heads.

"And the late Mr. Goldencalf, too, intimate with most of the substantial names on 'Change, and particularly with Sir Joseph Job!" added another.

Sir Joseph Job nodded his head, smiled, stroked his chin, and stood waiting for my reply.

"Property is in danger, Sir Joseph," I said, ironically; "but it matters not. If there is a will, it is as much my interest to know it as it can possibly be yours; and I am quite willing that a search be made on the spot."

Sir Joseph looked daggers at me; but, being a man of business, he took me at my word, and, receiving the keys I offered, a proper person was immediately set to work to open the drawers. The search was continued for four hours without success. Every private drawer was rummaged, every paper opened, and many a curious glance was cast at the contents of the latter, in order to get some clue to the probable amount of the assets of the deceased. Consternation and uneasiness very evidently increased among most of the spectators, as the fruitless examination proceeded; and when the notary ended, declaring that no will was to be found, nor any evidence of credits, every eye was fastened on me, as if I were suspected of stealing that which, in the order of nature, was likely to be my own without the necessity of crime.

"There must be a secret repository of papers somewhere," said Sir Joseph Job, as if he sus pected more than he wished just then to express—"Mr. Goldencalf is largely a creditor on the public books, and yet here is not so much as scrip for a pound!"

I left the room, and soon returned, bringing with me the bundle that had been committed to me by my father.

"Here, gentlemen," I said, "is a large packet of papers that were given to me by the deceased, on his death-bed, with his own hands. It is, as you see, sealed with his seal, and especially addressed to me, in his own hand-writing, and it is not violent to suppose that the contents concern me only. Still, as you take so great an interest in the affairs of the deceased, it shall now be opened, and those contents, so far as you can have any right to know them, shall not be hid from you."

I thought Sir Joseph looked grave when he saw the packet, and had examined the hand-writing of the envelope. All, however, expressed their satisfaction that the search was now most probably ended. I broke the seals, and exposed the contents of the envelope. Within it, there were several smaller packets, each sealed with the seal of the deceased, and each addressed to me, in his own hand-writing, like the external covering. Each of these smaller packets, too, had a separate endorsement of its contents. Taking them as they lay, I read aloud the nature of each, before I proceeded to the next They were also numbered.

"No. 1."—I commenced—"Certificates of public stock held by Tho: Goldencalf, June 12th, 1815." We were now at June 29th, of the same year. As I laid aside this packet, I observed that the sum endorsed on its back greatly exceeded a million 'No 2. Certificates of Bank of England stock.' This sum was several hundred thousands of pounds

"No. 3. South Sea Annuities." Nearly three hundred thousand pounds. "No. 4. Bonds and mortgages." Four hundred and thirty thousand pounds "No. 5. The Bond of Sir Joseph Job, for sixty-three thousand pounds."

I laid down the paper, and involuntarily exclaimed, "Property is in danger!" Sir Joseph turned pale, but he beckoned to me to proceed, saying,— "We shall soon come to the will, sir."

"No. 6.——" I hesitated; for it was an assignment to myself, which, from its very nature, I perceived was an abortive attempt to escape the payment of the legacy duty.

"Well, sir, No. 6.?" inquired Sir Joseph, with tremulous exultation.

"Is an instrument affecting myself, and with which you have no concern, sir."

"We shall see, sir—we shall see, sir—if you refuse to exhibit the paper, there are laws to compel you."

"To do what, Sir Joseph Job?—To exhibit to my father's debtors, papers that are exclusively addressed to me, and which can affect me only?— But here is the paper, gentlemen, that you so much desire to see. 'No. 7. The Last Will and Testament of Tho: Goldencalf, dated June 17th, 1816.'" (He died June the 24th, of the same year.)

"Ah! the precious instrument!" exclaimed Sir Joseph Job, eagerly extending his hand, as if expecting to receive the will.

"This paper, as you perceive, gentlemen," I said, holding it up in a manner that all present might see it, "is especially addressed to myself, and it shall not quit my hands until I learn that some other has a better right to it."

I confess my heart failed me as I broke the seals for I had seen but little of my father, and I knew that he had been a man of very peculiar opinions as well as habits. The will was all in his own hand writing, and it was very short. Summoning cou rage, I read it aloud, in the following words:—

"In the name of God,—Amen: I, Tho: Goldencalf, of the parish of Bow, in the city of London, do publish and declare this instrument to be my last Will and Testament:—

"That is to say; I bequeath to my only child and much beloved son, John Goldencalf; all my real estate in the parish of Bow, and city of London, aforesaid, to be held in fee-simple, by him, his heirs, and assigns, for ever.

"I bequeath to my said only child and much beloved son, John Goldencalf, all my personal property, of every sort and description whatever, of which I may die possessed, including bonds and mortgages, public debt, bank stock, notes of hand, goods and chattels, and all others of my effects, to him, his heirs, or assigns.

"I nominate and appoint my said much beloved son, John Goldencalf, to be the sole executor of this my last will and testament, counselling him not to confide in any of those who may profess to have been my friends; and particularly to turn a deaf ear to all the pretensions and solicitations of Sir Joseph Job, Knight.. In witness whereof," &c. &c.

The will was duly executed, and it was witnessed by the nurse, his confidential clerk, and the house-maid.

"Property is in danger, Sir Joseph!" I dryly remarked, as I gathered together the papers, in order to secure them.

"This will may be set aside, gentlemen!" cried the Knight, in a fury. "It contains a libel!"

"And for whose benefit, Sir Joseph?" I quietly

inquired. "With or without the will, my title to my father's assets would seem to be equally valid.'

This was so evidently true, that the more prudent retired in silence; and even Sir Joseph, after a short delay, during which he appeared to be strangely agitated, withdrew. The next week, his failure was announced, in consequence of som extravagant risks on 'Change, and eventually I received but three shillings and four-pence in the pound, for my bond of sixty-three thousand.

When the money was paid, I could not help exclaiming, mentally, "Property is in danger!"

The following morning, Sir Joseph Job balanced his account with the world, by cutting his throat.

CHAPTER V.

About the social-stake system, the dangers of concentration, and other moral and immoral curiosities.

The affairs of my father were almost as easy of settlement as those of a pauper. In twenty-four hours I was completely master of them, and found myself, if not the very richest, certainly one of the richest subjects of Europe. I say subjects, for sovereigns frequently have a way of appropriating the effects of others, that would render a pretension to rivalry ridiculous. Debts there were none; and if there had been, ready money was not wanting: the balance in cash in my favor at the bank amounted of itself to a fortune.

The reader may now suppose that I was perfectly happy. Without a solitary claim on either my time or my estate, I was in the enjoyment of an income that materially exceeded the revenues of many reigning princes. I had not an expensive nor a vicious habit of any sort. Of houses, horses, hounds, packs, and menials, there were none to vex or perplex me. In every particular save one, I was completely my own master. That one was the near, dear, cherished sentiment that rendered Anna in my eyes an angel, (and truly she was little short of it in those of other people,) and made her the polar star to which every wish pointed. How gladly would I have paid half a million, just then, to be the grandson of a baronet, with precedency from the seventeenth century!

There was, however, another and a present cause for uneasiness, that gave me even more concern than the fact that my family reached the dark ages with so much embarrassing facility. In witnessing the dying agony of my ancestor, I had got a dread lesson on the vanity, the hopeless character, the dangers and the delusions of wealth, that time can never eradicate. The history of its accumulation was ever present to mar the pleasure of its possession. I do not mean that I suspected what, by the world's convention, is deemed dishonesty—of that there had been no necessity—but simply that the heartless and estranged existence, the waste of energies, the blunted charities, and the isolated and distrustful habits of my father, appeared to me to be but poorly requited by the joyless ownership of his millions. I would have given largely to be directed in such a way as, while escaping the wastefulness of the shoals of Scylla, I might in my own case steer clear of the miserly rocks of Charybdis.

When I drove from between the smoky lines of the London houses, into the green fields, and amid the blossoming hedges, this earth looked beautiful, and as if it were made to be loved. I saw in it the workmanship of a divine and a beneficent Creator, and it was not difficult to persuade myself that he who dwelt in the confusion of a town, in order to transfer gold from the pocket of his neighbor to his own, had mistaken the objects of his being. My poor ancestor, who had never quitted London, stood before me with his dying regrets; and my first resolution was, to live in open communion with my kind. So intense, indeed, did my anxiety to execute this purpose become, that it might have led even to frenzy, had not a fortunate circumstance interposed to save me from so dire a calamity.

The coach in which I had taken passage, (for I purposely avoided the parade and trouble of a post-chaise and servants,) passed through a market town of known loyalty, on the eve of a contested election. This appeal to the intelligence and patriotism of the constituency, had occurred in consequence of the late incumbent having taken office. The new minister, for he was a member of the cabinet, had just ended his canvass, and he was about to address his fellow-subjects, from a window of the tavern in which he lodged. Fatigued, but ready to seek mental relief by any means, I threw myself from the coach, secured a room, and made one of the multitude.

The favorite candidate occupied a large balcony, surrounded by his principal friends, among whom it was delightful to see Earls, Lords John, Baronets, dignitaries of the church, tradesmen of influence in the borough, and even a mechanic or two, all squeezed together in the agreeable amalgamation of political affinity. 'Here then,' thought I, 'is an example of the heavenly charities! The candidate, himself the son and heir of a peer, feels that he is truly of the same flesh and blood as his constituents;—how amiably he smiles!—how bland are his manners!—and with what cordiality does he shake hands with the greasiest and the worst! There must be a corrective to human pride, a stimulus to the charities, a never-ending lesson of benevolence in this part of our excellent system, and I will look farther into it.'——The candidate appeared, and his harangue commenced.

Memory would fail me, were I to attempt recording the precise language of the orator, but his opinions and precepts are so deeply graven on my recollection, that I do not fear misrepresenting them. He commenced with a very proper and an eloquent eulogium on the constitution, which he fearlessly pronounced to be, in its way, the very perfection of human reason; in proof of which he adduced the well-ascertained fact, that it had always been known, throughout the vicissitudes and trials of so many centuries, to accommodate itself to circumstances, abhorring change. "Yes, my friends," he exclaimed, in a burst of patriotic and constitutional fervor—"whether under the roses, or the lilies—the Tudors, the Stuarts, or the illustrious house of Brunswick, this glorious structure has resisted the storms of faction, has been able to receive under its sheltering roof the most opposite elements of domestic strife, affording protection, warmth, ay, and food and raiment"—(here the orator happily laid his hand on the shoulder of a butcher, who wore a frieze over-coat that made him look not unlike a stall-fed beast)—"yes, food and raiment, victuals and drink, to the meanest subject in the realm. Nor is this all; it is a constitution peculiarly English: and who is there so base, so vile, so untrue to himself, to his fathers, to his descendants, as to turn his back on a constitution that is thoroughly and inherently English—a constitution that he has inherited from his ancestors, and which, by every obligation, both human and divine, he is bound to transmit unchanged to posterity;"—here the orator, who continued to speak, however, was deafened by shouts of applause, and that part of the subject might very fairly be considered as definitively settled.

From the constitution as a whole, the candidate next proceeded to extol the particular feature of it, that was known as the borough of Householder. According to his account of this portion of the government, its dwellers were animated by the noblest spirit of independence, the most rooted determination to uphold the ministry, of which he was the least worthy member, and were distinguished by what, in an ecstasy of political eloquence, he happily termed the most freeborn understanding of its rights and privileges. This loyal and judicious borough had never been known to waste its favors on those who had not a stake in the community. It understood that fundamental principle of good government, which lays down the axiom, that none were to be trusted but those who had a visible and an extended interest in the country; for without these pledges of honesty and independence, what had the elector to expect but bribery and corruption—a traffic in his dearest rights, and a bargaining that might destroy the glorious institutions under which he dwelt. This part of the harangue was listened to in respectful silence, and shortly after the orator concluded;—when the electors dispersed with, no doubt, a better opinion of themselves and the constitution, than it had probably been their good fortune to entertain since the previous election.

Accident placed me, at dinner, (the house being crowded,) at the same table with an attorney who had been very active the whole morning, among the householders, and who, I soon learned from himself, was the especial agent of the owner of the independent borough in question. He told me that he had come down with the expectation of disposing of the whole property to Lord Pledge, the ministerial candidate named; but the means had not been forthcoming, as he had been led to hope, and the bargain was unluckily off, at the very moment when it was of the utmost importance to know to whom the independent electors rightfully belonged.

"His Lordship, however," continued the attorney, winking, "has done what is handsome; and there can be no more doubt of his election, than there would be of yours, did you happen to own the borough."

"And is the property now open for sale?" I asked.

"Certainly—my principal can hold out no longer. The price is settled, and I have his power of attorney to make the preliminary bargain. 'Tis a thousand pities that the public mind should be left in this undecided state on the eve of an election."

"Then, sir, I will be the purchaser."

My companion looked at me with astonishment and doubt. He had transacted too much business of this nature, however, not to feel his way before he was either off or on.

"The price of the estate is three hundred and twenty-five thousand pounds, sir, and the rental is only six!"

"Be it so. My name is Goldencalf: by accompanying me to town, you shall receive the money."

"Goldencalf!—What, sir, the only son and heir of the late Thomas Goldencalf, of Cheapside?"

"The same. My father has not been dead a month."

"Pardon me, sir—convince me of your identity—we must be particular in matters of this sort—and you shall have possession of the property in season to secure your own election, or that of any of your friends. I will return Lord Pledge his small advances, and another time he will know better than to fail of keeping his promises. What is a borough good for, if a nobleman's word is not sacred? You will find the electors, in particular, every way worthy of your favor. They are as frank, loyal, and straight-forward a constituency, as any in England. No skulking behind the ballot for them!—and, in all respects, they are fearless Englishmen, who will do what they say, and say whatever their landlord shall please to require of them."

As I had sundry letters and other documents about me, nothing was easier than to convince the attorney of my identity. He called for pen and ink; drew out of his pocket the contract that had been prepared for Lord Pledge; gave it to me to read; filled the blanks; and affixing his name, called the waiters as witnesses, and presented me the paper with a promptitude and respect that I found really delightful. So much, thought I, for having given pledges to society by the purchase of a borough. I drew on my bankers foı three hundred and twenty-five thousand pounds, and arose from table, virtually, the owner of the estate of Householder, and of the political consciences of its tenantry.

A fact so important could not long be unknown; and in a few minutes all eyes in the coffee-room were upon me. The landlord presented himself, and begged I would do him the honor to take possession of his family parlour, there being no other at his disposal. I was hardly installed, before a servant in a handsome livery presented the following note:—

Dear Mr. GOLDENCALF,

I have this moment heard of your being in town, and am exceedingly rejoiced to learn it. A long intimacy with your late excellent and most loyal father, justifies my claiming you for a friend, and I waive all ceremony, (official, of course, is meant, there being no reason for any other between us,) and beg to be admitted for half an hour.

Dear Mr. Goldencalf,

Your's, very faithfully and sincerely,

PLEDGE.

——— GOLDENCALF, Esquire.

Monday evening.

I begged that the noble visiter might not be made to wait a moment. Lord Pledge met me like an old and an intimate friend. He made a hundred handsome inquiries after my dead ancestor; spoke feelingly of his regret at not having been summoned to attend his death-bed; and then very ingenuously and warmly congratulated me on my succession to so large a property.

"I hear, too, you have bought this borough, my dear sir.—I could not make it convenient, just at this particular moment, to conclude my own arrangement,—but it is a good thing. Three hundred and twenty thousand, I suppose, as was mentioned between me and the other party?"

"Three hundred and twenty-*five* thousand, Lord Pledge."

I perceived by the countenance of the noble candidate, that I had paid the odd five thousand as a fine,—a circumstance which accounted for the promptitude of the attorney in the transaction, he most probably pocketing the difference himself.

"You mean to sit, of course?"

"I do, my Lord, as one of the members, at the next general election; but at present, I shall be most happy to aid your return."

"My dear Mr. Goldencalf——"

"Really, without presuming to compliment, Lord Pledge, the noble sentiments I heard you express this morning, were so very proper, so exceedingly statesmanlike, so truly English, that I shall feel infinitely more satisfaction in knowing that you fill the vacant seat, than if it were in my own possession."

"I honor your public spirit, Mr. Goldencalf, and only wish to God, there was more of it in the world. But you can count on our friendship, sir. What you have just remarked, is true—very true—only too true—true to a hair—a–a–a I mean, my dear Mr. Goldencalf, most especially those sentiments of mine which—a–a–a—I say it, before God, without vanity—but which, as you have so very ably intimated, are so truly proper and English."

"I sincerely think so, Lord Pledge, or I should not have said it. I am peculiarly situated, myself. With an immense fortune, without rank, name, or connexions, nothing is easier than for one of my years to be led astray; and it is my ardent desire to hit upon some expedient that may connect me properly with society."

"Marry, my dear young friend—select a wife from among the fair and virtuous of this happy isle—unluckily I can propose nothing in this way myself—for both my own sisters are disposed of."

"I have made my choice, already, I thank you a thousand times, my dear Lord Pledge; although I scarcely dare execute my own wishes. There are objections,—if I were only the child, now, of a baronet's second son, or——"

"Become a baronet yourself," once more interrupted my noble friend, with an evident relief from suspense; for I verily believe he thought I was about to ask for something better. "Your affair shall be arranged by the end of the week—and if there is any thing else I can do for you, I beg you to name it without reserve."

"If I could hear a few more of those remarkale sentiments of yours, concerning the stake we should all have in society, I think it would relieve my mind."

My companion looked at me a moment, with a very awkward sort of intensity, drew his hand across his brows, reflected, and then obligingly complied.

"You attach too much importance, Mr. Goldencalf, to a few certainly very just, but very ill-arranged ideas. That a man, without a proper stake in society, is little better than the beast of the fields, I hold to be so obvious, that it is unnecessary to dwell on the point. Reason as you will, forward or backward, you arrive at the same result,—he that hath nothing, is usually treated by mankind little better than a dog, and he that is little better than a dog, usually has nothing.—Again,—What distinguishes the savage from the civilized man?—why, civilization, to be sure.—Now, what is civilization?—the arts of life.—What feeds, nourishes, sustains the arts of life?—money, or property. By consequence, civilization is property, and property is civilization. If the control of a country is in the hands of those who possess the property, the government is a civilized government; but, on the other hand, if it is in the hands of those who have no property, the government is necessarily an uncivilized government. It is quite impossible that any one should become a safe statesman, who does not possess a direct property interest in society. You know there is not a tyro of our political sect who does not fully admit the truth of this axiom."

"Mr. Pitt?"

"Why, Pitt was certainly an exception, in one way; but then, you will recollect, he was the immediate representative of the tories, who own most of the property of England."

"Mr. Fox?"

"Fox represented the whigs, who own all the rest, you know. No, my dear Goldencalf, reason as you will, we shall always arrive at the same results.—You will, of course, as you have just said, take one of the seats yourself, at the next general election?"

"I shall be too proud of being your colleague, to hesitate."

This speech sealed our friendship; for it was a pledge to my noble acquaintance of his future connexion with the borough. He was much too high-bred to express his thanks in vulgar phrases, (though high-breeding rarely exhibits all its finer qualities pending an election,) but, a man of the world, and one of a class whose main business it is to put the *suaviter in modo*, as the French have it, *en evidence*, the reader may be sure that when we parted that night, I was in perfect good humor with myself, and, as a matter of course, with my new acquaintance.

The next day the canvass was renewed, and we had another convincing speech on the subject of the virtue of "a stake in society;" for Lord Pledge was tactician enough to attack the citadel, once assured of its weak point, rather than expend his efforts on the out-works of the place. That night the attorney arrived from town with the title-deeds all properly executed, (they had been some time in preparation for Lord Pledge,) and the following morning early, the tenants were served with the usual notices, with a handsomely expressed sentiment, on my part, in favor of "a stake in society." About noon, Lord Pledge walked over the course, as it is expressed at New-Market and Doncaster. After dinner we separated, my noble friend returning to town, while I pursued my way to the Rectory.

Anna never appeared more fresh, more serene, more elevated above mortality, than when we met, a week after I had quitted Householder, in the breakfast-parlor of her father's abode.

"You are beginning to look like yourself again, Jack," she said, extending her hand, with the simple cordiality of an Englishwoman; "and I hope we shall find you more rational."

"Ah, Anna, if I could only presume to throw myself at your feet, and to tell you how much and what I feel, I should be the happiest fellow in all England."

"As it is, you are the most miserable!" the laughing girl answered, as, crimsoned to the temples, she drew away the hand I was foolishly pressing against my heart. "Let us go to breakfast, Mr. Goldencalf—my father has ridden across the country to visit Dr. Liturgy."

"Anna," I said, after seating myself, and taking a cup of tea from fingers that were rosy as the morn, "I fear you are the greatest enemy that I have on earth."

"John Goldencalf!" exclaimed the startled girl, turning pale, and then flushing violently. "Pray explain yourself."

"I love you to my heart's core—could marry

you, and then, I fear, worship you, as man never before worshipped woman."

Anna laughed faintly.

"And you feel in danger of the sin of idolatry?" she at length succeeded in saying.

"No, I am in danger of narrowing my sympathies—of losing a broad and safe hold of life—of losing my proper stake in society—of—in short, of becoming as useless to my fellows as my poor, poor father, and of making an end as miserable! Oh! Anna, could you have witnessed the hopelessness of that death-bed, you could never wish me a fate like his!"

My pen is unequal to convey an adequate idea of the expression with which Anna regarded me. Wonder, doubt, apprehension, affection, and anguish, were all beaming in her eyes; but the unnatural brightness of these conflicting sentiments was tempered by a softness that resembled the pearly lustre of an Italian sky.

"If I yield to my fondness, Anna, in what will my condition differ from that of my miserable father's? He concentrated his feelings in the love of money, and I—yes, I feel it here, I know it is here—I should love you so intensely, as to shut out every generous sentiment in favor of others. I have a fearful responsibility on my shoulders,—wealth—gold;—gold, beyond limits; and to save my very soul, I must extend, not narrow, my interest in my fellow-creatures. Were there a hundred such Annas, I might press you all to my heart,—but, one! no—no—'t would be misery—'t would be perdition! The very excess of such a passion would render me a heartless miser, unworthy of the confidence of my fellow-men!"

The radiant and yet serene eyes of Anna seemed to read my soul: and when I had done speaking, she arose, stole timidly to my side of the table, as woman approaches when she feels most, placed her velvet-like hand on my burning forehead, pressed its throbbing pulses gently to her heart, burst into tears, and fled.

We dined alone, nor did we meet again until the dinner hour. The manner of Anna was soothing, gentle, even affectionate; but she carefully avoided the subject of the morning. As for myself, I was constantly brooding over the danger of concentrating interests, and of the excellence of the social-stake system.

"Your spirits will be better, Jack, in a day or two," said Anna, when we had taken wine after the soup. "Country air, and old friends, will restore your freshness and color."

"If there were a thousand Annas, I could be happy, as man was never happy, before! But I must not, dare not, lessen my hold on society."

"All of which proves my insufficiency to render you happy. But here comes Francis, with yesterday morning's paper—let us see what society is about, in London."

After a few moments of intense occupation with the journal, an exclamation of pleasure and surprise escaped the sweet girl. On raising my eyes, I saw her gazing (as I fancied) fondly at myself.

"Read what you have, that seems to give you so much pleasure."

She complied, reading with an eager and tremulous voice the following paragraph:—

"His Majesty has been most graciously pleased to raise John Goldencalf, of Householder Hall, in the county of Dorset, and of Cheapside, Esquire to the dignity of a Baronet of the United Kingdoms of Great Britain and Ireland."

"Sir John Goldencalf, I have the honor to drink to your health and happiness!" cried the delighted girl, brightening like the dawn, and wetting her pouting lip with liquor less ruby than itself. "Here, Francis, fill a bumper, and drink to the new baronet."

The gray-headed butler did as ordered, with a very good grace, and then hurried into the servants' hall, to communicate the news.

"Here at least, Jack, is a new hold that society has on you, whatever hold you may have on society."

I was pleased, because she was pleased, and because it showed that Lord Pledge had some sense of gratitude, (although he afterwards took occasion to intimate that I owed the favor chiefly to *hope*,) and I believe my eyes never expressed more fondness.

"Lady Goldencalf would not have an awkward sound, after all, dearest Anna."

"As applied to one, Sir John, it might possibly do; but not as applied to a hundred." Anna laughed, blushed, burst into tears once more, and again fled.

"What right have I to trifle with the feelings of this single-hearted and excellent girl," said I to myself; "it is evident that the subject distresses her—she is unequal to its discussion, and it is unmanly and improper in me to treat it in this manner. I must be true to my character as a gentleman and a man—ay, and, under presen circumstances, as a baronet; and—I will never speak of it again as long as I live."

The following day I took leave of Dr. Etherington and his daughter, with the avowed intention of travelling for a year or two. The good rector gave me much friendly advice, flattered me with expressions of confidence in my discretion, and, squeezing me warmly by the hand, begged me to recollect that I had always a home at the rectory. When I had made my adieus to the father, I went, with a sorrowful heart, in quest of the daughter. She was still in the little breakfast parlor—that parlor so loved! I found her pale, timid, sensitive, bland, but serene. Little could ever disturb that heavenly quality in the dear girl; if she laughed, it was with a restrained and moderated joy; if she wept, it was like rain falling from a sky that still shone with the lustre of the sun. It was only when feeling and nature were unutterably big within her, that some irresistible impulse of her sex betrayed her into emotions like those I had twice witnessed so lately.

"You are about to leave us, Jack," she said, holding out her hand kindly, and without the affectation of an indifference she did not feel—"you will see many strange faces, but you will see none who——"

I waited for the completion of the sentence, but, although she struggled hard for self-possession, it was never finished.

"At my age, Anna, and with my means, it would be unbecoming to remain at home, when, if I may so express it, 'human nature is abroad.' I go to quicken my sympathies, to open my heart to my kind, and to avoid the cruel regrets that tortured the death-bed of my father."

"Well—well"—interrupted the sobbing girl, "we will talk of it no more. It is best that you should travel; and so adieu, with a thousand—nay millions of good wishes for your happiness and safe return.—You will come back to us, Jack when tired of other scenes?"

This was said with gentle earnestness, and a sincerity so winning, that it came near upsetting all my philosophy; but I could not marry the whole sex, and to bind down my affections in one, would have been giving the death-blow to the development of that sublime principle on which I was bent, and which I had already decided was to make me worthy of my fortune, and the ornament of my species. Had I been offered a kingdom, however, I could not speak. I took the unresisting girl in my arms, folded her to my heart, pressed a burning kiss on her cheek, and withdrew.

"You will come back to us, Jack?" she half whispered, as her hand was reluctantly drawn through my own.

Oh! Anna, it was indeed painful to abandon thy frank and gentle confidence, thy radiant beauty, thy serene affections, and all thy womanly virtues, in order to practise my newly discovered theory! Long did thy presence haunt me—nay, never did it entirely desert me—putting my constancy to a severe proof, and threatening, at each remove, to contract the lengthening chain that still bound me to thee, thy fire-side, and thy altars! But I triumphed, and went abroad upon the earth, with a heart expanding towards all the creatures of God, though thy image was still enshrined in its inmost core, shining in womanly glory, pure, radiant, and without spot, like the floating prism that forms the lustre of the diamond.

CHAPTER VI.

A theory of palpable sublimity—some practical ideas, and the commencement of adventures.

The recollection of the intense feelings of that important period of my life has, in some measure, disturbed the connexion of the narrative, and may possibly have left some little obscurity, in the mind of the reader, on the subject of the new sources of happiness that had broken on my own intelligence. A word here, in the way of elucidation, therefore, may not be misapplied, although it is my purpose to refer more to my acts, and to the wonderful incidents it will shortly be my duty to lay before the world, for a just understanding of my views, than to mere verbal explanations.

Happiness—happiness, here and hereafter, was my goal. I aimed at a life of useful and active benevolence, a death-bed of hope and joy, and an eternity of fruition. With such an object before me, my thoughts, from the moment that I witnessed the dying regrets of my father, had been intensely brooding over the means of attainment. Surprising as, no doubt, it will appear to vulgar minds, I obtained the clue to this sublime mystery, at the late election for the borough of Householder and from the lips of my Lord Pledge. Like other important discoveries, it is very simple when understood, being easily rendered intelligible to the dullest capacities, as, indeed, in equity, ought to be the case with every principle that is so intimately connected with the well-being of man.

It is an universally admitted truth, that happiness is the only legitimate object of all human associations. The ruled concede a certain portion of their natural rights for the benefits of peace, security and order, with the understanding that they are to enjoy the remainder as their own proper indefeasible estate. It is true, that there exist, in different nations, some material differences of opinion on the subject of the quantities to be bestowed and retained; but these aberrations from a just medium are no more than so many caprices of the human judgment, and in no manner do they affect the principle. I found also, that all the wisest and best of the species, or, what is much the same thing, the most responsible, uniformly maintain that he who has the largest stake in society, is, in the nature of things, the most qualified to administer its affairs. By a stake in society is meant, agreeably to universal convention, a multiplication of those interests which occupy us in our daily concerns—or what is vulgarly called, property. This principle works by exciting us to do right, through those heavy investments of our own which would inevitably suffer were we to do wrong. The proposition is now clear, nor can the premises readily be mistaken. Happiness is the aim of society; and property, or a vested interest in that society, is the best pledge of our disinterestedness and justice, and the best qualification for its proper control. It follows as a legitimate corollary, that a multiplication of those interests will increase the stake, and render us more and more worthy of the trust, by elevating us, as near as may be, to the pure and ethereal condition of the angels. One of those happy accidents which sometimes make men emperors and kings, had made me, perhaps, the richest subject of Europe. With this polar star of theory shining before my eyes, and with practical means so ample, it would have been clearly my own fault, had I not steered my bark into the right haven. If he who had the heaviest investments was the most likely to love his fellows, there could be no great difficulty for one in my situation to take the lead in philanthropy. It is true that, with superficial observers, the instance of my own immediate ancestor might be supposed to form an exception, or rather an objection, to the theory. So far from this being the case, however, it proves the very reverse. My father, in a great measure, had concentrated all his investments in the national debt. Now, beyond all cavil he loved the funds intensely; grew violent when they were assailed; cried out for bayonets when the mass declaimed against taxation; eulogized the gallows, when there were menaces of revolt, and, in a hundred other ways, proved that "where the treasure is, there will the heart be also." The instance of my father, therefore, like all exceptions, only went to prove the excellence of the rule. He had merely fallen into the error of contraction, when the only safe course was that of expansion. I resolved to expand; to do that which, probably, no political economist had ever yet thought of doing—in short, to carry out the principle of the social stake in such a way, as should cause me to love all things, and consequently to become worthy of being intrusted with the care of all things.

On reaching town, my earliest visit was one of thanks to my Lord Pledge. At first, I had felt some doubts whether the baronetcy would, or would not, aid the system of philanthropy; for, by raising me above a large portion of my kind, it was, in so much at least, a removal from philanthropical sympathies; but, by the time the patent was received, and the fees were paid, I found that it might fairly be considered a pecuniary investment, and that it was consequently brought within the rule I had prescribed for my own government

The next thing was to employ suitable agents to aid in making the purchases that were necessary to attach me to mankind. A month was diligently occupied in this way. As ready money was not wanting, and I was not very particular on the subject of prices, at the end of that time, I began to have certain incipient sentiments which went to prove the triumphant success of the experiment. In other words, I owned much, and was beginning to take a lively interest in all I owned.

I made purchases of estates in England, Scotland, Ireland and Wales. This division of real property was meant to equalize my sentiments justly, between the different portions of my native country. Not satisfied with this, however, I extended the system to the colonies. I had East India shares, a running ship, Canada land, a plantation in Jamaica, sheep at the Cape and at New South Wales, an indigo concern at Bengal, an establishment for the collection of antiques in the Ionian Isles, and a connexion with a shipping house, for the general supply of our various dependencies with beer, bacon, cheese, broadcloths and ironmongery. From the British Empire, my interests were soon extended into other countries. On the Garonne, and at Xeres, I bought vineyards. In Germany I took some shares in different salt and coal-mines; the same in South America, in the precious metals; in Russia, I dipped deeply into tallow; in Switzerland, I set up an extensive manufactory of watches, and bought all the horses for a voiturier on a large scale. I had silk-worms in Lombardy, olives and hats in Tuscany, a bath in Lucca, and a maccaroni establishment at Naples. To Sicily I sent funds for the purchase of wheat, and at Rome I kept a connoisseur to conduct a general agency in the supply of British articles; such as mustard, porter, pickles, and corned beef; as well as for the forwarding of pictures and statues to the lovers of the arts and of *virtù*.

By the time all this was effected, I found my hands full of business. Method, suitable agents, and a resolution to succeed, smoothed the way, however, and I began to look about me and to take breath. By way of relaxation, I now descended into details; and, for a few days, I frequented the meetings of those who are called "the Saints," in order to see if something might not be done towards the attainment of my object, through their instrumentality. I cannot say that this experiment met with all the success I had anticipated. I heard a great deal of subtle discussion, found that manner was of more account than matter, and had unreasonable and ceaseless appeals to my pocket. So near a view of charity had a tendency to expose its blemishes, as the brilliancy of the sun is known to exhibit defects on the face of beauty, which escape the eye when seen through the medium of that artificial light for which they are best adapted; and I soon contented myself with sending my contributions, at proper intervals, keeping aloof in person. This experiment gave me occasion to perceive, that human virtues, like little candles, shine best in the dark, and that their radiance is chiefly owing to the atmosphere of a "naughty world." From speculating I returned to facts.

The question of slavery had agitated the benevolent for some years, and finding a singular apathy in my own bosom on this important subject, I bought five hundred of each sex, to stimulate my sympathies. This led me nearer to the United States of America, a country that I had endeavored to blot out of my recollection; for, while thus encouraging a love for the species, I had scarcely thought it necessary to go so far from home. As no rule exists without an exception; I confess I was a good deal disposed to believe that a Yankee might very fairly be an omission in an Englishman's philanthropy. But, "in for a penny, in for a pound." The negroes led me to the banks of the Mississippi, where I was soon the owner of both a sugar and a cotton-plantation. In addition to these purchases, I took shares in divers South-Sea-men, owned a coral and pearl-fishery of my own, and sent an agent with a proposition to King Tamamamaah to create a monopoly of sandal-wood, in our joint behalf.

The earth and all it contained assumed new glories in my eyes. I had fulfilled the essential condition of the political economists, the jurists, the constitution-mongers, and all the "talents and decency," and had stakes in half the societies of the world. I was fit to govern, I was fit to advise, to dictate to most of the people of Christendom; for I had taken a direct interest in their welfares, by making them my own. Twenty times was I about to jump into a post-chaise, and to gallop down to the rectory, in order to lay my new-born alliance with the species, and all its attendant felicity, at the feet of Anna,—but the terrible thought of monogamy, and of its sympathy-withering consequences, as often stayed my course. I wrote to her, weekly, however, making her the participator of a portion of my happiness, though I never had the satisfaction of receiving a single line in reply.

Fairly emancipated from selfishness, and pledged to the species, I now quitted England on a tour of philanthropical inspection. I shall not weary the reader with an account of my journeys over the beaten tracks of the continent, but transport him and myself at once to Paris, in which city I arrived on the 17th of May, Anno Domini 1819. I had seen much, fancied myself improved, and, by constant dwelling on my system, saw its excellencies as plainly as Napoleon saw the celebrated star which defied the duller vision of his uncle, the Cardinal. At the same time, as usually happens with those who direct all their energies to a given point, the opinions originally formed of certain portions of my theory, began to undergo mutations, as nearer and more practical views pointed out inconsistencies and exposed defects. As regards Anna, in particular, the quiet, gentle, unobtrusive, and yet distinct picture of womanly loveliness, that was rarely absent from my mind, had, for the past twelve-month, haunted me with a constancy of argument that might have unsettled the Newtonian scheme of philosophy itself. I already more than questioned whether the benefit to be derived from the support of one so affectionate and true, would not fully counterbalance the disadvantage of a concentration of interest, so far as the sex was concerned. This growing opinion was fast getting to be conviction, when I encountered on the boule vards, one day, an old country neighbor of the rec tor's, who gave me the best account of the family adding, after descanting on the beauty and excel lence of Anna herself, that the dear girl had, quite lately, actually refused a peer of the realm, who enjoyed all the acknowledged advantages of youth, riches, birth, rank and a good name, and who had selected her, from a deep conviction of her worth, and of her ability to make any sensible man happy As to my own power over the heart of Anna, I never entertained a doubt. She had betrayed it in a thousand ways, and on a hundred occasions; nor had I been at all backward in letting her understand how highly I valued her dear self, although I had never yet screwed up my resolution so high as distinctly to propose for her hand. But all my unsettled purposes became concentrated on hearing this welcome intelligence; and, taking an abrupt leave of my old acquaintance, I hurried home and wrote the following letter:

Dear—very dear, nay—dearest ANNA:

I met your old neighbor ——, this morning, on the boulevards, and during an interview of an hour we did little else but talk of thee. Although it has been my most ardent and most predominant wish to open my heart to the whole species, yet, Anna, I fear I have loved thee alone! Absence, so far from expanding, appears to contract my affections, too many of which centre in thy sweet form and excellent virtues. The remedy I proposed is insufficient, and I begin to think that matrimony alone can leave me master of sufficient freedom of thought and action, to turn the attention I ought to the rest of the human race. Thou hast been with me in idea, in the four corners of the earth, by sea and by land, in dangers and in safety, in all seasons, regions and situations, and there is no sufficient reason why those who are ever present in the spirit, should be materially separated. Thou hast only to say a word, to whisper a hope, to breathe a wish, and I will throw myself, a repentant truant, at thy feet, and implore thy pity. When united, however, we will not lose ourselves in the sordid and narrow paths of selfishness, but come forth again, in company, to acquire a new and still more powerful hold on this beautiful creation, of which, by this act, I acknowledge thee to be the most divine portion.

Dearest, dearest Anna, thine and the species',

For ever,

JOHN GOLDENCALF

To Miss ETHERINGTON.

If there was ever a happy fellow on earth, it was myself, when this letter was written, sealed, and fairly dispatched. The die was cast; and I walked into the air, a regenerated and an elastic being. Let what might happen, I was sure of Anna. Her gentleness would calm my irritability; her prudence temper my energies; her bland but enduring affections soothe my soul. I felt at peace with all around me, myself included, and I found a sweet assurance of the wisdom of the step I had just taken in the expanding sentiment. If such were my sensations now that every thought centered in Anna, what would they not become when these personal transports were cooled by habit, and nature was left to the action of the ordinary impulses! I began to doubt of the infallibility of that part of my system which had given me so much pain, and to incline to the new doctrine, that by concentration on particular parts, we come most to love the whole. On examination, there was reason to question whether it was not on this principle even, that, as an especial landholder, I attained so great an interest in my native island; for, while I did not certainly own the whole of Great Britain, I felt that I had a profound respect for every thing in it, that was in any, even the most remote manner, connected with my own particular possessions.

A week flew by in delightful anticipations. The happiness of this short but heavenly period became so exciting, so exquisite, that I was on the point of giving birth to an improvement on my theory, (or rather on the theory of the political economists and constitution-mongers, for it is in fact theirs, and not mine,) when the answer of Anna was received. If anticipation be a state of so much happiness,—happiness being the great pursuit of man,—why not invent a purely probationary condition of society?—why not change its elementary features from positive to anticipating interests, which would give more zest to life, and bestow felicity unimpaired by the dross of realities? I had determined to carry out this principle in practice, by an experiment, and left the hotel to order an agent to advertise, and to enter into a treaty or two, for some new investments, (without the smallest intention of bringing them to a conclusion,) when the porter delivered me the ardently expected letter. I never knew what would be the effect of taking a stake in society by anticipation, therefore; the contents of Anna's missive driving every subject that was not immediately connected with the dear writer, and with sad realities, completely out of my head. It is not improbable, however, that the new theory would have proved to be faulty, for I have often had occasion to remark that heirs (in remainder, for instance,) manifest a hostility to the estate, by carrying out the principle of anticipation, rather than any of that prudent respect for social consequences, to which the legislator looks with so much anxiety.

The letter of Anna was in the following words:

Good—nay, Dear JOHN,

Thy letter was put into my hands yesterday. This is the fifth answer I have commenced, and you will therefore see that I do not write without reflection. I know thy excellent heart, John, better than it is known to thyself. It has either led thee to the discovery of a secret of the last importance to thy fellow-creatures, or it has led thee cruelly astray. An experiment so noble and so praiseworthy, ought not to be abandoned, on account of a few momentary misgivings concerning the result. Do not stay thy eagle flight, at the instant thou art soaring so near the sun! Should we both judge it for our mutual happiness, I can become thy wife at a future day. We are still young, and there is no urgency for an immediate union. In the mean time, I will endeavor to prepare myself to be the companion of a philanthropist, by practising on thy theory, and, by expanding my own affections, render myself worthy to be the wife of one who has so large a stake in society, and who loves so many and so truly.

Thine imitator and friend,

Without change,

ANNA ETHERINGTON.

To Sir JOHN GOLDENCALF, Bart.

P. S. You may perceive that I am in a state of improvement, for I have just refused the hand of Lord M'Dee, because I found I loved all his neighbors, quite as well as I loved the young peer himself.

Ten thousand furies took possession of my soul, in the shape of so many demons of jealousy. Anna expanding her affections!—Anna taking any other stake in society than that I made sure she would accept through me!—Anna teaching herself to love more than one, and that one myself!—The thought was madness. I did not believe in the sincerity of her refusal of Lord M'Dee. I ran for a copy of the Peerage, (for since my own elevation in life, I regularly bought both that work and the Baronetage,) and turned to the page that contained his name. He was a Scottish Viscount, who had just been created a Baron of the United Kingdom, and his age was precisely that of my own. Here was a rival to excite distrust! By a singular contradiction in sentiments, the more I dreaded his power to injure me, the more I undervalued his means. While I fancied Anna was merely playing with me, and had in secret made up her mind to be a peeress, I had no doubt that the subject of her choice was both ill-favored and awkward, and had cheek-bones like a Tartar While reading of the great antiquity of his family (which reached obscurity in the thirteenth century,)

I set it down as established, that the first of his unknown predecessors was a bare-legged thief, and, at the very moment that I imagined Anna was smiling on him, and retracting her coquettish denial, I could have sworn that he spoke with an unintelligible border accent, and that he had red hair!

The torment of such pictures grew to be intolerable, and I rushed into the open air for relief. How long, or whither I wandered, I know not; but on the morning of the following day I found I was seated in a *guinguette*, near the base of Montmartre, eagerly devouring a roll, and refreshing myself with sour wine. When a little recovered from the shock of discovering myself in a situation so novel, (for, having no investments in guinguettes, I had not taken sufficient interest in these popular establishments ever to enter one before,) I had leisure to look about and survey the company. Some fifty Frenchmen of the laboring classes were drinking on every side, and talking with a vehemence of gesticulation, and a clamor, that completely annihilated thought. This then, thought I, is a scene of popular happiness. These creatures are excellent fellows, enjoying themselves on liquor that has not paid the city-duty; and perhaps I may seize upon some point that favors my system among spirits so frank and clamorous. Doubtless, if any one among them is in possession of any important social secret, it will not fail to escape him here. From meditations of this philosophical character, I was suddenly aroused by a violent blow before me, accompanied with an exclamation, in very tolerable English, of the word—

"King!"

On the centre of the board which did the office of a table, and directly beneath my eyes, lay a clenched fist of fearful dimensions, that, in color and protuberances, bore a good deal of resemblance to a freshly unearthed Jerusalem artichoke. Its sinews seemed to be cracking with tension, and the whole knob was so expressive of intense pugnacity, that my eyes involuntarily sought its owner's face. I had unconsciously taken my seat directly opposite a man whose stature was nearly double that of the compact, bustling, sputtering, and sturdy little fellows, who were bawling on every side of us, and whose skinny lips, instead of joining in the noise, were so firmly compressed as to render the crevice of the mouth no more strongly marked than a wrinkle in the brow of a man of sixty. His complexion was naturally fair, but exposure had tanned the skin of his face to the color of the *crackle* of a roasted pig; those parts which a painter would be apt to term the "high lights" being indicated by touches of red, nearly as bright as fourth-proof brandy. His eyes were small, stern, fiery, and very gray; and just at the instant they met my admiring look, they resembled two stray coals, that, by some means, had got separated from the body of adjacent heat in the face. He had a prominent, well-shaped nose, athwart which the skin was stretched like leather in the process of being rubbed down on the currier's bench, and his ropy black hair was carefully smoothed over his temples and brows, in a way to show that he was abroad on a holiday excursion.

When our eyes met, this singular-looking being gave me a nod of friendly recognition, for no better reason that I could discover, than the fact that I did not appear to be a Frenchman.

"Did mortal man ever listen to such fools, Captain," he observed, as if certain we must think alike on the subject.

"Really I did not attend to what was said; there certainly is much noise."

"I don't pretend to understand a word of what they are saying, myself; but it *sounds* like thorough nonsense."

"My ear is not yet sufficiently acute to distinguish sense from nonsense by mere intonation and sound—but it would seem, sir, that you speak English, only."

"Therein you are mistaken; for, being a great traveller, I have been compelled to look about me, and as a nat'ral consequence, I speak a little of all languages. I do not say that I use the foreign parts of speech always fundamentally, but then I worry through an idee so as to make it legible and of use, especially in the way of eating and drinking. As to French, now, I can say '*don-nez-me some van*,' and '*don-nez-vous some pan*' as well as the best of them; but when there are a dozen throats bawling at once, as is the case with these here chaps, why one might as well go on the top of Ape's Hill, and hold a conversation with the people he will meet with there, as to pretend to hold a rational or a discussional discourse. For my part, where there is to be a conversation, I like every one to have his turn, keeping up the talk, as it might be, watch and watch; but among these Frenchmen it is pretty much as if their idees had been caged, and the door being suddenly opened, they fly out in a flock, just for the pleasure of saying they are at liberty."

I now perceived that my companion was a reflecting being, his ratiocination being connected by regular links, and that he did not boost his phiosop iy on the leaping-staff of impulse, like most of those who were sputtering, and arguing, and wrangling, with untiring lungs, in all corners of the *guinguette*. I frankly proposed, therefore, that we should quit the place, and walk into the road, where our discourse would be less disturbed, and consequently more satisfactory. The proposal was well received, and we left the brawlers, walking by the outer boulevards towards my hotel in the Rue de Rivoli, by the way of the Champs Elysées.

CHAPTER VII.

Touching an amphibious animal, a special introduction, and its consequences.

I SOON took an interest in my new acquaintance. He was communicative, shrewd, and peculiar; and though apt to express himself quaintly, it was always with the pith of one who had seen a great deal of, at least, one portion of his fellow-creatures. The conversation, under such circumstances, did not flag; on the contrary, it soon grew more interesting by the stranger's beginning to touch on his private interests. He told me that he was a mariner, who had been cast ashore by one of the accidents of his calling, and, by way of putting in a word in his own favor, he gave me to understand that he had seen a great deal, more especially of that caste of his fellow-creatures, who, like himself, live by frequenting the mighty deep.

"I am very happy," I said, "to have met with a stranger who can give me information touching an entire class of human beings, with whom I have, as yet, had but little communion. In order that we may improve the occasion to the utmost,

I propose that we introduce ourselves to each other at once, and swear an eternal friendship, or, at least, until we may find it convenient to dispense with the obligation."

"For my part, I am one who like the friendship of a dog better than his enmity," returned my companion, with a singleness of purpose that left him no disposition to waste his breath in idle compliments. "I accept the offer, therefore, with all my heart; and this the more readily, because you are the only one I have met, for a week, who can ask me how I do, without saying '*Come on, cong portez-vous.*' Being used to meet with squalls, however, I shall accept your offer under the last condition named."

I liked the stranger's caution. It denoted a proper care of character, and furnished a proof of responsibility. The condition was therefore accepted on my part, as frankly as it had been urged on his.

"And now, sir," I added, "when we had shaken each other very cordially by the hand, "may I presume to ask your name?"

"I am called Noah, and I don't care who knows it. I'm not ashamed of either of my names, whatever else I may be ashamed of."

"Noah ——?"

"Poke, at your service"—he pronounced the word slowly and very distinctly, as if what he had just said of his self-confidence were true. As I had afterwards occasion to take his signature, I shall at once give it in the proper form—"Capt Noah Poke."

"Of what part of England are you a native Mr. Poke?"

"I believe I may say, of the new parts."

"I did not know that any portion of the island

was so designated. Will you have the good-nature to explain yourself."

"I'm a native of Stunin'tun, in the state of Connecticut, in *old* New England. My parents being dead, I was sent to sea a four-year-old, and here I am, walking about the kingdom of France without a cent in my pocket, a shipwrecked mariner. Hard as my lot is, to say the truth, I'd about as leave starve as live by speaking their d——d lingo."

"Shipwrecked—a mariner—starving—and a Yankee!"

"All that, and maybe more, too; though, by your leave, commodore, we'll drop the last title. I'm proud enough to call myself a Yankee, but my back is apt to get up when I hear an Englishman use the word. We are yet friends, and it may be well enough to continue so, until some good comes of it, to one or the other of the parties."

"I ask your pardon, Mr. Poke, and will not offend again. Have you circumnavigated the globe?"

Capt. Poke snapped his fingers, in pure contempt of the simplicity of the question.

"Has the moon ever sailed round the 'arth! Look here a moment, commodore"—he took from his pocket an apple, of which he had been munching half-a-dozen during the walk, and held it up to view—"draw your lines which way you will on this sphere; crosswise, or lengthwise, up or down, zig-zag or parpendic'lar, and you will not find more traverses than I've worked about the old ball!"

"By land, as well as by sea?"

"Why, as to the land, I've had my share of that, too; for it has been my hard fortune to run upon it, when a softer bed would have given a more quiet nap. This is just the present difficulty with me, for I am now tacking about among these Frenchmen in order to get afloat again, like an alligator floundering in the mud. I lost my schooner on the north-east coast of Russia—somewhere hereabouts," pointing to the precise spot on the apple; "we were up there trading in skins—and finding no means of reaching home by the road I'd come, and smelling salt water down here-away, I've been shaping my course westward, for the last eighteen months, steering as near as might be directly athwart Europe and Asia; and here I am at last, within two days' run of Havre, which is, if I can get good Yankee planks beneath me once more, within some eighteen or twenty days' run of home."

"You allow me, then, to call the planks, Yankee?"

"Call 'em what you please, commodore; though I should prefar to call 'em the 'Debby and Dolly of Stunin'tun,' to any thing else, for that was the name of the craft I lost.—Well, the best of us are but frail, and the longest-winded man is no dolphin to swim with his head under water!"

"Pray, Mr. Poke, permit me to ask where you learned to speak the English language with so much purity?"

"Stunin'tun—I never had a mouthful of schooling but what I got at home. It's all homespun. I make no boast of scholarship; but as for navigation, or for finding my way about the 'arth, I'll turn my back on no man, unless it be to leave him behind. Now we have people with us, that think a great deal of their geometry and astronomics but I hold to no such slender threads. My way is when there is occasion to go anywhere, to settle it well in my mind as to the place, and then to make as straight a wake, as natur' will allow taking little account of the charts, which are as ap to put you wrong as right;—and when they do ge you into a scrape, it's a smasher! Depend on yourself and human natur', is my rule; though I admit there is some accommodation in a compass particularly in cold weather."

"Cold weather!—I do not well comprehend th distinction."

"Why, I rather conclude that one's scent gets to be dullish in a frost; but this may be no more than a conceit, after all, for the two times I've been wrecked were in summer, and both the accidents happened by sheer dint of hard blowing, and in broad day-light, when nothing human, short of a change of wind, could have saved us."

"And you prefer this peculiar sort of navigation?"

"To all others, especially in the sealing-business, which is my ra'al occupation. It's the very bes way in the world, to discover islands; and every body knows that we sealers are always on th look-out for su'thin' of that sort."

"Will you suffer me to inquire, Captain Poke, how many times you have doubled Cape Horn?"

My navigator threw a quick, jealous glance at me, as if he distrusted the nature of the question.

"Why, that is neither here nor there;—perhaps I don't double either of the capes, perhaps I do. I get into the South Sea with my craft, and it's of no great moment how it's done. A skin is worth just as much in the market, though the furrier may not happen to have a glossary of the road it has travelled."

"A glossary?"

"What matters a signification, commodore, when people understand each other? This over-land journey has put me to my wits, for you will understand, that I've had to travel among natives that cannot speak a syllable of the homespun; so I brought the schooner's dictionary with me as a sort of terrestrial almanac, and I fancied that, as they spoke gibberish to me, the best way was to give it to them back again, as near as might be in their own coin, hoping I might hit on su'thin' to their liking. By this means, I've come to be rather more voluble than formerly."

"The idea was happy."

"No doubt it was, as is just evinced. But, having given you a pretty clear insight into my natur' and occupation, it is time that I ask a few questions of you. This is a business, you must know, at which we do a good deal at Stunin'tun, and at which we are commonly thought to be handy."

"Put your questions, Capt. Poke; I hope the answers will be satisfactory."

"Your name?"

"John Goldencalf—by the favor of His Majesty, Sir John Goldencalf, Baronet."

"'Sir John Goldencalf—by the favor of His Majesty, a Baronet!' Is Baronet a calling? or what sort of crittur or thing is it?"

"It is my rank, in the kingdom to which I belong."

"I begin to understand what you mean. Among your nation, mankind is what we call stationed, like a ship's people that are called to go about;—you have a certain birth in that kingdom of yours, much as I should have in a sealing schooner."

"Exactly so; and I presume you will allow that order, and propriety, and safety, result from this method, among mariners?"

"No doubt—no doubt; we station anew, however, each v'yage, according to experience: I'm not so sure that it would do to take even the cook from father to son, or we might have a pretty mess of it."

Here the sealer commenced a series of questions which he put with a vigor and perseverance that, I fear, left me without a single fact of my life unrevealed, except those connected with the sacred sentiment that bound me to Anna, and which were far too hallowed to escape me, even under the ordeal of a Stunin'tun inquisitor. In short, finding that I was nearly helpless in such hands, I made a merit of necessity, and yielded up my secrets, as wood in a vice discharges its moisture. It was scarcely possible that a mind like mine, subjected to the action of such a pair of moral screws, should not yield some hints touching its besetting propensities. The Captain seized this clue, and he went at the theory like a bull-dog at the muzzle of an ox.

To oblige him, therefore, I entered, at some length, into an explanation of my system. After the general remarks that were necessary to give a stranger an insight into its leading principles, I gave him to understand that I had long been looking for one like him, for a purpose that shall now be explained to the reader. I had entertained some negotiations with Tamaahmaah, and had certain investments in the pearl and whale-fisheries, it is true; but, on the whole, my relations with all that portion of mankind who inhabit the islands of the Pacific, the north-west coast of America, and the north-east coast of the old continent, were rather loose, and generally in an unsettled and vague condition; and it appeared to me that I had been singularly favored, in having a man so well adapted to their regeneration, thrown, as it were, by Providence, and in a manner so unusual, directly in my way. I now frankly proposed, therefore, to fit out an expedition, that should be partly of trade and partly of discovery, in order to expand my interests in this new direction, and to place my new acquaintance at its head. Ten minutes of earnest explanation on my part, sufficed to put my companion in possession of the leading features of the plan.—When I had ended this direct appeal to his love of enterprise, I was answered by the favorite exclamation of—

"King!"

"I do not wonder, Captain Poke, that your admiration breaks out in this manner; for, I believe, few men fairly enter into the beauty of this benevolent system, who are not struck equally with its grandeur and its simplicity. May I count on your assistance?"

"This is a new idee, Sir Goldencalf——"

"Sir John Goldencalf, if you please, sir."

"A new idee, Sir John Goldencalf, and it needs circumspection. Circumspection in a bargain, is the certain way to steer clear of misunderstandings. You wish a navigator to take your craft, let her be what she will, into unknown seas, and I wish, naturally, to make a straight course for Stunin'tun.—You see the bargain is in apogee, from the start."

"Money is no consideration with me, Captain Poke."

"Well, this is an idee that has brought many a more difficult contract at once into perigee, Sir John Goldencalf. Money is always a considerabl consideration with me, and I may say, also, just now it is rather more so than usual. But when a gentleman clears the way as handsomely as you have now done, any bargain may be counted as a good deal more than half made."

A few explicit explanations disposed of this part of the subject, and Captain Poke accepted of my terms in the spirit of frankness with which they were made. Perhaps his decision was quickened by an offer of twenty Napoleons, which I did not neglect making on the spot. Amicable, and in some respects confidential, relations were now established between my new acquaintance and myself; and we pursued our walk, discussing the details necessary to the execution of our project. After an hour or two passed in this manner, I invited my companion to go to my hotel, meaning that he should partake of my board until we could both depart for England, where it was my intention to purchase, without delay, a vessel for the contemplated voyage, in which I also had decided to embark in person.

We were obliged to make our way through the throng that usually frequents the lower part of the Champs Elysées, during the season of good weather and towards the close of day. This task was nearly over, when my attention was particularly drawn to a group that was just entering the place of general resort, apparently with the design of adding to the scene of thoughtlessness and amusement. But, as I am now approaching the most material part of this extraordinary work, it will be proper to reserve the opening for a new chapter

CHAPTER VIII.

An introduct.on to four new characters, some touches of pri-losophy, and a few capital thoughts on political economy.

The group which drew my attention was composed of six individuals, two of which were animals of the genus *homo*, or what is vulgarly termed *man;* and the remainder were of the order *primates*, and of the class *mammalia;* or what, in common parlance, are called *monkeys*.

The first were Savoyards, and may be generally described as being *unwashed, ragged* and *carnivorous;* in colour, *swarthy;* in lineaments and expression, *avaricious* and *shrewd*, and in appetites *voracious*. The latter were of the common species, of the usual size, and of approved gravity. There were two of each sex; being very equally paired as to years and external advantages.

The monkeys were all habited with more or less of the ordinary attire of our modern European civilization; but peculiar care had been taken with the toilet of the senior of the two males. This individual had on the coat of a hussar, a cut that would have given a particular part of his body a more military *contour* than comported with his real character, were it not for a red petticoat, that was made shorter than common; less, however, with a view to show a pretty foot and ankle, than to leave the nether limbs at liberty to go through with certain extravagant efforts, which the Savoyards were unmercifully exacting from his natural agility. He wore a Spanish hat, decorated with a few bedraggled feathers, a white cockade, and a wooden sword. In addition to the latter, he carried in his hand a small broom.

Observing that my attention was strongly attracted to this party, the ill-favored Savoyards immediately commenced a series of experiments in saltation, with the sole view, beyond a question, to profit by my curiosity. The inoffensive victims of this act of brutal tyranny, submitted with a patience worthy of the profoundest philosophy, meeting the wishes of their masters with a readiness and dexterity that was beyond all praise. One swept the earth, another leaped on the back of a dog, a third threw himself head-over-heels, again and again, without a murmur; and the fourth moved gracefully to and fro, like a young girl in a quadrille. All this might have passed without calling for particular remark, (since, alas! the spectacle is only too common,) were it not for certain eloquent appeals that were made to me, through the eyes, by the individual in the hussar jacket. His look was rarely averted from my face for a moment, and, in this way, a silent communion was soon established between us. I observed that his gravity was indomitable. Nothing could elicit a smile, or a change of countenance. Obedient to the whip of his brutal master, he never refused the required leap; for minutes at a time, his legs and petticoat described confused circles in the air, appearing to have taken a final leave of the earth; but, the effort ended, he invariably descended to the ground with a quiet dignity and composure, that showed how little the inward monkey partook of the antics of the outward animal. Drawing my companion a little aside, I ventured to suggest a few thoughts to him on the subject.

"Really, Captain Poke, it appears to me there is great injustice in the treatment of these poor creatures!" I said. "What right have these two foul-looking blackguards to seize upon beings much more interesting to the eye, and, I dare say, far more intellectual, than themselves, and cause them to throw their legs about in this extravagant manner, under the penalty of stripes, and without regard to their feelings, or to their convenience?—I say, sir, the measure appears to me to be intolerably oppressive, and it calls for prompt redress."

"King!"

"King or subject, it does not alter the moral deformity of the act. What have these innocent beings done, that they should be subjected to this disgrace? Are they not flesh and blood, like ourselves—do they not approach nearer to our form and, for aught we know to the contrary, to our reason, than any other animal? and is it tolerable that our nearest imitations, our very cousins, should be thus dealt by? Are they dogs, that they are treated like dogs?"

"Why, to my notion, Sir John, there isn't a dog on 'arth that can take such a summerset. Their flapjacks are quite extraor'nary!"

"Yes, sir, and more than extraordinary; they are oppressive. Place yourself, Mr. Poke, for a single instant, in the situation of one of these persons; fancy that you had a hussar jacket squeezed upon your brawny shoulders, a petticoat placed over your lower extremities, a Spanish hat with bedraggled feathers set upon your head, a wooden sword stuck at your side, and a broom put into your hand; and that these two Savoyards were to menace you with stripes unless you consented to throw summersets for the amusement of strangers—I only ask you to make the case your own, sir, and then say what course you would take, and what you would do?"

"I would lick both of these young blackguards Sir John, without remorse, break the sword and the broom over their heads, kick their sensibilities till they couldn't see, and take my course for Stunin'tun, where I belong."

"Yes, sir, this might do with the Savoyards who are young and feeble"——

"'Twouldn't alter the case much, if two of these Frenchmen were in their places"—put in the Captain, glaring wolfishly about him. "To be plain with you, Sir John Goldencalf, being human, I'd submit to no such monkey tricks."

"Do not use the term reproachfully, Mr. Poke, I entreat of you. We call these animals monkeys, it is true; but we do not know what they call themselves. Man is merely an animal, and you must very well know"——

"Harkee, Sir John"—interrupted the Captain, "I'm no botanist, and do not pretend to more schooling than a sealer has need of, for finding his way about the 'arth; but, as for a man's being an animal, I just wish to ask you, now, if, in your judgment, a hog is also an animal?"

"Beyond a doubt—and fleas, and toads, and sea-serpents, and lizards, and water-devils—we are all, neither more nor less than animals."

"Well, if a hog is an animal, I am willing to allow the relationship; for, in the course of my experunce, which is not small, I have met with men that you might have mistaken for hogs, in every thing but the bristles, the snout, and the tail. I'll never deny what I've seen with my own eyes, though I suffer for it; and therefore I admit that hogs being animals, it is more than likely that some men must be animals too."

"We call these interesting beings monkeys; but how do we know that they do not return the compliment and call us, in their own particular dialect, something quite as offensive. It would become our species to manifest a more equitable and philosophical spirit, and to consider these interesting strangers as an unfortunate family which has fallen into the hands of brutes, and which is, in every way, entitled to our commiseration and our active interference. Hitherto, I have never sufficiently stimulated my sympathies for the animal world, by any investment in quadrupeds; but it is my intention to write to-morrow to my English agent to purchase a pack of hounds and a suitable stud of horses; and by way of quickening so laudable a resolution, I shall forthwith make propositions to the Savoyards for the speedy emancipation of this family of amiable foreigners. The slave trade is an innocent pastime, compared to the cruel oppression that the gentleman in the Spanish hat, in particular, is compelled to endure."

"King!"

"He may be a king, sure enough, in his own country, Captain Poke;—a fact that would add tenfold agony to his unmerited sufferings."

Hereupon, I proceeded, without more ado, to open a negotiation with the Savoyards. The judicious application of a few Napoleons soon brought about a happy understanding between the contracting parties, when the Savoyards transferred to my hands the strings which confined their vassals, as the formal and usual acknowledgment of the right of ownership. Committing the three others to the keeping of Mr. Poke, I led the individual in the hussar-jacket a little on one side, and, raising my hat, to show that I was superior to the vulgar feeling of feudal superiority, I addressed him, briefly, in the following words:—

"Although I have ostensibly bought the right

which these Savoyards professed to have in your persons and services, I seize an early occasion to inform you that, virtually, you are now free. As we are among a people accustomed to see your race in subjection, however, it may not be prudent to proclaim the nature of the present transaction, lest there might be some further conspiracies against your natural rights. We will retire to my hotel, forthwith, therefore, where your future happiness shall be the subject of our more mature and of our united deliberations."

The respectable stranger in the hussar-jacket heard me with inimitable gravity and self-command. until, in the warmth of feeling, I raised an arm in earnest gesticulation, when, most probably overcome by the emotions of delight that were naturally awakened in his bosom by this sudden change of fortune, he threw three summersets, or flapjacks, as Captain Poke had quaintly designated his evolutions, in so rapid succession, as to render it, for a moment, a matter of doubt whether nature had placed his head or his heels uppermost.

Making a sign for Captain Poke to follow, I now took my way directly to the rue de Rivoli. We were attended by a constantly increasing crowd, until the gate of the hotel was fairly entered; and glad was I to see my charge safely housed, for there were abundant indications of another design upon their rights, in the taunts and ridicule of the living mass that rolled up, as it were, upon our heels. On reaching my own apartment, a courier, who had been waiting my return, and who had just arrived express from England, put a packet into my hands, stating that it came from my principal English agent. Hasty orders were given to attend to the comfort and wants of Captain Poke and the strangers, (orders that were in no danger of being neglected, since Sir John Goldencalf, with the reputed annual revenue of three millions of francs, had unlimited credit with all the inhabitants of the hotel,) and I hurried into my cabinet, and sat down to the eager perusal of the different communications.

Alas! there was not a line from Anna! The obdurate girl still trifled with my misery; and, in revenge, I entertained a momentary resolution of adopting the notions of Mahmoud, in order to qualify myself to set up a harem.

The letters were from a variety of correspondents, embracing many of those who were entrusted with the care of my interests in very opposite quarters of the world. Half an hour before, I had been dying to open more intimate relations with the interesting strangers; but my thoughts instantly took a new direction, and I soon found that the painful sentiments I had entertained touching their welfare and happiness, were quite lost in the newly awakened interests that lay before me. It is in this simple manner, no doubt, that the system to which I am a convert effects no small part of its own great purposes. No sooner does any one interest grow painful by excess, than a new claim arises to divert the thoughts, a new demand is made on the sensibilities; and, by lowering our affections from the intensity of selfishness, to the more bland and equable feeling of impartiality, forms that just and generous condition of the mind at which the political economists aim, when they dilate on the glories and advantages of their favorite theory of the social stake.

In this happy frame of mind, I fell to reading the letters with avidity, and with the god-like determination to reverence Providence and to do justice.—Fiat justitia ruat cœlum!

The first epistle was from the agent of the principal West-India estate. He acquainted me with the fact that all hopes from the expected crop were destroyed by a hurricane, and he begged that I would furnish the means necessary to carry on the affairs of the plantation, until another season might repair the loss. Priding myself on punctuality as a man of business, before I broke another seal, a letter was written to a banker in London, requesting him to supply the necessary credits, and to notify the agent in the West-Indies of the circumstance. As he was a member of parliament, I seized the occasion, also, to press upon him the necessity of government's introducing some early measure for the protection of the sugar-growers, a most meritorious class of his fellow-subjects, and one whose exposures and actual losses called loudly for relief of this nature. As I closed the letter. I could not help dwelling, with complacency, on the zeal and promptitude with which I had acted—the certain proof of the usefulness of the theory of investments.

The second communication was from the man ager of an East-India property, that very happily came with its offering to fill the vacuum left by the failure of the crops just mentioned. Sugar was likely to be a drug in the peninsula, and my correspondent stated that the cost of transportation being so much greater than from the other colonies this advantage would be entirely lost, unless go vernment did something to restore the East-Indian to his natural equality. I enclosed this letter in one to my Lord Say and Do, who was in the ministry, asking of him, in the most laconic and pointed terms, whether it were possible for the empire to prosper, when one portion of it was left in possession of exclusive advantages, to the prejudice of all the others? As this question was put with a truly British spirit, I hope it had some tendency to open the eyes of his Majesty's ministers; for much was shortly after said, both in the journals and in Parliament, on the necessity of protecting our East-Indian fellow-subjects, and of doing natural justice by establishing the national prosperity on the only firm basis, that of Free Trade.

The next letter was from the acting partner of a large manufacturing house, to which I had advanced quite half the capital, in order to enter into a sympathetic communion with the cotton-spinners. The writer complained heavily of the import duty on the raw article; made some poignant allusions to the increasing competition on the continent and in America; and pretty clearly intimated that the Lord of the manor of Householder ought to make himself felt by the administration, in a question of so much magnitude to the nation. On this hint I spake. I sat down, on the spot, and wrote a long letter to my friend, Lord Pledge, in which I pointed out to him the danger that threatened our political economy; that we were imitating the false theories of the Americans, (the countrymen of Captain Poke); that trade was clearly never so prosperous as when it was the most successful; that succes depended on effort, and effort was the most efficien when the least encumbered; and, in short that, as it was self-evident a man would jump fart ier without being in foot-irons, or strike harder without being handcuffed, so it was equally apparent, that a merchant would make a better bargain for himself, when he could have things all his own way, than when his enterprise and industry were shackled by the impertinent and selfish interposition of the interests of others. In conclusion, there was an eloouent description of the demoralizing consequences of smuggling, and a pungent attack on the tendencies of taxation in general. I have written and said some good things in my time, as several of my dependants have sworn to me, in a way that even my natural modesty cannot repudiate; but I shall be excused for the weakness, if I now add, that I believe this letter to Lord Pledge contained some as clever points, as any thing I remember, in their way; the last paragraph, in particular, being positively the neatest and the best turned moral I ever produced.

Letter fourth was from the steward of the Householder estate. He spoke of the difficulty of getting the rents; a difficulty that he imputed altogether to the low price of corn. He said that it would soon be necessary to re-let certain farms; and he feared that the unthinking cry against the corn-laws would affect the conditions. It was incumbent on the landed interest to keep an eye on the popular tendencies, as respected this subject; for any material variation from the present system would lower the rental of all the grain-growing counties in England, thirty per cent., at least, at a blow. He concluded with a very hard rap at the Agrarians, a party that was just coming a little into notice in Great Britain, and, by a very ingenious turn, in which he completely demonstrated that the protection of the landlord and the support of the Protestant religion were indissolubly connected. There was also a vigorous appeal to the common sense of the subject, on the danger to be apprehended by the people from themselves; which he treated in a way that, a little more expanded, would have made a delightful homily on the rights of man.

I believe I meditated on the contents of this letter fully an hour. Its writer, John Dobbs, was as worthy and upright a fellow as ever breathed; and I could not but admire the surprising knowledge of men which shone through every line he had indited. Something must be done, it was clear; and, at length, I determined to take the bull by the horns, and to address Mr. Huskisson at once, as the shortest way of coming at the evil. He was the political sponsor for all the new notions on the subject of our foreign mercantile policy; and, by laying before him, in a strong point of view, the fatal consequences of carrying his system to extremes, I hoped something might yet be done for the owners of real estate, the bones and sinews of the land.

I shall just add, in this place, that Mr. Huskisson sent me a very polite and a very statesman-like reply, in which he disclaimed any intention of meddling improperly with British interests, in any way; that taxation was necessary to our system, and of course every nation was the best judge of its own means and resources; but that he merely aimed at the establishment of just and generous principles, by which nations that had no occasion for British measures should not unhandsomely resort to them; and that certain eternal truths should stand, like so many well-constructed tubs, each on its own bottom. I must say I was pleased with this attention from a man generally reputed as clever as Mr. Huskisson, and from that time I became a convert to most of his opinions.

The next communication that I opened, was from the overseer of the estate in Louisiana, who informed me that the general aspect of things in that quarter of the world was favorable, but the small-pox had found its way among the negroes, and the business of the plantation would immediately require the services of fifteen able-bodied men, with the usual sprinkling of women and children. He added, that the laws of America prohibited the further importation of blacks from any country without the limits of the Union, but that there was a very pretty and profitable internal trade in the article; and that the supply might be obtained, in sufficient season, either from the Carolinas, Virginia, or Maryland. He admitted, however, that there was some choice between the different stocks of these several states, and that some discretion might be necessary in making the selection. The negro of the Carolinas was the most used to the cotton-field, had less occasion for clothes, and it had been proved by experiment, could be fattened on red herrings; while, on the other hand, the negro farther north had the highest instinct, could sometimes reason, and that he had even been known to preach, when he had got as high up as Philadelphia. He much affected, also, bacon and poultry. Perhaps it might be well to purchase samples of lots from all the different stocks in market.

In reply, I assented to the latter idea, suggesting the expediency of getting one or two of the higher castes from the north; I had no objection to preaching, provided they preached work; but I cautioned the overseer particularly against schismatics. Preaching, in the abstract, could do no harm; all depending on doctrine.

This advice was given as the result of much earnest observation. Those European states that had the most obstinately resisted the introduction of letters, I had recently had occasion to remark, were changing their systems, and were about to act on the principle of causing "fire to fight fire." They were fast having recourse to school-books, using no other precaution than the simple expedient of writing them themselves. By this ingenious invention, poison was converted into food, and truths of all classes were at once put above the dangers of disputations and heresies.

Having disposed of the Louisianian, I very gladly turned to the opening of the sixth seal. The letter was from the efficient trustee of a company to whose funds I had largely contributed, by way of making an investment in charity. It had struck me, a short time previously to quitting home, that interests positive as most of those I had embarked in, had a tendency to render the spirit worldly; and I saw no other check to such an evil, than by seeking for some association with the saints, in order to set up a balance against the dangerous propensity. A lucky occasion offered through the wants of the Philo-african-anti-compulsion-free-labour Society, whose meritorious efforts were about to cease for want of the great charity-power—gold. A draft for five thousand pounds had obtained me the honor of being advertised as a shareholder and a patron; and, I know not why!—but it certainly caused me to inquire into the results with far more interest than I had ever before felt in any similar institution. Perhaps this benevolent anxiety arose from that principle in our nature, which induces us to look after whatever has been our own, as long as any part of it can be seen.

The principal trustee of the Philo-african-anti-compulsion-free-labour Society now wrote to state that some of the speculations which had gone *pari passu* with the charity, had been successful, and that the shareholders were, by the fundamental provisions of the association, entitled to a dividend, but—how often that awkward word stands between the cup and the lip!—*but*, that he was of opinion the establishment of a new factory, near a point where the slavers most resorted, and where gold-dust and palm-oil were also to be had in the greatest quan tities, and consequently at the lowest prices, would equally benefit trade and philanthropy; that, by a judicious application of our means, these two interests might be made to see-saw very cleverly, as cause and effect, effect and cause; that the black man would be spared an incalculable amount of misery, the white man a grievous burthen of sin, and the particular agents of so manifest a good might quite reasonably calculate on making, at the very least, forty per cent. per annum on their money, besides having all their souls saved, in the bargain. Of course I assented to a proposition so reasonable in itself, and which offered benefits so plausible!

The next epistle was from the head of a great commercial house in Spain, in which I had taken some shares, and whose interests had been temporarily deranged by the throes of the people in their efforts to obtain redress for real or imaginary wrongs. My correspondent showed a proper indignation on the occasion, and was not sparing in his language whenever he was called to speak of popular tumults. "What do the wretches wish!' he asked, with much point—"Our lives, as well as our property? Ah! my dear sir, this bitter fact impresses us all (by us, he meant the mercantile interests) with the importance of strong executives. Where should we have been, but for the bayonets of the king? or what would have become of our altars, our firesides and our persons, had it not pleased God to grant us a monarch indomitable in will, brave in spirit, and quick in action?" I wrote a proper answer of congratulation, and turned to the next epistle, which was the last of the communications.

The eighth letter was from the acting head of

another commercial house, in New-York, United States of America, or the country of Captain Poke, where it would seem the President, by a decided exercise of his authority, had drawn upon himself the execrations of a large portion of the commercial interests of the country; since the effect of the measure, right or wrong, as a legitimate consequence or not, by hook or by crook, had been to render money scarce. There is no man so keen in his philippics, so acute in discovering and so prompt in analyzing facts, so animated in his philosophy, and so eloquent in his complaints, as your debtor, when money unexpectedly gets to be scarce Credit, comfort, bones, sinews, marrow and all, appear to depend on the result; and it is no wonder that, under so lively impressions, men who have hitherto been content to jog on in the regular and quiet habits of barter, should suddenly start up into logicians, politicians, ay, or even into magicians. Such had been the case with my present correspondent, who seemed to know and to care as little in general of the polity of his own country as if he had never been in it, but who now was ready to split hairs with a metaphysician, and who could not have written more complacently of the constitution if he had even read it. My limits will not allow an insertion of the whole letter, but one or two of its sentences shall be given. "Is it tolerable, my dear sir," he went on to say, "that the executive of *any* country, I will not say merely of our own, should possess, or exercise, even admitting that he does possess them, such unheard of powers? Our condition is worse than that of the Mussulmans, who, in losing their money, usually lose their heads and are left in a happy insensibility to their sufferings: but, alas! there is an end of the much boasted liberty of America! The executive has swallow ed up all the other branches of the government, and the next thing will be to swallow up us. Our altars, our firesides, and our persons will shortly be invaded; and I much fear that my next letter will be received by you, long after all correspondence shall be prohibited, every means of communication cut off, and we ourselves shall be precluded from writing, by being chained, like beasts of burthen, to the car of a bloody tyrant." Then followed as pretty a string of epithets as I remember to have heard from the mouth of the veriest shrew at Billingsgate.

I could not but admire the virtue of the "social-stake system," which kept men so sensibly alive to all their rights, let them live where they would, or under what form of government, which was so admirably suited to sustain truth and render us just. In reply, I sent back epithet for epithet, echoed all the groans of my correspondent, and railed as became a man who was connected with a losing concern.

This closed my correspondence for the present and I arose wearied with my labors, and yet greatly rejoicing in their fruits. It was now late, but excitement prevented sleep; and before retiring for the night, I could not help looking in upon my guests. Captain Poke had gone to a room in another part of the hotel, but the family of amiable strangers were fast asleep in the ante-chamber. They had supped heartily, as I was assured, and were now indulging in a happy but temporary oblivion—to use an approved expression—of all their wrongs Satisfied with this state of things, I now sought my own pillow, or, according to a favorite phrase of Mr. Noah Poke, I also "turned in."

CHAPTER IX.

The commencement of wonders, which are the more extraordinary on account of their truth.

I DARE say my head had been on the pillow fully an hour, before sleep closed my eyes. During this time, I had abundant occasion to understand th activity of what are called the "busy thoughts."—Mine were feverish, glowing, and restless. They wandered over a wide field;—one that included Anna, with her beauty, her mild truth, her womanly softness and her womanly cruelty; Captain Poke and his peculiar opinions; the amiable family of quadrupeds and their wounded sensibilities; the excellencies of the social-stake system; and, in short, most of that which I had seen and heard during the last four-and-twenty hours. When sleep did tardily arrive, it overtook me at the very moment that I had inwardly vowed to forget my heartless mistress, and to devote the remainder of my life to the promulgation of the doctrine of the expansive-super-human-generalized-affection-principle, to the utter exclusion of all narrow and selfish views, and in which I resolved to associate myself with Mr. Poke, as with one who had seen a great deal of this earth and its inhabitants, without narrowing down his sympathies in favor of any one place or person, in particular, Stunin'tun and himself very properly excepted.

It was broad day-light when I awoke on the following morning. My spirits were calmed by rest, and my nerves had been soothed by the balmy freshness of the atmosphere. It appeared that my valet had entered and admitted the morning air and then had withdrawn, as usual, to await the signa of the bell, before he presumed to reappear. I lay many minutes, in delicious repose, enjoying the periodical return to life and reason, bringing with it, the pleasures of thought and its ten thousand agreeable associations. The delightful reverie into which I was insensibly dropping, was, however, ere long arrested by low, murmuring, and, as I thought, plaintive voices, at no great distance from my own bed. Seating myself erect, I listened intently, and with a good deal of surprise; for it was not easy to imagine whence sounds, so unusual for that place and hour, could proceed. The discourse was earnest, and even animated; but it was carried on in so low a tone that it would have been utterly inaudible, but for the deep quiet of the hotel. Occasionally a word reached my ear, and I was completely at fault in endeavoring to ascertain even the language. That it was in neither of the five great European tongues, I was certain, for all these I either spoke or read; and there were particular sounds and inflexions that induced me to think that it savored of the most ancient of the two classics. It is true that the prosody of these dialects, at the same time that is is a shibboleth of learning, is a disputed point, the very sounds of the vowels even being a matter of national convention;—the Latin word *dux*, for instance, becoming *ducks* in England, *dooks* in Italy, and *dukes* in France: yet there is a '*je ne sais quoi*,' a delicacy in the auricular taste of a true scholar, that will rarely lead him astray, when his ears are greeted with words that have been used by Demosthenes or Cicero.* In the present instance, I distinctly heard the word, *my-bom-y-nos-fos-kom-i-ton*,

* Or Chichero, or Kickero, whichever may happen to sui the prejudices of the reader.

which I made sure was a verb in the dual number and second person, of a Greek root, but of a signification that I could not, on the instant, master, but which, beyond a question, every scholar will recognize as having a strong analogy to a well-known line in Homer. If I was puzzled with the syllables that accidentally reached me, I was no less perplexed with the intonations of the voices of the different speakers. While it was easy to understand they were of the two sexes, they had no direct affinity to the mumbling sibilations of the English, the vehement monotony of the French, the gagging sonorousness of the Spaniards, the noisy melody of the Italians, the ear-splitting octaves of the Germans, or the undulating, head-over-heels enunciation of the countrymen of my particular acquaintance, Captain Noah Poke. Of all the living languages of which I had any knowledge, the resemblance was nearer to the Danish and Swedish, than to any other; but I much doubted, at the time I first heard the syllables, and still question, if there is exactly such a word as *my-bom-y-nos-fos-kom-i-ton* to be found in even either of those tongues. I could no longer support the suspense. The classical and learned doubts that beset me, grew intensely painful; and, arising with the greatest caution, in order not to alarm the speakers, I prepared to put an end to them all, by the simple and natural process of actual observation.

The voices came from the ante-chamber, the door of which was slightly open. Throwing on a dressing-gown, and thrusting my feet into slippers, I moved on tiptoe to the aperture, and placed my eye in such a situation as enabled me to command a view of the persons of those who were still earnestly talking in the adjoining room All surprise vanished the moment I found that the four monkeys were grouped in a corner of the apartment, where they were carrying on a very animated dialogue, the two oldest of the party (a male and a female) being the principal speakers. It was not to be expected that even a graduate of Oxford, although belonging to a sect so proverbial for classical lore, that many of them knew nothing else, could, at the first hearing, decide upon the analogies and character of a tongue that is so little cultivated even in that ancient seat of learning. Although I had now certainly a direct clue to the root of the dialect of the speakers, I found it quite impossible to get any useful acquaintance with the general drift of what was passing among them. As they were my guests, however, and might possibly be in want of some of the conveniences that were necessary to their habits, or might even be suffering under still graver embarrassments, I conceived it to be a duty to waive the ordinary usages of society, and at once offer whatever it was in my power to bestow, at the risk of interrupting concerns that they might possibly wish to consider private. Using the precaution, therefore, to make a little noise, as the best means of announcing my approach, the door was gently opened, and I presented myself to view. At first I was a little at a loss in what manner to address the strangers; but, believing that a people who spoke a language so difficult of utterance and so rich as that I had just heard, like those who use dialects derived from the Slavonian root, were most probably the masters of all others; and remembering, moreover, that French was a medium of thought among all polite people, I determined to have recourse to that tongue.

"*Messieurs et mesdames*," I said, inclining my

body in salutation, "*mille pardons pour cette intrusion peu convenable*"—but, as I am writing in English it may be well to translate the speeches as I proceed; although I abandon with regret the advantage of going through them literally, and in the appropriate dialect in which they were originally spoken.

"Gentlemen and ladies," I said, inclining my body in salutation, "I ask a thousand pardons for this inopportune intrusion on your retirement; but overhearing a few of what I much fear are but too well grounded complaints, touching the false position in which you are placed, as the occupant of this apartment, and in that light your host, I have ventured to approach, with no other desire than the wish that you would make me the repository of all your griefs, in order, if possible, that they may be repaired as soon as circumstances shall in any manner allow."

The strangers were very naturally a little startled at my unexpected appearance, and at the substance of what I had just said. I observed that the two ladies were apparently, in some slight degree, even distressed, the younger turning her head on one side in maiden modesty, while the elder, a duenna-sort-of-looking person, dropped her eyes to the floor, but succeeded in better maintaining her self-possession and gravity. The eldest of the two gentlemen approached me with dignified composure, after a moment of hesitation; and, returning my salute, by waving his tail with singular grace and decorum, he answered as follows.—I may as well state in this place, that he spoke the French about as well as an Englishman who has lived long enough on the continent to fancy he can travel in the provinces without being detected for a foreigner. *Au reste*, his accent was slightly Russian, and his enunciation whistling and harmonious. The females, especially in some of the lower keys of their voices, made sounds not unlike the sighing tones of the Eolian harp. It was really a pleasure to hear them; but I have often had occasion to remark that, in every country but one which I do not care to name, the language, when uttered by the softer sex, takes new charms, and is rendered more delightful to the ear.

"Sir," said the stranger, when he had done waving his tail, "I should do great injustice to my feelings and to the monikin character in general, were I to neglect expressing some small portion of the gratitude I feel on the present occasion. Destitute, houseless, insulted wanderers and captives, fortune has at length shed a ray of happiness on our miserable condition, and hope begins to shine through the cloud of our distress, like a passing gleam of the sun. From my very tail, sir, in my own name and in that of this excellent and most prudent matron, and in those of these two noble and youthful lovers, I thank you—Yes! honorable and humane being of the genus *homo*, species *Anglicus*, we all return our most tail-felt acknowledgments of your goodness!"

Here the whole party gracefully bent the ornaments in question over their heads, touching their receding foreheads with the several tips, and bowed.—I would have given ten thousand pounds, at that moment, to have had a good investment in tails, in order to emulate their form of courtesy; but naked, shorn and destitute as I was, with a feeling of humility, I was obliged to put my head a little on one shoulder, and give the ordinary English bob, in return for their more elaborate politeness.

"If I were merely to say, sir," I continued, when the opening salutations were thus properly exchanged, "that I am charmed at this accidental interview, the word would prove very insufficient to express my delight. Consider this hotel as your own; its domestics as your domestics; its stores of condiments as your stores of condiments, and its nominal tenant as your most humble servant and friend. I have been greatly shocked at the indignities to which you have hitherto been exposed, and now promise you liberty, kindness, and all those attentions to which, it is very apparent, you are fully entitled by your birth, breeding, and the delicacy of your sentiments. I congratulate myself a thousand times for having been so fortunate as to make your acquaintance. My greatest desire has always been to stimulate the sympathies; but, until to-day, various accidents have confined the cultivation of this heaven-born property, in a great measure, to my own species; I now look forward, however, to a delicious career of new-born interests in the whole of the animal creation, I need scarcely say, in that of quadrupeds of your family in particular."

"Whether we belong to the class of quadrupeds or not, is a question that has a good deal embarrassed our own *savans*," returned the stranger. "There is an ambiguity in our physical action that renders the point a little questionable; and therefore, I think, the higher castes of our natural philosophers rather prefer classing the entire monikin species, with all its varieties, as caudæ-jactans, or tail-wavers; adopting the term from the nobler part of the animal formation. Is not this the better opinion at home, my Lord Chatterino?" he asked, turning to the youth, who stood respectfully at his side.

"Such, I believe, my dear Doctor, was the last classification sanctioned by the academy," the young noble replied, with a readiness that proved him to be both well-informed and intelligent, and, at the same time, with a reserve of manner that did equal credit to his modesty and breeding. "The question of whether we are or are not bipeds has greatly agitated the schools for more than three centuries."

"The use of this gentleman's name," I hastily rejoined, "my dear sir, reminds me that we are but half acquainted with each other. Permit me to waive ceremony, and to announce myself, at once, as Sir John Goldencalf, Baronet, of Householder-Hall, in the Kingdom of Great Britain, a poor admirer of excellence wherever it is to be found, or under whatever form, and a devotee of the system of the 'social-stake.'"

"I am happy to be admitted to the honor of this formal introduction, Sir John. In return, I beg you will suffer me to say that this young nobleman is, in our own dialect, No. 6, purple; or, to translate the appellation, my Lord Chatterino. This young lady is No. 4, violet, or, my Lady Chatterissa. This excellent and prudent matron is No. 4,626,243, russet, or, Mistress Vigilance Lynx, to translate her appellation also into the English tongue; and that I am No. 22,817, brown-study-color, or, Dr. Reasono, to give you a literal signification of my name,—a poor disciple of the philosophers of our race, an LL. D., and a F. U. D. G. E., the travelling tutor of this heir of one of the most illustrious and the most ancient houses of the island of Leaphigh, in the monikin section of mortality."

"Every syllable, learned Dr. Reasono, that falls from your revered lips, only whets curiosity, and adds fuel to the flame of desire, tempting me to inquire further into your private history, your future intentions, the polity of your species, and all those interesting topics that will readily suggest themselves to one of your quick apprehension and extensive acquirements. I dread being thought indiscreet; and yet, putting yourself in my position, I trust you will overlook a wish so natural and ardent."

"Apology is unnecessary, Sir John, and nothing would afford me greater satisfaction than to answer any and every inquiry you may be disposed to make."

"Then, sir, to cut short all useless circumlocution, suffer me to ask at once an explanation of the system of enumeration, by which you indicate individuals?—You are called No. 22,817, brown-study-color——"

"Or, Dr. Reasono. As you are an Englishman you will perhaps understand me better, if I refer to a recent practice of the new London police. You may have observed that the men wear letters in red or white, and numbers on the capes of their coats. By the letters, the passenger can refer to the company of the officer, while the number indicates the individual. Now, the idea of this improvement came, I make no doubt, from our system, under which society is divided into castes, for the sake of harmony and subordination, and these castes are designated by colors and shades of colors, that are significant of their stations and pursuits—the individual, as in the new police, being known by the number. Our own language being exceedingly sententious, is capable of expressing the most elaborate of these combinations in a very few sounds. I should add that there is no difference in the manner of distinguishing the sexes, with the exception that each is numbered apart, and each has a counterpart-color to that of the same caste in the other sex. Thus, purple and violet are both noble, the former being masculine and the latter feminine, and russet being the counterpart of brown-study-color."

"And—excuse my natural ardor to know more —and do you bear these numbers and colors marked on your attire, in your own region?"

"As for attire, Sir John, the monikins are too highly improved, mentally and physically, to need any. It is known that in all cases, extremes meet. The savage is nearer to nature than the merely civilized being, and the creature that has passed the mistifications of a middle state of improvement, finds himself again approaching nearer to the habits, the wishes, and the opinions of our common mother. As the real gentleman is more simple in manners than the distant imitator of his deportment; as fashions and habits are always more exaggerated in provincial towns than in polished capitals; or, as the profound philosopher has less pretensions than the tyro, so does our common genus, as it draws nearer to the consummation of its destiny, and its highest attainments, learn to reject the most valued usages of the middle condition, and to return, with ardor, towards nature, as to a first love. It is on this principle, sir, that the monikin family never wears clothes."

"I could not but perceive that the ladies have manifested some embarrassment ever since I entered,—is it possible, that their delicacy has taken the alarm, at the state of my toilet?"

"At the toilet itself, Sir John, rather than at its state, if I must speak plainly. The female mind, trained as it is with us, from infancy upward, in the habits and usages of nature, is shocked by any departure from her rules. You will know how to make allowances for the squeamishness of the sex for I believe it is much alike, in this particular, le come from what quarter of the earth it may."

"I can only excuse the seeming want of politeness by my ignorance, Dr. Reasono. Before I ask another question, the oversight shall be repaired. I must retire into my own chamber for an instant, gentlemen and ladies, and I beg you will find such sources of amusement as first offer, until I can return. There are nuts, I believe, in this closet; sugar is usually kept on that table, and perhaps the ladies might find some relaxation by exercising themselves on the chairs. In a single moment I shall be with you again."

Hereupon, I withdrew into my bed-chamber, and began to lay aside the dressing-gown, as well as my shirt. Remembering, however, that I was but too liable to colds in the head, I returned to ask Dr. Reasono to step in where I was for an instant. On mentioning the difficulty, this excellent person assumed the office of preparing his female friends to overlook the slight innovation of my still wearing the night-cap and slippers.

"The ladies would think nothing of it," the philosopher good-humoredly remarked, by way of lessening my regrets at having wounded their sensibilities, "were you even to appear in a military cloak and Hessian boots, provided, it was not thought that you were of their acquaintance, and in their immediate society. I think you must have often remarked among the sex of your own species, who are frequently quite indifferent to nudities (their prejudices running counter to ours,) that appear in the streets, but which would cause them instantly to run out of the room, when exhibited in the person of an acquaintance; these conventional asides being tolerated everywhere, by a judicious concession of punctilios that might otherwise become insupportable."

"The distinction is too reasonable to require another word of explanation, dear sir. Now, let us rejoin the ladies, since I am, at length, in some degree, fit to be seen."

I was rewarded for this bit of delicate attention, by an approving smile from the lovely Chatterissa, and good Mistress Lynx no longer kept her eyes riveted on the floor, but bent them on me, with looks of admiration and gratitude.

"Now that this little *contre-tems* is no longer an obstacle," I resumed, "permit me to continue those inquiries which you have hitherto answered with so much amenity, and so satisfactorily. As you have no clothes, in what manner is the parallel between your usage and that of the new London police practically completed?"

"Although we have no clothes, Nature, whose laws are never violated with impunity, but who is as beneficent as she is absolute, has furnished us with a downy covering to supply their places, wherever clothes are needed for comfort. We have coats that defy fashions, require no tailors, and never lose their naps. But it would be inconvenient to be totally clad in this manner; and, therefore, the palms of our hands are, as you see, ungloved; the portions of the frame on which we seat ourselves are left uncovered, most probably lest some inconvenience should arise from taking accidental and unfavorable positions. This is the part of the monikin frame the best adapted for receiving paint, and the numbers of which I have spoken are periodically renewed there, at public offices appointed for that purpose. Our characters are so minute as to escape the human eye; but by using that opera glass, I make no doubt that you may still see some of my own enregistration, although, alas! unusual friction, great misery, and, I may say, unmerited wrongs, have nearly un-monikined me in this, as well as in various other, particulars."

As Dr. Reasono had the complaisance to turn round, and to use his tail like the index of a black board, by aid of the glass, I very distinctly traced the figures to which he alluded. Instead of being in paint, however, as he had given me reason to anticipate, they seemed to be branded, or burnt in, indelibly, as we commonly mark horses, thieves, and negroes. On mentioning the fact to the philosopher, it was explained with his usual facility and politeness.

"You are quite right, sir," he said; "the omission of paint was to prevent tautology, an offence against the simplicity of the monikin dialect, as well as against monikin taste, that would have been sufficient, under our opinions, even to overturn the government."

"Tautology!"

"Tautology, Sir John; on examining the background of the picture, you will perceive that it is already of a dusky, sombre hue; now, this being of a meditative and grave character, has been denominated by our academy the 'brown-study-color;' and it would clearly have been supererogatory to lay the same tint upon it. No, sir; we avoid repetitions even in our prayers, deeming them to be so many proofs of an illogical and of an anti-consecutive mind."

"The system is admirable, and I see new beauties at each moment. You enjoy the advantage, for instance, under this mode of enumeration, of knowing your acquaintances from behind, quite as well as if you met them face to face!"

"The suggestion is ingenious, showing an active and an observant mind; but it does not quite reach the motive of the politico-numerical-identity-system of which we are speaking. The objects of this arrangement are altogether of a higher and more useful nature; nor do we usually recognize our friends by their countenances, which at the best are no more than so many false signals, but by their tails."

"This is admirable! What a facility you possess for recognizing an acquaintance, who may happen to be up a tree! But may I presume to inquire, Dr. Reasono, what are the most approved of the advantages of the politico-numerical-identity-system? For impatience is devouring my vitals."

"They are connected with the interests of government. You know, sir, that society is established for the purposes of governments, and governments, themselves, mainly to facilitate contributions and taxations. Now, by the numerical system, we have every opportunity of including the whole monikin race in the collections, as they are periodically checked off by their numbers. The idea was a happy thought of an eminent statician of ours, who gained great credit at court by the invention, and, in fact, who was admitted to the academy in consequence of its ingenuity."

"Still it must be admitted, my dear Doctor," put in Lord Chatterino, always with the modesty, and perhaps I might add, with the generosity of youth, "that there are some among us who deny that society was made for governments, and who maintain that governments were made for society; or, in other words, for monikins."

"Mere theorists, my good Lord; and their opinions, even if true, are never practised on. Practice is every thing in political matters; and theories are of no use, except as they confirm practice."

"Both theory and practice are perfect," I cried

"and I make no doubt that the classification into colors, or castes, enables the authorities to commence the imposts with the richest, or the 'purples.'"

"Sir, monikin prudence never lays the foundation-stone at the summit; it seeks the base of the edifice; and as contributions are the walls of society, we commence with the bottom. When you shall know us better, Sir John Goldencalf, you will begin to comprehend the beauty and benevolence of the entire monikin economy."

I now adverted to the frequent use of this word "monikin;" and, admitting my ignorance, desired an explanation of the term, as well as a more general insight into the origin, history, hopes, and polity of the interesting strangers; if they can be so called who were already so well known to me. Dr. Reasono admitted that the request was natural and was entitled to respect; but he delicately suggested the necessity of sustaining the animal functions by nutriment, intimating that the ladies had supped but in an indifferent way the evening before, and acknowledging that, philosopher as he was, he should go through the desired explanations after improving the slight acquaintance he had already made with certain condiments in one of the *armoires*, with far more zeal and point, than could possibly be done in the present state of his appetite. The suggestion was so very plausible that there was no resisting it; and, suppressing my curiosity as well as I could, the bell was rung, I retired to my bed-chamber to resume so much of my attire as was necessary to the semi-civilization of man, and then the necessary orders were given to the domestics, who, by the way, were suffered to remain under the influence of those ordinary and vulgar prejudices that are pretty generally entertained by the human, against the monikin family.

Previously to separating from my new friend Dr. Reasono, however, I took him aside, and stated that I had an acquaintance in the hotel, a person of singular philosophy, after the human fashion, and a great traveller; and that I desired permission to let him into the secret of our intended lecture on the monikin economy, and to bring him with me as an auditor. To this request, No. 22,817, brown-study-color, or Dr. Reasono, gave a very cordial assent; hinting delicately, at the same time, his expectation that this new auditor, who, of course, was no other than Captain Noah Poke, would not deem it disparaging to his manhood, to consult the sensibilities of the ladies, by appearing in the garments of that only decent and respectable tailor and draper, nature. To this suggestion I gave a ready approval; when each went his way, after the usual salutations of bowing and tail-waving, with a mutual promise of being punctual to the appointment.

CHAPTER X.

A great deal of negotiation, in which human shrewdness is completely shamed, and human ingenuity is shown to be of a very secondary quality.

Mr. Poke listened to my account of all that had passed, with a very sedate gravity. He informed me that he had witnessed so much ingenuity among the seals, and had known so many brutes that seemed to have the sagacity of men, and so many men who appeared to have the stupidity of brutes, that he had no difficulty whatever in be lieving every word I told him. He expressed his satisfaction, too, at the prospect of hearing a lecture on natural philosophy and political economy from the lips of a monkey; although he took occasion to intimate that no desire to learn anything lay at the bottom of his compliance; for, in his country, these matters were very generally studied in the district schools, the very children who ran about the streets of 'Stunin'tun' usually knowing more than most of the old people in foreign parts. "Still a monkey might have some new ideas; and, for his part, he was willing to hear what every one had to say; for, if a man did'nt put in a word for himself, in this world, he might be certain no one else would take the pains to speak for him." But when I came to mention the details of the *programme* of the forthcoming interview, and stated that it was expected the audience would wear their own skins, out of respect to the ladies, I greatly feared that my friend would have so far excited himself as to go into fits. The rough old sealer swore some terrible oaths, protesting "that he would not make a monkey of himself, by appearing in this garb, for all the monikin philosophers, or high-born females, that could be stowed in a ship's hold; that he was very liable to tak cold; that he once knew a man who undertook to play beast in this manner, and the first thing the poor devil knew, he had great claws and a tail sprouting out of him; a circumstance that he had always attributed to a just judgment for striving to make himself more than Providence had intended him for; that, provided a man's ears were naked, he could hear just as well as if his whole body was naked; that he did not complain of the monkeys going in their skins, and that they ought, in reason, not to meddle with his clothes; that he should be scratching himself the whole time, and thinking what a miserable figure he cut; that he would have no place to keep his tobacco; that he was apt to be deaf when he was cold; that he would be d——d if he did any such thing; that human natur' and monkey natur' were not the same, and it was not to be expected that men and monkeys should follow exactly the same fashions; that the meeting would have the appearance of a boxing-match, instead of a philosophical lecture; that he never heard of such a thing at Stunin'tun; that he should feel sneaking at seeing his own shins in the presence of ladies; that a ship always made better weather under some canvas, than under bare poles; that he might possibly be brought to his shirt and pantaloons, but as for giving up these, he would as soon think of cutting the sheet-anchor off his bows, with the vessel driving on a lee-shore; that flesh and blood were flesh and blood, and they liked their comfort; that he should think the whole time he was about to go in a swimming, and should be looking about for a good place to dive;" together with a great many more similar objections, that have escaped me in the multitude of things of greater interest which have since occupied my time. I have frequently had occasion to observe, that, when a man has one good, solid reason for his decision, it is no easy matter to shake it; but, that he who has a great many, usually finds them of far less account in the struggle of opinions. Such proved to be the fact with Captain Poke on the present occasion. I succeeded in stripping him of his garments, one by one, until I got him reduced to the shirt, where, like a stout ship that is easily brought to her bearings by the breeze, he 'stuck and hung' in a manner to manifest it would require a heavy strain to bring him down any lower. A lucky thought relieved us all from the dilemma. There were a couple of good large bison-skins among my effects, and on suggesting to Dr. Reasono the expediency of encasing Captain Poke in the folds of one of them, the philosopher cheerfully assented, observing that any object of a *natural* and *simple* formation was agreeable to the monikin senses; their objections were merely to the deformities of art, which they deemed to be so many offences against Providence. On this explanation, I ventured to hint that, being still in the infancy of the new civilization, it would be very agreeable to my ancient habits, could I be permitted to use one of the skins, also, while Mr. Poke occupied the other. Not the slightest objection was raised to the proposal, and measures were immediately taken to prepare us to appear in good company. Soon after I received from Dr. Reasono a *protocol* of the conditions that were to regulate the approaching interview. This document was written in Latin, out of respect to the ancients, and as I afterwards understood, it was drawn up by my Lord Chatterino, who had been educated for the diplomatic career at home, previously to the accident which had thrown him, alas! into human hands. I translate it freely, for the benefit of the ladies, who usually prefer their own tongues to any others.

PROTOCOL of an interview that is to take place between Sir John Goldencalf, Bart., of Householder Hall, in the kingdom of Great Britain, and No. 22,817, brown-study-colour, or Socrates Reasono, F. U. D G. E., Professor of Probabilities in the University of Monikinia, and in the kingdom of Leaphigh:

The contracting parties agree as follows, viz.—

ARTICLE 1. That there shall be an interview.

ART. 2. That the said interview shall be a peaceable interview, and not a belligerent interview.

ART. 3. That the said interview shall be logical, explanatory, and discursory.

ART. 4. That during said interview, Dr. Reasono shall have the privilege of speaking most, and Sir John Goldencalf the privilege of hearing most.

ART. 5. That Sir John Goldencalf shall have the privilege of asking questions, and Dr. Reasono the privilege of answering them.

ART. 6. That a due regard shall be had to both human and monikin prejudices and sensibilities.

ART. 7. That Dr. Reasono, and any monikins who may accompany him, shall smooth their coats, and otherwise dispose of their natural vestments, in a way that shall be as agreeable as possible to Sir John Goldencalf and his friend.

ART. 8. That Sir John Goldencalf, and any man who may accompany him, shall appear in bison-skins, wearing no other clothing, in order to render themselves as agreeable as possible to Dr. Reasono and his friends.

ART. 9. That the conditions of this *protocol* shall be respected.

ART. 10. That any doubtful significations in this *protoçol* shall be interpreted, as near as may be, in favor of both parties.

ART. 11. That no precedent shall be established to the prejudice of either the human or the monikin dialect, by the adoption of the Latin language on this occasion.

Delighted with this proof of attention on the part of my Lord Chatterino, I immediately left a card for that young nobleman, and then seriously set about preparing myself, with an increased scrupu-

.ousness, for the fulfilment of the smallest condition of the compact. Capt. Poke was soon ready, and I must say that he looked more like a quadruped on its hind legs, in his new attire, than a human being. As for my own appearance, I trust it was such as became my station and character.

At the appointed time all the parties were assembled, Lord Chatterino appearing with a copy of the *protocol* in his hand. This instrument was formally read, by the young peer, in a very creditable manner, when a silence ensued, as if to invite comment. I know not how it is, but I never yet heard the positive stipulations of any bargain, that I did not feel a propensity to look out for weak places in them. I had begun to see that the discussion might lead to argument, argument to comparisons between the two species, and something like an *esprit de corps* was stirring within me. It now struck me that a question might be fairly raised as to the propriety of Dr. Reasono's appearing with *three* backers, while I had but *one*. The objection was, therefore, urged on my part, I hope in a modest and conciliatory manner. In reply, my Lord Chatterino observed, it was true the *protocol* spoke in general terms of mutual supporters, but if—

"Sir John Goldencalf would be at the trouble of referring to the instrument itself, he would see that the backers of Dr. Reasono were mentioned in the *plural* number, while that of Sir John himself was alluded to only in the *singular* number."

"Perfectly true, my Lord; but you will, however, permit me to remark, that *two* Monikins would completely fulfil the conditions in favor of Dr. Reasono, while he appears here with *three*; there certainly must be some limits to this plurality, or the Doctor would have a right to attend the interview accompanied by all the inhabitants of Leaphigh."

"The objection is highly ingenious, and creditable in the last degree to the diplomatic abilities of Sir John Goldencalf; but, among monikins, two *females* are deemed equal to only one male, in the eye of the law. Thus, in cases which require two witnesses, as in conveyances of real estate, two *male* monikins are sufficient, whereas it would be necessary to have *four female* signatures, in order to give the instrument validity. In the legal sense, therefore, I conceive that Dr. Reasono is attended by only *two* monikins."

Captain Poke hereupon observed that this provision in the law of Leaphigh was a good one; for he had often had occasion to remark that women, quite half the time, did not know what they were about; and he thought, in general, that they require more ballast than men.

"This reply would completely cover the case, my Lord," I answered, "were the *protocol* purely a monikin document, and this assembly purely a monikin assembly. But the facts are notoriously otherwise. The document is drawn up in a common vehicle of thought among scholars, and I gladly seize the opportunity to add, that I do not remember to have seen a better specimen of modern latinity."

"It is undeniable, Sir John," returned Lord Chatterino, waving his tail in acknowledgment of the compliment, "that the *protocol* itself, is in a language that has now become common property; but the mere medium of thought, on such occasions, is of no great moment, provided it is neutral as respects the contracting parties; moreover in this particular case, article 11th of the *protocol* contains a stipulation that no legal consequences whatever are to follow the use of the Latin language; a stipulation that leaves the contracting parties in possession of their original rights. Now, as the lecture is to be a monikin lecture, given by a monikin philosopher, and on monikin grounds, I humbly urge that it is proper the interview should generally be conducted on monikin principles."

"If by monikin grounds, is meant monikin ground, (which I have a right to assume, since the greater necessarily includes the less,) I beg leave to remind your Lordship, that the parties are, at this moment, in a neutral country, and that, if either of them can set up a claim of territorial jurisdiction, or the rights of the flag, these claims must be admitted to be human, since the *locataire* of this apartment is a man, in control of the *locus in quo,* and *pro hac vice*, the suzerain."

"Your ingenuity has greatly exceeded my construction, Sir John, and I beg leave to amend my plea.—All I mean is, that the leading consideration in this interview, is a monikin interest—that we are met to propound, explain, digest, animadvert on, and embellish a monikin theme—that the accessory must be secondary to the principal—that the lesser must merge, not in your sense, but in my sense, in the greater—and, by consequence, that——"

"You will accord me your pardon, my dear Lord, but I hold——"

"Nay, my good Sir John, I trust to your inteligence to be excused if I say——"

"One word, my Lord Chatterino, I pray you, n order that——"

"A thousand, very cheerfully, Sir John, but——"

"My Lord Chatterino!"

"Sir John Goldencalf!"

Hereupon we both began talking at the same time, the noble young monikin gradually narrowing down the direction of his observations to the single person of Mrs. Vigilance Lynx, who, I afterwards had occasion to know, was an excellent listener; and I, in my turn, after wandering from eye to eye, settled down into a sort of oration that was especially addressed to the understanding of Captain Noah Poke. My auditor contrived to get one ear entirely clear of the bison's skin, and nodded approbation of what fell from me, with a proper degree of human and clannish spirit. We might possibly have harangued in this desultory manner, to the present time, had not the amiable Chatterissa advanced, and, with the tact and delicacy which distinguish her sex, by placing her pretty *patte* on the mouth of the young nobleman, she effectually checked his volubility. When a horse is running away, he usually comes to a dead stop, after driving through lanes, and gates, and turnpikes, the moment he finds himself master of his own movements, in an open field. Thus, in my own case, no sooner did I find myself in sole possession of the argument, than I brought it to a close. Dr. Reasono improved the pause, to introduce a proposition that, the experiment already made by myself and Lord Chatterino being evidently a failure, he and Mr. Poke should retire and make an effort to agree upon an entirely new *programme* of the proceedings. This happy thought suddenly restored peace; and, while the two negotiators were absent, I improved the opportunity to become better acquainted with the lovely Chatterissa and her female Mentor. Lord Chatterino, who possessed all the graces of diplomacy, who could turn from a hot and angry discussion, on the instant, to the most bland and win ning courtesy, was foremost in promoting my wishes, inducing his charming mistress to throw aside the reserve of a short acquaintance, and to enter, at once, into a free and friendly discourse.

Some time elapsed before the plenipotentiaries returned; for it appears that, owing to a constitutional peculiarity, or, as he subsequently explained it himself, a 'Stunin'tun principle,' Captain Poke conceived he was bound, in a bargain, to dispute every proposition which came from the other party. This difficulty would probably have proved insuperable, had not Dr. Reasono luckily bethought him of a frank and liberal proposal to leave every other article, without reserve, to the sole dictation of his colleague, reserving to himself the same privilege for all the rest. Noah, after being well assured that the philosopher was no lawyer, assented; and the affair, once begun in this spirit of concession, was soon brought to a close. And here I would recommend this happy expedient to all negotiators of knotty and embarrassing treaties, since it enables each party to gain his point, and probably leaves as few openings for subsequent disputes, as any other mode that has yet been adopted. The new instrument ran as follows, it having been written, in duplicate, in English and in Monikin. It will be seen that the pertinacity of one of the negotiators gave it very much the character of a capitulation.

Protocol of an interview, &c. &c. &c.

The contracting parties agree as follows, viz.—

Article 1. There shall be an interview.

Art. 2. Agreed; provided all the parties can come and go at pleasure.

Art. 3. The said interview shall be conducted generally, on philosophical and liberal principles

Art. 4. Agreed; provided tobacco may be used at discretion.

Art. 5. That either party shall have the privilege of propounding questions, and either party the privilege of answering them.

Art. 6. Agreed; provided no one need listen, or no one talk, unless so disposed.

Art. 7. The attire of all present shall be conformable to the abstract rules of propriety and decorum.

Art. 8. Agreed; provided the bison-skins may be reefed, from time to time, according to the state of the weather.

Art. 9. The provisions of this protocol shall be rigidly respected.

Art. 10. Agreed; provided no advantage be taken by lawyers.

Lord Chatterino and myself pounced upon the respective documents like two hawks, eagerly looking for flaws, or the means of maintaining the opinions we had before advanced, and which we had both shown so much cleverness in supporting.

"Why, my Lord, there is no provision for the appearance of any Monikins at all at this interview!"

"The generality of the terms leaves it to be inferred that all may come and go who may be so disposed."

"Your pardon, my Lord; article 8 contains a direct allusion to *bison-skins* in the *plural*, and under circumstances from which it follows, by a just deduction, that it was contemplated that more than *one* wearer of the said skins should be present at the said interview."

"Perfectly just, Sir John; but you will suffer me to observe that by article 1, it is conditioned that there shall be an interview; and by article 3, it is furthermore agreed that the said interview shall be conducted 'on philosophical and *liberal* principles;' now, it need scarcely be urged, good Sir John, that it would be the extreme of *illiberality* to deny to one party any privilege that was possessed by the other."

"Perfectly just, my Lord, were this an affair of mere courtesy; but legal constructions must be made on legal principles, or else, as jurists and diplomatists, we are all afloat on the illimitable ocean of conjecture."

"And yet article 10 expressly stipulates that 'no advantage shall be taken by lawyers.' By considering articles 3, and 10, profoundly and in conjunction, we learn that it was the intention of the negotiators to spread the mantle of liberality, apart from all the subtilties and devices of mere legal practitioners, over the whole proceedings. Permit me, in corroboration of what is now urged, to appeal to the voices of those who framed the very conditions about which we are now arguing. Did *you*, sir," continued my Lord Chatterino, turning to Captain Poke, with emphasis and dignity; "did you, sir, when you drew up this celebrated article 10—did you deem that you were publishing authority of which the lawyers could take advantage?"

A deep and very sonorous "No," was the energetic reply of Mr. Poke.

My Lord Chatterino, then turning, with equal grace, to the Doctor, first diplomatically waving his tail three times, continued:—

"And you, sir, in drawing up article 3—did you conceive that you were supporting and promulgating *illiberal* principles?"

The question was met by a prompt negative

when the young noble paused, and looked at me, like one who had completely triumphed.

"Perfectly eloquent, completely convincing, irrefutably argumentative, and unanswerably just, my Lord," I put in; "but I must be permitted to hint that the validity of all laws is derived from the *enactment:* now the enactment, or, in the case of a treaty, the virtue of the stipulation, is not derived from the *intention* of the party who may happen to *draw up a law* or *a clause*, but from the *assent* of the *legal deputies.* In the present instance, there are two negotiators, and I now ask permission to address a few questions to them, reversing the order of your own interrogatories; and the result may possibly furnish a clue to the *quo animo*, in a new light." Addressing the philosopher, I continued—"Did *you*, sir, in assenting to article 10, imagine that you were defeating justice, countenancing oppression, and succouring might to the injury of right?"

The answer was a solemn, and, I do not doubt, a very conscientious, "No."

"And *you*, sir," turning to Captain Poke, "did you, in assenting to article 3, in the least conceive that, by any possibility, the foes of humanity could torture your approbation into the means of determining that the bison-skin wearers were not to be upon a perfect footing with the best Monikins of the land?"

"Blast me, if I did!"

"But, Sir John Goldencalf, the Socratic method of reasoning——"

"Was first resorted to by yourself, my Lord—

"Nay, good Sir——"

"Permit me, my dear Lord——"

"Sir John——"

"My Lord——"

Hereupon the gentle Chatterissa again advanced, and by another timely interposition of her graceful tact, she succeeded in preventing the reply. The parallel of the runaway horse was acted over, and I came to another stand-still. Lord Chatterino now gallantly proposed that the whole affair should be referred, with full powers, to the ladies. I could not refuse; and the plenipotentiaries retired, under a growling accompaniment of Captain Poke, who pretty plainly declared that women caused more quarrels than all the rest of the world, and, from the little he had seen, he expected it would turn out the same with monikinas.

The female sex certainly possess a facility of composition that is denied our portion of the creation. In an incredibly short time, the referees returned with the following *programme*.

Protocol of an interview between, &c. &c.

The contracting parties agree as follows, viz.—

Article 1. There shall be an amicable, logical philosophical, ethical, liberal, general, and controversial interview.

Art. 2. The interview shall be amicable

Art. 3. The interview shall be general.

Art. 4. The interview shall be logical.

Art. 5. The interview shall be ethical.

Art. 6. The interview shall be philosophical.

Art. 7. The interview shall be liberal.

Art. 8. The interview shall be controversial.

Art. 9. The interview shall be controversial, liberal, philosophical, ethical, logical, general, and amicable.

Art. 10. The interview shall be as particularly agreed upon.

The cat does not leap upon the mouse with more avidity than Lord Chatterino and myself pounced upon the third *protocol*, seeking new grounds for the argument that each was resolved on.

"*Auguste! cher Auguste!*" exclaimed the lovely Chatterissa, in the prettiest Parisian accent I thought I had ever heard—"Pour moi!"

"*A moi!* Monseigneur," I put in, flourishing my copy of the protocol—I was checked in the midst of this controversial ardor, by a tug at the bison-skin; when, casting a look behind me, I saw Captain Poke winking and making other signs that he wished to say a word in a corner.

"I think, Sir John," observed the worthy sealer, "if we ever mean to let this bargain come to a catastrophe, it might as well be done now. The females have been cunning, but the deuce is in it if we can't weather upon two women before the matter is well over. In Stunin'tun, when it is thought best to accommodate proposals, why we object and raise a breeze in the beginning, but towards the end we kinder soften and mollify, or else trade would come to a stand. The hardest gale must blow its pipe out. Trust to me to floor the best argument the best monkey of them all can agitate!"

"This matter is getting serious, Noah, and I am filled with an *esprit de corps*. Do you not begin yourself to feel human?"

"Kinder; but more bisonish than any thing else. Let them go on, Sir John; and, when the time comes, we will take them aback, or set me down as a pettifogger."

The Captain winked knowingly; and I began to see that there was some sense in his opinion. On rejoining our friends, or allies, I scarce know which to call them, I found that the amiable Chat terissa had equally calmed the diplomatic ardor of her lover, again; and we now met on the best possible terms. The *protocol* was accepted by acclamation; and preparations were instantly commenced for the lecture of Dr. Reasono.

CHAPTER XI.

A philosophy that is bottomed on something substantial—Some reasons plainly presented, and cavilling objections put to flight, by a charge of logical bayonets.

Dr. Reasono was quite as reasonable, in the personal embellishments of his lyceum, as any public lecturer I remember to have seen, who was required to execute his functions in the presence of ladies. If I say that his coat had been brushed, his tail newly curled, and that his air was a little more than usually "solemnized," as Captain Poke described it in a decent whisper, I believe all will be said that is either necessary or true. He placed himself behind a footstool, which served as a table, smoothed its covering a little with his paws, and at once proceeded to business. It may be well to add that he lectured without notes, and, as the subject did not immediately call for experiments, without any apparatus.

Waving his tail towards the different parts of the room in which his audience were seated, th philosopher commenced.

"As the present occasion, my hearers," he said, "is one of those accidental calls upon science, to which all belonging to the academies are liable, and does not demand more than the heads of our thesis to be explained, I shall not dig into the roots of the subject, but limit myself to such general remarks as may serve to furnish the outlines of our philosophy, natural, moral and political——"

"How, sir," I cried, "have you a political as well as a moral philosophy?"

"Beyond a question; and a very useful philosophy it is. No interests require more philosophy than those connected with politics.—To resume our philosophy, natural, moral and political, reserving most of the propositions, demonstrations, and corollaries, for greater leisure, and a more advanced state of information in the class.—Prescribing to myself these salutary limits, therefore, I shall begin only with Nature.

"Nature is a term that we use to express the pervading and governing principle of created things. It is known both as a generic and a specific term, signifying in the former character the elements and combinations of omnipotence, as applied to matter in general, and in the latter, its particular subdivisions, in connexion with matter in its infinite varieties. It is moreover subdivided into its physical and moral attributes, which admit also of the two grand distinctions just named. Thus, when we say Nature, in the abstract, meaning physically, we would be understood as alluding to those general, uniform, absolute, consistent, and beautiful laws, which control and render harmonious, as a great whole, the entire action, affinities, and destinies of the universe; and when we say Nature in the speciality, we would be understood to speak of the nature of a rock, of a tree, of air, fire, water, and land. Again; in alluding to a moral Nature in the abstract, we mean sin, and its weaknesses, its attractions, its deformities; in a word, its totality; while, on the other hand, when we use the term, in this sense, under the limits of a speciality, we confine its signification to the particular shades of natural qualities that mark the precise object named. Let us illustrate our positions by a few brief examples.

"When we say 'O Nature! how art thou glorious, sublime, instructive!'—we mean that her laws emanate from a power of infinite intelligence and perfection; and when we say 'O Nature! how art thou frail, vain and insufficient!' we mean that she is, after all, but a secondary quality, inferior to that which brought her into existence, for definite, limited, and, doubtless, useful purposes. In these examples, we treat the principle in the abstract.

"The examples of nature in the speciality will be more familiar, and, although in no degree more true, will be better understood by the generality of my auditors. Especial nature, in the physical signification, is apparent to the senses, and is betrayed in the outward forms of things, through their force, magnitude, substance, and proportions and, in its more mysterious properties, to examination, by their laws, harmony, and action. Especial moral nature is denoted in the different propensities, capacities and conduct of the different classes of all moral beings. In this latter sense we have monikin nature, dog nature, horse nature, hog nature, human nature——"

"Permit me, Dr. Reasono," I interrupted, "to inquire if, by this classification, you intend to convey more than may be understood by the accidental arrangement of your examples?"

"Purely the latter, I do assure you, Sir John."

"And do you admit the great distinctions of animal and vegetable natures?"

"Our academies are divided on this point. One school contends that all living nature is to be em braced in a great comprehensive genus, while another admits of the distinctions you have named. I am of the latter opinion, inclining to the belief that Nature herself has drawn the line between the two classes, by bestowing on one the double gift of the moral and physical nature. and by withholding the former from the other. The existence of the moral nature is denoted by the presence of the will. The academy of Leaphigh has made an elaborate classification of all the known animals, of which the sponge is at the bottom of the list, and the monikin at the top."

"Sponges are commonly uppermost," growled Noah.

"Sir," said I, with a disagreeable rising at the throat, "am I to understand that your savans account man an animal in a middle state between a sponge and a monkey?"

"Really, Sir John, this warmth is quite unsuited to philosophical discussion—if you continue to indulge in it, I shall find myself compelled to postpone the lecture."

At this rebuke I made a successful effort to restrain myself, although my *esprit de corps* nearly choked me. Intimating, as well as I could, a change of purpose, Dr. Reasono, who had stood suspended over his table with an air of doubt, waved his tail, and proceeded:—

"Sponges, oysters, crabs, sturgeons, clams, toads, snakes, lizards, skunks, opossums, ant-eaters, baboons, negroes, wood-chucks, lions, esquimaux, sloths, hogs, hottentots, ourang-outangs, men and monikins are, beyond a question, all animals. The only disputed point among us is, whether they are all of the same genus, forming varieties or species, or whether they are to be divided into the three great families of the *improvables*, the *unimprova-*

bles, and the *retrogressives*. They who maintain that we form but one great family, reason by certain conspicuous analogies, that serve as so many links to unite the great chain of the animal world. Taking man as a centre, for instance, they show that this creature possesses, in common with every other creature, some observable property. Thus, man is, in one particular, like a sponge; in another, he is like an oyster; a hog is like a man; the skunk has one peculiarity of a man; the ourang-outang another; the sloth another——"

"King!"

"And so on, to the end of the chapter. This school of philosophers, while it has been very ingeniously supported, is not, however, the one most in favor, just at this moment, in the academy of Leaphigh——"

"Just at this moment, Doctor!"

"Certainly, sir. Do you not know that truths, physical as well as moral, undergo their revolutions, the same as all created nature? The academy has paid great attention to this subject; and it issues annually an almanack, in which the different phases, the revolutions, the periods, the eclipses, whether partial or total, the distances from the centre of light, the *apogee* and *perigee* of all the more prominent truths, are calculated, with singular accuracy; and by the aid of which the cautious are enabled to keep themselves, as near as possible, within the bounds of reason. We deem this effort of the monikin mind as the sublimest of all its inventions, and as furnishing the strongest known evidence of its near approach to the consummation of our earthly destiny. This is not the place to dwell on that particular point of our philosophy, however; and. for the present we will postpone the subject."

"Yet you will permit me, Dr. Reasono, in virtue of clause 1, article 5, *protocol* No. 1, (which *protocol*, if not absolutely adopted, must be supposed to contain the *spirit* of that which was,) to inquire whether the calculations of the revolutions of truth, do not lead to dangerous moral extravagancies, ruinous speculations in ideas, and serve to unsettle society?"

The philosopher withdrew a moment with my Lord Chatterino, to consult whether it would be prudent to admit of the validity of *protocol* No. 1, even in this indirect manner; whereupon it was decided between them, that, as such admission would lay open all the vexatious questions that had just been so happily disposed of, clause 1 of article 5 having a direct connexion with clause 2; clauses 1 and 2 forming the whole article; and the said article 5, in its entirety, forming an integral portion of the whole instrument; and the doctrine of constructions enjoining that instruments are to be construed, like wills, by their general, and not by their especial, tendencies, it would be dangerous to the objects of the interview to allow the application to be granted. But, reserving a protest against the concession being interpreted into a precedent, it might be well to concede that, as an act of courtesy, which was denied as a right. Hereupon, Dr. Reasono informed me that these calculations of the revolutions of truth *did* lead to certain moral extravagancies, and in many instances to ruinous speculations in ideas; that the academy of Leaphigh, and so far as his information extended, the academy of every other country, had found the subject of *truth*, more particularly *moral* truth, the one of all others the most difficult to manage, the most likely to be abused, and the most dangerous to promulgate. I was moreover promised, at a future day, some illustrations of this branch of the subject.

"To pursue the more regular thread of my lecture," continued Dr. Reasono, when he had politely made this little digression, "we now divide these portions of the created world into animated and vegetable nature; the former is again divided into the *improvable* and the *unimprovable*, and the *retrogressive*. The improvable embraces all those species which are marching, by slow, progressive, but immutable mutations, towards the perfection of terrestrial life, or to that last, elevated, and sublime condition of mortality, in which the material makes its final struggle with the immaterial—mind with matter. The improvable class of animals, agreeably to the monikin dogmas, commences with those species in which matter has the most unequivocal ascendency, and terminates with those in which mind is as near perfection as this mortal coil will allow. We hold that mind and matter, in that mysterious union which connects the spiritual with the physical being, commence in the medium state, undergoing, not, as some men have pretended, transmigrations of the soul only, but such gradual and imperceptible changes of both soul and body, as have peopled the world with so many wonderful beings; wonderful, mentally and physically; and all of which (meaning all of the *improvable* class) are no more than animals of the same great genus, on the high road of tendencies, who are advancing towards the last stage of improvement, previously to their final translation to another planet, and a new existence.

"The *retrogressive* class is composed of those specimens which, owing to their destiny, take a false direction; which. instead of tending to the immaterial, tend to the material; which gradually become more and more under the influence of matter, until, by a succession of physical translations, the will is eventually lost, and they become incorporated with the earth itself. Under this last transformation, these purely materialized beings are chymically analyzed in the great laboratory of nature, and their component parts are separated:—thus the bones become rocks, the flesh earth, the spirits air, the blood water, the grizzle clay, and the ashes of the will are converted into the element of fire. In this class we enumerate whales, elephants, hippopotami, and divers other brutes, which visibly exhibit accumulations of matter that must speedily triumph over the less material portions of their natures."

"And yet, Doctor, there are facts that militate against the theory; the elephant, for instance, is accounted one of the most intelligent of all the quadrupeds."

"A mere false demonstration, sir. Nature delights in these little equivocations: thus, we have false suns, false rainbows, false prophets, false vision, and even false philosophy. There are entire races of both our species, too, as the Congo and the Esquimaux, for yours, and baboons and the common monkeys, that inhabit various parts of the world possessed by the human species, for ours, which are mere shadows of the forms and qualities that properly distinguish the animal in its state of perfection."

"How, sir; are you not, then, of the same family as all the other monkeys that we see hopping and skipping about the streets?"

"No more, sir, than you are of the same family as the flat-nosed, thick-lipped, low-browed, ink-skinned negro, or the squalid, passionless, brutalized

Esquimaux. I have said that nature delights in vagaries; and all these are no more than some of her mistifications. Of this class is the elephant, who, while verging nearest to pure materialism, makes a deceptive parade of the quality he is fast losing. Instances of this species of playing trumps. if I may so express it, are common in all classes of beings. How often, for instance, do men, just as they are about to fail, make a parade of wealth, women seem obdurate an hour before they capitulate, and diplomatists call Heaven to be a witness of their resolutions to the contrary, the day before they sign and seal! In the case of the elephant, however, there is a slight exception to the general rule, which is founded on an extraordinary struggle between mind and matter, the former making an effort that is unusual, and which may be said to form an exception to the ordinary warfare between these two principles, as it is commonly conducted in the retrogressive class of animals. The most infallible sign of the triumph of mind over matter, is in the development of the tail——"

"King!"

"Of the tail, Dr. Reasono?"

"By all means, sir,—that seat of reason, the tail! Pray, Sir John, what other portion of our frames did you imagine was indicative of intellect?"

"Among men, Dr. Reasono, it is commonly thought the head is the more honorable member, and, of late, we have made analytical maps of this part of our physical formation, by which it is pretended to know the breadth and length of a moral quality, no less than its boundaries."

"You have made the best use of your materials, such as they were, and I dare say the map in question, all things considered, is a very clever performance. But in the complication and abstruseness of this very moral chart (one of which I perceive standing on your mantel-piece,) you may learn the confusion which still reigns over the human intellect. Now, in regarding us, you can understand the very converse of your dilemma. How much easier, for instance, is it to take a yard-stick, and by a simple admeasurement of a tail, come to a sound, obvious and incontrovertible conclusion as to the extent of the intellect of the specimen, than by the complicated, contradictory, self-balancing and questionable process to which you are reduced! Were there only this fact, it would abundantly establish the higher moral condition of the monikin race, as it is compared with that of man."

"Dr. Reasono, am I to understand that the monikin family seriously entertain a position so extravagant as this: that a monkey is a creature more intellectual and more highly civilized than man?".

"Seriously, good Sir John!—Why you are the first respectable person it has been my fortune to meet, who has even affected to doubt the fact. It is well known that both belong to the *improveable* class of animals, and that monkeys, as you are pleased to term us, were once men, with all their passions, weaknesses, inconsistencies, modes of philosophy, unsound ethics, frailties, incongruities and subserviency to matter; that they passed into the monikin state by degrees, and that large divisions of them are constantly evaporating into the imma terial world, completely spiritualized and free fron the dross of flesh. I do not mean in what is called death—for that is no more than an occasional deposit of matter to be resumed in a new aspect, and with a nearer approach to the grand results, (whether of the *improveable* or of the *retrogressive* classes;) but those final mutations which transfer us to another planet, to enjoy a higher state of be ing, and leaving us always on the high road towards final excellence."

"All this is very ingenious, sir; but, before you can persuade me into the belief that man is an animal inferior to a monkey, Dr. Reasono, you will allow me to say that you must prove it."

"Ay, ay, or me, either," put in Captain Poke waspishly.

"Were I to cite my proofs, gentlemen," continued the philosopher, whose spirit appeared to be much less moved by our doubts than ours were by his position—"I should, in the first place, refer you to history. All the monikin writers are agreed in recording the gradual translation of the species from the human family——"

"This may do very well, sir, for the latitude of Leaphigh, but permit me to say that no human historian, from Moses down to Buffon, has ever taken such a view of our respective races. There is not a word in any of all these writers on the subject."

"How should there be, sir?—History is not a prediction, but a record of the past. Their silence is so much negative proof in our favor. Does Tacitus, for instance, speak of the French revolution? Is not Herodotus silent on the subject of the independence of the American continent?—or do any of the Greek and Roman writers give us the annals of Stunin'tun,—a city whose foundations were most probably laid some time after the commencement of the Christian era? It is morally impossible that men or monikins can faithfully relate events that have never happened; and as it has never yet happened to any man, who is still a man, to be translated to the monikin state of being, it follows, as a necessary consequence. that he can know nothing about it. If you want historical proofs, therefore, of what I say, you must search the monikin annals for the evidence. There it is to be found, with an infinity of curious details; and I trust the time is not far distant, when I shall have great pleasure in pointing out to you some of the most approved chapters of our best writers on this subject. But we are not confined to the testimony of history, in establishing our condition to be of the secondary formation. The internal evidence is triumphant: we appeal to our simplicity, our philosophy, the state of the arts among us; in short, to all those concurrent proofs which are dependent on the highest possible state of civilization. In addition to this, we have the infallible testimony which is to be derived from the development of our tails. Our system of caudology is, in itself, a triumphant proof of the high improvement of the monikin reason."

"Do I comprehend you aright, Dr. Reasono, when I understand your system of caudology, or tailology, to render it into the vernacular, to dogmatize on the possibility that the seat of reason in a man, which to day is certainly in his brains, can ever descend into a tail?"

"If you deem development, improvement and simplification, a descent, beyond a question, sir. But your figure is a bad one, Sir John; for ocular demonstration is before you, that a monikin can carry his tail as high as a man can possibly carry his head. Our species, in this sense, is morally nicked; and it costs us no effort to be on a level with human kings. We hold, with you, that the brain is the seat of reason, while the animal is in what we call the human probation, but that it is a reason undeveloped, imperfect and confused; cased, as it were, in an envelope unsuited to its functions; but that, as it gradually oozes out of this straitened receptacle towards the base of the animal, it ac quires solidity, lucidity, and, finally, by elongation and development, point. If you examine the human brain, you will find it, though capable of being stretched to a great length, compressed in a diminutive compass, involved and snarled; whereas the same physical portion of the genus gets simplicity, a beginning and an end, a directness and consecutiveness, that are necessary to logic, and, as has just been mentioned, a point, in the monikin seat of reason, which, by all analogy, go to prove the superiority of the animal possessing advantages so great."

"Nay, sir, if you come to analogies, they will be found to prove more than you may wish. In vegetation, for instance, saps ascend for the purposes of fructification and usefulness; and, reasoning from the analogies of the vegetable world, it is far more probable that tails have ascended into brains, than that brains have descended into tails; and, consequently, that men are much more likely to be an improvement on monkeys, than monkeys an improvement on men."

I spoke with warmth, I know; for the doctrine of Dr. Reasono was new to me; and, by this time, my *esprit de corps* had pretty effectually blinded reflection.

"You gave him a red-hot shot that time, Sir John," whispered Captain Poke at my elbow; "now, if you are so disposed, I will wring the necks of all these little blackguards, and throw them out of the window."

I immediately intimated that any display of brute force would militate directly against our cause; as the object, just at that moment, was to be as immaterial as possible.

"Well, well, manage it in your own way, Sir John, and I'm quite as immaterial as you can wish; but should these cunning varments ra'ally get the better of us in the argument, I shall never dare look at Miss Poke, or show my face ag'in in Stunin'tun."

This little aside was secretly conducted, while Dr. Reasono was drinking a glass of *eau sucrée*; but he soon returned to the subject, with the dignified gravity that never forsook him.

"Your remark touching saps has the usual savor of human ingenuity, blended, however, with the proverbial short-sightedness of the species. It is very true that saps ascend for the purposes of fructification; but what is this fructification, to which you allude? It is no more than a false demonstration of the energies of the plant. For all the purposes of growth, life, durability, and the final conversion of the vegetable matter into an element, the root is the seat of power and authority; and, in particular, the tap-root above, or rather below all others. This tap-root may be termed the tail of vegetation. You may pluck fruits with impunity—nay, you may even top all the branches, and the tree shall survive; but, put the axe to the root, and the pride of the forest falls!"

All this was too evidently true to be denied, and I felt worried and badgered; for no man likes to be beaten in a discussion of this sort, and more especially by a monkey. I bethought me of the elephant, and determined to make one more thrust, by the aid of his powerful tusks, before I gave up the point.

"I am inclined to think, Dr. Reasono," I put in as soon as possible, "that your *savans* have not been very happy in illustrating their theory by means of the elephant. This animal, besides being a mass of flesh, is too well provided with intellect to be passed off for a dunce; and he not only has *one*, but he might almost be said to be provided with *two* tails."

"That has been his chief misfortune, sir. Matter, in the great warfare between itself and mind, has gone on the principle of divide and conquer. You are nearer the truth than you imagined, for the trunk of the elephant is merely the abortion of a tail; and yet, you see, it contains nearly all the intelligence that the animal possesses. On the subject of the fate of the elephant, however, theory is confirmed by actual experiment. Do not your geologists and naturalists speak of the remains of animals, which are no longer to be found among living things?"

"Certainly, sir; the mastodon—the megatherium, iguanodon; and the plesiosaurus——"

"And do you not also find unequivocal evidences of animal matter incorporated with rocks?"

"This fact must be admitted, too."

"These phenomena, as you call them, are no more than the final deposits which nature has made in the cases of those creatures in which matter has completely overcome its rival, mind. So soon as the will is entirely extinct, the being ceases to live; or it is no longer an animal. It falls and reverts altogether to the element of matter. The processes of decomposition and incorporation are longer, or shorter, according to circumstances; and these fossil remains of which your writers say so much, are merely cases that have met with accidental obstacles to their final decomposition. As respects our two species, a very cursory examination of their qualities ought to convince any candid mind of the truth of our philosophy. Thus, the physical part of man is much greater in proportion to the spiritual, than it is in the monikin; his habits are grosser and less intellectual; he requires sauce and condiments in his food; he is farther removed from simplicity, and, by necessary implication, from high civilization; he eats flesh, a certain proof that the material principle is still strong in the ascendant he has no *cauda*——"

"On this point, Dr. Reasono, I would inquire if your scholars attach any weight to traditions?"

"The greatest possible, sir. It is the monikin tradition that our species is composed of men refined, of diminished matter and augmented minds, with the seat of reason extricated from the confinement and confusion of the *caput*, and extended, unravelled, and rendered logical and consecutive, in the *cauda*."

"Well, sir, *we* too have our traditions; and an eminent writer, at no great distance of time, has laid it down as incontrovertible, that men once *had caudæ*."

"A mere prophetic glance into the future, as coming events are known to cast their shadows before."

"Sir, the philosopher in question establishes his position, by pointing to the stumps."

"He has unluckily mistaken a foundation-stone for a ruin! Such errors are not unfrequent with the ardent and ingenious. That men *will* have tails, I make no doubt; but that they *have* ever reached this point of perfection, I do most solemnly deny. There are many premonitory symptoms of their approaching this condition; the current opinions of the day, the dress, habits, fashions, and philosophy of the species, encourage the belief; but hitherto you have never reached the enviable distinction. As to traditions, even your own are al in favor of our theory. Thus, for instance, you have a tradition that the earth was once peopled by giants. Now, this is owing to the fact that men were formerly more under the influence of matter, and less under that of mind, than to-day. You admit that you diminish in size, and improve in moral attainments; all of which goes to establish the truth of the monikin philosophy. You begin to lay less stress on physical, and more on moral excellencies and, in short, many things show that the time fo the final liberation and grand development of youı brains, is not far distant. This much I very gladly concede; for, while the dogmas of our schools are not to be disregarded, I very cheerfully admit that you are our fellow-creatures, though in a more infant and less improved condition of society."

"King!"

Here Dr. Reasono announced the necessity of taking a short intermission, in order to refresh himself. I retired with Captain Poke, to have a little communication with my fellow-mortal, under the peculiar circumstances in which we were placed, and to ask his opinion of what had been said. Noah swore bitterly at some of the conclusions of the monikin philosopher, affirming he should like no better sport than to hear him lecture in the streets of Stunin'tun, where, he assured me, such doctrine would not be tolerated any longer than was necessary to sharpen a harpoon, or to load a gun. Indeed, he did not know but the Doctor would be incontinently kicked over into Rhode Island, without ceremony.

"For that matter," continued the indignant old sealer, "I should ask no better sport, than to have permission to put the big toe of my right foot, under full sail, against the part of the blackguard where his beloved tail is stepped. That would soon bring him to reason. Why, as for his *caudæ*, if you will believe me, Sir John, I once saw a man, on the coast of Patagonia—a savage, to be sure, and not a philosopher, as this fellow pretends to be—who had an outrigger of this sort, as long as a ship's ring-tail-boom. And what was he, after all out a poor devil who did not know a sea-lion from a grampus!"

This assertion of Captain Poke relieved my mind considerably; and, laying aside the bison-skin, I asked him to have the goodness to examine the localities, with some particularity, about the termination of the dorsal bone, in order to ascertain if there were any encouraging signs to be discovered. Capt. Poke put on his spectacles, for time had brought the worthy mariner to their use, as he said, "whenever he had occasion to read fine print;" and, after some time, I had the satisfaction to hear him declare, that if it was a *cauda* I wanted, there was as good a place to step one, as could be found about any monkey in the universe; "and you have only to say the word, Sir John, and I will just step into the next room, and by the help of my knife and a little judgment in choosing, I'll fit you out with a jury-article, which, if there be any ra'al vartue in this sort of thing, will qualify you at once to be a judge, or, for that matter, a bishop."

We were now summoned again to the lecture-room, and I had barely time to thank Captain Poke for his obliging offer, which circumstances just then, however, forbade my accepting.

CHAPTER XII.

Better and better—A higher flight of reason—More obvious truths, deeper philosophy, and facts that even an ostrich might digest.

"I GLADLY quit what I fear some present may have considered the personal part of my lecture," resumed Dr. Reasono, "to turn to those portions of the theme that should possess a common interest, awaken common pride, and excite common felicitations. I now propose to say a few words on that part of our natural philosophy which is connected with the planetary system, the monikin location,—and, as a consequence from both, the creation of the world."

"Although dying with impatience to be enlightened on all these interesting points, you will grant me leave to inquire, *en passant*, Dr. Reasono, if your *savans* receive the Mosaic account of the creation or not."

"As far as it corroborates our own system, sir, and no farther. There would be a manifest inconsistency in our giving an antagonist validity to any hostile theory, let it come from Moses or Aaron; as one of your native good sense and subsequent cultivation will readily perceive."

"Permit me to intimate, Dr. Reasono, that the distinction your philosophers take in this matter, is directly opposed to a very arbitrary canon in the law of evidence, which dictates the necessity of repudiating the whole of a witness's testimony, when we repudiate a part."

"That may be a human, but it is not a monikin, distinction. So far from admitting the soundness of the principle, we hold that no monikin is ever wholly right, or that he will be wholly right, so long as he remain in the least under the influence of matter; and we therefore winnow the false from the true, rejecting the former as worse than useless while we take the latter as the nutriment of facts."

"I now repeat my apologies for so often interrupting you, venerable and learned sir; and I entreat you will not waste another moment in replying to my interrogatories, but proceed at once to an explanation of your planetary system, or of any other little thing it may suit your convenience to mention. When one listens to a real philosopher, one is certain to learn something that is either useful or agreeable, let the subject be what it may."

"By the monikin philosophy, gentlemen," continued Dr. Reasono, "we divide the great component parts of this earth into land and water. These two principles we term the *primary* elements. Human philosophy has added air and fire to the list; but these we reject either entirely, or admit them only as *secondary* elements. That neither air nor fire is a *primary* element, may be proved by experiment Thus, air can be formed, in the quality of gases can be rendered pure or foul; is dependent on evaporation, being no more than ordinary matter in a state of high rarefaction. Fire has no independent existence; requires fuel for its support, and is evidently a property that is derived from the combinations of other principles. Thus, by putting two or more billets of wood together, by rapid friction you produce fire. Abstract the air suddenly, and your fire becomes extinct; abstract the wood, and you have the same result. From these two experiments it is shown that fire has no independent existence, and therefore is not an element. On the other hand, take a billet of wood and let it be completely saturated with water: the wood acquires a new property, (as also by the application of fire, which converts it into ashes and air,) for its specific gravity is increased, it becomes less inflammable, emits vapor more readily, and yields less readily to the blow of the axe. Place the same billet under a powerful screw, and a vessel beneath. Compress the billet, and by a sufficient application of force, you will have the wood, perfectly dry, left beneath the screw, and the vessel will contain water. Thus is it shown that land (all vegetable matter being no more than fungi of the earth) is a *primary* element, and that water is also a *primary* element; while air and fire are not.

"Having established the elements, I shall, for brevity's sake, suppose the world created. In the beginning, the orb was placed in vacuum, stationary, and with its axis perpendicular to the plane of what is now called its orbit. Its only revolution was the diurnal."

"And the changes of the seasons?"

"Had not yet taken place. The days and nights were equal; there were no eclipses; the same stars were always visible. This state of the earth is supposed, from certain geological proofs, to have continued about a thousand years, during which time the struggle between mind and matter was solely confined to quadrupeds. Man is thought to have made his appearance, so far as our documents go to establish the fact, about the year of the world one thousand and three. About this period, too, it is supposed that fire was generated by the friction of the earth's axis, while making the diurnal movement; or, as some imagine, by the friction of the periphery of the orb, rubbing against vacuum at the rate of so many thousand miles in a minute. The fire penetrating the crust, soon got access to the bodies of water that fill the cavities of the earth. From this time is to be dated the existence of a new and most important agent in the terrestrial phenomena, called *steam.* Vegetation now began to appear, as the earth received warmth from within——"

"Pray, sir, may I ask in what manner all th animals existed previously?"

"By feeding on each other. The strong devoured the weak, until the most diminutive of the animal cula was reached, when these turned on their persecutors, and, profiting by their insignificance, commenced devouring the strongest. You find daily parallels to this phenomenon in the history of man. He who, by his energy and force, has triumphed over his equals, is frequently the prey of the insignificant and vile. You doubtless know that the polar regions, even in the original attitude of the earth, owing to their receiving the rays of the sun obliquely, must have possessed a less genial climate than the parts of the orb that lie between the arctic and the antarctic circles. This was a wise provision of Providence to prevent a premature occupation of those chosen regions, or to cause them to be left uninhabited, until mind had so far mastered matter, as to have brought into existence the first monikin."

"May I venture to ask to what epoch you refer the appearance of the first of your species?"

"To the Monikin Epocha, beyond a doubt, sir—but if you mean to ask in what year of the world this event took place, I should answer, about the year 4017. It is true, that certain of our writers affect to think that divers men were approaching to the sublimation of the monikin mind, previously to this period; but the better opinion is, that these cases were no more than what are termed premonitory

Thus, Socrates, Plato, Confucius, Aristotle, Euclid, Zeno, Diogenes, and Seneca, were merely so many admonishing types of the future condition of man, indicating their near approach to the monikin, or to the final translation."

"And Epicurus——"

"Was an exaggeration of the material principle, that denoted the retrogression of a large portion of the race towards brutality and matter. These phenomena are still of daily occurrence."

"Do you then hold the opinion, for instance, Dr. Reasono, that Socrates is now a monikin philosopher, with his brain unravelled and rendered logically consecutive, and that Epicurus is transformed perchance into a hippopotamus or a rhinoceros, with tusks, horns, and hide?"

"You quite mistake our dogmas, Sir John. We do not believe in transmigration in the individual at all, but in the transmigration of classes. Thus, we hold that whenever a given generation of men, in a peculiar state of society, attain, in the aggregate, a certain degree of moral improvement, or *mentality*, as we term it in the schools, that there is an admixture of their qualities in masses, some believe by scores, others think by hundreds, and others again pretend by thousands; and if it is found, by the analysis that is regularly instituted by nature, that the proportions are just, the material is consigned to the monikin birth; if not, it is repudiated, and either kneaded anew for another human experiment, or consigned to the vast stores of dormant matter. Thus all individuality, so far as it is connected with the past, is lost."

"But, sir, existing facts contradict one of the most important of your propositions; while you admit that a want of a change in the seasons would be a consequence of the perpendicularity of the earth's axis to the plane of its present orbit, this change in the seasons is a matter not to be denied. Flesh and blood testify against you here, no less than reason."

"I spoke of things as they were, sir, previously to the birth of the monikinia; since which time a great, salutary, harmonious, and contemplated alteration has occurred. Nature had reserved the polar regions for the new species, with divers obvious and benevolent purposes. It was rendered uninhabitable by the obliquity of the sun's rays; and though matter, in the shape of mastodons and whales, with an instinct of its antagonist destination, had frequently invaded their precincts, it was only to leave the remains of the first embedded in fields of ice, memorials of the uselessness of struggling against destiny, and to furnish proofs of the same great truth in the instance of the others; who, if they *did* enter the polar basins as masters of the great deep, either left their bones there, or returned in the same characters as they went. From the appearance of animal nature on the earth, down to the period when the monikin race arose, the regions in question were not only uninhabited, but virtually uninhabitable. When, however, Nature, always wary wise, beneficent, and never to be thwarted, had prepared the way, those phenomena were exhibited that cleared the road for the new species. I have alluded to the internal struggle between fire and water, and to their progeny, steam. This new agent was now required to act. A moment's attention to the manner in which the next great step in the progress of civilization was made, will show with what foresight and calculation our common mother had established her laws. The earth is flattened at the poles, as is well imagined by some of the human philosophers, in consequence of its diurnal movement commencing while the ball was still in a state of fusion, which naturally threw off a portion of the unkneaded matter, towards the periphery. This was not done without the design of accomplishing a desired end. The matter that was thus accumulated at the equator, was necessarily abstracted from other parts; and, in this manner, the crust of the globe became thinnest at the poles. When a sufficiency of steam had been generated in the centre of the ball, a safety-valve was evidently necessary to prevent a total disruption. As there was no other machinist than Nature, she worked with her own tools, and agreeably to her own established laws. The thinnest portions of the crust opportunely yielded to prevent a catastrophe, when the superfluous and heated vapor escaped, in a right line with the earth's axis, into vacuum. This phenomenon occurred, as nearly as we have been able to ascertain, about the year 700 before the Christian era commenced, or some two centuries previously to the birth of the first monikins."

"And why so early, may I presume to inquire, Doctor?"

"Simply that there might be time for the new climate to melt the ice that had accumulated about the islands and continents of that region, (for it was only at the southern extremity of the earth that the explosion had taken place,) in the course of so many centuries. Two hundred and seventy years of the active and unremitted agency of steam sufficed for this end; since the accomplishment of which, the monikin race has been in the undisturbed enjoyment of the whole territory, together with its blessed fruits."

"Am I to understand," asked Captain Poke, with more interest than he had before manifested in the philosopher's lecture, "that your folks, when at hum', live to the south'ard of the belt of ice that we mariners always fall in with somewhere about the parallel of 77° south latitude?"

"Precisely so—alas! that we should, this day be so far from those regions of peace, delight, intelligence, and salubrity! But the will of Providence be done!—doubtless, there is a wise motive for our captivity and sufferings, which may yet lead to the further glory of the monikin race!"

"Will you have the kindness to proceed with your explanations, Doctor? If you deny the annual revolution of the earth, in what manner do you account for the changes of the seasons, and other astronomical phenomena, such as the eclipses which so frequently occur?"

"You remind me that the subject is not yet exhausted," the philosopher hurriedly rejoined, hastily and covertly dashing a tear from his eye. "Prosperity produced some of its usual effects, among the founders of our species. For a few centuries, they went on multiplying in numbers, elongating and rendering still more consecutive their *caudæ*, improving in knowledge and the arts, until some spirits, more audacious than the rest, became restive under the slow march of events, which led them towards perfection at a rate ill-suited to their fiery impatience. At this time, the mechanic arts were at the highest pitch of perfection amongst us—we have since, in a great measure, abandoned them, as unsuited to, and unnecessary for, an advanced state of civilization—we wore clothes, constructed canals, and effected other works that were greatly esteemed among the species from which we had emigrated. At this time, also, the whole monikin family lived together as one people, enjoyed the same laws, and pursued the same objects. But a political sect arose in the region, under the direction of misguided and hot-headed leaders, who brought down upon us the just judgment of Providence, and a multitude of evils that it will require ages to remedy. This sect soon had recourse to religious fanaticism and philosophical sophisms, to attain its ends. It grew rapidly in power and numbers; for we monikins, like men, as I have had occasion to observe, are seekers of novelties. At last it proceeded to absolute overt acts of treason against the laws of Providence itself. The first violent demonstration of its madness and folly, was setting up the doctrine that injustice had been done the monikin race, by causing the safety-valve of the world to be opened within their region. Although we were manifestly indebted to this very circumstance for the benignity of our climate, the value of our possessions, the general healthfulness of our families—nay, for our separate existence itself, as an independent species, yet did these excited and ill-judging wretches absolutely wage war upon the most benevolent and the most unequivocal friend they had. Specious premises led to theories, theories to declamations, declamation to combination, combination to denunciation, and denunciation to open hostilities. The matter in dispute was debated for two generations, when the necessary degree of madness having been excited, the leaders of the party, who by this time had worked themselves through their hobby, into the general control of the monikin affairs, called a meeting of all their partisans, and passed certain resolutions, which will never be blotted from the monikin memory, so fatal were their consequences, so ruinous, for a time their effects! They were conceived in the following terms:—

"At a full and overflowing meeting of the most monikinized of the monikin race, holden at the house of Peleg Pat, (we still used the human appellations, at that epoch,) in the year of the world 3,007, and of the monikin era 317, Plausible Shout was called to the chair, and Ready Quill was named secretary

"After several excellent and eloquent addresses from all present, it was unanimously resolved as follows, viz.

"That steam is a curse, and not a blessing; and that it deserves to be denounced by all patriotic and true monikins.

"That we deem it the height of oppression and injustice in Nature, that she has placed the great safety-valve of the world, within the lawful limits of the monikin territories.

"That the said safety-valve ought to be removed forthwith; and that it shall be so removed, peaceably if it can, forcibly if it must.

"That we cordially approve of the sentiments of John Jaw, our present estimable chief magistrate, the incorruptible partisan, the undaunted friend of his friends, the uncompromising enemy of steam and the sound, pure, orthodox, and true monikin.

"That we recommend the said Jaw to the confidence of all monikins.

"That we call upon the country to sustain us in our great, holy, and glorious design, pledging ourselves, posterity, the bones of our ancestors, and all who have gone before or who may come after us, to the faithful execution of our intentions.

"Signed,

"Plausible Shout, Chairman.

"Ready Quill, Secretary."

"No sooner were these resolutions promulgated (for instead of being passed at a full meeting, it is now understood they were drawn up between Messrs. Shout and Quill, under the private dictation of Mr. Jaw,) than the public mind began seriously to meditate proceeding to extremities That perfection in the mechanic arts which had hitherto formed our pride and boast, now proved to be our greatest enemy. It is thought that the leaders of this ill-directed party meant, in truth, to confine themselves to certain electioneering effects; but who can stay the torrent, or avert the current of prejudice! The stream was setting against steam; the whole invention of the species was put in motion; and in one year from the passage of the resolutions I have recited, mountains were transported, endless piles of rocks were thrown into the gulf, arches were constructed, and the hole of the safety-valve was hermetically sealed. You will form some idea of the waste of intelligence and energy on this occasion, when I add, that it was found, by actual observation, that this artificial portion of the earth was thicker, stronger, and more likely to be durable than the natural. So far did infatuation lead the victims, that they actually caused the whole region to be sounded, and, having ascertained the precise locality of the thinnest portion of the crust, John Jaw, and all the most zealous of his followers, removed to the spot, where they established the seat of their government in triumph. All this time Nature rested upon her arms, in the quiet of conscious force. It was not long, however, before our ancestors began to perceive the consequences of their act, in the increase of the cold, in the scarcity of fruits, and in the rapid augmentation of the ice. The monikin enthusiasm is easily awakened in favor of any plausible theory, but it invariably yields to physical pressure. No doubt the human race, better furnished with the material of physical resistance, does not exhibit so much of this weakness, but——"

"Do not flatter us with the exception, Doctor. I find so many points of resemblance between us that I really begin to think we must have had the same origin; and if you would only admit that man is of the secondary formation and the monikins of the primary, I would accept the whole of your philosophy without a moment's delay."

"As such an admission would be contrary to both fact and doctrine, I trust, my dear sir, you will see the utter impossibility of a Professor in the University of Leaphigh making the concession, even in this remote part of the world.—As I was about to observe, the people began to betray uneasiness at the increasing and constant inclemency of the weather; and Mr. John Jaw found it necessary to stimulate their passions by a new development of his principles. His friends and partisans were all assembled in the great square of the new capital, and the following resolutions were, to use the language of a handbill that is still preserved in the archives of the Leaphigh Historical Society, (for it would seem they were printed before they were passed,) "unanimously, enthusiastically, and finally adopted," viz.

Resolved, That this meeting has the utmost contempt for steam.

Resolved, That this meeting defies snow, and sterility, and all other natural disadvantages.

Resolved, That we will live for ever.

Resolved, That we will henceforward go naked, as the most effectual means of setting the frost at defiance.

Resolved, That we are now over the thinnest part of the earth's crust in the polar regions.

Resolved, That henceforth we will support no monikin for any public trust, who will not give a pledge to put out all his fires, and to dispense with cooking altogether.

Resolved, That we are animated by the true spirit of patriotism, reason, good faith, and firmness.

Resolved, That this meeting now adjourn *sine die.*

"We are told that the last resolution was just carried by acclamation, when Nature arose in her might, and took ample vengeance for all her wrongs. The great boiler of the earth burst, with a tremendous explosion, carrying away, as the thinnest part of the workmanship, not only Mr. John Jaw, and all his partisans, but forty thousand square miles of territory. The last that was seen of them was about thirty seconds after the occurrence of the explosion, when the whole mass disappeared near the northern horizon, going at a rate a little surpassing that of a cannon-ball which has just left its gun."

"King!' exclaimed Noah; "that is what we sailors call, to cut and run."

"Was nothing ever heard of Mr. Jaw and his companions, my good Doctor?"

"Nothing that could be depended on. Some of our naturalists assume that the monkeys which frequent the other parts of the earth are their descendants, who, stunned by the shock, have lost their reasoning powers, while, at the same time, they show glimmerings of their origin. This is, in truth, the better opinion of our *savans;* and it is usual with us, to distinguish all the human species of monkeys by the name of "the lost monikins." Since my captivity, chance has thrown me in the way of several of these animals, who were equally under the control of the cruel Savoyards; and in conversing with them, in order to inquire into their traditions and to trace the analogies of language, I have been led to think there is some foundation for the opinion. Of this, however, hereafter."

"Pray, Dr. Reasono, what became of the forty thousand square miles of territory?"

"Of that, we have a better account; for one of our vessels, which was far to the northward, on an exploring expedition, fell in with it in longitude 2° from Leaphigh, latitude 6° S., and by her means it was ascertained that divers islands had been already formed by falling fragments; and, judging from the direction of the main body when last seen, the fertility of that part of the world, and various geological proofs, we hold that the great western Archipelago is the deposit of the remainder."

"And the monikin region, sir,—what was the consequence of this phenomenon to that part of the world?"

"Awful—sublime—various—and durable! The more important, or the personal consequences, shall be mentioned first. Fully one-third of the monikin species was scalded to death. A great many contracted asthmas and other diseases of the lungs, by inhaling steam. Most of the bridges were swept away by the sudden melting of the snows, and large stores of provisions were spoilt by the unexpected appearance and violent character of the thaw. These may be enumerated among the unpleasant consequences. Among the pleasant, we esteem a final and agreeable melioration of the climate, which regained most of its ancient char acter, and a rapid and distinct elongation of our *caudæ*, by a sudden acquisition of wisdom.

"The secondary, or the terrestrial consequences were as follow.—By the suddenness and force with which so much steam rushed into space, finding its outlet several degrees from the pole, the earth was canted from its perpendicular attitude, and remained fixed with its axis having an inclination of 23° 27°° to the plane of its orbit. At the same time, the orb began to move in vacuum, and, restrained by antagonist attractions, to perform what is called its annual revolution."

"I can very well understand, friend Reasono," observed Noah, "why the 'arth should heel under so sudden a flaw, though a well-ballasted ship would right again when the puff was over; but I cannot understand how a little steam leaking out at one end of a craft should set her a-going at the rate we are told this world travels?"

"If the escape of the steam were constant, the diurnal motion giving it every moment a new position, the earth would not be propelled in its orbit, of a certainty, Captain Poke; but as, in fact, this escape of the steam has the character of pulsation, being periodical and regular, nature has ordained that it shall occur but once in the twenty-four hours, and this at such a time as to render its action uniform, and its impulsion always in the same direction. The principle on which the earth receives this impetus, can be easily illustrated by a familiar experiment. Take, for instance, a double-barrelled fowling-piece, load both barrels with extra quantities of powder, introduce a ball and *two* wads into each barrel, place the breech within $4\frac{628}{1000}$ inches of the abdomen, and take care to fire both barrels at once. In this case, the balls will give an example of the action of the forty thousand square miles of territory, and the person experimenting will not fail to imitate the impulsion, or the backward movement, of the earth."

"While I do not deny that such an experiment would be likely to set both parties in motion, friend Reasono, I do not see why the 'arth should not finally stop, as the man would be sure to do, after he had got through with hopping, and kicking, and swearing."

"The reason why the earth, once set in motion in vacuum, does not stop, can also be elucidated by experiment, as follows.—Take Captain Noah Poke, provided as he is by nature with legs and the power of motion; lead him to the *Place Vendôme;* cause him to pay three sous, which will gain him admission to the base of the column; let him ascend to the summit; thence let him leap with all his energy, in a direction at right angles with the shaft of the column, into the open air; and it will be found that, though the original impulsion would not probably impel the body more than ten or twelve feet, motion would continue until it had reached the earth.—Corollary: hence it is proved, that all bodies in which the *vis inertia* has been overcome, will continue in motion, until they come in contact with some power capable of stopping them."

"King!—Do you not think, Mr. Reasono, that the arth makes its circuit, as much owing to this said steam of yours shoving, as it were, always a little on one side, acting thereby in some fashion as a rudder, which causes her to keep waring, as we seamen call it, and as big crafts take more room than small ones in waring, why, she is compelled to run so many millions of miles before, as it might be, she comes up to the wind ag'in? Now, there s reason in such an idee; whereas, I never could reconcile it to my natur', that these little bits of stars should keep a craft like the 'arth in her course, with such a devil of a way on her, as we know in reason she must have, to run so far in a twelve-month. Why, the smallest yaw—and, for a hooker of her keel, a thousand miles would n't be a broader yaw than a hundred feet in a ship—the smallest yaw would send her aboard of the Jupiter, or the Marcury, when there would be a smashing of out-board work such as mortal never before witnessed!"

"We rather lean to the opinion of the efficacy of attraction, sir;—nor do I see that your proposition would at all obviate your own objection."

"Then, sir, I will just explain myself. Let us suppose there was a steamer with a hundred miles of keel; let us suppose the steam up, and the craft with a broad offing; let us suppose her helm lash'd hard a-port, and she going at the rate of ten thousand knots the hour, without bringing up or shortening sail for years at a time. Now, all this being admitted, what would be her course? Why, sir, any child could tell you, she would keep turning in a circle of some fifty or a hundred thousand miles in circumference; and such, it appears to me, it is much more rational to suppose is the natur' of the 'arth's traversing, than all this steering-smal among stars and attractions."

"There is truly something very plausible, Captain Poke, in your suggestion; and I propose that you shall profit by the first occasion to lay your opinions on the subject, more at large, before the Academy of Leaphigh."

"With all my heart, Doctor; for I hold that knowledge, like good liquor, is given to be passed round from one to another, and not to be gulped in a corner by any particular individdle. And now I'm throwing out hints of this natur'. I will just intimate another, that you may add to your next demonstration, by way of what you call a corollary:—which is this,—that is to say—if all you tell us about the bursting of the boiler and the polar kick be true, then is the 'arth the first steam-boat that was ever invented, and the boastings of the French, and the English, and the Spaniards, and the Italians, on this point, are no more than so much smoke."

"And of the Americans, too, Captain Poke,' I ventured to observe.

"Why, Sir John, that is as it may happen.—I don't well see how Fulton could have stolen the idee, seeing that he did not know the Doctor, and most probably never heard of Leaphigh in his life."

We all smiled, even to the amiable Chatterissa, at the nicety of the navigator's distinctions; and the philosopher's lecture, in its more didactic form, being now virtually at an end, a long and desultory conversation took place, in which a multitude of ingenious questions were put by Captain Poke and myself, and which were as cleverly answered by the Doctor and his friends.

At length, Dr. Reasono, who, philosopher as he was, and much as he loved science, had not given himself all this trouble, without a view to what are called ulterior considerations, came out with a frank *exposé* of his wishes. Accident had apparently combined all the means for gratifying the burning desire I betrayed to be let into further details of the monikin polity, morals, philosophy, and all the other great social interests of the part of the world they inhabit. I was wealthy beyond bounds, and the equipment of a proper vessel would be an expenditure of no moment; both the

Doctor and Lord Chatterino were good practical geographers, after they were once within the parallel of 77° south, and Captain Poke, according to his own account of himself, had passed half his life in poking about among the sterile and uninhabited islands of the frozen ocean. What was there to prevent the most earnest wishes of all present from being gratified? The Captain was out of employment, and no doubt would be glad to get the command of a good tight sea-boat; the strangers pined for home, and it was my most ardent wish to increase my stake in society, by taking a further interest in monikins.

On this hint, I frankly made a proposal to the old sealer, to undertake the task of restoring these amiable and enlightened strangers to their own fire-sides and families. The Captain soon began to discover a little of his Stunin'tun propensity; for, the more I pressed the matter on him, the more readily he found objections. The several motives he urged for declining the proposal, may be succinctly given as follows:—

It was true that he wanted employment, but then he wanted to see Stunin'tun too; he doubted whether monkeys would make good sailors; it was no joke to run in among the ice, and it might be still less of one to find our way back again; he had seen the bodies of dead seals and bears that were frozen as hard as stone, and which might, for any thing he knew, have lain in that state a hundred years, and, for his part, he should like to be buried when he was good for nothing else; how did he know these monikins might not catch the men, when they had once fairly got them in their country, and strip them, and make them throw summersets, as the Savoyards had compelled the Doctor, and even the Lady Chatterissa, to do?—he knew he should break his neck the very first flap-jack, if he were ten years younger, perhaps he should like the frolic; he did not believe the right sort of craft could be found in England, and, for his part, he liked sailing under the stars and stripes; he didn't know but he might go, if he had a crew of Stunin'tunners; he always knew how to get along with such people; he could scare one by threatening to tell his *marm* how he behaved, and bring another to reason by hinting that the gals would shy him, if he wasn't more accommodating; then there might be no such place as Leaphigh, after all; or, if there was, he might never find it; as for wearing a bison-skin under the equator, it was quite out of the question, a human skin being a heavy load to carry in the calm latitudes; and finally, that he didn't exactly see what he was to get by it."

These objections were met, one by one, reversing the order in which they were made, and commencing with the last.

I offered a thousand pounds sterling as the reward. This proposal brought a gleam of satisfaction into Noah's eyes, though he shook his head, as if he thought it very little. It was then suggested that there was no doubt we should discover certain islands that were well stored with seals, and that I would waive all claims as owner, and that hereafter he might turn these discoveries to his own private account. At this bait he nibbled, and, at one time, I thought he was about to suffer himself to be caught. But he remained obstinate. After trying all our united rhetoric, and doubling the amount of the pecuniary offer, Dr. Reasono luckily bethought him of the universal engine of human weakness, and the old sealer, who had resisted money—an influence of known efficacy at Stunin'tun—ambition, the secret of new sealing grounds, and all the ordinary inducements that might be thought to have weight with men of his class, was, in the end, hooked by his own vanity!

The philosopher cunningly expatiated on the pleasure there would be in reading a paper before the academy of Leaphigh, on the subject of the captain's peculiar views touching the earth's annual revolution, and of the virtue of sailing planets with their helms lashed hard-a-port, when all the dogmatical old navigator's scruples melted away like snow in a thaw.

CHAPTER XIII.

A chapter of preparations—Discrimination in character—A tight fit, and other conveniences, with some judgment.

I SHALL pass lightly over the events of the succeeding month. During this time, the whole party was transferred to England, a proper ship had been bought and equipped, the family of strangers were put in quiet possession of their cabins, and I had made all my arrangements for being absent from England for the next two years. The vessel was a stout-built, comfortable ship of about three hundred tons burthen, and had been properly constructed to encounter the dangers of the ice. Her accommodations were suitably arranged to meet all the exigencies of both monikin and human wants, the apartments of the ladies being very properly separated from those of the gentlemen, and otherwise rendered decorous and commodious. The Lady Chatterissa very pleasantly called their private room the *gynecée*, which, as I afterwards ascer tained, was a term for the women's apartments, obtained from the Greek, the monikins being quite as much addicted as we are ourselves, to showing their acquirements by the introduction of words from foreign tongues.

Noah showed great care in the selection of the ship's company, the service being known to be arduous, and the duties of a very responsible character. For this purpose, he made a journey expressly to Liverpool, (the ship lying in the Greenland Dock at London,) where he was fortunate enough to engage five Yankees, as many Englishmen, two Norwegians and a Swede, all of whom had been accustomed to cruising as near the poles as ordinary men ever succeed in reaching. He was also well suited in his cook and mates; but I observed that he had great difficulty in finding a cabin-boy to his mind. More than twenty applicants were rejected, some for the want of one qualification, and some for the want of another. As I was present at several examinations of different candidates for the office, I got a little insight into his manner of ascertaining their respective merits.

The invariable practice was, first, to place a bottle of rum, and a pitcher of water, before the lad, and to order him to try his hand at mixing a glass of grog. Four applicants were incontinently rejected for manifesting a natural inaptitude at hitting the *juste milieu*, in this important part of the duty of a cabin-boy. Most of the candidates, however, were reasonably expert in the art; and the captain soon came to the next requisite, which was, to say "Sir," in a tone, as Noah expressed it, somewhere between the snap of a steel-trap and the mendicant whine of a beggar. Fourteen were rejected for deficiencies on this score, the captain remarking that most of them "were the sa'ciest blackguards" he had ever fallen in with. When he had, at length, found one who could mix a tumbler of grog, and answer "Sir," to his liking, he proceeded to make experiments on their abilities in carrying a soup-tureen over a slushed plank; in wiping plates without a napkin, and without using their shirt-sleeves; in snuffing candles with their fingers; in making a soft bed with few materials besides boards; in mixing the various compounds of burgoo lob-skous, and dough, (which he affectedly pro nounced *duff*); in fattening pigs on beef-bones, and ducks on the sweepings of the deck; in looking at molasses without licking his lips; and in various other similar accomplishments, which he maintained were as familiar to the children of Stunin'tun, as their singing-books and the ten commandments. The nineteenth candidate to my uninstructed eyes seemed perfect; but Noah rejected him for the want of a quality that he declared was indispensable to the quiet of the ship. It appeared he was too bony about an essential part of his anatomy, a peculiarity that was very dangerous to a captain, as he himself was once so unfortunate as to put his great toe out of joint, by kicking one of these ill-formed youngsters with unpremeditated violence; a thing that was very apt to happen to a man in a hurry. Luckily, number twenty passed, and was immediately promoted to the vacant birth. The very next day the ship put to sea, in good condition, and with every prospect of a fortunate voyage.

I will here state that a general election occurred the week before we sailed; and I ran down to Householder and got myself returned, in order to protect the interests of those who had a natural right to look up to me for that small favor.

We discharged the pilot when we had the Scilly Islands over the taffrail, and Mr. Poke took command of the vessel, in good earnest. Coming down channe., he had done little more than rummage about in the cabin, examine the lockers, and make his foot acquainted with the anatomy of poor Bob as the cabin-boy was called; who, judging from the amount of the captain's practice, was admirably well suited for his station, in the great requisite of a kickee. But, the last hold of the land loosened by the departure of the pilot, our navigator came forth in his true colours, and showed the stuff of which he was really made. The first thing he did was to cause a pull to be made on every halyard, bowline and brace in the ship; he then rattled off both mates, in order to show them (as he afterwards told me in confidence) that he was captain of his own vessel; gave the people to understand he did not like to speak twice on the same subject and on the same occasion, which he said was a privilege he very willingly left to congress-men and women; and then he appeared satisfied with himself and all around him.

A week after we had taken our departure, I ventured to ask Captain Poke if it might not be well enough to take an observation, and to resort to some means in order to know where the ship was. Noah treated this idea with great disrespect. He could see no use in wearing out quadrants without any necessity for it. Our course was south, we knew, for we were bound to the south pole; all we had to do was to keep America on the starboard, and Africa on the larboard, hand. To be sure, there was something to be said about the trades, and a little allowance to be made for currents, now and then; but he and the ship would get to be better acquainted before a great while, and then all would go on like clockwork. A few days after this conversation, I was on deck just as day dawned, and to my surprise Noah, who was in his birth, called out to the mate, through the sky-light, to let him know exactly how the land bore. No one had yet seen any land; but at this summons we began to look about us, and sure enough there was an island dimly visible in the eastern board! Its position by compass was immediately communicated to the captain, who seemed well satisfied with the result. Renewing his admonition to the officer of the deck to take care and keep Africa on the larboard hand, he turned over in his bed to resume his nap.

I afterwards understood from the mates, that we had made a very capital fall upon the trades, and that we were getting on wonderfully well, though it was quite as great a mystery to them as it was to me, how the captain could know where the ship was; for he had not touched his quadrant, except to wipe it with a silk handkerchief, since we left England. About a fortnight after we had passed the Cape de Verds, Noah came on deck in a great rage, and began to storm at the mate and the man at the wheel for not keeping the ship her course. To this the former answered with spirit, that the only order he had received in a fortnight, was "to keep her jogging south, allowing for variation," and that she was heading at that moment according to orders. Hereupon Noah gave Bob, who happened to pass him just then, a smart application à posteriori, and swore "that the compass was as big a fool as the mate; that the ship was two points off her course; that south was hereaway, and not thereaway; that he knew by the feel of the wind that it had no northin' in it, and we had got it away on the quarter, whereas it ought to be for'ard of the beam; that we were running for Rio instead of Leaphigh, and that if we ever expected to get to the latter country, we must haul up on a good taut bowline." The mate, to my surprise, suddenly acquiesced, and immediately brought the ship by the wind. He afterwards told me, in a half whisper, that the second mate having been sharpening some harpoons, had unwittingly left them much too close to the binnacle; and that, in fact, the magnet had been attracted by them, so as to deceive the man at the wheel and himself, fully twenty degrees as to the real points of the compass. I must say this little occurrence greatly encouraged me, leaving no doubt about our eventual and safe arrival as far, at least, as the boundary of ice which separates the human from the monikin region. Profiting by this feeling of security, I now began to revive the intercourse with the strangers, which had been partially interrupted by the novel and disagreeable circumstances of a sea life.

The Lady Chatterissa and her companion, as is much the case with females at sea, rarely left the gynecée; but, as we drew near the equator, the philosopher and the young peer passed most of their time on deck, or aloft. Dr. Reasono and I spent half of the mild nights in discussing subjects connected with my future travels; and, as soon as we were well clear of the rain and the thunder and lightning of the calm latitudes, Captain Poke, Robert, and myself, began to study the language of Leaphigh. The cabin-boy was included in this arrangement, Noah intimating we should find it convenient to take him on shore with us, since a wish to conceal my destination had induced me to bring no servant along. Luckily for us, the monikin ingenuity had greatly diminished the labor of the acquisition. The whole language was spoken and written on a system of decimals, which rendered it particularly easy, after the elementary principles were once acquired. Thus, unlike most human tongues, in which the rule usually forms the exception, no departure from its laws was ever allowed, under the penalty of the pillory. This provision, the captain protested, was the best rule of them all, and saved a vast deal of trouble; for, as he knew by experience, a man might be a perfect adept in the language of Stunin'tun, and then be laughed at in New-York for his pains. The comprehensiveness of the tongue was also another great advantage; though, like all other eminent advantages or excessive good, it was the next-door neighbor to as great an evil. Thus, as my Lord Chatterino obligingly explained, "*we-witch-it-me-cum,*" means "Madam, I love you from the crown of my head to the tip of my tail; and as I love no other half as well, it would make me the happiest monikin on earth, if you would consent to become my wife, that we might be models of domestic propriety before all eyes, from this time henceforth and for ever." In short, it was the usual and the most solemn expression for asking in marriage; and, by the laws of the land, was binding on the proposer until as formally declined by the other party. But, unluckily, the word "we-*s*witch-it-me-cum," means "Madam, I love you from the crown of my head to the tip of my tail; and, *if I did not love another better*, it would make me the happiest monikin on earth, if you would consent to become my wife, that we might be models of domestic propriety before all eyes, from this time henceforth and for ever." Now this distinction, subtle and insignificant as it was to the eye and the ear, caused a vast deal of heart-burning and disappointment among the young people of Leaphigh. Several serious lawsuits had grown out of this cause, and two great political parties had taken root in the unfortunate mistake of a young monikin of quality, who happened to lisp, and who used the fatal word indiscreetly

That feud, however, was now happily appeased having lasted only a century; but it would be wise as we were all three bachelors, to take note of the distinction. Captain Poke said he thought, on the whole, he was sufficiently safe, as he was much accustomed to the use of the word "*switchel;*" but he thought it might be very well to go before some consul, as soon as the ship anchored, and enter a formal protest of our ignorance of all these niceties, lest some advantage should be taken of us by the reptiles of lawyers; that he in particular was not a bachelor, and that Miss Poke would be as furious as a hurricane, if, by an accident, he should happen to forget himself. The matter was deferred for future deliberation.

About this time, too, I had some more interesting communications with Dr. Reasono, on the subject of the private histories of all the party of which he was the principal member. It would seem that the philosopher, though rich in learning, and the proprietor of one of the best developed *caudæ* in the entire monikin world, was poor in the more vulgar attributes of monikin wealth. While he bestowed freely, therefore, from the stores of his philosophy, and through the medium of the academy of Leaphigh, on all his fellows, he was obliged to seek an especial recipient for his surplus knowledge, in the shape of a pupil, in order to provide for the small remains of the animal that still lingered in his habits. Lord Chatterino, the orphan heritor of one of the noblest and wealthiest, as well as one of the most ancient houses of Leaphigh, had been put under his instruction at a very tender age, as had my Lady Chatterissa under that of Mrs. Lynx, with very much the same objects. This young and accomplished pair had early distinguished each other, in monikin society, for their unusual graces of person, general attainments, mutual amiableness of disposition, harmony of thought, and soundness of principles. Every thing was propitious to the gentle flame which was kindled in the vestal bosom of Chatterissa, and which was met by a passion so ardent, and so respectful, as that which glowed in the heart of young No. 8 purple. The friends of the respective parties, so soon as the budding sympathy between them was observed, in order to prevent the blight of wishes so appropriate, had called in the aid of the matrimonial surveyor-general of Leaphigh, an officer especially appointed by the king in council, whose duty it is to take cognizance of the proprieties of all engagements that are likely to assume a character as grave and durable as that of marriage. Dr. Reasono showed me the certificate issued from the Marriage Department on this occasion, and which, in all his wanderings, he had contrived to conceal within the lining of the Spanish hat the Savoyards had compelled him to wear, and which he still preserved as a document that was absolutely indispensable on his return to Leaphigh; else he would never be permitted to travel a foot in company with two young people of birth and of good estates, who were of the different sexes. I translate the certificate, as literally as the poverty of the English language will allow.

EXTRACT from the Book of Fitness, Marriage Department, Leaphigh, season of nuts, day of brightness.

Vol. 7243, p. 82.

Lord Chatterino: Domains; 126,952¾ acres of and; meadow, arable and wood in just proportions.

Lady Chatterissa: Domains; 115,999½ acres of and; mostly arable.

Decree, as of record; it is found that the lands

of my Lady Chatterissa possess in quality what they want in quantity.

Lord Chatterino: Birth; sixteen descents pure; one bastardy—four descents pure—a suspicion—one descent pure—a certainty.

Lady Chatterissa: Birth; six descents pure—three bastardies—eleven descents pure—a certainty—a suspicion—unknown.

Decree as of record; it is found that the advantage is on the side of my Lord Chatterino, but the excellence of the estate on the other side is believed to equalize the parties.

(Signed) No. 6 ermine. A true copy,
(Counter signed) No. 1,000,003 ink-color.

Ordered, that the parties make the Journey of Trial together, under the charge of Socrates Reasono, Professor of Probabilities in the University of Leaphigh, L. L. D., F. U. D. G. E., and of Mrs. Vigilance Lynx, licensed duenna.

The Journey of Trial is so peculiar to the monikin system, and it might be so usefully introduced into our own, that it may be well to explain it. Whenever it is found that a young couple are agreeable (to use a peculiarly anglicized anglicism), in all the more essential requisites of matrimony, they are sent on the journey in question, under the care of prudent and experienced mentors, with a view to ascertain how far they may be able to support, in each other's society, the ordinary vicissitudes of life. In the case of candidates of the more vulgar classes, there are official overseers, who usually drag them through a few mud-puddles, and then set them to work at some hard labor that is especially profitable to the public functionaries, who commonly get the greater part of their own year's work done in this manner. But, as the moral provisions of all laws are invented less for those who own 126,952$\frac{3}{4}$ acres of land, divided into meadow arable and wood, in just proportions, than for those whose virtues are more likely to yield to the fiery ordeal of temptation, the rich and noble, after making a proper and useful manifestation of their compliance with the usage, ordinarily retire to their country-seats, where they pass the period of probation as agreeably as they can; taking care to cause to be inserted in the Leaphigh gazette however, occasional extracts from their letters describing the pains and hardships they are compelled to endure, for the consolation and edification of those who have neither birth nor country-houses In a good many instances the journey is actually performed by proxy. But the case of my Lord Chatterino and my Lady Chatterissa formed an exception even to these exceptions. It was thought by the authorities, that the attachment of a pair so illustrious offered a good occasion to distinguish the Leaphigh impartiality; and, on the well-known principle which induces us sometimes to hang an Earl in England, the young couple was commanded actually to go forth with all useful éclat, (secret orders being given to their guardians to allow every possible indulgence, at the same time,) in order that the lieges might see and exult in the sternness and integrity of their rulers.

Dr. Reasono had accordingly taken his departure from the capital for the mountains, where he instructed his wards in a practical commentary on the ups and downs of life, by exposing them on the verges of precipices and in the delights of the most fertile valleys, (which, as he justly observed, was the greater danger of the two,) leading them over flinty paths, hungry and cold, in order to try their tempers; and setting up establishments with the most awkward peasants for servants, to ascertain the depth of Chatterissa's philosophy; with a variety of similar ingenious devices, that will readily suggest themselves to all who have any matrimonial experience, whether they live in palaces or cottages. When this part of the trial was successfully terminated, (the result having shown that the gentle Chatterissa was of proof, so far as mere temper was concerned,) the whole party was ordered off to the barrier of ice, which divides the monikin from the human region, with a view to ascertain whether the warmth of their attachment was of a nature likely to resist the freezing collisions of the world. Here, unfortunately, (for the truth must be said,) an unlucky desire of Dr. Reasono, who was already F. U. D. G. E., but who had a devouring ambition to become also M. O. R. E., led him into the extreme imprudence of pushing through an opening, where he had formerly discovered an island, on an ancient expedition of the same sort; and on which island he thought he saw a rock, that formed a stratum of what he believed to be a portion of the 43,000 square miles, that were discomposed by the great eruption of the earth's boiler. The philosopher foresaw a thousand interesting results that were dependent on the ascertaining of this important fact; for all the learning of Leaphigh having been exhausted, some five hundred years before, in establishing the *greatest* distance to which any fragment had been thrown on that memorable occasion, great attention had latterly been given to the discovery of the *least* distance any fragment had been hurled. Perhaps I ought to speak tenderly of the consequences of a learned zeal, but it was entirely owing to this indiscretion that the whole party fell into the hands of certain mariners who were sealing on the northern shores of this very island, (friends and neighbours, as it afterwards appeared, of Captain Poke,) who remorselessly seized upon the travellers, and sold them to a homeward-bound Indiaman, which they afterwards fell in with, near the island of St. Helena—St. Helena! the tomb of him who is a model to all posterity, for the moderation of his desires, the simplicity of his character, a deep veneration for truth, profound reverence for justice, unwavering faith, and a clear appreciation of all the nobler virtues!

We came in sight of the island in question, just as Dr. Reasono concluded his interesting narrative; and, turning to Captain Poke, I solemnly asked that discerning and shrewd seaman,—

"If he did not think the future would fully avenge itself of the past—if history would not do ample justice to the mighty dead—if certain names would not be consigned to everlasting infamy for chaining a hero to a rock; and whether *his* country, the land of freemen, would ever have disgraced itself, by such an act of barbarism and vengeance?"

The Captain heard me very calmly; then deliberately helping himself to some tobacco, he replied:—

"Harkee, Sir John. At Stunin'tun, when we catch a ferocious crittur', we always put it in a cage. I'm no great mathematician, as I've often told you but if my dog bites me once, I kick him—twice, I beat him—thrice, I chain him."

Alas!—there are minds so unfortunately constituted, that they have no sympathies with the sublime. All their tendencies are direct and common sense-like. To such men, Napoleon appears little better than one who lived among his fellows more in the character of a tiger than in that of a man. They condemn him because he could not reduce his own sense of the attributes of greatness to the level of their homebred morality. Among this number, it would now seem, was to be classed Captain Noah Poke.

A wish to relate the manner in which Dr Reasono and his companions fell into human hands, has caused me to overlook one or two matters of lighter moment, that should not, in justice to myself, however, be entirely omitted.

When we had been at sea two days, a very agreeable surprise for the monikin party, was prepared and executed. I had caused a certain number of jackets and trowsers to be made of the skins of different animals, such as dogs, cats, sheep, tigers, leopards, hogs, &c. &c., with the proper accompaniments of snouts, hoofs, and claws; and, when the ladies came on deck, after breakfast, their eyes were no longer offended by our rude innovations upon nature, but the whole crew were flying about the rigging, like so many animals of the different species named. Noah and myself appeared in the characters of sea-lions, the former having intimated that he understood the nature of that beast better than any other. Of course, this delicate attention was properly appreciated, and handsomely acknowledged.

I had taken the precaution to order imitation-skins to be made of cotton, which were worn in the low latitudes; and, as we got near the Falkland Islands, the real skins were resumed, with promptitude, and I might add, with pleasure.

Noah had, at first, raised some strong objections to the scheme, saying that he should not feel safe in a ship manned and officered altogether by wild beasts; but, at last, he came to enjoy the thing as a good joke, never failing to hail the men, not by their names as formerly, but, as he expressed it himself, "by their natur's;" calling out

You cat, scatch this;" "You tiger, jump here;" You hog, out of that dirt;" "You dog, scamper here;" "You horse, haul away," and divers other similar conceits, that singularly tickled his fancy The men themselves took up the ball, which they kept rolling, embellished with all sorts of nautical witticisms; their surname—they had but one, viz. Smith—being entirely dropped for the new appellations. Thus, the sounds of "Tom Dog," "Jack Cat," "Bill Tiger," "Sam Hog," and "Dick Horse," were flying about the decks, from morning to night.

Good humour is a great alleviator of bodily privation. From the time the ship lost sight of Staten Land, we had heavy weather, with hard gales from the southward and westward; and we had the utmost difficulty in making our southing. Observations now became a very difficult matter, the sun being invisible for a week at a time. The marine instinct of Noah, at this crisis, was of the last importance to all on board. He gave us the cheering assurance, however, from time to time, that we were going south, although the mates declared that they knew not where the ship was, or whither she was running; neither sun, moon, nor star having now been seen for more than a week.

We had been in this state of anxiety and doubt for about a fortnight, when Captain Poke suddenly appeared on deck, and called for the cabin-boy, in his usual stentorian and no-denial voice, by the name of "You Bob Ape;" for the duty of Robert requiring that he should be much about the persons of the monikins, I had given him a dress of apes' skins, as a garb that would be more congenial to their tastes than that of a pig, or a weasel. Bob Ape was soon forthcoming, and, as he approached his m ter, he quietly turned his face from him, receiving, as a matter of course, three or four smart admonitory hints, by way of letting him know that he was to be active in the performance of the duty on which he was about to be sent. On this occasion I made an odd discovery. Bob had profited by the dimensions of his lower garment, which had been cut for a much larger boy, (one of those who had broken down in essaying the true Doric of "Sir,") by stuffing it with an old union-jack—a sort of "sarvice," as he afterwards told me, that saved him a good deal of wear and tear of skin. To return to passing events, however: when Robert had been duly kicked, he turned about manfully, and demanded the captain's pleasure. He was told to bring the largest and the fairest pumpkin he could find, from the private stores of Mr. Poke, that navigator never going to sea without a store of articles, that he termed "Stunin'tun food." The Captain took the pumpkin between his legs, and carefully peeled off the whole of its greenish-yellow coat, leaving it a globe of a whitish colour. He then asked for the tar-bucket; and, with his fingers, traced various marks, which were pretty accurate outlines of the different continents and the larger islands of the world. The region near the south pole, however, he left untouched; intimating that it contained certain sealing islands, which he considered pretty much as the private property of the Stunin'tunners.

"Now, Doctor," he said, pointing to the pumpkin, "there is the 'arth, and nere is the tar-pot—just mark down the position of your island of Leaphigh, if you please, according to the best accounts your academy has of the matter. Make a dab, here and there, if you happen to know of any rocks and shoals. After that, you can lay down the island where you were captured, giving a general idee of its headlands and of the trending of the coast."

Dr. Reasono took a fidd, and with its end he traced all the desired objects with great readiness and skill. Noah examined the work, and seemed satisfied that he had fallen into the hands of a monikin who had very correct notions of bearings and distances, one, in short, on whose local knowedge it might do to run even in the night. He then projected the position of Stunin'tun, an occupation in which he took great delight, actually designing the meeting-house and the principal tavern; after which, the chart was laid aside.

CHAPTER XIV.

How to steer small—How to run the gauntlet with a ship How to go clear—A new-fashioned screw-dock, and certain mile-stones.

Captain Poke no longer deliberated about the course we were to steer. With his pumpkin fo a chart, his instinct for an observation, and his nose for a compass, the sturdy sealer stood boldly to the southward; or, at least, he ran dead before a stiff gale, which, as he more than once affirmed, was as true a norther as if bred and born in the Canadas.

After coursing over the billows, at a tremendous rate, for a day and a night, the Captain appeared on deck, with a face of unusual meaning and a mind loaded with its own reflections, as was proved by his winking knowingly whenever he delivered himself of a sentiment; a habit that he had most probably contracted, in early youth, at Stunin'tun, for it seemed to be quite as inveterate as it was thorough-bred.

"We shall soon know, Sir John," he observed, hitching the sea-lion skin into symmetry, "whether it is sink or swim!"

"Pray explain yourself, Mr. Poke," cried I, in a little alarm. "If any thing serious is to happen, you are bound to give timely notice."

"Death is always untimely to some crittur's, Sir John."

"Am I to understand, sir, that you mean to cast away the ship?"

"Not if I can help it, Sir John; but a craft that is foreordained to be a wrack, will be a wrack, in spite of reefing and bracing. Look ahead, you Dick Lion—ay, there you have it!"

There we had it, sure enough! I can only compare the scene which now met my eyes, to a sudden view of the range of the Oberland Alps, when the spectator is unexpectedly placed on the verge of the precipice of the Weissenstein. There he would see before him a boundless barrier of glittering ice, broken into the glorious and fantastic forms of pinnacles, walls and valleys; while here, we saw all that was sublime in such a view, heightened by the fearful action of the boisterous ocean, which beat upon the impassable boundary, in ceaseless violence.

"Good God! Captain Poke," I exclaimed, the instant I caught a glimpse of the formidable danger that menaced us, "you surely do not mean to continue madly on, with such a warning of the consequences in plain view?"

"What would you have, Sir John? Leaphigh lies on the t'other side of these ice-islands?"

"But you need not run the ship against them—why not go round them?"

"Because *they* go round the 'arth, in this latitude. Now is the time to speak, Sir John. If we are bound to Leaphigh, we have the choice of three pretty desperate chances; to go through, to go under, or to go over that there ice. If we are to put back, there is not a moment to lose, for it may be even now questioned whether the ship would claw off, as we are, with a sending sea, and this heavy norther."

I believe I would, at that moment, gladly have given up all my social stakes to be well rid of the adventure. Still pride, that substitute for so many virtues, the greatest and the most potent of all hypocrites, forbade my betraying the desire to retreat. I deliberated, while the ship flew; and when, at length, I turned to the captain to suggest a doubt that might, at an earlier notice, possibly have changed the whole aspect of affairs, he bluntly told me it was too late. It was safer to proceed than to return, if, indeed, return were possible, in the present state of the winds and waves. Making a merit of necessity, I braced my nerves to meet the crisis, and remained a submissive, and, apparently, a calm spectator, of that which followed.

The Walrus, (such was the name of our good ship,) by this time, was under easy canvas, and yet, urged by the gale, she rolled down, with alarming velocity, towards the boundary of foam, where the congealed and the still liquid element held their strife. The summits of the frozen crags waved in their glittering glory, in a way just to show that they were afloat; and I remembered to have heard that, at times, as their bases melted, entire mountains had been known to roll over, engulphing all that lay beneath. To me it seemed but a moment, before the ship was fairly overshadowed by these shining cliffs, which gently undulating, waved their frozen summits nearly a thousand feet in air. I looked at Noah, in alarm. for it appeared to me, that he intentionally precipi tated us to destruction. But, just as I was about to remonstrate, he made a sign with his hand, and the vessel was brought to the wind. Still retreat was impossible; for the heave of the sea was too powerful, and the wind too heavy, to leave us any hope of long keeping the Walrus from drifting down upon the ragged peaks that bristled in icy glory to leeward. Nor did Captain Poke, himself, seem to entertain any such design; for, instead of hugging the gale, in order to haul off from the danger, he had caused the yards to be laid perfectly square, and we were now running, at a great rate, in a line nearly parallel with the frozen coast, though gradually setting upon it.

"Keep full! Let her go through water, you Jim Tiger," said the old sealer, whose professional ardor was fairly aroused. "Now, Sir John, unluckily, we are on the wrong side of these ice-mountains, for the plain reason, that Leaphigh lies to the south'ard of them. We must be stirring, therefore, for no craft that was ever launched could keep off these crags, with such a gale driving home upon them, for more than an hour or two. Our great concern, at present, is to look out for a hole to run into."

"Why have you come so close to the danger, with your knowledge of the consequences?"

"To own the truth, Sir John, natur' is natur' and I'm getting to be a little near-sighted as I grow old; besides, I'm not so sartain that danger is the more dangerous, for taking a good steady look plump in its face."

Noah raised his hand, as much as to say he wished no answer, and both of us were immediately occupied in gazing anxiously to leeward. The ship was just opening a small cove in the ice, which might have been a cable's length in depth and a quarter of a mile across its outer, or the widest, part. Its form was regular, being that of a semicircle; but, at its bottom, the ice, instead of forming a continued barrier, like all the rest we had yet passed, was separated by a narrow opening, that was bounded on each side by a frowning precipice. The two bergs were evidently drawing nearer to each other, but there was still a strait, or a watery gorge between them, of some two hundred feet in width. As the ship plunged onward, the pass was opened, and we caught a glimpse of the distant view to leeward. It was merely a glimpse—the impatient Walrus allowing us but a moment for examination,—but it appeared sufficient for the purposes of the old sealer. We were already across the mouth of the cove, and within a cable's length of the ice again; for as we drew near what may be called the little cape, we found ourselves once more in closer proximity to the menacing mountain. It was a moment when all depended on decision; and, fortunately, our sealer, who was so wary and procrastinating in a bargain, never had occasion to make two drafts on his thoughts, in situations of emergency. As the ship cleared the promontory on the easter side of the cove, we again opened a curvature of the ice, which gave a little more water to leeward. Tacking was impossible, and the helm was put hard-a-weather. The bow of the Walrus fell off, and as she rose on the next wave, I thought its send would carry us helplessly down upon the berg. But the good craft, obedient to her rudder, whirled round, as if sensible herself of the danger, and, in less time than I had ever before known her to ware, we felt the wind on the other quarter. Our cats and dogs bestirred themselves for there was no one there, Captain Noah Poke excepted, whose heart did not beat quick and hard. In much less time than usual, the yards were braced up on the other tack, and the ship was ploughing heavily against the sea, with her head to the westward. It is impossible to give one who has never been in such a situation, a just idea of the feverish impatience, the sinking and mounting of hope, as we watch the crab-like movement of a vessel, that is clawing off a lee shore, in a gale. In the present case, it being well known that the sea was fathomless, we had run so near the danger that not even the smallest of its horrors was veiled from sight.

While the ship labored along, I saw the clouds fast shutting in to windward, by the interposition of the promontory of ice,—the certain sign that our drift was rapid,—and, as we drew nearer to the point, breathing became labored and even audible. Here Noah took a chew of tobacco, I presume on the principle of enjoying a last quid should the elements prove fatal; and then he went to the wheel in person.

"Let her go through the water," he said, easing the helm a little—"let her jog ahead, or we shall lose command of her in this devil's-pot!"

The vessel felt the slight change, and drew faster through the foaming brine, bringing us, with increasing velocity, nearer to the dreaded point. As we came up to the promontory, the water fell back in spray on the decks, and there was an instant when it appeared as if the wind was about to desert us. Happily the ship had drawn so far ahead, as to feel the good effects of a slight change of current that was caused by the air rushing obliquely into the cove; and, as Noah, by easing the helm still more, had anticipated this alteration, which had been felt adversely but a moment before, while struggling to the eastward of the promontory, we drew swiftly past the icy cape, opening the cove handsomely, with the ship's head falling off fast towards the gorge.

There was but a minute, or two, for squaring the yards and obtaining the proper position to windward of the narrow strait. Instead of running down in a direct line for the latter, Captain Poke kept the ship on such a course as to lay it well open, before her head was pointed toward the passage. By this time, the two bergs had drawn so near each other as actually to form an arch across its mouth; and this too, at a part so low as to render it questionable whether there was sufficient elevation to permit the Walrus to pass beneath. But retreat was impossible, the gale urging the ship furiously onward. The width of the passage was now but little more than a hundred feet, and it actually required the nicest steerage to keep our yard-arms clear of the opposite precipices, as the vessel dashed, with foaming bows, into the gorge. The wind drew through the opening with tremendous violence, fairly howling, as if in delight at discovering a passage by which it might continue its furious career. We may have been aided by the sucking of the wind and the waves, both of which were irresistibly drawn towards the pass, or it is quite probable that the skill of Captain Poke did us good service, on this awful occasion; but, owing to the one or the other, or to the two causes united, the Walrus shot into the gorge so accurately, as to avoid touching either of the lateral margins of the ice. We were not so fortunate, however, with the loftier spars; for, scarcely was the vessel beneath the arch, wnen she lifted on a swell, and her main-top-gallant-mast snapped off in the cap.

The ice groaned and cracked over our heads and large fragments fell both ahead and astern of us, several of them even tumbling upon our decks One large piece came down within an inch of the extremity of Dr. Reasono's tail, just escaping the dire calamity of knocking out the brains of that profound and philo-monikin philosopher. In another instant, the ship was through the pass, which completely closed, with the crash of an earthquake, as soon as possible afterwards.

Still driven by the gale, we ran rapidly towards the south, along a channel less than a quarter of a mile in width, the bergs evidently closing on each side of us, and the ship, as if conscious of her jeopardy, doing her utmost, with Captain Poke still at the wheel. In little more than an hour, the worst was over; the Walrus issuing into an open basin of several leagues in extent, which was, however, completely encircled by the frozen mountains. Here Noah took a look at the pumpkin, after which he made no ceremony in plumply telling Dr. Reasono that he had been greatly mistaken in laying down the position of Captivity Island, as he himself had named the spot where the amiable strangers had fallen into human hands. The philosopher was a little tenacious of his opinion; but what is argument in the face of facts? Here was the pumpkin, and there were the blue waters! The Captain now quite frankly declared that he had great doubts whether there was any such place as Leaphigh at all; and as the ship had a capital position for such an object, he bluntly, though privately, proposed to me, that we should throw all the monikins overboard, project the entire polar basin on his chart as being entirely free from islands, and then go a sealing. I rejected the propositions, firstly, as premature; secondly, as inhuman; thirdly, as inhos pitable; fourthly, as inconvenient; and lastly, as impracticable.

There might have arisen a disagreeable controversy between us, on this point; for Mr. Poke had begun to warm, and to swear that one good seal, of the true quality of fur, was worth a hundred monkeys; when most happily the panther at the mast-head cried out that two of the largest of the mountains, to the southward of us, were separating, and that he could discern a passage into another basin. Hereupon Captain Poke concentrated his oaths, which he caused to explode like a bomb, and instantly made sail, again, in the proper direction. By three o'clock, P. M., we had run the gauntlet of the bergs, a second time, and were at least a degree nearer the pole, in the basin just alluded to.

The mountains had now entirely disappeared in the southern board; but the sea was covered, far as the eye could reach, with field-ice. Noah stood on, without apprehension; for the water had been smooth ever since we entered the first opening, the wind not having rake enough to knock up a swell. When about a mile from the margin of the frozen and seemingly interminable plain, the ship was brought to the wind, and hove-to.

Ever since the vessel left the docks, there had been six sets of spars of a form so singular, lying among the booms, that they had often been the subject of conversation between the mates and myself, neither of the former being able to tell their uses. These sticks were of no great length, some fifteen feet at the most, of sound English oak. Two or three pairs were alike, for they were in pairs, each pair having one of the sides of a shape resembling different parts of the ship's bottom, with the exception that they were chiefly concave, while the bottom of a vessel is mainly convex. At one extremity each pair was firmly connected by a short, massive, iron link, of about two feet in length; and, at its opposite end, a large eye-bolt was driven into each stick, where it was securely forelocked. When the Walrus was stationary, we learned, for the first time, the uses of these unusual preparations. A pair of the timbers, which were of great solidity and strength, were dropped over the stern, and, sinking beneath the keel, their upper extremities were separated, by means of lanyards turned into the eye-bolts. The lanyards were then brought forward to the bilge of the vessel, where, by the help of tackles, the timbers were rowsed up in such a manner, that the link came close to the false-keel, and the timbers themselves were laid snug against each side of the ship. As great care had been taken, by means of marks on the vessel, as well as in forming the skids themselves, the fit was perfect. No less than five pairs were secured in and near the bilge, and as many more were distributed forward and aft, according to the shape of the bottom. Fore-and-aft pieces, that reached from one skid to the other, were then placed between those about the bilge of the ship, each of them having a certain number of short ribs, extending upwards and downwards. These fore-and-aft pieces were laid along the water-line, their ends entering the skids by means of mortices and tenons, where they were snugly bolted. The result of the entire arrangement was to give the vessel an exterior protection against the field-ice, by means of a sort of net-work of timber, the whole of which had been so accurately fitted in the dock, as to bear equally on her frame. These preparations were not fairly completed before ten o'clock on the following morning, when Noah stood direct y for an opening in the ice before us, which, just about that time began to be apparent.

"We sha'n't go so fast for our armour," observed the cautious old sealer; "but what we want in heels, we'll make up in bottom."

For the whole of that day, we worked our devious course, by great labor, and at uncertain intervals, to the southward; and at night, we fastened the Walrus to a floe, in waiting for the return of light. Just as the day dawned, however, I heard a tremendous grating sound against the side of the vessel; and, rushing on deck, I found that we were completely caught between two immense fields, which seemed to be attracted towards each other for no other apparent purpose than to crush us. Here it was that the expedient of Captain Poke made manifest its merits. Protected by the massive timbers, and false ribs, the bilge of the ship resisted the pressure; and as, under such circumstances, something must yield, luckily nothing but the attraction of gravitation was overcome. The skids, through their inclination, acted as wedges, the links pressing against the keel; and, in the course of an hour, the Walrus was gradually lifted out of the water, maintaining her upright position, in consequence of the powerful nip of the floes. No sooner was this experiment handsomely effected, than Mr. Poke jumped upon the ice, and commenced an examination of the ship's bottom.

"Here's a dry dock for you, Sir John!" exclaimed the old sealer, chuckling. "I'll have a patent for this, the moment I put foot ag'in in Stunin'tun."

A feeling of security, to which I had been a stranger ever since we entered the ice, was created by the composure of Noah, and by his self-congratulation at what he called his project to get a look at the Walrus's bottom. Notwithstanding all the fine declarations of exultation and success, however, that he flourished among us who were not mariners, I was much disposed to think that, like other men of extraordinary genius, he had blundered on the grand result of his "ice-screws," and that it was not foreseen and calculated. Let this be as it may, however, all hands were soon on the floe, with brooms, scrapers, hammers, and nails, and the opportunity of repairing and cleaning was thoroughly improved.

For four-and-twenty hours the ship remained in the same attitude, stiff as a church, and some of us began to entertain apprehensions, that she might be kept on her frozen blocks for ever. The accident had happened, according to the statements of Captain Poke, in lat. 78° 13′ 26″—although I never knew in what manner he ascertained the important particular of our precise situation. Thinking it might be well to get some more accurate ideas on this subject, after so long and ticklish a run, I procured the quadrant from Bob Ape, and brought it down upon the ice, where I made it a point, as an especial favor, the weather being favorable and the proper hour near, that our commander would correct his instinct by a solar observation. Noah protested that your old seaman, especially if a sealer and a Stunin'tunner, had no occasion for such geometry-operations, as he termed them; that it might be well enough, perhaps necessary, for your counting-house, silk-gloved captains, who run between New-York and Liverpool, to be rubbing up their glasses and polishing their sextants, for they hardly ever knew where they were, except at such times; but as for himself, he had little need of turning star-gazer at his time of life, and that, as he had already told me, he was getting to be near-sighted, and had some doubts whether he could discern an object like the sun, that was known to be so many thousands of millions of miles from the earth. These scruples, however, were overcome by my cleaning the glasses, preparing a barrel for him to stand on, that he might be at the customary elevation above his horizon, and putting the instrument into his hands, the mates standing near, ready to make the calculations, when he gave the sun's declination.

"We are drifting south'ard, I know," said Mr. Poke, before he commenced his sight—"I feel it in my bones. We are, at this moment, in 79° 36′ 14″—having made a southerly drift of more than eighty miles, since yesterday noon. Now, mind my words, and see what the sun will say about it."

When the calculations were made, our latitude was found to be 79° 35′ 47″. Noah was somewhat puzzled by the difference, for which he could in no plausible way account, as the observation had been unusually good and certain. But an opinionated and an ingenious man is seldom at a loss to find a sufficient reason to establish his own correctness, or to prove the mistakes of others.

"Ay, I see how it is," he said, after a little cogitation; "the sun must be wrong—it should be no wonder if the sun did get a little out of his track, in these high, cold latitudes. Yes, yes: the sun must be wrong."

I was too much delighted at being certain we were going on our course to dispute the point, and the great luminary was abandoned to the imputation of sometimes being in error. Dr Reasono took occasion to say, in my private ear that there was a sect of philosophers in Leaphigh who had long distrusted the accuracy of the planetary system, and who had even thrown out hints that the earth, in its annual revolution, moved in a direction absolutely contrary to that which Nature had contemplated when she gave the original polar impulse; but that, as regarded himself, he thought very little of these opinions, as he had frequent occasion to observe that there was a large class of monikins whose ideas always went up hill.

For two more days and as many nights, we continued to drift with the floes to the southward, or as near as might be, towards the haven of our wishes. On the fourth morning, there was a suitable change in the weather; both thermometer and barometer rose; the air became more bland, and most of our cats and dogs, notwithstanding we were still surrounded by the ice, began to cast their skins. Dr. Reasono noted these signs, and stepping on the floe he brought back with him a considerable fragment of the frozen element.—This was carried to the camboose, where it was subjected to the action of fire, which, within a given number of minutes, pretty much as a matter of course, as I thought, caused it to melt. The whole process was watched with an anxiety the most intense, by the whole of the monikins, however; and when the result was announced, the amiable and lovely Chatterissa clapped her pretty little *pattes* with joy, and gave all the other natural indications of delignt, which characterize the emoticns of that gentle sex of which she was so bright an ornament. Dr. Reasono was not backward in explaining the cause of so much unusual exhilaration, for hitherto her manner had been characterized by the well-bred and sophisticated restraint which marks high training. The experiment had shown, by the infallible and scientific tests of monikin chemistry, that we were now within the influence of a steam-climate, and there could no longer be any rational doubt of our eventual arrival in the polar basin.

The result proved that the philosopher was right. About noon the floes, which all that day had begun to assume what is termed a 'sloppy character,' suddenly gave way, and the Walrus settled down into her proper element, with great equanimity and propriety. Captain Poke lost no time in unshipping the skids; and, a smacking breeze, that was well saturated with steam, springing up from the westward, we made sail. Our course was due south, without regard to the ice, which yielded before our bows like so much thick water, and, just as the sun set, we entered the open sea, rioting in the luxuriance of its genial climate, in triumph.

Sail was carried on the ship all that night; and just as the day dawned, we made the first milestone, a proof, not to be mistaken, that we were now actually in the monikin region. Dr. Reasono had the goodness to explain to us the history of these aquatic phenomena. It would seem that when the earth exploded, its entire crust, throughout the whole of this part of the world, was started upward in such a way as to give a very uniform depth to the sea, which in no place exceeds four fathoms. It follows, as a consequence, that no prevalence of northerly winds can force the icebergs beyond 78° of south latitude, as they invariably ground on reaching the outer edge of the polar bank. The floes, being thin, are melted of course; and thus, by this beneficent prevention, the monikin world is kept entirely free from the very danger to which a vulgar mind would be the most apt to believe it is the most exposed.

A congress of nations had been held, about five

centuries since, which was called the Holy-philo-marine-safety-and-find-the-way Alliance. At this Congress the high contracting parties agreed to name a commission to make provision, generally, for the secure navigation of the seas. One of the expedients of this commission, which, by the way, is said to have been composed of very illustrious monikins, was to cause massive blocks of stone to be laid down, at measured distances, throughout the whole of the basin, and in which other stone uprights were secured. The necessary inscriptions were graved on proper tablets, and as we approached the one already named, I observed that it had the image of a monikin, carved also in stone, with his tail extended in a right line, pointing, as Mr. Poke assured me, S. and by W. half W. I had made sufficient progress in the monikin language, to read, as we glided past this water-mark — "To Leaphigh, 15 miles." One monikin mile, however, we were next told, was equal to nine English statute miles; and, consequently, we were not quite so near our port as was at first supposed. I expressed great satisfaction at finding ourselves so fairly on the road, however, and paid Dr. Reasono some well-merited compliments on the high state of civilization to which his species had evidently arrived. The day was not distant, I added, when, it was reasonable to suppose, our own seas would have floating *restaurants* and *cafés*, with suitable pot-houses for the mariners; though I did not well see how we were to provide a substitute for their own excellent organization of mile-stones. The Doctor received my compliments with a proper modesty, saying that he had no doubt mankind would do all that ay in their power to have good eating and drinking-houses, wherever they could be established; but, as to the marine mile-stones, he agreed with me, that there was little hope of their being planted, until the crust of the earth should be driven upward, so as to rise within four fathoms of the surface of the water. On the other hand, Captain Poke held this latter improvement very cheap. He affirmed it was no sign of civilization at all, for, as a man became civilized, he had less need of primers and finger-boards; and, as for Leaphigh, any tolerable navigator might see it bore S. by W. half W. allowing for variation, distant 135 English miles. To these objections I was silent, for I had had frequent occasions to observe that men very often underrate any advantage of which they have come into the enjoyment by a providential interposition.

Just as the sun was in the meridian, the cry of 'land ahead' was heard from aloft. The monikins were all smiles and gratitude; the crew was excited by admiration and wonder; and, as for myself, I was literally ready to jump out of my skin, not only with delight, but, in some measure also, from the exceeding warmth of the atmosphere. Our cats and dogs began to uncase; Bob was obliged to unmask his most exposed frontier, by removing the union-jack; and Noah himself fairly appeared on deck in his shirt and night-cap. The amiable strangers were too much occupied to be particular, and I slipped into my state-room to change my toilet to a dress of thin silk, that was painted to resemle the skin of a polar bear,—a contradiction between appearances and the substance of things, that is much too common in our species ever to be deemed out of fashion.

We neared the land with great rapidity, impelled by a steam-breeze, and just as the sun sunk in the horizon our anchor was let go, in the outer harbor of the city of Aggregation.

CHAPTER XV.

An arrival, forms of reception; several new christenings an official document, and terra firma.

It is always agreeable to arrive safe, at the end of a long, fatiguing and hazardous journey. But the pleasure is considerably augmented when the visit is paid to a novel region, with a steam-climate, and which is peopled by a new species. My own satisfaction, too, was coupled with the reflection that I had been of real service to four very interesting and well-bred strangers, who had been cast, by an adverse fortune, into the hands of humanity, and who owed to me a boon far more precious than that of life itself,—a restoration to their natural and acquired rights, their proper stations in society, and sacred liberty! The reader will judge, therefore, with what inward self-congratulation I now received the acknowledgments of the whole monikin party, and listened to their most solemn protestations ever to consider, not only all they might jointly and severally possess in the way of estates and dignities, at my entire disposal, but their persons as my slaves. Of course, I made as light as possible of any little service I might have done them, protesting, in my turn, that I looked upon the whole affair more in the light of a party of pleasure than a tax, reminding them that I had not only obtained an insight into a new philosophy, but that I was already, thanks to the decimal system, a tolerable proficient in their ancient and learned language. These civilities were scarcely well over, before we were boarded by the boat of the port-captain.

The arrival of a human ship was an event likely to create excitement in a monikin country; and, as our approach had been witnessed for several hours, preparations had been made to give us a proper reception. The section of the academy to whom is committed the custody of the "Science of Indications," was hastily assembled, by order of the King, who, by the way, never speaks except through the mouth of his oldest male first cousin, who, by the fundamental laws of the realm, is held responsible for all his official acts, (in private, the King is allowed almost as many privileges as any other monikin,) and who, as is due to him in simple justice, is permitted to exercise, in a public point of view, the functions of the eyes, ears, nose, conscience, and tail of the monarch. The *savans* were active, and as they proceeded with method, and on well-established principles, their report was quickly made. It contained, as we afterwards understood, seven sheets of premises, eleven of argument, sixteen of conjecture, and two lines of deduction. This heavy draft on the monikin intellect, was duly achieved by dividing the work into as many parts as there were members of the section present, viz. forty. The substance of their labors was, to say that the vessel in sight was a strange vessel; that it came to a strange country, on a strange errand, being manned by strangers; and that its objects were more likely to be peaceful than warlike, since the glasses of the academy did not enable them to discover any means of annoyance, with the exception of certain wild beasts, who appeared, however, to be peaceably occupied in working the ship. All this was sententiously expressed in the purest monikin language. The effect of the report was to cause all hostile preparations to be abandoned.

No sooner did the boat of the port-captain return to the shore, with the news that the strange ship had arrived with my Lord Chatterino, my Lady Chatterissa and Dr. Reasono, than there was a general burst of joy along the strand. In a very short time, the King—alias his eldest first cousin of the male gender—ordered the usual compliments to be paid to his distinguished subjects. A deputation of young Lords, the hopes of Leaphigh, came off to receive their colleague; whilst a bevy of beautiful maidens, of noble birth, crowded around the smiling and graceful Chatterissa, gladdening her heart with their caressing manners and felicitations. The noble pair left us in separate boats, each attended by an appropriate escort. We overlooked the little neglect of forgetting to take leave of us, for joy had quite set them both beside themselves. Next came a long procession composed of high numbers, all of the "brown-study-color." These learned and dignified persons were a deputation from the academy, which had sent forth no less than forty of its number to receive Dr. Reasono. The meeting between these loving friends of monikinity and of knowledge, was conducted on the most approved principles of reason. Each section (there are forty in the academy of Leaphigh) made an address, to all of which the Doctor returned suitable replies, always using exactly the same sentiments, but varying the subject by transpositions, as dictionaries are known to be composed by the ingenious combinations of the twenty-six letters of the alphabet. Dr. Reasono withdrew with his coadjutors, to my surprise, paying not a whit more attention to Captain Poke and myself, than would be paid, in any highly civilized country of Christendom, on a similar occasion, by a collection of the learned, to the accidental pre sence of two monkeys. I thought this augured badly, and began to feel as became Sir John Goldencalf, Bart., of Householder Hall, in the Kingdom of Great Britain, when my sensations were nipped in the bud by the arrival of the Officers of Registration and Circulation. It was the duty of the latter to give us the proper passports to enter into and to circulate within the country, after the former had properly enregistered our numbers and colors, in such a way as to bring us within the reach of taxation. The officer of Registration was very expeditious from long practice. He decided, at once, that I formed a new class by myself; of which, of course, I was No. 1. The Captain and his two mates formed another, Nos. 1, 2 and 3. Bob had a class also to himself, and the honors of No. 1; and the crew formed a fresh class, being numbered according to height, as the register deemed their merits to be altogether physical. Next came the important point of color, on which depended the quality of the class or *caste*, the numbers merely indicating our respective stations in the particular divisions. After a good deal of deliberation, and many interrogatories, I was enregistered as No. 1, flesh-color. Noah as No. 1, sea-water-color, and his mates 2 and 3, accordingly. Bob as No. 1, smut-colour; and the crew as Nos. 1, 2, 3, &c. tar-color. The officer now called upon an assistant to come forth with a sort of knitting-needle heated red-hot, in order to affix the official stamp to each in succession. Luckily for us all, Noah happened to be the first to whom the agent of the stamp-office applied, to uncase and to prepare for the operation. The result was one of those bursts of eloquent and logical vituperation, and of remonstrating outcries, to which any new personal exaction never failed to give birth in the sealer. His discourse on this occasion might be divided into the several following heads, all of which were very ingeniously embellished by the usual expletives and imagery—'He was not a beast to be branded like a horse, nor a slave to be treated like a Congo nigger; he saw no use in applying the marks to men, who were sufficiently distinguished from monkeys already; Sir John had a handle before his name, and if he liked it, he might carry his name behind his body, by way of counterpoise, but, for his part, he wanted no outriggers of the sort, being satisfied with plain Noah Poke; he was a republican, and it was anti-republican for a man to carry about with him graven images; he thought it might be even flying in the face of the Scriptures, or, what was worse, turning his back on them; he said that the Walrus had her name, in good legible characters, on her starn, and that might answer for both of them; he protested, d——n his eyes, that he wouldn't be branded like a thief; he incontinently wished the keeper of the privy-seal to the d——l; he insisted there was no use in the practice, unless one threw all aback and went starn foremost into society, a rudeness at which human natur' revolted; he knew a man at Stunin'tun who had five names, and he should like to know what they would do with him, if this practice should come into fashion there; he had no objection to a little paint, but no red-hot knitting-needle should make acquaintance with his flesh, so long as he walked his quarter-deck."

The keeper of the seals listened to this remonstrance with singular patience and decorum; a forbearance that was probably owing to his not understanding a word that had been said. But there is a language that is universal, and it is not less easy to comprehend when a man is in a passion, than it is to comprehend any other irritated animal. The officer of the Registration Department, on this hint, politely inquired of me, if some part of his official duties were not particularly disagreeable to No. 1, sea-water-color. On my admitting that the captain was reluctant to be branded, he merely shrugged his shoulders, and observed, that the exactions of the public were seldom agreeable, but that duty was duty, that the stamp-act was peremptory, and not a foot of ours could touch Leaphigh, until we were all checked off in this manner, in exact conformity with the registration. I was much puzzled what to do, by this indomitable purpose to perform his duty in the officer: for, to own the truth, my own cuticle had quite as much aversion to the operation, as that of Captain Poke himself. It was not the principle, so much as the novelty of its application, which distressed me; for I had travelled too much not to know that a stranger rarely enters a *civilized* country without being more or less skinned, the merest savages only permitting him to pass unscathed. It suddenly came to my recollection that the monikins had left all the remains of their particular stores on board, consisting of an ample supply of delicious nuts. Sending for a bag of the best of them, I ordered it to be put into the register's boat, informing him, at the same time, that I was conscious they were quite unworthy of him, but that I hoped, such as they were, he would allow me to make an offering of them to his wife. This attention was properly felt and received; and a few minutes afterwards, a certificate in the following words was put into my hands, viz.—

"Leaphigh, season of promise, day of performance: *Whereas,* certain persons of the human species have lately presented themselves to be enregistered, according to the statute 'For the promotion of order and classification, and for the collection of contributions;' and *whereas,* these persons are yet in the second class of the animal probation, and are more subject to bodily impressions than the higher, or monikin species; Now, know all monikins, &c., that they are *stamped* in paint, and that only by their numbers; each class among them being easily to be distinguished from the others, by outward and indelible proofs.

"Signed,

"No. 8,020 office-color."

I was told that all we had to do now, was to mark ourselves with paint or tar, as we might choose, the latter being recommended for the crew; taking no farther trouble than to number ourselves: and, when we went ashore, if any of the gens-d'armes inquired why we had not the legal impression on our persons, which quite possibly would be the case, as the law was absolute in its requisitions, all we had to do was to show the certificate; but, if the certificate was not sufficient, we were men of the world, and understood the nature of things so well, that we did not require to be taught so simple a proposition in philosophy, as that which says, "like causes produce like effects;" and he presumed I could not have so far overrated his merits, as to have sent the whole of my nuts into his boat. I avow that I was not very sorry to hear the officer throw out these hints, for they convinced me that my journey through Leaphigh would be accompanied with less embarrassment than I had anticipated, since

I now plainly perceived that monikins act on principles that are not very essentially different from those of the human race in general.

The complaisant register and the keeper of the privy-seal took their departure together, when we forthwith proceeded to number ourselves in compliance with his advice. As the principle was already settled, we had no difficulty with its application, Noah, Bob, myself, and the largest of the seamen being all No's. 1, and the rest ranking in order. By this time it was night. The guard-boats began to appear on the water, and we deferred disembarking until morning.

All hands were early afoot. It had been arranged that Captain Poke and myself, attended by Bob, as a domestic, were to land, in order to make a journey through the island, while the Walrus was to be left in charge of the mates and the crew; the latter having permission to go ashore, from time to time, as is the practice with all seamen in port. There was a great deal of preliminary scrubbing and shaving, before the whole party could appear on deck, properly attired for the occasion. Mr. Poke wore a thin dress of linen, admirably designed to make him look like a sea-lion; a conceit that he said was not only agreeable to his feelings and habits, but which had a cool and pleasant character, that was altother suited to a steam-climate. For my own part, I agreed with the worthy sealer, seeing but little difference between his going in this garb, and his going quite naked. My dress was made, on a design of my own, after the social-stake system; or, in other words, it was so arranged as to take an interest in half of the animals of Exeter 'Change, to which *menagerie* the artist, by whom it had been painted, was sent expressly, in order to consult nature. Bob wore the effigy, as his master called it, of a turnspit.

The monikins were by far too polished to crowd about us when we landed, with an impertinent and troublesome curiosity. So far from this, we were permitted to approach the capital itself without let or hindrance. As it is less my intention to describe physical things than to dwell upon the philosophy and the other moral aspects of the Leaphigh world, little more will be said of their houses, domestic economy, and other improvements in the arts, than may be gathered incidentally, as the narrative shall proceed. Let it suffice to say, on these heads, that the Leaphigh monikins, like men, consult, or think they consult—which, so long as they know no better, amounts to pretty much the same thing—their own convenience in all things, the pocket alone excepted; and that they continue very laudably to do as their fathers did before them, seldom making changes, unless they may happen to possess the recommendation of being exotics; when, indeed, they are sometimes adopted, probably on account of their possessing the merit of having been proved suitable to another state of things.

Among the first persons we met, on entering the great square of Aggregation, as the capital of Leaphigh is called when rendered into English, was my Lord Chatterino. He was gaily promenading with a company of young nobles, who all seemed to be enjoying their youth, health, rank and privileges, with infinite gusto. We met this party in a way to render an escape from mutual recognition impossible. At first I thought, from his averted eye, that it was the intention of our late shipmate to consider our knowledge of each other as one of those accidental acquaintances which, it is known, we all form at watering-places, on journeys, or in the country, and which it is ill-mannered to press upon others in town; or, as Captain Poke afterwards expressed it, like the intimacy between an Englishman and a Yankee, that has been formed in the house of the latter, on better wine than is met with anywhere else, and which was never yet known to withstand the influence of a British fog. "Why, Sir John," the sealer added, "I once tuck (he meant to say *took*, not *tucked*) a countryman of yours under my wing, at Stunin'tun, during the last war. He was a prisoner, as we make prisoners; that is, he went and did pretty much as he pleased; and the fellow had the best of every thing—molasses that a spoon would stand up in, pork that would do to slush down a top-mast, and New-England rum, that a king might sit down to, but could not get up from—well, what was the end on't? why, as sure as we are among these monkeys, the fellow *booked* me. Had I *booked* but the half of what he guzzled, the amount, I do believe, would have taken the transaction out of any justice's court in the state He said my molasses was meagre, the pork lean and the liquor infernal. There were truth and gratitude for you! He gave the whul account, too, as a specimen of what he called American living!"

Hereupon I reminded my companion, that an Englishman did not like to receive even favors, on compulsion; that when he meets a stranger in his own country, and is master of his own actions, no man understands better what true hospitality is, as I hoped one day to show him, at Householder Hall: as to his first remark, he ought to remember that an Englishman considered America as no more than the country, and that it would be ill-mannered to press an acquaintance made there.

Noah, like most other men, was very reasonable on all subjects that did not interfere with his prejudices or his opinions; and he very readily admitted the general justice of my reply.

"It's pretty much as you say, Sir John," he continued. "In England you may press men, but it wun't do to press hospitality. Get a volunteer in this way, and he is as good a fellow as heart can wish. I shouldn't have cared so much about the chap's book, if he had said nothin' ag'in the rum. Why, Sir John, when the English bombarded Stunin'tun with eighteen-pounders, I proposed to load our old twelve with a gallon out of the very same cask, for I do think it would have huv' the shot the best part of a mile!"

——— But this digression is leading me from the narrative. My Lord Chatterino turned his head a little on one side, as we were passing; and I was deliberating whether, under the circumstances, it would be well-bred to remind him of our old acquaintance, when the question was settled by the decision of Captain Poke, who placed himself in such a position that it was no easy matter to get round him, through him, or over him; or who laid himself what he called "athwart hawse."

"Good morning, my Lord," said the straight forward seaman, who generally went at a subject, as he went at a seal. "A fine warm day; and the smell of the land, after so long a passage, is quite agreeable to the nose, whatever its ups and downs may be to the legs."

The companions of the young peer looked amazed; and some of them, I thought, notwithstanding gravity and earnestness are rather characteristic of the monikin physiognomy, betrayed a slight disposition to laugh. Not so with my Lord Chatterino himself.

He examined us a moment through a glass, and then seemed suddenly and on the whole, agreeably struck at seeing us.

"How, Goldencalf!" he cried, in surprise, "you

in Leaphigh! This is, indeed, an unexpected satisfaction; for it will now be in my power to prove some of the facts that I am telling my friends, by actual observation. Here are two of the humans, gents, of whom I was but this moment giving you some account—"

Observing a disposition to merriment in his associates, he continued, looking exceedingly grave:—

"Restrain yourselves, gentlemen, I pray you. These are very worthy people, I do assure you, in their own way, and are not at all to be ridiculed. I scarcely know, even in our own marine, a better or a bolder navigator than this honest seaman; and, as for the one in the parti-colored skin, I will take upon myself to say, that he is really a person of some consideration in his own little circle. He is, I believe, a member of par—par—par—am I right, Sir John?—a member of——"

"Parliament, my Lord—an M. P."

"Ay—I thought I had it—an M. P. or a member of parliament in his own country, which, I dare say, now, is some such thing among his people, as a public proclaimer of those laws which come from His Majesty's eldest first-cousin of the masculine gender, may be among us. Some such thing—eh—now—eh—is it not, Sir John?"

"I dare say it is, my Lord."

"All very true, Chatterino," put in one of the young monikins, with a very long, elaborated tail, which he carried nearly perpendicular—"but what would be even a law-*maker*—to say nothing of law-*breakers* like ourselves—among men! You should remember, my dear fellow, that a mere title, or a profession, is not the criterion of true greatness; but that the prodigy of a village may be a very common monikin in town."

"Poh—poh"—interrupted Lord Chatterino, "thou

art ever for refining, Hightail—Sir John Goldencalf is a very respectable person in the island of—a—a—a—what do you call that said island of yours, Goldencalf?—a—a——"

"Great Britain, my Lord."

"Ay, Great Breeches, sure enough: yes, he is a respectable person—I can take it upon myself to say, with confidence, a very respectable person, in Great Breeches. I dare say he owns no small portion of the island himself. How much, now, Sir John, if the truth were told?"

"Only the estate and village of Householder, my Lord, with a few scattered manors, here and there."

"Well, that is a very pretty thing, there can be no doubt,—then you have money at use?"

"And who is the debtor?" sneeringly inquired the jack-a-napes Hightail.

"No other, my Lord Hightail, than the realm of Great Britain."

"Exquisite, that, egad! A noble's fortune in the custody of the realm of a—Greek—a——"

"Great Breeches," interrupted my Lord Chatterino; who, notwithstanding he swore he was excessively angry with his friend for his obstinate incredulity, very evidently had to exercise some forbearance to keep from joining in the general laugh. "It is a very respectable country, I do protest; and I scarcely remember to have tasted better gooseberries than they grow in that very island."

"What! have they really gardens, Chatterino?"

"Certainly—after a fashion—and houses, and public conveyances—and even universities."

"You do not mean to say, certainly, that they have a system!"

"Why, as to system, I believe they are a littl

at sixes and sevens. I really can't take it upon myself to say that they have a system."

"Oh, yes, my Lord,—of a certainty we have one—the Social-stake System.

"Ask the creature," whispered audibly the filthy coxcomb Hightail, "if he himself, now, has any income."

"How is it, Sir John,—have you an income?"

"Yes, my Lord, of one hundred and twelve thousand sovereigns a year."

"Of what?—of what?" demanded two or three voices, with well-bred, subdued eagerness.

"Of sovereigns—why that means kings!"

It would appear that the Leaphighers, while they obey only the King's eldest first-cousin of the masculine gender, perform all their official acts in the name of the sovereign himself, for whose person and character they pretty uniformly express the profoundest veneration; just as we men express admiration for a virtue that we never practise. My declaration, therefore, produced a strong sensation, and I was soon required to explain myself. This I did, by simply stating the truth.

"Oh, gold, y'clept sovereigns!" exclaimed three or four, laughing heartily. "Why then, your famous Great Breeches people, after all, Chatterino, are so little advanced in civilization, as to use gold! Harkee, Signior—a—a—Boldercraft, have you no currency in 'promises'?"

"I do not know, sir, that I rightly comprehend the question."

"Why, we poor barbarians, sir, who live as you see us, only in a state of simplicity and nature,"—there was irony in every syllable the impudent scoundrel uttered,—"we poor wretches, or rather our ancestors, made the discovery, that, for the purposes of convenience, having, as you perceive, no pockets, it might be well to convert all our currency into 'promises.' Now, I would ask if you have any of that coin?"

"Not as coin, sir, but as collateral to coin, we have plenty."

"He speaks of collaterals in currency, as if he were discussing a pedigree! Are you really, Mynherr Shouldercalf, so little advanced in your country, as not to know the immense advantages of a currency of 'promises'?"

"As I do not understand exactly what the nature of this currency is, sir, I cannot answer as readily as I could wish."

"Let us explain it to him; for, I vow, I am really curious to hear his answer. Chatterino, do you, who have some knowledge of the thing's habits, be our interpreter."

"The matter is thus, Sir John. About five hundred years ago, our ancestors having reached that pass in civilization when they came to dispense with the use of pockets, began to find it necessary to substitute a new currency for that of the metals, which it was inconvenient to carry, of which they might be robbed, and which also were liable to be counterfeited. The first expedient was to try a lighter substitute. Laws were passed giving value to linen and cotton, in the raw material; then, compounded and manufactured; next, written on, and reduced in bulk, until, having passed through the several gradations of wrapping-paper, brown-paper, foolscap and blotting-paper, and having set the plan fairly at work, and got confidence thoroughly established, the system was perfected by a *coup de main*;—'promises' in words, were substituted for all other coin. You see the advantage at a glance.—A monikin can travel, without pockets or baggage, and still carry a million; the money cannot be counterfeited, nor can it be stolen or burned."

"But, my Lord, does it not depreciate the value of property?"

"Just the contrary:—an acre that formerly could be bought for one promise, would now bring a thousand."

"This certainly is a great improvement, unless frequent failures——"

"Not at all; there has not been a bankruptcy in Leaphigh since the law was passed making promises a legal tender."

"I wonder no Chancellor of the Exchequer ever thought of this, at home!"

"So much for your Great Breeches, Chatterino!" And then there was another and a very general laugh. I never before felt so deep a sense of national humility.

"As they have universities," cried another cox comb, "perhaps this person has attended one of them."

"Indeed, sir," I answered, "I am regularly graduated."

"It is not easy to see what he has done with his knowledge,—for, though my sight is none of the worst, I can not trace the smallest sign of a *cauda* about him."

"Ah!" Lord Chatterino good-naturedly explained, "the inhabitants of Great Breeches carry their brains in their heads."

"Their heads!"

"Heads!"

"That's excellent, by His Majesty's prerogative! Here's civilization, with a vengeance!"

I now thought that the general ridicule would overwhelm me. Two or three came closer, as if in pity or curiosity; and, at last, one cried out that I actually wore clothes.

"Clothes—the wretch! Chatterino, do all your human friends wear clothes?"

The young peer was obliged to confess the truth: and then there arose such a clamor as may be fancied took place among the peacocks, when they discovered the daw among them in masquerade. Human nature could endure no more; and, bowing to the company, I wished Lord Chatterino, very hurriedly good morning, and proceeded towards the tavern.

"Don't forget to step into Chatterino-house, Goldencalf, before you sail," cried my late fellow-traveller, looking over his shoulder, and nodding in quite a friendly way towards me.

"King!" exclaimed Captain Poke. "That black guard ate a whole bread-locker-full of nuts, on our outward passage, and, now, he tells us to step into his Chatterino-house, before we sail!"

I endeavoured to pacify the sealer, by an appeal to his philosophy. It was true that men never forgot obligations, and were always excessively anxious to repay them; but the monikins were an exceedingly instructed species; they thought more of their minds than of their bodies, as was plain by comparing the smallness of the latter with the length and development of the seat of reason; and one of his experience should know that good-breeding is decidedly an arbitrary quality, and that we ought to respect its laws, however opposed to our own previous practices.

"I dare say, friend Noah, you may have observed some material difference in the usages of Paris, for instance, and those of Stunin'tun."

"That I have, Sir John, that I have; and altogether to the advantage of Stunin'tun be they."

"We are all addicted to the weakness of believing our own customs best; and it requires that we should travel much, before we are able to decide on points so nice."

"And do you not call me a traveller! Haven't I been sixteen times a sealing, twice a whaling, without counting my cruise over-land, and this last run to Leaphigh!"

"Ay, you have gone over much land and much water, Mr. Poke; but your stay in any given place has been just long enough to find fault. Usages must be worn, like a shoe, before one can judge of the fit."

It is possible Noah would have retorted, had not Mrs. Vigilance Lynx, at that moment, come wriggling by, in a way to show she was much satisfied with her safe return home. To own the truth, while striving to find apologies for it, I had been a little *contrarié*, as the French term it, by the indifference of my Lord Chatterino, which, in my secret heart, I was not slow in attributing to the manner in which a peer of the realm of Leaphigh regarded, *de haut en bas*, a mere Baronet of Great Britain—or Great Breeches, as the young noble so pertinaciously insisted on terming our illustrious island. Now, as Mrs. Vigilance was of "russet-color," a caste of an inferior standing, I had little doubt that she would be as glad to own an intimacy with Sir John Goldencalf of Householder Hall, as the other might be willing to shuffle it off.

"Good morrow, good Mrs. Vigilance," I said familiarly, endeavoring to wriggle in a way that *would* have shaken a tail, had it been my good fortune to be the owner of one—"Good morrow, good Mrs. Vigilance—I'm glad to meet you again on shore."

I do not remember that Mrs. Vigilance, during

the whole period of our acquaintance, was particularly squeamish, or topping in her deportment On the contrary, she had rather made herself remarkable for a modest and commendable reserve. But, on the present occasion, she disappointed all reasonable expectation, by shrinking on one side, uttering a slight scream, and hurrying past as if she thought we might bite her. Indeed, I can only compare her deportment to that of a female of our own, who is so full of vanity as to fancy all eyes on her, and who gives herself airs about a dog or a spider, because she thinks they make her look so much the more interesting. Conversation was quite out of the question; for the duenna hurried on, bending her head downward, as if heartily ashamed of an involuntary weakness.

"Well, good madam," said Noah, whose stern eye followed her movements until she was quite lost in the crowd, "you would have had a sleepless v'yage, if I had fore-imagined this! Sir John, these people stare at us as if we were wild beasts!"

"I cannot say I am of your way of thinking, Captain Poke. To me they seem to take no more notice of us, than we should take of two curs in the streets of London."

"I begin, now, to understand what the parsons mean when they talk of the lost condition of man. It's ra'ally awful to witness to what a state of unfeelingness a people can be abandoned! Bob, get out of the way, you grinning blackguard."

Hereupon Bob received a salutation which would have demolished his stern-frame, had it not been for the union-jack. Just then I was glad to see Dr. Reasono advancing towards us, surrounded by a group of attentive listeners, all of whom, by their years, gravity and deportment, I made no question were *savans*. As he drew near. I found he was discoursing of the marvels of his late voyage. When within six feet of us the whole party stopped the Doctor continuing his descant, with a very proper gesticulation, and in a way to show that his subject was of infinite interest to his listeners. Accidentally turning his eye in our direction, he caught a glimpse of our figures, and making a few hurried apologies to those around him, the excellent philosopher came eagerly forward, with both hands extended. Here was a difference, indeed, between his treatment and that of Lord Chatterino and the duenna! The salutation was warmly returned; and the Doctor and myself stepped a little apart, as he lost no time in informing me he wished to say a word in private.

"My dear Sir John," the philosopher began, "our arrival has been the most happily-timed thing imaginable! All Leaphigh, by this time, is filled with the subject; and you can scarcely conceive the importance that is attached to the event. New sources of trade, scientific discoveries, phenomena both moral and physical, and results that it is thought may serve to raise the monikin civilization still higher than ever. Fortunately, the academy holds its most solemn meeting of the year this very day, and I have been formally requested to give the assembly an outline of those events which have lately passed before my eyes. The King's eldest first-cousin of the masculine gender is to attend openly; and it is even conjectured, in a way to be quite authentic, that the King himself will be present in his own royal person."

"How!" I exclaimed; "have you a mode, in Leaphigh, of rendering conjectures certain?"

"Beyond a doubt, sir, or what would our civilization be worth? As to the King's Majesty, we always deal in the most direct ambiguities Now as respects many of our ceremonies, the sovereign is known morally to be present, when he may be actually and physically eating his dinner at the other extremity of the island; this important illustration of the royal ubiquity is effected by means of a legal fiction. On the other hand, the King often indulges his natural propensities, such as curiosity, love of fun, or detestation of ennui, by coming in person, when, by the court-fiction, he is thought to be seated on his throne, in his own royal palace. Oh! as to all these little accomplishments and graces in the art of Truths, we are behind no people in the universe!"

"I beg pardon, Doctor—so his Majesty is expected to be at the academy, this morning?"

"In a private box. Now this affair is of the last importance to me as a *savant*, to you as a human being—for it will have a direct tendency to raise your whole species in the monikin estimation—and, lastly, to learning. It will be indispensably necessary that you should attend, with as many of your companions as possible—more especially the better specimens. I was coming down to the landing, in the hope of meeting you; and a messenger has gone off to the ship to require that the people be sent ashore forthwith. You will have a tribune to yourselves; and, really, I do not like to express beforehand what I think concerning the degree of attention you will all receive; but this much I think I can say—you will see."

"This proposition, Doctor, has taken me a little by surprise, and I hardly know what answer to give."

"You cannot say no, Sir John; for, should his Majesty hear that you have refused to come to a meeting at which he is to be present, it would seriously, and. I might add, justly offend him:—nor could I answer for the consequences."

"Why, I was told that all the power was in the hands of his Majesty's eldest first-cousin of the masculine gender; in which case I thought I might snap my fingers at his Majesty himself."

"Not in opinion, Sir John, which is one of the three estates of the government. Ours is a government of three estates—viz. the Law, Opinion, and Practice. By law the king rules, by practice his cousin rules, and by opinion the king again rules Thus is the strong point of practice balanced by law and opinion. This it is that constitutes the harmony and perfection of the system. No, it would never do to offend his Majesty."

Although I did not very well comprehend the Doctor's argument, yet, as I had often found in human society, theories political, moral, theological, and philosophical, that everybody had faith in, and which nobody understood, I thought discussion useless, and gave up the point by promising the Doctor to be at the academy in half an hour, which was the time named for our appearance. Taking the necessary directions to find the place, we separated; he to hasten to make his preparations, and I to reach the tavern, in order to deposit our baggage, that no decency might be overlooked on an occasion so solemn.

CHAPTER XVI.

An inn—Debts paid in advance, and a singular touch of human nature found closely incorporated with monikin nature

We soon secured rooms, ordered dinner, brushed our clothes, and made the other little arrangements that it was necessary to observe for the credit of the species. Everything being ready, we left the inn, and hurried towards the "*Palais des Arts et des Sciences.*" We had not got out of sight of the inn, however, before one of its *garçons* was at our heels with a message from his mistress. He told us, in very respectful tones, that his master was out, and that he had taken with him the key of the strong-box; that there was not actually money enough in the drawer to furnish an entertainment for such great persons as ourselves, and she had taken the liberty to send us a bill receipted, with a request that we would make a small advance, rather than reduce her to the mortification of treating such distinguished guests in an unworthy manner. The bill read as follows:—

No. 1 parti-color and friends

To No. 82,763 grape color	Dr.
To use of apartments, with meals and lights, as per agreement, *p. p.* 300 per diem—one day,	*p. p.* 300
By cash advanced,	50
Balance due *p. p.*	250

"This seems all right," I observed to Noah; "but I am, at this moment, as penniless as the good woman herself. I really do not see what we are to do, unless Bob sends her back his store of nuts——"

"Harkee, my nimble-go-hop," put in the seaman, "what is your pleasure?"

The waiter referred to the bill, as expressing his mistress's wants.

"What are these p. p. that I find noted in the bill—play or pay, hey?"

"Promises, of course, your honor."

"Oh! then you desire fifty promises, to provide our dinner."

"Nothing more, sir. With that sum you shall dine like noblemen—ay, sir, like aldermen."

I was delighted to find that this worthy class of beings have the same propensities in all countries.

"Here, take a hundred," answered Noah, snapping his fingers, "and make no bones of it. And harkee, my worthy—lay out every farthing of them in the fare. Let there be good cheer, and no one will grumble at the bill. I am ready to buy the inn, and all it holds, at need."

The waiter departed well satisfied with these assurances, and apparently in the anticipation of good vails for his own trouble.

We soon got into the current that was setting towards our place of destination. On reaching the gate, we found we were anxiously expected; for there was an attendant in waiting, who instantly conducted us to the seats that were provided for our special reception. It is always agreeable to be among the privileged, and I must own that we were all not a little flattered, on finding that an elevated tribune had been prepared for us, in the centre of the rotunda in which the academy held its sittings, so that we could see, and be seen by, every individual of the crowded assembly. The whole crew even to the negro-cook, had preceded us; an additional compliment, that I did not fail to acknowledge, by suitable salutations to all the members present. After the first feelings of pleasure and surprise were a little abated, I had leisure to look about me and to survey the company.

The academicians occupied the whole of th body of the rotunda, the space taken up by the erection of our temporary tribune alone excepted; while there were sofas, chairs, tribunes and benches arranged for the spectators, in the outer circles, and along the side-walls of the hall. As the edifice itself was very large, and mind had so essentially reduced matter in the monikin species, there could not have been less than fifty thousand tails present. Just before the ceremonies commenced, Dr. Reasono approached our tribune, passing from one to another of the party, saying a pleasant and an encouraging word to each, in a way to create high expectations in us all, as to what was to follow. We were so very evidently honored and distinguished, that I struggled hard to subdue any unworthy feeling of pride, as unbecoming human meekness, and in order to maintain a philosophical equanimity under the manifestations of respect and gratitude that I knew were about to be lavished upon even the meanest of our party. The Doctor was yet in the midst of his pointed attentions, when the King's eldest first-cousin of the masculine gender entered, and the business of the meeting immediately began I profited by a short pause, however, to say a few words to my companions. I told them there would soon be a serious demand on their modesty. We had performed a great and generous exploit, and it did not become us to lessen its merit by betraying a vain-glorious self-esteem. I implored them all to take pattern by me; promising, in the end, that their new friends would trebly prize their hardihood, self-denial and skill.

There was a new member of the academy of Latent Sympathies to be received and installed. A long discourse was read by one of this department of the monikin learning, which pointed out and enlarged on the rare merits of the new academician. He was followed by the latter; who, in a very elaborate production, that consumed just fifty-five minutes in the reading, tried all he could to persuade the audience that the defunct was a loss to the world, that no accident or application would ever repair; and that he himself was precisely the worst person who could have been selected to be his successor. I was a little surprised at the perfect coolness with which the learned body listened to a reproach, that was so very distinctly and perseveringly thrown, as it were, into their very teeth. But a more intimate acquaintance with monikin society satisfied me, that any one might say just what he pleased, so long as he allowed that every one else was an excellent fellow, and he himself the poorest devil going. When the new member had triumphantly established his position, and just as I thought his colleagues were bound, in common honesty, to reconsider their vote, he concluded and took his seat among them, with quite as much assurance as the best philosopher of them all.

After a short pause, and an abundance of felicitations on his excellent and self-debasing discourse, the newly-admitted member again rose, and began to read an essay on some discoveries he had made in the science of Latent Sympathies. According to his account of the matter, every monikin possessed a fluid which was invisible, like the animalcula which pervade nature, and which required only

.o be brought into command, and to be reduced to more rigid laws, to become the substitutes for the senses of sight, touch, taste, hearing and smelling. This fluid was communicable; and had already been so far rendered subject to the will, as to make it of service in seeing in the dark, in smelling when the operator had a bad cold, in tasting when the palate was down, and in touching by proxy. Ideas had been transmitted, through its agency, sixty-two leagues in one minute and a half. Two monikins, who were afflicted with diseased tails, had, during the last two years, been insulated and saturated, and had then lost those embellishments, by operations; a quantity of the fluid having been substituted in their places so happily, that the patients fancied themselves more than ever conspicuous for the length and *finesse* of their *caudæ*. An experiment had also been successfully tried on a member of the lower house of parliament, who, being married to a monikina of unusual mind, had for a long time been supplied with ideas from this source, although his partner was compelled to remain at home, in order to superintend the management of their estate, forty-two miles from town, during the whole session. He particularly recommended to government the promotion of this science, as it might be useful in obtaining evidence for the purposes of justice, in detecting conspiracies, in collecting the taxes, and in selecting candidates for trusts of a responsible nature. The suggestion was well received by the King's cousin, more especially those parts that alluded to sedition and the revenue.

This essay was also perfectly well received by the *savans*, for I afterwards found very little came amiss to the academy; and the members named a committee forthwith, to examine into "the facts concerning invisible and unknown fluids, their agency, importance, and relations to monikin happiness."

We were next favored with a discussion on the different significations of the word *gorstchwzyb;* which, rendered into English, means "eh!" The celebrated philologist who treated the subject, discovered amazing ingenuity in expatiating on its ramifications and deductions. First, he tried the letters by transpositions, by which he triumphantly proved that it was derived from all the languages of the ancients; the same process showed that it possessed four thousand and two different significations; he next reasoned most ably and comprehensively for ten minutes, backwards and forwards, using no other word but this, applied in its various senses; after which, he incontrovertibly established that this important part of speech was so useful as to be useless, and he concluded by a proposition, in which the academy coincided by acclamation, that it should be for ever and incontinently expunged from the Leaphigh vocabulary. As the vote was carried by acclamation, the King's cousin arose, and declared that the writer who should so far offend against good taste, as hereafter to make use of the condemned word, should have two inches cut off the extremity of his tail. A shudder among the ladies, who, I afterwards ascertained, loved to carry their *caudæ* as high as our women like to carry their heads, proved the severity of the decree.

An experienced and seemingly much respected member now arose to make the following proposal. He said it was known that the monikin species was fast approaching perfection; that the increase of mind and the decrease of matter was so very apparent as to admit of no denial; that, in his own case, he found his physical powers diminish daily while his mental acquired new distinctness and force that he could no longer see without spectacles, near without a tube, or taste without high seasoning: from all this he inferred that they were drawing near to some important change, and he wished that portion of the science of Latent Sympathies which was connected with the unknown fluid, just treated on, might be referred to a committee of the whole, in order to make some provision for the wants of a time when monikins should finally lose their senses. There was nothing to say against a proposition so plausible, and it was accepted *nemine contradicente,* with the exception of a few in the minority.

There was now a good deal of whispering, much wagging of tails, and other indications that the real business of the meeting was about to be touched upon. All eyes were turned on Dr. Reasono, who, after a suitable pause, entered a tribune prepared for solemn occasions, and began his discourse.

The philosopher, who, having committed his essay to memory, spoke extempore, commenced with a beautiful and most eloquent apostrophe to learning, and to the enthusiasm which glows in the breasts of all her real votaries, rendering them alike indifferent to their personal ease, their temporal interests, danger, suffering, and tribulations of the spirit. After this exordium, which was pronounced to be *unique* for its simplicity and truth, he entered, at once, on the history of his own recent adventures.

First alluding to the admirable character of that Leaphigh usage which prescribes the Journey of Trial, our philosopher spoke of the manner in which he had been selected to accompany my Lord Chatterino on an occasion so important to his future hopes. He dwelt on the physical preparations, the previous study, and the moral machinery that he had employed with his pupil, before they quitted town: all of which, there is reason to think, were well fitted to their objects, as he was constantly interrupted by murmurs of applause. After some time spent in dilating on these points, I had, at length, the satisfaction to find him, Mrs. Lynx, and their two wards, fairly setting out on a journey which, as he very justly mentioned, proved "to be pregnant with events of so much importance to knowledge in general, to the happiness of the species, and to several highly interesting branches of monikin science, in particular." I say the satisfaction, for, to own the truth, I was eager to witness the effect that would be made on the monikin sensibilities, when he came to speak of my own discernment in detecting their real characters beneath the contumely and disgrace in which it had been my good fortune to find them, the promptitude with which I had stepped forward to their relief, and the liberality and courage with which I had furnished the means and encountered the risks, that were necessary to restore them to their native land. The anticipation of this human triumph could not but diffuse a general satisfaction in our tribune,—even the common mariners, as they recalled the dangers through which they had passed, feeling a consciousness of deserving, mingled with that soothing sentiment which is ever the companion of a merited reward. As the philosopher drew nearer to the time when it would be necessary to speak of us, I threw a look of triumph at Lord Chatterino, which, however, failed of its intended effect,—the young peer continuing to whisper to his noble companions with just as much self-importance and coolness as if he had not been one of the rescued captives.

Dr. Reasono was justly celebrated, among his colleagues, for ingenuity and eloquence. The ex cellent morals that he threw in o every possible opening of his subject, the beauty of the figures with which they were illustrated, and the masculine tendencies of his argument, gave general delight to the audience. The Journey of Trial was made to appear, what it had been intended to be by the fathers and sages of the Leaphigh institutions, a probation replete with admonitions and instruction. The aged and experienced, who had grown callous by time, could not conceal their exultation; the mature and suffering looked grave and full of meditation; while the young and sanguine fairly trembled, and, for once, doubted. But, as the philosopher led his party from precipice to precipice in safety, as rocks were scaled and seductive valleys avoided, a common feeling of security began to extend itself among the audience; and we all followed him in his last experiment among the ice, with that sort of blind confidence which the soldier comes, in time, to entertain in the orders of a tried and victorious general.

The Doctor was graphic in his account of the manner in which he and his wards plunged among these new trials. The lovely Chatterissa (for all his travelling companions were present,) bent aside her head and blushed, as the philosopher alluded to the manner in which the pure flame that glowed in her gentle bosom resisted the chill influence of that cold region; and when he recited an ardent declaration that my Lord Chatterino had made on the centre of a floe, and the kind and amorous answer of his mistress, I thought the applause of the old academicians would have actually brought the vaulted dome clattering about our ears.

At length he reached the point in the narrative, where the amiable wanderers fell in with the sealers, on that unknown island to which chance and an adverse fortune had unhappily led them, in their pilgrimage. I had taken measures secretly to instruct Mr. Poke and the rest of my companions, as to the manner in which it became us to demean ourselves, while the Doctor was acquainting the academy with that first outrage committed by human cupidity, or the seizure of himself and friends. We were to rise, in a body, and, turning our faces a little on one side, veil our eyes in sign of shame. Less than this, it struck me, could scarcely be done, without manifesting an improper indifference to monikin rights; and more than this, might have been identifying ourselves with the particular individuals of the species who had perpetrated the wrong. But there was no occasion to exhibit this delicate attention to our learned hosts. The Doctor, with a refinement of feeling that did credit, indeed, to monikin civilization, gave an ingenious turn to the whole affair, which at once removed all cause of shame from our species · and which, if it left reason for any to blush, by a noble act of disinterestedness, threw the entire onus of the obligation on himself. Instead of dwelling on the ruthless manner in which he and his friends had been seized, the worthy Doctor very tranquilly informed his listeners that, finding himself, by hazard, brought in contact with another species, and that the means of pushing important discoveries were unexpectedly placed in his power; conscious it had long been a desideratum with the *savans* to obtain a nearer view and more correct notions of human society; believing he had a discretion in the matter of his wards, and knowing that the inhabitants of Leaplow, a republic which all disliked, were seriously talking of sending out an expedition for this very purpose, he had promptly decided to profit by events, to push inquiry to the extent of his abilities.

and to hazard all in the cause of learning and truth, by at once engaging the vessel of the sealers, and sailing, without dread of consequences, forthwith into the very bosom of the world of man!

I have listened with awe to the thunder of the tropics,—I have held my breath as the artillery of a fleet vomited forth its fire, and rent the air with sudden concussions,—I have heard the roar of the tumbling river of the Canadas, and I have stood aghast at the crashing of a forest in a tornado;—but never before did I feel so life-stirring, so thrilling an emotion, of surprise, alarm and sympathy, as that which arose within me, at the burst of commendation and delight with which this announcement of self-devotion and enterprise was received by the audience. Tails waved, *pattes* met each other in ecstasy, voice whistled to voice, and there was one common cry of exultation, of rapture and of glorification, at this proof, not of monikin, for that would have been frittering away the triumph, but at this proof of Leaphigh courage!

During the clamor, I took an opportunity to express my satisfaction at the handsome manner in which our friend the Doctor had passed over an acknowledged human delinquency, and the ingenuity with which he had turned the whole of the unhappy transaction to the glory of Leaphigh. Noah answered that the philosopher had certainly 'shown a knowledge of human natur', and he presumed of monikin natur', in the matter; no one would now dispute his statement, since, as he knew by experience, no one was so likely to be set down as a liar, as he who endeavored to unsettle the good opinion that either a community or an individual entertained of himself. This was the way at Stunin'tun, and he believed this was pretty much the way at New-York, or he might say with the whole 'arth, from pole to pole. As for himself, however, he owned he should like to have a few minutes' private conversation with the sealer in question, to hear his account of the matter; he didn't know any owner in his part of the world, who would bear a captain out, should he abandon a v'yage in this way, on no better security than the promises of a monkey, and of a monkey, too, who must, of necessity, be an utter stranger to him."

When the tumult of applause had a little abated, Dr. Reasono proceeded with his narrative. He touched lightly on the accommodations of the schooner, which he gave us reason to think were altogether of a quality beneath the condition of her passengers, and he added that, falling in with a larger and fairer vessel, which was making a passage between Bombay and Great Britain, he profited by the occasion, to exchange ships. This vessel touched at the island of St. Helena, where, according to the Doctor's account of the matter, he found means to pass the greater part of a week on shore.

Of the island of St. Helena he gave a long, scientific, and certainly an interesting account. It was reported to be volcanic, by the human *savans*, he said, but a minute examination and a comparison of the geological formation, &c., had quite satisfied him that their own ancient account, which was contained in the mineralogical works of Leaphigh, was the true one; or, in other words, that this rock was a fragment of the polar world that had been blown away at the great eruption, and which had become separated from the rest of the mass at this spot, where it had fallen and become a fixture of the ocean. Here the Doctor produced certain specimens of rock, which he submitted to the learned present, inviting their attention to its character, and asking, with great mineralogical confidence, if it did not intimately resemble a well-known stratum of a mountain within two leagues of the very spot they were in? This triumphant proof of the truth of his proposition was admirably received; and the philosopher was in particular rewarded by the smiles of all the females present; for ladies usually are well-pleased with any demonstration that saves them the trouble of comparison and reflection.

Before quitting this branch of his subject, the Doctor observed that, interesting as were these proofs of the accuracy of their histories, and of the great revolutions of inanimate nature, there was another topic connected with St. Helena, which, he felt certain, would excite a lively emotion in the breasts of all who heard him. At the period of his visit, the island had been selected as a prison for a great conqueror and disturber of his fellow-creatures; and public attention was much drawn to the spot by this circumstance, few *men* coming there who did not permit all their thoughts to be absorbed by the past acts, and the present fortunes, of the individual in question. As for himself, there was of course no great attraction in any events connected with mere human greatness, the little struggles and convulsions of the species containing no particular interest for a devotee of the monikin philosophy; but the manner in which all eyes were drawn in one direction, afforded him a liberty of action that he had eagerly improved, in a way that, he humbly trusted, would not be thought altogether unworthy of their approbation. While searching for minerals among the cliffs, his attention had been drawn to certain animals that are called monkeys, in the language of those regions; which, from very obvious affinities of a physical nature, there was some reason to believe might have had a common origin with the monikin species. The academy would at once see how desirable it was to learn all the interesting particulars of the habits, language, customs, marriages, funerals, religious opinions, traditions, state of learning, and general moral condition of this interesting people, with a view to ascertain whether they were merely one of those abortions to which, it is known, nature i in the practice of giving birth, in the outward appearance of their own species, or whether, as several of their best writers had plausibly maintained, they were indeed a portion of those whom they had been in the habit of designating as the "Lost Monikins." He had succeeded in getting access to a family of these beings, and in passing an entire day in their society. The result of his investigations was, that they were truly of the monikin family, retaining much of the ingenuity and many of the spiritual notions of their origin, but with their intellects sadly blunted, and perhaps their improvable qualities annihilated, by the concussion of the elements that had scattered them abroad upon the face of the earth, houseless, hopeless, regionless wanderers. The vicissitudes of climate, and a great alteration of habits, had certainly wrought some physical changes; but there still remained a sufficient scientific identity to prove they were monikins. They even retained, in their traditions, some glimmerings of the awful catastrophe by which they were separated from the rest of their fellow-creatures; but they necessarily were vague and profitless. Having touched on several other points connected with these very extraordinary facts, the Doctor concluded by saying that he saw but one way in which this discovery could be turned to any practical advantage, beyond the confirmation it afforded of the truth of their own annals. He suggested the expediency of fitting out expeditions to go among these islands and seize upon a number of families, which, being transported into Leaphigh, might found a race of useful menials, who, while they would prove much less troublesome than those who possessed all the knowledge of monikins, would probably be found more intelligent and useful than any domestic animal which they at present owned. This happy application of the subject met with decided commendation. I observed that most of the elderly females put their heads together on the spot, and appeared to be congratulating each other on the prospect of being speedily relieved from their household cares.

Dr. Reasono next spoke of his departure from St. Helena, and of his finally landing in Portugal. Here, agreeably to his account, he engaged certain Savoyards to act as his *couriers* and guides during a tour he intended to make through Portugal, Spain, Switzerland, France, &c. &c. &c. I listened with admiration. Never before had I so lively a perception of the vast difference that is effected in our views of matters and things, by the agency of an active philosophy, as was now furnished by the narrative of the speaker. Instead of complaining of the treatment he had received, and of the degradations to which he and his companions had been subjected, he spoke of it all as so much prudent submission, on his part, to the customs of the countries in which he happened to find himself, and as the means of ascertaining a thousand important facts, both moral and physical, which he proposed to submit to the academy in a separate memoir, another day. At present, he was admonished by the clock to conclude, and he would therefore hasten his narrative, as much as possible.

The Doctor, with great ingenuousness, confessed

that he could gladly have passed a year or two longer in those distant and highly interesting portions of the earth; but he could not forget that he had a duty to perform to the friends of two noble families. The Journey of Trial had been completed under the most favorable auspices, and the ladies naturally became anxious to return home. They had accordingly passed into Great Britain, a country remarkable for maritime enterprise, where he immediately commenced the necessary preparations for their sailing. A ship had been procured under the promise of allowing it to be freighted, free of custom-house charges, with the products of Leaphigh. A thousand applications had been made to him for permission to be of his party, the natives naturally enough wishing to see a civilized country; but prudence had admonished him to accept of those only who were the most likely to make themselves useful. The King of Great Britain, no mean prince in human estimation, had committed his only son and heir-apparent to his care, with a view to his improvement by travelling; and the Lord High Admiral himself had asked permission to take command of an expedition that was of so much importance to knowledge in general, and to his own profession in particular.

Here Dr. Reasono ascended our tribune, and presented Bob to the academy as the Prince-Royal of Great Britain, and Captain Poke as her Lord High Admiral! He pointed out certain peculiarities about the former, the smut in particular, which had become pretty effectually incorporated with the skin, as so many signs of royal birth; and ordering the youngster to uncase, he drew forth the union-jack that the lad carefully kept about his nether part as a fender, and exhibited it as his armorial bearings—a modification of its uses that would not have been very far out of the way, had another limb been substituted for the agent. As for Captain Poke, he requested the academicians to study his nautical air, in general, as furnishing sufficient proof of his pursuits, and of the ordinary appearance of human seamen.

Turning to me, I was then introduced to all present as the travelling governor and personal attendant of Bob, and as a very respectable person in my way. He added, that he believed, also, I had some pretension to be the discoverer of something that was called the social-stake system; which, he dared to say, was a very creditable discovery for one of my opportunities.

By this prompt substitution of employments, I found I had effectually changed places with the cabin-boy; who, instead of waiting on me, was, in future, to receive that trifling attention at my hands. The mates were presented as two rear-admirals at nurse, and the crew was said to be composed of so many post-captains in the navy of Great Britain. To conclude, the audience was given to understand that we were all brought to Leaphigh, like the minerals from St. Helena, as so many specimens of the human species!

I shall not deny that Dr. Reasono had taken a very different view of himself and his acts, as well as of me and my acts, from those I had all along entertained myself; and yet, on reflection, it is so common to consider ourselves in lights very different from those in which we are viewed by others, that I could not, on the whole, complain as much of his representations as I had at first thought it might become me to do. At all events, I was completely spared the necessity of blushing for my generosity and disinterestedness, and in other respects was saved the pain of viewing any part of my own conduct under a consciousness of its attracting attention by its singularity on the score of merit. I must say, nevertheless, that I was both surprised, and a little indignant; but the sudden and unexpected turn that had been given to the whole affair threw me so completely off my centre, that, for the life of me, I could not say a word in my own behalf. To make the matter worse, that monkey Chatterino nodded to me kindly, as if he would show the spectators that, on the whole, he thought me a very good sort of a fellow!

After the lecture was over, the audience approached to examine us, taking a great many amiable liberties with our persons, and otherwise showing that we were deemed curiosities worthy of their study. The King's cousin, too, was not neglectful of us, but he had it announced to the assembly that we were entirely welcome to Leaphigh; and that, out of respect to Dr. Reasono we were all promoted to the dignity of "Honorary Monikins," for the entire period of our stay in the country. He also caused it to be proclaimed, that if the boys annoyed us in the streets, they should have their tails curled with birch curling-irons. As for the Doctor himself, it was proclaimed that, in addition to his former title of F.U.D.G.E., he was now preferred to be even M.O.R.E., and that he was also raised to the dignity of an H.O.A.X., the very highest honor to which any savant of Leaphigh could attain.

At length curiosity was appeased, and we were permitted to descend from the tribune; the company ceasing to attend to us, in order to pay attention to each other. As I had time, now, to recollect myself, I did not lose a moment in taking the two mates aside, to present a proposition that we should go, in a body, before a notary, and enter a protest against the unaccountable errors into which Dr. Reasono had permitted himself to fall, whereby the truth was violated, the rights of persons invaded, humanity dishonored, and the Leaphigh philosophy misled. I cannot say that my arguments were well received; and I was compelled to quit the two rear-admirals, and to go in quest of the crew, with the conviction that the former had been purchased. An appeal to the reckless, frank, loyal natures of the common seamen, I thought, would not fail to meet with better success. Here, too, I was fated to encounter disappointment. The men swore a few hearty oaths, and affirmed that Leaphigh was a good country. They expected pay and rations, as a matter of course, in proportion to their new rank; and having tasted the sweets of command, they were not yet prepared to quarrel with their good fortune, and to lay aside the silver tankard for the tar-pot.

Quitting the rascals, whose heads really appeared to be turned by their unexpected elevation, I determined to hunt up Bob, and, by dint of Mr. Poke's ordinary application, compel him, at least, in despite of the union-jack, to return to a sense of his duty, and to reassume his old post as the servitor of my wants. I found the little blackguard in the midst of a bevy of monikinas of all ages, who were lavishing their attentions on his worthless person, and otherwise doing all they could to eradicate everything like humility, or any good quality that might happen to remain in him. He certainly gave me a fair opportunity to commence the attack, for he wore the union-jack over his shoulder, in the manner of a royal mantle, while the females of inferior rank pressed about him to kiss its hem! The air with which he received this adulation, fairly imposed on even me; and, fearful that the monikinas might mob me, should I attempt to undeceive them

—for monikinas, let them be of what species they may, always hug a delusion,—I abandoned my hostile intentions, for the moment, and hurried after Mr. Poke, little doubting my ability of bringing one of his natural rectitude of mind, to a right way of thinking.

The Captain heard my remonstrances with a decent respect. He even seemed to enter into my feelings with a proper degree of sympathy He very frankly admitted that I had not been well treated by Dr. Reasono, and he appeared to think that a private conversation with that individual might yet possibly have the effect of bringing him to a more reasonable representation of facts. But, as to any sudden and violent appeal to public opinion for justice, or an ill-advised recourse to a notary, he strenuously objected to both. The purport of his remarks was somewhat as follows:—

"He was not acquainted with the Leaphigh law of protests, and, in consequence, we might spend our money in paying fees, without reaping any advantage; the Doctor, moreover, was a philosopher, an F. U. D. G. E., and an H. O. A. X., and these were fearful odds to contend against in any country, and more especially in a foreign country; he had an innate dislike for law-suits; the loss of my station was certainly a grievance, but, still, it might be borne; as for himself, he never asked for the office of Lord High Admiral of Great Britain, but, as it had been thrust upon him, why, he would do his best to sustain the character; he knew his friends at Stunin'tun would be glad to hear of his promotion, for, though in his country there were no Lords, nor even any Admirals, his countrymen were always exceedingly rejoiced whenever any of their fellow-citizens were preferred to those stations by any body but themselves, seeming to think an honor conferred on one, was an honor conferred on the whole nation; he liked to confer honor on his own nation, for no people on 'arth tuck up a notion of this sort, and divided it among themselves in a way to give each a share, sooner than the people of the States, though they were very cautious about leaving any portion of the credit in first hands, and, therefore, he was disposed to keep as much as he could, while it was in his power; he believed he was a better seaman than most of the Lord High Admirals who had gone before him, and he had no fears on that score; he wondered whether his promotion made Miss Poke Lady High Admiral; as I seemed greatly *put out* about my own rank, he would give me the acting appointment of a chaplain, (he did n't think I was qualified to be a sea-officer,) and no doubt I had interest enough at home to get it confirmed; a great statesman in his country had said, "that few die and none resigned," and he did n't like to be the first to set new fashions; for his part, he rather looked upon Dr. Reasono as his friend, and it was unpleasant to quarrel with one's friends; he was willing to do any thing, in reason, but resign, and if I could persuade the Doctor to say he had fallen into a mistake in my particular case, and that I had been sent to Leaphigh as a Lord High Ambassador, Lord High Priest, or Lord High any thing else, except Lord High Admiral, why, he was ready to swear to it—though he now gave notice that, in the event of such an arrangement, he should claim to rank me in virtue of the date of his own commission; if he gave up his appointment a minute sooner than was absolutely necessary, he should lose his own self-respect, and never dare look Miss Poke in the face, again; on the whole, he should do no such thing; and, finally, he wished me a good morning, as he was about to make a call on the Lord High Admiral of Leaphigh.'

CHAPTER XVII.

New lords, new laws—Gyration, rotation, and another nation;—also an invitation.

I FELT that my situation had now become exceedingly peculiar. It is true that my modesty had been unexpectedly spared, by the very ingenious turn Dr. Reasono had given to the history of our connexion with each other; but I could not see that I had gained any other advantage by the expedient. All my own species had, in a sense, cut me; and I was obliged to turn despondingly, and not without humiliation, towards the inn, where the banquet ordered by Mr. Poke waited our appearance.

I had reached the great square, when a tap on the knee drew my attention to one at my side. The applicant for notice was a monikin, who had all the physical peculiarities of a subject of Leaphigh, and yet, who was to be distinguished from most of the inhabitants of that country, by a longer and less cultivated nap to his natural garment, greater shrewdness about the expression of the eyes and the mouth, a general air of business, and, for a novelty, a bob-*cauda*. He was accompanied by positively the least well-favored being of the species I had yet seen. I was addressed by the former.

"Good morning, Sir John Goldencalf," he commenced, with a sort of jerk, that I afterwards learned was meant for a diplomatic salutation; "you have not met with the very best treatment to-day, and I have been waiting for a good opportunity to make my condolences, and to offer my services."

"Sir, you are only too good. I do feel a little wronged; and I must say, sympathy is most grateful to my feelings. You will, however, allow me to express my surprise at your being acquainted with my real name, as well as with my misfortunes?"

"Why, sir, to own the truth, I belong to an examining people. The population is very much scattered in my country, and we have fallen into a practice of inquiry that is very natural to such a state of things. I think you must have observed that in passing along a common highway, you rarely meet another without a nod; while thousands are met in a crowded street without even a glance of the eye. We develop this principle, sir; and never let any fact escape us, for the want of a laudable curiosity."

"You are not a subject of Leaphigh, then?"

"God forbid!—No, sir, I am a citizen of Leaplow, a great and a glorious republic that lies three days' sail from this island; a new nation, which is in the enjoyment of all the advantages of youth and vigor, and which is a perfect miracle for the boldness of its conceptions, the purity of its institutions, and its sacred respect for the rights of monikins. I have the honor to be, moreover, the Envoy Extraordinary and Minister Plenipotentiary of the republic to the King of Leaphigh, a nation from which we originally sprung, but which we have left far behind us in the race of glory and usefulness. I ought to acquaint you with my name, sir, in return for the advantage I possess on this head, in relation to yourself."

Hereupon my new acquaintance put into my hand one of his visiting-cards, which contained as follows:—

General-Commodore-Judge-Colonel,
People's Friend:
Envoy Extraordinary and Minister Plenipotentiary from the Republic of Leaplow near his Majesty the King of Leaphigh.

"Sir," said I, pulling off my hat with a profound reverence, "I was not aware to whom I had the honor of speaking. You appear to fill a variety of employments, and I make no doubt, with equal skill."

"Yes, sir, I believe I am about as good at one of my professions, as at another."

"You will permit me to observe, however, General—a—a—Judge—a—a—I scarcely know, dear sir, which of these titles is the most to your taste?"

"Use which you please, sir.—I began with General, but had got as low as Colonel before I left home. People's Friend is the only appellation of which I am at all tenacious. Call me People's Friend, sir, and you may call me anything else you find most convenient."

"Sir, you are only too obliging. May I venture to ask if you have really, *propriâ personâ*, filled all these different stations in life?"

"Certainly, sir—I hope you do not mistake me for an impostor!"

"As far from it as possible.—But a judge and a commodore, for instance, are characters whose duties are so utterly at variance, in human affairs, that I will allow I find the conjunction, even in a monikin, a little extraordinary."

"Not at all, sir. I was duly elected to each, served my time out in them all, and have honorable discharges to show in every instance."

"You must have found some perplexity in the performance of duties so very different?"

"Ah—I see you have been long enough in Leap high to imbibe some of its prejudices! It is a sad country for prejudice. I got my foot mired in some of them myself, as soon as it touched the land. Why, sir, my card is an illustration of what we call, in Leaplow, rotation in office."

"Rotation in office!"

"Yes, sir, rotation in office; a system that w invented for our personal convenience, and which is likely to be firm, as it depends on principles that are eternal."

"Will you suffer me to inquire, Colonel, if it has any affinity to the social-stake system?"

"Not in the least. That, as I understand it, is a stationary, while this is a rotatory system. Nothing is simpler. We have in Leaplow two enormous boxes made in the form of wheels. Into one we put the names of the citizens, and into the other the names of the offices. We then draw forth, in the manner of a lottery; and the thing is settled for a twelvemonth."

"I find this rotatory plan exceedingly simple—pray, sir, does it work as well as it promises?"

"To perfection.—We grease the wheels, of course, periodically."

"And are not frauds sometimes committed by those who are selected to draw the tickets?"

"Oh! they are chosen precisely in the same way."

"But those who draw *their* tickets?"

"All rotatory—they are drawn exactly on the same principle."

"But there must be a beginning. Those, again, who draw *their* tickets—they may betray their trusts?"

"Impossible—*they* are always the most Patriotic Patriots of the land! No, no, sir—we are not such dunces as to leave anything to corruption. Chance does it all. Chance makes me a commodore to-day—a judge to-morrow. Chance makes the lottery boys, and chance makes the patriots. It is necessary to see in order to understand how much purer and useful is your chance patriot, for instance, than one that is bred to the calling."

"Why, this savors, after all, of the doctrine of descents, which is little more than a matter of chance."

"It would be so, sir, I confess, were it not that our chances centre in a system of patriots. Our approved patriots are our guarantees against abuses——"

"Hem!"—interrupted the companion of Commodore People's Friend, with an awkward distinctness, as if to recall himself to our recollection.

"Sir John, I crave pardon for great remissness—allow me to present my fellow-citizen, Brigadier Downright, a gentleman who is on his travels, like yourself; and as excellent a fellow as is to be found in the whole monikin region."

"Brigadier Downright, I crave the honor of your acquaintance.—But, gentlemen, I too have been sadly negligent of politeness. A banquet that has cost a hundred promises is waiting my appearance; and, as some of the expected guests are unavoidably absent, if you would favor me with your excellent society, we might spend an agreeable hour in the further discussion of these important interests."

As neither of the strangers made the smallest objection to the proposal, we were all soon comfortably seated at the dinner-table. The Commodore, who, it would seem, was habitually well fed merely paid a little complimentary attention to the banquet; but Mr. Downright attacked it tooth and nail, and I had no great reason to regret the absence of Mr. Poke. In the mean time, the con versation did not flag.

"I think I understand the outline of your system Judge People's Friend," I resumed, "with the exception of the part that relates to the Patriots. Would it be asking too much to request a little explanation on that particular point?"

"Not in the least, sir. Our social arrangement is founded on a hint from nature; a base, as you will concede, that is broad enough to sustain the universe. As a people, we are a hive that formerly swarmed from Leaphigh; and finding ourselves free and independent, we set about forthwith building the social system on not only a sure foundation, but on sure principles. Observing that nature dealt in duplicates, we pursued the hint, as the leading idea——"

"In duplicates, Commodore!"

"Certainly, Sir John—a monikin has two eyes, two ears, two nostrils, two lungs, two arms, two hands, two legs, two feet, and so on to the end of the chapter. On this hint, we ordered that there should be drawn, morally, in every district of Leaplow, two distinct and separate lines, that should run at right angles to each other. These were termed the "political land-marks" of the country; and it was expected that every citizen should range himself along one or the other.—All this you will understand, however, was a moral contrivance, not a physical one."

"Is the obligation of this moral contrivance imperative?"

"Not legally, it is true; but then, he who does not respect it is like one who is out of fashion, and he is so generally esteemed a poor devil, that the usage has a good deal more than the force of a law. At first, it was intended to make it a part of the constitution; but one of our most experienced statesmen so clearly demonstrated that, by so doing, we should not only weaken the nature of the obligation, but most probably raise a party against it, the idea was abandoned. Indeed, if any thing, both the letter and the spirit of the fundamental law have been made to lean a little against the practice; but having been cleverly introduced, in the way of construction, it is now bone of our bone, and flesh of our flesh. Well, sir, these two great political landmarks being fairly drawn, the first effort of one who aspires to be thought a Patriot, is to acquire the practice of 'toeing the mark' promptly and with facility. But should I illustrate my positions by a few experiments, you might comprehend the subject all the better.—For though, in fact, the true evolutions are purely moral, as I have just had the honor to explain, yet we have instituted a physical parallel that is very congenial to our habits, with which the neophyte always commences."

Here the Commodore took a bit of chalk and drew two very distinct lines, crossing each other at right angles, through the centre of the room. When this was done, he placed his feet together, and then he invited me to examine if it were possible to see any part of the planks between the extremities of his toes and the lines. After a rigid look, I was compelled to confess it was not.

"This is what we call 'toeing the mark;' it is Social Position, No. 1.' Almost every citizen gets to be expert in practising it, on one or the other of the two great political lines. After this, he who would push his fortunes further, commences his career on the great rotatory principle."

"Your pardon, Commodore;—we call the word rotary, in English."

"Sir, it is not expressive enough for our meaning; and therefore we term it 'rotatory.' I shall now give you an example of Position No. 2."

Here the Commodore made a spring, throwing his body, as a soldier would express it, to the "right about," bringing, at the same time, his feet entirely on the other side of the line; always rigidly toeing the mark.

"Sir," said I, "this was extremely well done; but is this evolution as useful as certainly it is dexterous?"

"It has the advantage of changing front, Sir John; a manœuvre quite as useful in politics as in war. Most all in the line get to practise this, too, as my friend Downright, there, could show you, were he so disposed."

"I don't like to expose my flanks, or my rear, more than another," growled the Brigadier.

"If agreeable, I will now show you Gyration 2d, or Position No. 3."

On my expressing a strong desire to see it, the Commodore put himself again in Position No. 1; and then he threw what Captain Poke was in the habit of calling a 'flap-jack,' or a summerset; coming down in a way tenaciously to toe the mark.

I was much gratified with the dexterity of the Commodore, and frankly expressed as much; inquiring, at the same time, if many attained to the same skill. Both the Commodore and the Brigadier laughed at the simplicity of the question; the former answering that the people of Leaplow were exceedingly active and adventurous, and both lines had got to be so expert, that, at the word of command, they would throw their summersets in as exact time, and quite as promptly, as a regi ment of guards would go through the evolution of slapping their cartridge-boxes.

"What, sir," I exclaimed, in admiration, "the entire population!"

"Virtually, sir. There is, now and then, a stumbler; but he is instantly kicked out of sight, and uniformly counts for nothing."

"But as yet, Commodore, your evolutions are altogether too general to admit of the chance selection of patriots, since patriotism is usually a monopoly."

"Very true, Sir John; I shall therefore come to the main point without delay. Thus far, it is pretty much an affair of the whole population, as you say; few refusing to toe the mark, or to throw the necessary flap-jacks, as you have ingeniously termed them. The lines, as you may perceive, cross each other at right angles; and there is consequently some crowding, and, occasionally, a good deal of jostling, at and near the point of junction. We begin to term a monikin a Patriot, when he can perform this evolution."

Here the Commodore threw his heels into the air with such rapidity that I could not very well tell what he was about, though it was sufficiently apparent that he was acting entirely on the rotatory principle. I observed that he alighted, with singular accuracy, on the very spot where he had stood before, toeing the mark with beautiful precision.

"That is what we call Gyration 3d, or Position No. 4. He who can execute it is considered an adept in our politics; and he invariably takes his position near the enemy, or at the junction of the hostile lines."

"How, sir, are these lines, then, manned as they

are with citizens of the same country, deemed hostile!"

"Are cats and dogs hostile, sir?—Certainly, although standing, as it might be, face to face, acting on precisely the same principle, or the rotatory impulse, and professing to have exactly the same object in view, viz. the common good, they are social, political, and I might almost say, the moral antipodes of each other. They rarely intermarry, never extol, and frequently refuse to speak to one another. In short, as the Brigadier could tell you, if he were so disposed, they are antagonist, body and soul. To be plain, sir, they are enemies."

"This is very extraordinary for fellow-citizens!"

"'Tis the monikin nature," observed Mr. Downright; "no doubt, sir, men are much wiser?"

As I did not wish to divert the discourse from the present topic, I merely bowed to this remark, and begged the Judge to proceed.

"Well, sir," continued the latter, "you can easily imagine that they who are placed near the point where the two lines meet, have no sinecures. To speak the truth, they blackguard each other with all their abilities, he who manifests the most inventive genius in this high accomplishment, being commonly thought the cleverest fellow. Now, sir, none but a patriot could, in the nature of things, endure this without some other motive than his country's good, and so we esteem them."

"But the most Patriotic Patriots, Commodore?"

The minister of Leaphigh now toed the mark again, placing himself within a few feet of the point of junction between the two lines; and then he begged me to pay particular attention to his evolution. When all was ready, the Commodore threw himself, as it were, invisibly into the air again head over heels, so far as I could discover and alighted on the antagonist line, toeing the mark with a most astonishing particularity. It was a clever gyration, beyond a doubt; and the performer looked towards me, as if inviting commendation.

"Admirably executed, Judge, and in a way to induce one to believe that you must have paid great attention to the practice."

"I have performed this manœuvre, Sir John, five times in real life; and my claim to be a Patriotic Patriot is founded on its invariable success. A single false step might have ruined me; but as you say, practice makes perfect, and perfection is the parent of success."

"And yet I do not rightly understand how so sudden a desertion of one's own side, to go over, in this active manner, head over heels, I may say, to another side, constitutes a fair claim to be deemed so pure a character as that of a patriot."

"What, sir, is not he who throws himself defencelessly into the very middle of the ranks of the enemy, the hero of the combat? Now, as this is a political struggle, and not a warlike struggle, but one in which the good of the country is alone uppermost, the monikin who thus manifests the greatest devotion to the cause, must be the purest patriot. I give you my honor, sir, all my own claims are founded entirely on this particular merit."

"He is right, Sir John; you may believe every word he says," observed the Brigadier, nodding.

"I begin to understand your system, which is certainly well adapted to the monikin habits, and must give rise to a noble emulation in the practice of the rotatory principle. But I understood you to say, Colonel, that the people of Leaplow are from the hive of Leaphigh?"

"Just so, sir."

"How happens it then, that you dock yourselves of the nobler member, while the inhabitants of this country cherish it as the apple of the eye—nay, as the seat of reason itself?"

"You allude to our tails?—Why, sir, Nature has dealt out these ornaments with a very unequal hand, as you may perceive on looking out of the window. We agree that the tail is the seat of reason, and that the extremities are the most intellectual parts; but, as governments are framed to equalize these natural inequalities, we denounce them as anti-republican. The law requires, therefore, that every citizen, on attaining his majority, shall be docked agreeably to a standard measure, that is kept in each district. Without some such expedient, there might be an aristocracy of intellect among us, and there would be an end of our liberties. This is the qualification of a voter, too, and of course we all seek to obtain it."

Here the Brigadier leaned across the table and whispered that a great patriot, on a most trying occasion, had succeeded in throwing a summerset out of his own into the antagonist line, and that, as he carried with him all the sacred principles for which his party had been furiously contending for many years, he had been unceremoniously dragged back by his tail, which unfortunately came within reach of those quondam friends on whom he had turned his back; and that the law had, in truth, been passed in the interests of the patriots. He added, that the lawful measure allowed a longer stump than was commonly used; but that it was considered under-bred for any one to wear a dock that reached more than two inches and three quarters of an inch into society, and that most of their political aspirants, in particular, chose to limit themselves to one inch and one quarter of an inch, as a proof of excessive humility.

Thanking Mr. Downright for his clear and sensible explanation, the conversation was resumed.

"I had thought, as your institutions are founded on reason and nature, Judge," I continued, "that you would be more disposed to cultivate this member than to mutilate it; and this the more especially, as I understand all monikins believe it to be the very quintessence of reason."

"No doubt, sir; we do cultivate our tails, but it is on the vegetable principle, or as the skilful gardener lops the branch that it may throw out more vigorous shoots. It is true, we do not expect to see the tail itself sprouting out anew; but then we look to the increase of its reason, and to its more general diffusion in society. The extremities of our *caudæ*, as fast as they are lopped, are sent to a great intellectual mill, where the mind is extracted from the matter, and the former is sold, on public account, to the editors of the daily journals. This is the reason our Leaplow journalists are so distinguished for their ingenuity and capacity, and the reason, too, why they so faithfully represent the average of the Leaplow knowledge."

"And honesty, you ought to add," growled the Brigadier.

"I see the beauty of the system, Judge, and very beautiful it is! This essence of lopped tails represents the average of Leaplow brains, being a compound of all the tails of the country; and as a daily journal is addressed to the average intellect of the community, there is a singular fitness between the readers and the readees. To complete my stock of information on this head, however, will you just allow me to inquire what is the effect of this system on the totality of Leaplow intelligence?"

"Wonderful! As we are a commonwealth, it is necessary to have a unity of sentiment on all leading matters, and by thus compounding all the extremes of our reasons, we get what is called 'public opinion;' which public opinion is uttered through the public journals——"

"And a most Patriotic Patriot is always chosen to be the inspector of the mill," interrupted the Brigadier.

"Better and better! you send all the finer parts of your several intellects to be ground up and kneaded together; the compound is sold to the journalists, who utter it anew, as the results of the united wisdom of the country!"

"Or, as public opinion.—We make great account of reason in all our affairs, invariably calling ourselves the most enlightened nation on earth; but then we are especially averse to anything like an insulated effort of the mind, which is offensive, anti-republican, aristocratic and dangerous. We put all our trust in this representation of brains, which is singularly in accordance with the fundamental base of our society, as you must perceive."

"We are a commercial people, too," put in the Brigadier; "and being much accustomed to the laws of insurance, we like to deal in averages."

"Very true, brother Downright; very true. We are particularly averse to anything like inequality. Ods zooks! it is almost as great an offence for a monikin to know more than his neighbors, as it is for him to act on his own impulses. No—no—we are truly a free and an independent commonwealth, and we hold every citizen as amenable to public opinion, in all he does, says, thinks or wishes."

"Pray, sir, do both of the two great political

lines send their tails to the same mills, and respect the same general sentiments?"

"No, sir; we have two public opinions, in Leaplow."

"*Two* public opinions!"

"Certainly, sir; the horizontal and the perpendicular."

"This infers a most extraordinary fertility of thought, and one that I hold to be almost impossible!"

Here the Commodore and the Brigadier incontinently both laughed as hard as they could; and that, too, directly in my face.

"Dear me, Sir John—why, my dear Sir John! you are really the drollest creature!"—gasped the Judge, holding his sides,—"the very funniest question I have ev—ev—ever encountered!" He now stopped to wipe his eyes; after which he was better able to express himself. "The same public opinion, forsooth!—Dear me—dear me, that I should not have made myself understood!—I commenced, my good Sir John, by telling you that we deal in duplicates, on a hint from Nature; and that we act on the rotatory principle. In obedience to the first, we have always *two* public opinions; and, although the great political land-marks are drawn in what may be called a stationary sense, they, too, are in truth rotatory. One, which is thought to lie parallel to the fundamental law, or the constitutional meridian of the country, is termed the horizontal, and the other the perpendicular line. Now, as nothing is really stationary in Leaplow, these two great land-marks are always acting, likewise, on the rotatory principle, changing places periodically; the perpendicular becoming the horizontal, and *vice versâ;* they who toe their respective marks, necessarily taking new views of things, as they vary the line of sight These great revolutions are, however, very slow, and are quite as imperceptible to those who accompany them, as are the revolutions of our planet to its inhabitants."

"And the gyrations of the patriots, of which the Judge has just now spoken," added the Brigadier, "are much the same as the eccentric movements of the comets that embellish the solar system, without deranging it by their uncertain courses."

"No, sir, we should be poorly off, indeed, if we had but *one* public opinion," resumed the Judge. "Ecod, I do not know what would become of the most Patriotic Patriots, in such a dilemma!"

"Pray, sir, let me ask, as you draw for places, if you have as many places as there are citizens?"

"Certainly, sir. Our places are divided, firstly, into the two great subdivisions of the "inner" and the "outer." Those who toe the mark on the most popular line occupy the former, and those who toe the mark on the least popular line take all the rest, as a matter of course. The first, however, it is necessary to explain, are the only places worth having. As great care is had to keep the community pretty nearly equally divided——"

"Excuse the interruption—but in what manner is this effected?"

"Why, as only a certain number can *toe the mark*, we count all those who are not successful in getting up to the line, as outcasts; and, after fruitlessly hanging about our skirts for a time, they invariably go over to the other line; since it is better to be first in a village, than second in Rome. We thus keep up something like an equilibrium in the state, which, as you must know, is necessary to liberty. The minority take the outer places, and all the inner are left to the majority

Then comes another subdivision of the places; that is to say, one division is formed of the honorary, and another of the profitable places. The honorary, or about nine-tenths of all the inner places, are divided, with great impartiality, among the mass of those who have toed the mark on the strongest side, and who usually are satisfied with the glory of the victory. The names of the remainder are put into the wheels to be drawn for against the prizes, on the rotatory principle."

"And the patriots, sir;—are they included in this chance-medley?"

"Far from it. As a reward for their dangers, they have a little wheel to themselves, although they, also, are compelled to submit to the rotatory principle. Their cases differ from those of the others, merely in the fact that they always get *something*."

I would gladly have pursued the conversation, which was opening a flood of light upon my political understanding; but, just then, a fellow with the air of a footman entered, carrying a packet tied to the end of his *cauda*. Turning round, he presented his burthen, with profound respect, and withdrew. I found that the packet contained three notes, with the following addresses:—

"To his Royal Highness Bob, Prince of Wales, &c. &c. &c.
"To my Lord High Admiral Poke, &c. &c. &c."
"To Master Goldencalf, Clerk, &c. &c. &c."

Apologizing to my guests, the seal of my own note was eagerly opened. It read as follows:

"The Right Honorable the Earl of Chatterino, Lord of the Bed-Chamber in waiting on his Majesty, informs Master John Goldencalf, Clerk, that he is commanded to attend the drawing-room, this evening, when the nuptial ceremony will take place between the Earl of Chatterino and the Lady Chatterissa, the first Maid of Honor to her Majesty the Queen.

"N. B. *The gentlemen will appear in full dress.*"

On explaining the contents of my note to the Judge, he informed me that he was aware of the approaching ceremony, as he had also an invitation to be present, in his official character. I begged, as a particular favor, England having no representative at Leaphigh, that he would do me the honor to present me, in his capacity of a foreign minister. The Envoy made no sort of objection, and I inquired as to the costume necessary to be observed; as, so far as I had seen, it was good breeding at Leaphigh to go naked. The Envoy had the goodness to explain, that, although, in point of mere attire, clothing was extremely offensive to the people of both Leaphigh and Leaplow, yet, in the former country, no one could present himself at court, foreign ministers excepted, without a *cauda.* As soon as we understood each other on these points, we separated, with an understanding that I was to be in readiness (together with my companions, of whose interest I had not been forgetful) to attend the Envoy and the Brigadier, when they should call for me, at an hour that was named.

CHAPTER XVIII.

A court, a court-dress, and a courtier—Justice in various aspects, as well as honor.

My guests were no sooner gone, than I sent for the landlady, to inquire if any court-dresses were to be had in the neighborhood. She told me, plenty might certainly be had, that were suited to the monikin dimensions, but she much doubted whether there was a tail in all Leaphigh, natural or artificial, that was at all fit for a person of my stature. This was vexatious; and I was in a brown-study, calling up all my resources for the occasion, when Mr. Poke entered the inn, carrying in his hand two as formidable ox-tails as I remember ever to have seen. Throwing one towards me, he said the Lord High Admiral of Leaphigh had acquainted him, that there was an invitation out for the Prince and himself, as well as for the governor of the former, to be present at court within an hour. He had hurried off from what he called a very good dinner, considering there was nothing solid, (the Captain was particularly fond of pickled pork,) to let me know the honor that was intended us; and, on the way home, he had fallen in with Dr. Reasono, who, on being acquainted with his errand, had not failed to point out the necessity of the whole party coming *en habit de cour*. Here was a dilemma, with a vengeance; for the first idea that struck the Captain was "the utter impossibility of finding any thing in this way, in all Leaphigh, befitting a Lord High Admiral of his length of keel; for, as to going in an ordinary monikin *queue*, why, he should look like a three-decked ship, with a brig's spar stepped for a lower mast!" Dr. Reasono, however, had kindly removed the embarrassment, by conducting him to the Cabinet of Natural History, where three suitable appendages had been found, viz. two fine relics of oxen,* and another, a capital specimen, that had formerly been the mental lever, or, as the Captain expressed it, "the steering oar" of a kangaroo. The latter had been sent off, express, with a kind consideration for the honor of Great Britain, to Prince Bob, who was at a villa of one of the royal family, in the neighborhood of Aggregation.

I was greatly indebted to Noah, for his dexterity in helping me to a good fit with my court-dress. There was not time for much particularity, for we were in momentary expectation of Judge People's Friend's return. All we could do, therefore, was to make a belt of canvas, (the Captain being always provided with needles, palm, &c., in his bag,) and to introduce the smaller end of the tail through a hole in the belt, drawing its base tight up to the cloth, which, in its turn, was stitched round our bodies. This was but an indifferent substitute for the natural appendage, it is true; and the hide had got to be so dry and unyielding, that it was impossible for the least observant person to imagine there was a particle of brains in it. The arrangement had, also, another disadvantage. The *cauda* stuck out nearly at right angles with the position of the body, and, besides occupying much more space than would probably be permitted in the royal presence, "it gave any jackanapes," as Noah observed, "the great advantage over us, of making us yaw at pleasure, since he might use the outriggers as levers." But a seaman is inex-

* *Caudæ Bovium.*—BUF

haustible in expedients. Two "back-stays," or "bob-stays," (for the Captain facetiously gave them both appellations,) were soon "turned in," and the tails were "stayed in, in a way to bring them as upright as try-sail-masts;" to which spars, indeed, according to Noah's account of the matter, they bore no small resemblance.

The Envoy Extraordinary of Leaplow, accompanied by his friend, Brigadier Downright, arrived just as we were dressed; and a most extraordinary figure the former cut, if truth must be said. Although obliged to be docked, according to the Leaplow law, to six inches, and brought down to a real bob, by both the public opinions of his country, for this was one of the few points on which these antagonist sentiments were perfectly agreed, he now appeared in just the largest brush I remember to have seen appended to a monikin! I felt a strong inclination to joke the rotatory republican on this coquetry; but then I remembered how sweet any stolen indulgence becomes; and, for the life of me, I could not give utterance to a *bon mot.* The elegance of the Minister was rendered the more conspicuous by the simplicity of the Brigadier, who had contrived to *moustache* his dock, a very short one at the best, in such a manner as to render it nearly invisible. On my expressing a doubt to Mr. Downright about his being admitted in such a costume, he snapped his fingers, and gave me to understand he knew better. He appeared as a Brigadier of Leaplow, (I found afterwards that he was in truth no soldier, but that it was a fashion among his countrymen to travel under the title of Brigadier,) and this was his uniform; and he should like to see the chamberlain who would presume to call in question the state of his wardrobe! As it was no affair of mine, I prudently dropped the subject, and we were soon in the court of the palace.

I shall pass over the parade of guards, the state bands, the sergeant-trumpeters, the crowd of footmen and pages, and conduct the reader at once to the antechamber. Here we found the usual throng composed of those who live in the smiles of princes. There was a great deal of politeness, much bowing and curtseying, and the customary amount of genteel *empressement* to be the first to bask in the sunshine of royalty. Judge People's Friend, in his character of a foreign minister, was privileged; and we had enjoyed the private *entrée*, and were now, of right, placed nearest to the great doors of the royal apartments. Most of the diplomatic corps were already in attendance, and, quite as a matter of course, there were a great many cordial manifestations of the ardent attachment that bound them and their masters together, in the inviolable bonds of a most sacred amity. Judge People's Friend, according to his own account of the matter, represented a great nation—a very great nation—and yet I did not perceive that he met with a warm—a very warm—reception. However, as he seemed satisfied with himself, and all around him, it would have been unkind, not to say rude, in a stranger to disturb his self-esteem; and I took especial care, therefore, not to betray, by the slightest hint, my opinion that a good many near his person seemed to think him and his artificial *queue* somewhat in the way. The courtiers of Leaphigh, in particular, who are an exceedingly exclusive and fastidious corps, appeared to regard the privileges of the Judge with an evil eye; and one or two of them actually held their noses as he flourished his brush a little too near their sacred faces, as if they found its odo-

out of fashion. While making these silent observations, a page cried out from the lower part of the saloon, "Room for his Royal Highness the Crown Prince of Great Britain!" The crowd opened, and that young blackguard Bob walked up the avenue, in state. He wore the turnspit garment as the base of his toilet; but the superstructure was altogether more in keeping with the rascal's assumed character. The union-jack was thrown over his shoulder in the fashion of a mantle, and it was supported by the cook and steward of the Walrus, (two blacks,) both clothed as alligators. The kangaroo's tail was rigged in a way to excite audible evidences of envy in the heart of Mr. Poke. The stepping of it, the Captain whispered, "did the young dog great credit, for it looked as natural as the best wig he had ever seen; and then, in addition to the bob-stay, it had two guys, which acted like the yoke-lines of a boat, or in such a way, that by holding one in each hand, the brush could be worked 'starboard and larboard' like a rudder." I have taken this description mainly from the mouth of the Captain, and most sincerely do I hope it may be intelligible to the reader.

Bob appeared to be conscious of his advantages; for, on reaching the upper end of the room, he began whisking his tail, and flourishing it to the right and left, so as to excite a very perceptible and lively admiration in the mind of Judge People's Friend,—an effect that so much the more proved the wearer's address, for that high functionary was bound *ex officio* to entertain a sovereign contempt for all courtly vanities. I saw the eye of the Captain kindle, however; and when the insolent young coxcomb actually had the temerity to turn his back on his master, and to work his brush under his very nose, human nature could endure no more. The right leg of my Lord High Admiral slowly retired, with somewhat of the caution of the cat about to spring, and then it was projected forward, with a rapidity that absolutely lifted the Crown Prince from the floor.

The royal self-possession of Bob could not prevent an exclamation of pain, as well as of surprise; and some of the courtiers ran forward involuntarily to aid him,—for courtiers always run involuntarily to the succor of princes. At least a dozen of the ladies offered their smelling-bottles, with the most amiable assiduity and concern. To prevent any disagreeable consequences, however, I hastened to acquaint the crowd that, in Great Britain, it is the usage to cuff and kick the whole royal family; and that, in short, it is no more than the customary tribute of the subject to the prince. In proof of what I said, I took good care to give the saucy young scoundrel a touch of my own homage. The monikins, who know that different customs prevail in different nations, hastened to compliment the young scion of royalty in the same manner; and both the cook and steward relieved their *ennui* by falling into the track of imitation. Bob could not stand the last applications; and he was about to beat a retreat, when the master of ceremonies appeared, to conduct him to the royal presence.

The reader is not to be misled by the honors that were paid to the imaginary Crown Prince, and to suppose that the court of Leaphigh entertained any peculiar respect for that of Great Britain. It was merely done on the principle that governed the conduct of our own learned sovereign, King James I., when he refused to see the amiable Pocahontas of Virginia, because she had degraded royalty by intermarrying with a subject

The respect was paid to the caste, and not to the individual, to his species, or to his nation.

Let his privileges come from what cause they would, Bob was glad enough to get out of the presence of Captain Poke,—who had already pretty plainly threatened, in the Stunnin'tun dialect, to unship his *cauda*,—into that of the Majesty of Leaphigh. A few minutes afterwards, the doors were thrown open, and the whole company advanced into the royal apartments.

The etiquette of the court of Leaphigh differs, in many essential particulars, from the etiquette of any other court in the monikin region. Neither the King, nor his royal consort, is ever visible to any one in the country, so far as is vulgarly known. On the present occasion, two thrones were placed at opposite extremities of the saloon, and a magnificent, crimson, damask curtain was so closely drawn before each, that it was quite impossible to see who occupied it. On the lowest step there stood a chamberlain or a lady of the bed-chamber, who, severally, made all the speeches, and otherwise enacted the parts of the illustrious couple. The reader will understand, therefore, that all which is here attributed to either of these great personages, was in fact performed by one or the other of the substitutes named, and that I never had the honor of actually standing, face to face, with their Majesties. Every thing that is now about to be related, in short, was actually done by deputy, on the part of the monarch and his wife.

The King himself merely represents a sentiment, all the power belonging to his eldest first-cousin of the masculine gender, and any intercourse with him is entirely of a disinterested or of a sentimental character. He is the head of the church,—after a very secular fashion, however: —all the bishops and clergy therefore got down on their knees and said their prayers; though the Captain suggested that it might be their catechisms: I never knew which. I observed, also, that all his law officers did the same thing; but as *they* never pray, and do not know their catechisms, I presume the genuflections were to beg something better than the places they actually filled. After this, came a long train of military and naval officers, who, soldier-like, kissed his paw. The civilians next had a chance, and then it was our turn to be presented.

"I have the honor to present the Lord High Admiral of Great Britain, to your Majesty," said Judge People's Friend, who had waived his official privilege of going first, in order to do us this favor in person; it having been decided, on a review of all the principles that touched the case, that nothing human could take precedence of a monikin at court, always making the exception in favor of royalty, as in the case of Prince Bob.

"I am happy to see you at my court, Admiral Poke," the King politely rejoined, manifesting the tact of high rank in recognizing Noah by his family name, to the great surprise of the old sealer.

"King!"

"You were about to remark?——" most graciously inquired his Majesty, a little at a loss to understand what his visiter would be at.

"Why, I could not contain my astonishment at your memory, Mr. King, which has enabled you to recall a name that you probably never before heard!"

There was now a great, and, to me, a very unaccountable confusion in the circle. It would seem, that the Captain had unwittingly trespassed on two of the most important of the rules of etiquette, in very mortal points. He had confessed to the admission of an emotion as vulgar as that of astonishment in the royal presence and he had intimated that his Majesty had a memory; a property of the mind which, as it might prove dangerous to the liberties of Leaphigh, were it left in the keeping of any but a responsible minister, it had long been decided it was felony to impute to the King. By the fundamental law of the land, the King's eldest first-cousin of the masculine gender may have as many memories as he please, and he may use them, or abuse them, as he shall see fit, both in private or in the public service; but it is held to be utterly unconstitutional and unparliamentary, and, by consequence, extremely underbred, to insinuate, even in the most remote manner, that the King himself has either a memory, a will, a determination, a resolution, a desire, a conceit, an intention, or, in short, any other intellectual property, that of a "royal pleasure" alone excepted. It is both constitutional and parliamentary to say the King has a "royal pleasure," provided the context goes to prove that this "royal pleasure" is entirely at the disposition of his eldest first-cousin of the masculine gender.

When Mr. Poke was made acquainted with his mistake, he discovered a proper contrition; and the final decision of the affair was postponed, in order to have the opinion of the judges on the propriety of taking bail, which I promptly offered to put in, in behalf of my old ship-mate. This disagreeable little interruption temporarily disposed of, the business of the drawing-room went on.

Noah was next conducted to the Queen, who was much inclined (always by deputy) to overlook the little mistake into which he had fallen with her royal consort, and to receive him graciously

"May it please your Majesty, I have the honor to present to your Majesty's royal notice, the Lord Noah Poke, the Lord High Admiral of a distant and but little known country, called Great Britain," said the gold stick of the evening,—Judge People's Friend being afraid of committing Leaplow, and declining to introduce the Captain to any one else.

"Lord Poke is a countryman of our royal cousin the Prince Bob!" observed the Queen, in an exceedingly gracious manner.

"No marm," put in the sealer, promptly, "your cousin Bob is no cousin of mine; and if it were lawful for your Majesty to have a memory, or an inclination, or any thing else in that way, I should beg the favor of you, to order the young blackguard to be soundly threshed."

The Majesty of Leaphigh stood aghast, by proxy! It would seem Noah had now actually fallen into a more serious error, than the mistake he had made with the King. By the law of Leaphigh, the Queen is not a *femme couverte*. She can sue and be sued in her own name, holds her separate estate, without the intervention of trustees and *is* supposed to have a memory, a will, an inclination, or any thing else in that way, except a "royal pleasure," to which she cannot, of right, lay claim. As to her, the King's first-cousin is a dead letter; he having no more control over her conscience, than he has over the conscience of an apple-woman. In short, her Majesty is quite as much the mistress of her own convictions and conscience, as it probably ever falls to the lot of women in such high stations to be the mistress of interests that are of so much importance to those around them. Noah, innocently enough, I do firmly believe, had seriously wounded all those nice sensibilities which are naturally dependent on such an improved condition of society. Forbearance could go no farther, and I saw, by the dark looks around me, that the Captain had committed a serious crime. He was immediately arrested, and conducted from the presence to an adjoining room, into which I obtained admission, after a good deal of solicitation and some very strong appeals to the sacred character of the rights of hospitality.

It now appeared, that in Leaphigh, the merits of a law are decided on a principle very similar to the one we employ in England in judging of the quality of our wines; viz., its age. The older a law, the more it is to be respected, no doubt because, having proved its fitness by outlasting all the changes of society, it has become more mellow, if not more palatable. Now, by a law of Leaphigh, that is coeval with the monarchy, he who offends the Queen's Majesty at a levee, is to lose his head; and he who, under the same circumstances, offends the King's Majesty, necessarily the more heinous offence, is to lose his tail. In consequence of the former punishment, the criminal is invariably buried, and he is consigned to the usual course of monikin regeneration and resuscitation; but in consequence of the latter, it is thought that he is completely thrown without the pale of reason, and is thereby consigned to the class of the retrogressive animals. His mind diminishes, and his body increases; the brain, for want of the means of development, takes the ascending movement of sap again; his forehead dilates; bumps re-appear; and, finally, after passing gradually downward in the scale of intellect, he becomes a mass of insensible matter. Such, at least, is the theory of his punishment.

By another law, that is even older than the monarchy, any one who offends in the King's palace may be tried by a very summary process, the King's pages acting as his judges; in which case, the sentence is to be executed without delay.

Such was the dilemma to which Noah, by an indiscretion at court, was suddenly reduced; and, but for my prompt interference, he would probably have been simultaneously decapitated at both extremities, in obedience to an etiquette which prescribes that, under the circumstances of a court trial, neither the King's nor the Queen's rights shall be entitled to precedence. In defence of my client I urged his ignorance of the usages of the country, and, indeed, of all other civilized countries, Stunnin'tun alone excepted. I stated that the criminal was an object altogether unworthy of their notice; that he was not a Lord High Admiral at all, but a mere pitiful sealer; I laid some stress on the importance of maintaining friendly relations with the sealers, who cruise so near the monikin region; I tried to convince the judges that Noah meant no harm in imputing moral properties to the King, and that so long as he did not impute immoral properties to his royal consort, she might very well afford to pardon him. I then quoted Shakspeare's celebrated lines on mercy, which seemed to be well enough received, and committed the whole affair to their better judgment.

I should have got along very creditably, and most probably obtained the immediate discharge of my friend, had not the Attorney-General of Leaphigh been drawn by curiosity into the room. Although he had nothing to say to the merits of my arguments, he objected to every one of them, on the ground of formality. This was too long, and that was too short; one was too high, and another too low; a fifth was too broad, and a sixth too narrow; in short, there was no figure of speech of this nature, to which he did not resort, in order to prove their worthlessness, with the exception that I do not remember he charged any of my reasons with being too deep.

Matters were now beginning to look serious for poor Noah, when a page came skipping in to say that the wedding was about to take place and that if his comrades wished to witness it, they must sentence the prisoner without delay. Many a man, it is said, has been hanged, in order that the judge might dine; but, in the present instance, I do believe Captain Poke was spared, in order that his judges might not miss a fine spectacle. I entered into recognizance, in fifty thousand promises, for the due appearance of the criminal on the following morning; and we all returned, in a body, to the presence-chamber, treading on each other's tails, in the eagerness to be foremost.

Any one who has ever been at a human court, must very well know that, while it is the easiest thing in the world to throw it into commotion by a violation of etiquette, matters of mere life and death are not at all of a nature to disturb its tranquillity. There, everything is a matter of routine and propriety; and, to judge from experience, nothing is so unseemly as to appear to possess human sympathies. The fact is not very different at Leaphigh, for the monikin sympathies, apparently, are quite as obtuse as those of men; although justice compels me to allow, that in the case of Captain Poke, the appeal was made in behalf of a creature of a different species. It is also a settled principle of Leaphigh jurisprudence, that it would be monstrous for the King to interfere in behalf of justice,—justice, however, being always administered in his name; although it certainly is not held to be quite so improper for him to interfere in behalf of those who have offended justice.

As a consequence of these nice distinctions, which it requires a very advanced stage of civilization fully to comprehend, both the King and Queen received our whole party, when we came back into the presence, exactly as if nothing particular had occurred. Noah wore both head and tail erect, like another; and the Lord High Admiral of Leaphigh dropped into a familiar conversation with him, on the subject of ballasting ships, in just as friendly a manner as if he were on the best possible terms with the whole royal family. This moral *sang froid* is not to be ascribed to phlegm, but is, in fact, the result of high mental discipline, which causes the courtier to be utterly destitute of all feeling, except in cases that affect himself.

It was high time, now, that I should be presented. Judge People's Friend, who had witnessed the dilemma of Noah with diplomatic unconcern, very politely renewed the offer of his services in my favor, and I went forward and stood before the throne.

"Sire, allow me to present a very eminent literary character among men, a cunning clerk, by name Goldencalf," said the envoy, bowing to his Majesty.

"He is welcome to my court," returned the King by proxy. "Pray, Mr. People's Friend, is not this one of the human beings who have lately arrived in my dominions, and who have shown so much cleverness in getting Chatterino and his governor through the ice?"

"The very same, please your Majesty; and a very arduous service it was, and right cleverly performed."

"This reminds me of a duty.—Let my cousin be summoned."

I now began to see a ray of hope, and to feel the truth of the saying which teaches us that justice, though sometimes slow, never fails to arrive at last. I had also, now, and for the first time, a good view of the King's eldest first-cousin of the masculine gender, who drew near at the summons; and, while he had the appearance of listening with the most profound attention to the instructions of the King of Leaphigh, was very evidently telling that potentate what he ought to do. The conference ended, his Majesty's proxy spoke in a way to be heard by all who had the good fortune to be near the royal person.

"Reasono did a good thing," he said; "really a very good thing, in bringing us these specimens of the human family. But for his cleverness, I might have died without ever dreaming that men were gifted with tails." (Kings never get hold of the truth at the right end.) "I wonder if the Queen knew it. Pray, did you know, my Augusta, that men had tails?"

"Our exemption from state affairs gives us females better opportunities than your Majesty enjoys, to study these matters," returned his roya consort, by the mouth of her Lady of the Bed-Chamber.

"I dare say I'm very silly,—but our cousin, here, thinks it might be well to do something for these good people, for it may encourage their King himself to visit us some day."

An exclamation of pleasure escaped the ladies; who declared, one and all, it would be delightful to see a real human King,—it would be so funny!

"Well, well," added the good-natured monarch, "Heaven knows what may happen, for I have seen stranger things. Really, we ought to do something for these good people; for, although we owe the pleasure of their visit, in a great degree, to the cleverness of Reasono,—who, by the way, I'm glad to hear is declared an H. O. A. X.,—yet he very handsomely admits, that but for their exertions—none of our seamikins being within reach—it would have been quite impossible to get through the ice. I wish I knew, now, which was the cleverest and the most useful of their party."

Here the Queen, always thinking and speaking by proxy, suggested the propriety of leaving the point to Prince Bob.

"It would be no more than is due to his rank; for though they are men, I dare say they have feelings like ourselves."

The question was now submitted to Bob, who sat in judgment on us all, with as much gravity as if accustomed to such duties from infancy. It is said that men soon get to be familiar with elevation, and that, while he who has fallen never fails to look backward, he who has risen invariably limits his vision to the present horizon. Such proved to be the case with the princely Bob.

"This person," observed the jack-a-napes, pointing to me, "is a very good sort of a person, it is true, but he is hardly the sort of person your Majesty wants just now. There is the Lord High Admiral, too,—but—" (Bob's but was envenomed by a thousand kicks!)—"but—you wish, sire, to know which of my father's subjects was the most useful in getting the ship to Leaphigh?"

"That is precisely the fact I desire to know."

Bob, hereupon, pointed to the cook; who, it will be remembered, was present as one of his train-bearers.

"I believe I must say, sire, that this is the man. He fed us all; and without food, and that in considerable quantities, too, nothing could have been done."

The little blackguard was rewarded for his impudence, by exclamations of pleasure from all around him.—"It was so clever a distinction."—"it showed so much reflection,"—"it was so very profound,"—"it proved how much he regarded the base of society."—in short, "it was evident England would be a happy country, when he should be called to the throne!" In the mean time, the cook was required to come forth, and kneel before his Majesty.

"What is your name?" whispered the Lord of the Bed-Chamber, who now spoke for himself.

"Jack Coppers, your honor."

The Lord of the Bed-Chamber made a communication to his Majesty, when the sovereign turned round by proxy, with his back towards Jack, and, giving him the *accolade* with his tail, he bade him rise, as "Sir Jack Coppers."

I was a silent, an admiring, an astounded witness of this act of gross and flagrant injustice. Some one pulled me aside, and then I recognized the voice of Brigadier Downright.

"You think that honors have alighted where they are least due. You think that the saying of your Crown Prince has more smartness than truth, more malice than honesty. You think that the court has judged on false principles, and acted on an impulse rather than on reason; that the King has consulted his own ease in affecting to do justice; that the courtiers have paid a homage to their master, in affecting to pay a homage to merit; and that nothing in this life is pure or free from the taint of falsehood, selfishness or vanity. Alas! this is too much the case with us monikins, I must allow; though, doubtless, among men you manage a vast deal more cleverly."

CHAPTER XIX.

About the humility of professional saints, a succession of tails, a bride and bridegroom, and other heavenly matters,—diplomacy included.

PERCEIVING that Brigadier Downright had an observant mind, and that he was altogether superior to the clannish feeling which is so apt to render a particular species inimical to all others, I asked permission to cultivate his acquaintance; begging, at the same time, that he would kindly favor me with such remarks as might be suggested by his superior wisdom and extensive travels, on any of those customs or opinions that would naturally present themselves in our actual situation. The Brigadier took the request in good part, and we began to promenade the rooms in company. As the Archbishop of Aggregation, who was to perform the marriage ceremony, was shortly expected, the conversation very naturally turned on the general state of religion in the monikin region.

I was delighted to find that the clerical dogmas of this insulated portion of the world were based on principles absolutely identical with those of all Christendom. The monikins believe that they are a miserable lost set of wretches, who are so debased by nature, so eaten up by envy, uncharitableness and all other evil passions, that it is quite impossible they can do anything that is good of themselves; that their sole dependence is on the moral interference of the great superior power of creation; and that the very first, and the one needful step of their own, is to cast themselves entirely on this power for support, in a proper spirit of dependence and humility. As collateral to, and consequent on this condition of the mind, they lay the utmost stress on a disregard of all the vanities of life, a proper subjection of the lusts of the flesh and an abstaining from the pomp and vain-glory of ambition, riches, power and the faculties. In short, the one thing needful was humility—humility—humility. Once thoroughly humbled to a degree that put them above the danger of backsliding, they obtained glimpses of security, and were gradually elevated to the hopes and the condition of the just.

The Brigadier was still eloquently discoursing on this interesting topic, when a distant door opened, and a gold stick, or some other sort of stick, announced the Right Reverend Father in God, his Grace the most eminent and most serene Prelate, the very puissant and thrice gracious and glorified saint, the Primate of all Leaphigh!

The reader will anticipate the eager curiosity with which I advanced to get a glimpse of a saint under a system as sublimated as that of the great monikin family. Civilization having made such progress as to strip all the people, even to the King and Queen, entirely of every thing in the shape of clothes, I did not well see under what new mantle of simplicity the heads of the church could take refuge! Perhaps they shaved off all the hair from their bodies in sign of supereminent self-abasement, leaving themselves naked to the cuticle, that they might prove, by ocular evidence, what a poor ungainly set of wretches they really were, carnally considered; or perhaps they went on all-fours to heaven, in sign of their unfitness to enter into the presence of the pure of mind, in an attitude more erect and confident. Well, these fancies of mine only went to prove how erroneous and false are the conclusions of one whose capacity has not been amplified and concatenated by the ingenuities of a very refined civilization! His Grace, the most gracious Father in God, wore a mantle of extraordinary fineness and beauty, the material of which was composed of every tenth hair taken from all the citizens of Leaphigh, who most cheerfully submitted to be shaved, in order that the wants of his most eminent humility might be decently supplied. The mantle, wove from such a warp and such a woof, was necessarily very large; and it really appeared to me that the prelate did not very well know what to do with so much of it, more especially as the contributions include a new robe annually. I was now desirous of getting a sight of his tail; for, knowing that the Leaphighers take great pride in the length and beauty of that appurtenance, I very naturally supposed that a saint who wore so fine and glorious a robe, by way of humility, must have recourse to some novel expedient to mortify himself on this sensitive subject, at least. I found that the ample proportions of the mantle concealed, not only the person, but most of the movements of the Archbishop; and it was with many doubts of my success, that I led the Brigadier behind the episcopal train to reconnoitre. The result disappointed expectation again. Instead of being destitute of a tail, or of concealing that with which Nature had supplied him beneath his mantle, the most gracious dignitary wore no less than six *caudæ*, viz. his own, and five others added to it, by some subtle process of clerical ingenuity that I shall not attempt to explain; one "bent on to the other," as the Captain described them, in a subsequent conversation. This extraordinary train was allowed to sweep the floor; the only sign of humility, according to my uninstructed faculties, I could discern about the person and appearance of this illustrious model of clerical self-mortification and humility.

The Brigadier, however, was not tardy in setting me right. In the first place, he gave me to understand that the hierarchy of Leaphigh was illustrated by the order of their tails. Thus, a deacon wore one and a half; a curate, if a minister, one and three quarters, and a rector, two; a dean, two and a half; an archdeacon, three; a bishop four; the Primate of Leaphigh, five, and the Primate of *all* Leaphigh, six. The origin of the custom, which was very ancient, and of course very much respected, was imputed to the doctrine of a saint of great celebrity, who had satisfactorily proved that as the tail was the intellectual, or the spiritual part of a monikin, the farther it was removed from the mass of matter, or the body, the more likely it was to be independent, consecutive, logical and spiritualized. The idea had succeeded astonishingly at first; but time, which will wear out even a *cauda*, had given birth to schisms in the church on this interesting subject; one party contending that two more joints ought to be added to the Archbishop's embellishment, by way of sustaining the church, and the other that two joints ought to be incontinently abstracted, in the way of reform.

These explanations were interrupted by the appearance of the bride and bridegroom, at different doors. The charming Chatterissa advanced with a most prepossessing modesty, followed by a glorious train of noble maidens, all keeping their eyes, by a rigid ordinance of hymeneal etiquette, dropped to the level of the Queen's feet. On the other hand, my Lord Chatterino, attended by that coxcomb Hightail, and others of his kidney, stepped towards the altar with a lofty confidence, which the same etiquette exacted of the bridegroom. The parties were no sooner in their places, than the prelate commenced.

The marriage ceremony, according to the formula of the established church of Leaphigh, is a very solemn and imposing ceremony. The bridegroom is required to swear that he loves the bride and none but the bride; that he has made his choice solely on account of her merits, uninfluenced even by her beauty; and that he will so far command his inclinations as, on no account, ever to love another a jot. The bride, on her part, calls heaven and earth to witness, that she will do just what the bridegroom shall ask of her; that she will be his bondwoman, his slave, his solace and his delight; that she is quite certain no other monikin could make her happy, but, on the other hand, she is absolutely sure that any other monikin would be certain to make her miserable. When these pledges, oaths and asseverations were duly made and recorded, the Archbishop caused the happy pair to be wreathed together, by encircling them with his episcopal tail, and they were then pronounced monikin and monikina. I pass over the congratulations, which were quite in rule, to relate a short conversation I held with the Brigadier.

"Sir," said I, addressing that person, as soon as the prelate said 'amen,' "how is this? I have seen a certificate, myself, which showed that there was a just admeasurement of the fitness of this union, on the score of other considerations than those mentioned in the ceremony!"

"That certificate has no connexion with this ceremony."

"And yet this ceremony repudiates all the considerations enumerated in the certificate!"

"This ceremony has no connexion with that certificate."

"So it would seem; and yet both refer to the same solemn engagement!"

"Why, to tell you the truth, Sir John Goldencalf, we monikins (for in these particulars Leaphigh is Leaplow) have two distinct governing principles in all that we say or do, which may be divided into the theoretical and the practical—moral and immoral would not be inapposite—but, by the first we control all our interests, down as far as facts, when we immediately submit to the latter There may possibly be something inconsistent in appearance in such an arrangement; but then our most knowing ones say that it works well. No doubt among men, you get along without the embarrassment of so much contradiction."

I now advanced to pay my respects to the Countess of Chatterino, who stood supported by the Countess-dowager, a lady of great dignity and elegance of demeanor. The moment I appeared, the elaborate air of modesty vanished from the charming countenance of the bride, in a look of natural pleasure; and, turning to her new mother, she pointed me out as a man! The courteous old dowager gave me a very kind reception, inquiring if I had enough good things to eat, whether I was not much astonished at the multitude of strange sights I beheld in Leaphigh, said I ought to be much obliged to her son for consenting to bring me over, and invited me to come and see her, some fine morning.

I bowed my thanks, and then returned to join the Brigadier, with a view to seek an introduction to the Archbishop. Before I relate the particulars of my interview with that pious prelate, however, it may be well to say that this was the last I ever saw of any of the Chatterino set, as they retired from the presence immediately after the congratulations were ended. I heard, however, previously to leaving the region, which was within a month of the marriage, that the noble pair kept separate establishments, on account of some disagreement about an incompatibility of temper—or a young officer of the guards—I never knew exactly which; but as the estates suited each other so well, there is little doubt that, on the whole, the match was as happy as could be expected.

The Archbishop received me with a great deal of professional benevolence, the conversation dropping very naturally into a comparison of the respective religious systems of Great Britain and Leaphigh. He was delighted when he found we had an establishment; and I believe I was indebted to his knowledge of this fact, for his treating me more as an equal than he might otherwise have done, considering the difference in species. I was much relieved by this; for, at the commencement of the conversation, he had sounded me a little on doctrine, at which I am far from being expert, never having taken an interest in the church, and I thought he looked frowning at some of my answers; but, when he heard that we really had a national religion, he seemed to think all safe, nor did he once, after that, inquire whether we were pagans or presbyterians. But when I told him we had actually a hierarchy, I thought the good old prelate would have shaken my hand off, and beatified me on the spot!

"We shall meet in heaven some day!" he exclaimed, with holy delight; "men or monikins, it can make no great difference, after all. We shall meet in heaven; and that, too, in the upper mansions!"

The reader will suppose that, an alien, and otherwise unknown, I was much elated by this distinction. To go to heaven in company with the Archbishop of Leaphigh was in itself no small favor; but to be thus noticed by him at court was really enough to upset the philosophy of a stranger I was sorely afraid, all the while, he would descend to particulars, and that he might have found some essential points of difference to nip his new-born admiration. Had he asked me, for instance, how many *caudæ* our bishops wear, I should have been badgered; for, as near as I could recollect, their personal illustration was of another character. The venerable prelate, however, soon gave me his blessing, pressed me warmly to come to his palace before I sailed, promised to send some tracts by me to England, and then hurried away, as he said,'to sign a sentence of excommunication against an unruly presbyter, who had much disturbed the harmony of the church, of late, by an attempt to introduce a schism that he called "piety."

The Brigadier and myself discussed the subject of religion at some length, when the illustrious prelate had taken his leave. I was told that the monikin world was pretty nearly equally divided into two parts, the old and the new. The latter had remained uninhabited, until within a few generations, when certain monikins, who were too good to live in the old world, emigrated in a body, and set up for themselves in the new. This, the Brigadier admitted, was the Leaplow account of the matter; the inhabitants of the old countries, on the other hand, invariably maintaining that they had peopled the new countries by sending all those of their own communities there, who were not fit to stay at home. This little obscurity in the history of the new world, he considers of no great moment, as such trifling discrepancies must always depend on the character of the historian. Leaphigh was by no means the only country in the elder monikin region. There were among others, for instance, Leapup and Leapdown; Leapover and Leapthrough; Leaplong and Leapshort; Leapround and Leapunder. Each of these countries had a religious establishment, though Leaplow, being founded on a new social principle, had none. The Brigadier thought, himself, on the whole, that the chief consequences of the two systems were, that the countries which had establishments had a great reputation for possessing religion, and those that had no establishments were well enough off in the article itself, though but indifferently supplied on the score of reputation.

I inquired of the Brigadier if he did not think an establishment had the beneficial effect of sustaining truth, by suppressing heresies, limiting and curtailing prurient theological fancies, and otherwise setting limits to innovations. My friend did not absolutely agree with me in all these particulars; though he very frankly allowed that it had the effect of keeping *two* truths from falling out, by separating them. Thus, Leapup maintained one set of religious dogmas under its establishment, and Leapdown maintained their converse. By keeping these truths apart, no doubt, religious harmony was promoted, and the several ministers of the gospel were enabled to turn all their attention to the sins of the community, instead of allowing it to be diverted to the sins of each other, as was very apt to be the case when there was an antagonist interest to oppose.

Shortly after, the King and Queen gave us all our congés. Noah and myself got through the crowd without injury to our trains, and we separated in the court of the palace; he to go to his bed and dream of his trial on the morrow, and I to go home with Judge People's Friend and the Brigadier, who had invited me to finish the evening with a supper. I was left chatting with the last, whi e the first went into his closet to indite a dispatch to his government, relating to the events of the evening.

The Brigadier was rather caustic in his comments on the incidents of the drawing-room. A republican himself, he certainly did love to give royalty and nobility some occasional rubs; though I must do this worthy, upright monikin the justice to say, he was quite superior to that vulgar hostility which is apt to distinguish many of his caste and which is founded on a principle as simple as the fact that they cannot be kings and nobles themselves.

While we were chatting very pleasantly, quite at our ease, and in undress, as it were, the Brigadier in his bob, and I with my tail laid aside, Judge People's Friend rejoined us, with his dispatch open in his hand. He read aloud what he had written, to my great astonishment, for I had been accustomed to think diplomatic communications sacred. But the Judge observed, that in this case it was useless to affect secresy, for two very good reasons; firstly, because he had been obliged to employ a common Leaphigh scrivener to copy what he had written,—his government depending on a noble republican economy, which taught it that, if it did get into difficulties by the betrayal of its correspondence, it would still have the money that a clerk would cost, to help it out of the embarrassment; and, secondly, because he knew the government itself would print it, as soon as it arrived. For his part, he liked to have the publishing of his own works. Under these circumstances, I was even allowed to take a copy of the letter, of which I now furnish a fac-simile.

SIR,

The undersigned, Envoy Extraordinary and Minister Plenipotentiary of the North-Western Leaplow Confederate Union, has the honor to inform the Secretary of State, that our interests in this portion of the earth are in general, on the best possible footing; our national character is getting every day to be more and more elevated; our rights are more and more respected, and our flag is more and more whitening every sea. After this flattering and honorable account of the state of our general concerns, I hasten to communicate the following interesting particulars.

The treaty between our beloved North-Western Confederate Union and Leaphigh, has been dishonored in every one of its articles; nineteen Leaplow seamen have been forcibly impressed into a Leapthrough vessel of war; the King of Leapup has made an unequivocal demonstration with a very improper part of his person, at us; and the King of Leapover has caused seven of our ships to be seized and sold, and the money to be given to his mistress.

Sir, I congratulate you on this very flattering condition of our foreign relations; which can only be imputed to the glorious constitution of which we are the common servants, and to the just dread which the Leaplow name has so universally inspired in other nations.

The King has just had a drawing-room, in which I took great care to see that the honor of our beloved country should be faithfully attended to. My *cauda* was at least three inches longer than that of the representative of Leapup, the Minister most favored by Nature in this important particular; and I have the pleasure of adding, that her Majesty the Queen deigned to give me a very gracious smile. Of the sincerity of that smile there can be no earthly doubt, sir; for, though there is abundant evidence that she did apply certain unseemly words to our beloved country, lately, it would quite exceed the rules of diplomatic courtesy, and be unsustained by proof, were we to call in question her royal sincerity on this public occasion. Indeed, sir, at all the recent drawing-rooms I have received smiles of the most sincere and encouraging character, not only from the King, but from all his ministers, his first-cousin in particular; and I trust they will nave the most beneficial effects on the questions at issue between the Kingdom of Leaphigh and our beloved country. If they would now only do us justice in the very important affair of the long-standing and long-neglected redress, which we have been seeking in vain at their hands, for the last seventy-two years, I should say that our relations were on the best possible footing.

Sir, I congratulate you on the profound respect with which the Leaplow name is treated, in the most distant quarters of the earth, and on the benign influence this fortunate circumstance is likely to exercise on all our important interests.

I see but little probability of effecting the object of my special mission, but the utmost credit is to be attached to the sincerity of the smiles of the King and Queen, and of all the royal family.

In a late conversation with his Majesty, he inquired in the kindest manner after the health of the Great Sachem, [this is the title of the head of the Leaplow government,] and observed that our growth and prosperity put all other nations to shame; and that we might, on all occasions, depend on his most profound respect and perpetual friendship. In short, sir, all nations, far and near, desire our alliance, are anxious to open new sources of commerce, and entertain for us the profoundest respect, and the most inviolable esteem.—You can tell the Great Sachem that this feeling is surprisingly augmented under his administration, and that it has at least quadrupled during my mission. If Leaphigh would only respect its treaties, Leapthrough would cease taking our seamen, Leapup have greater deference for the usages of good society, and the King of Leapover would seize no more of our ships to supply his mistress with pocket-money, our foreign relations might be considered to be without spot. As it is, sir, they are far better off than I could have expected, or indeed, had ever hoped to see them; and of one thing you may be diplomatically certain, that we are universally respected, and tha the Leaplow name is never mentioned without all in company rising and waving their *caudæ*.

(Signed.) JUDAS PEOPLE'S FRIEND.

Hon. ——— ———, &c

P. S. [Private.]

DEAR SIR,—If you publish this dispatch, omit the part where the difficulties are *repeated*. I beg you will see that my name is put in with those of the other patriots, against the periodical rotation of the little wheel; as I shall certainly be obliged to return home soon, having consumed all my means. Indeed, the expense of maintaining a tail, of which our people have no notion, is so very great, that I think none of our missions should exceed a week in duration.

I would especially advise that the message should dilate on the subject of the high standing of the Leaplow character, in foreign nations; for, to be frank with you, facts require that this statement should be made as often as possible.

When this letter was read, the conversation reverted to religion. The Brigadier explained that the law of Leaphigh had various peculiarities on this subject, that I do not remember to have heard of before. Thus, a monikin could not be born, without paying something to the church, a practice which early initiated him into his duties towards that important branch of the public welfare; and, even when he died, he left a fee behind him, for the parson, as an admonition to those who still existed in the flesh, not to forget their obligations. He added that this sacred interest was, in short, so rigidly protected, that, whenever a monikin refused to be plucked for a new clerical or episcopal mantle, there was a method of fleecing him, by the application of red-hot iron rods, which generally singed so much of his skin, that he was commonly willing, in the end, to let the hair-proctors pick and choose, at pleasure.

I confess I was indignant at this picture, and did not hesitate to stigmatize the practice as barbarous.

"Your indignation is very natural, Sir John, and is just what a stranger would be likely to feel when he found mercy, and charity, and brotherly love, and virtue, and, above all, humility, made the stalking-horses of pride, selfishness, and avarice. But this is the way with us monikins; no doubt, men manage better."

CHAPTER XX.

A very common case—or a great deal of law, and very little justice. Heads and tails—with the dangers of each.

I WAS early with Noah on the following morning. The poor fellow, when it is remembered that he was about to be tried for a capital offence, in a foreign country, under novel institutions, and before a jury of a different species, manifested a surprising degree of fortitude. Still, the love of life was strong within him, as was apparent by the way in which he opened the discourse.

"Did you observe how the wind was, this morning, Sir John, as you came in?" the straight-forward sealer inquired, with a peculiar interest.

"It is a pleasant gale from the southward."

"Right off shore! If one knew where all them blackguards of Rear Admirals and Post Captains were to be found—I don't think, Sir John, that you would care much about paying those fifty thousand promises?"

"My recognizes?—Not in the least, my dear friend, were it not for our honor. It would scarcely be creditable for the Walrus to sail, however, eaving an unsettled account of her Captain's behind us. What would they say at Stunnin'tun—what would your own consort think of an act so unmanly?"

"Why, at Stunnin'tun, we think him the smartest who gets the easiest out of any difficulty; and I don't well see why Miss Poke should know it,—or, if she did, why she should think the worse of her husband, for saving his life."

"Away with these unworthy thoughts, and brace yourself to meet the trial. We shall, at least, get some insight into the Leaphigh jurisprudence.—Come, I see you are already dressed for the occasion; let us be as prompt as duellists."

Noah made up his mind to submit with dignity; although he lingered in the great square, in order to study the clouds, in a way to show he might have settled the whole affair with the fore-topsail, had he known where to find his crew. Fortunately for the reputations of all concerned, however, he did not; and, discarding everything like apprehension from his countenance, the sturdy mariner entered the Old Bailey with the tread of a man, and the firmness of innocence. I ought to have said sooner, that we had received notice early in the morning, that the proceedings had been taken from before the pages, on appeal, and that a new *venue* had been laid in the High Criminal Court of Leaphigh.

Brigadier Downright met us at the door; where also a dozen, grave, greasy-looking counsellors gathered about us, in a way to show that they were ready to volunteer in behalf of the stranger, on receiving no more than the customary fee. But I had determined to defend Noah myself, (the court consenting,) for I had forebodings that our safety would depend more on an appeal to the rights of hospitality, than on any legal defence it was in our power to offer. As the Brigadier kindly volunteered to aid me for nothing, I thought proper not to refuse his services, however.

I pass over the appearance of the court, the empannelling of the jury, and the arraignment; for, in matters of mere legal *forms,* there is no great difference between civilized countries, all of them wearing the same semblance of justice. The first indictment, for unhappily there were two, charged Noah with having committed an assault, with malice prepense, on the King's dignity, with "sticks, daggers, muskets, blunderbusses, air-guns, and other unlawful weapons, *more especially with the tongue,* in that he had accused his Majesty, face to face, with having a memory, &c. &c." The other indictment, repeating the formula of the first, charged the honest sealer with feloniously accusing her Majesty the Queen, "in defiance of the law, to the injury of good morals and the peace of society, with having no memory, &c. &c." To both these charges, the plea of "Not Guilty," was entered as fast as possible, in behalf of our client.

I ought to have said before, that both Brigadier Downright and myself had applied to be admitted of counsel for the accused, under an ancient law of Leaphigh, as next of kin; I as a fellow human being, and the Brigadier by adoption.

The preliminary forms observed, the Attorney-General was about to go into proof, in behalf of the crown, when my brother Downright arose and said that he intended to save the precious time of the court, by admitting the facts; and that it was intended to rest the defence altogether on the law of the case. He presumed that the jury was the judge of the law as well as of the facts, according to the rule of Leaplow, and that "he and his brother Goldencalf were quite prepared to show that the law was altogether with us, in this affair." The court received the admission, and the facts were submitted to the jury, by consent, as proven; although the Chief-Justice took occasion to remark, Longbeard dissenting, that, while the jury were certainly judges of the law, in one sense, yet there was another sense in which they were not judges of the law. The dissent of Baron Longbeard went to maintain that while the jury were the judges of the law in the "another sense" mentioned, they were not judges of the law in the "one sense" named. This difficulty disposed of, Mr. Attorney-General arose and opened for the crown.

I soon found that we had one of a very comprehensive and philosophical turn of mind against us, in the advocate of the other side. He commenced his argument by a vigorous and lucid sketch of the condition of the world previously to the subdivisions of its different inhabitants into nations, and tribes, and clans, while in the human or chrysalis condition. From this statement, he deduced the regular gradations by which men became separated into communities, and subjected to the laws of civilization, or what is called society. Having proceeded thus far, he touched lightly on the different phases that the institutions of men had presented, and descended gradually and consecutively to the fundamental principles of the social compact, as they were known to exist among monikins. After a few general observations that properly belonged to the subject, he came to speak of those portions of the elementary principles of society that are connected with the rights of the sovereign. These he divided into the rights of the King's prerogative, the rights of the King's person, and the rights of the King's conscience. Here he again generalized a little, and in a very happy manner, so well, indeed, as to leave all his hearers in doubt as to what he would next be at; when, by a fierce logical swoop, he descended suddenly on the latter of the King's rights, as the one that was most connected with the subject.

He triumphantly showed that the branch of the royal immunities that was chiefly affected by the offence of the prisoner at the bar, was very clearly connected with the rights of the King's conscience. "The attributes of royalty," observed the sagacious advocate, "are not to be estimated in the same manner as the attributes of the subject. In the sacred person of the King are centred many, if not most, of the interesting privileges of monikinism. That royal personage, in a political sense, can do no wrong; official infallibility is the consequence. Such a being has no occasion for the ordinary faculties of the monikin condition. Of what use, for instance, is a judgment, or a conscience, to a functionary who can do no wrong? The law, in order to relieve one on whose shoulders was imposed the burthen of the state, had, consequently, placed the latter especially in the keeping of another. His Majesty's first-cousin is the keeper of his conscience, as is known throughout the realm of Leaphigh. A memory is the faculty of the least account to a personage who has no conscience; and, while it is not contended that the sovereign is relieved from the possession of his memory by any positive statute law, or direct constitutional provision, it follows, by unavoidable implication, and by all legitimate construction, that, having no occasion to possess such a faculty, it is the legal presumption he is altogether without it."

"That simplicity, lucidity and distinctness, my Lords," continued Mr. Attorney-General, "which are necessary to every well-ordered mind, would be impaired, in the case of his Majesty, were his intellectual faculties unnecessarily crowded in this useless manner, and the state would be the sufferer. My Lords, the King reigns, but he does not govern. This is a fundamental principle of the constitution; nay, it is more—it is the palladium of our liberties! My Lords, it is an easy matter to reign in Leaphigh. It requires no more than the rights of primogeniture, sufficient discretion to understand the distinction between reigning and governing, and a political moderation that is unlikely to derange the balance of the state. But it is quite a different thing to govern. His Majesty is required to govern nothing, the slight interests just mentioned excepted; no, not even himself. The case is far otherwise with his first cousin. This high functionary is charged with the important trust of governing. It had been found, in the early ages of the monarchy, that one conscience, or indeed one set of faculties generally, scarcely sufficed for him whose duty it was both to reign and to govern. We all know, my Lords, how insufficient for our personal objects are our own private faculties; how difficult we find it to restrain even ourselves, assisted merely by our own judgments, consciences and memories; and in this fact, do we perceive the great importance of investing him who governs others, with an additional set of these grave faculties. Under a due impression of the exigency of such a state of things, the common law—not statute law, my Lords, which is apt to be tainted with the imperfections of monikin reason in its isolated or individual state, usually bearing the impress of the single *cauda* from which it emanated; but the common law, the known receptacle of all the common sense of the nation—in such a state of things, then, has the common law long since decreed that his Majesty's first-cousin should be the keeper of his Majesty's conscience; and, by necessary legal implication, endowed with his Majesty's judgment, his Majesty's reason, and, finally, his Majesty's *memory*.

"My Lords, this is the legal presumption. It would, in addition, be easy for me to show, in a thousand facts, that not only the sovereign of Leaphigh, but most other sovereigns, are and ever have been, destitute of the faculty of a memory. It might be said to be incompatible with the royal condition to be possessed of this obtrusive faculty. Were a prince endowed with a memory, he might lose sight of his high estate, in the recollection that he was born, and that he is destined, like another, to die; he might be troubled with visions of the past; nay, the consciousness of his very dignity might be unsettled and weakened by a vivid view of the origin of his royal race. Promises, obligations, attachments, duties, principles, and even debts, might interfere with the due discharge of his sacred trusts, were the sovereign invested with a memory; and it has, therefore, been decided, from time immemorial, that his Majesty is utterly without the properties of reason, judgment, and memory, as a legitimate inference from his being destitute of a conscience."

Mr. Attorney-General now directed the attention of the court and jury to a statute of the 3d of Firstborn 6th, by which it was enacted that any person attributing to his Majesty the possession of any faculty, with felonious intent, that might endanger the tranquillity of the state, should suffer decaudisation, without benefit of clergy. Here he rested the case on behalf of the crown.

There was a solemn pause, after the speaker had resumed his seat. His argument, logic, and above all his good sense and undeniable law, made a very sensible impression; and I had occasion to observe that Noah began to chew tobacco ravenously. After a decent interval, however, Brigadier Downright, who, it would seem, in spite of his military appellation, was neither more nor less than a practising attorney and counsellor in the city of Bivouac, the commercial capital of the republic of Leaplow, arose and claimed a right to be heard in reply. The court now took it into its head to start the objection, for the first time, that the advocate had not been duly qualified to plead, or to argue, at their bar. My brother Downright instantly referred their Lordships to the law of adoption, and to that provision of the criminal code which permitted the accused to be heard by his next of kin.

"Prisoner at the bar," said the Chief-Justice, "you hear the statement of counsel. Is it your desire to commit the management of your defence to your next of kin?"

"To anybody, your honors, if the court please," returned Noah, furiously masticating his beloved weed; "to anybody who will do it well, my honorables, and do it cheap."

"And do you adopt, under the provisions of the statute in such cases made and provided, Aaron Downright as one of your next of kin, and if so, in what capacity?"

"I do—I do—my Lords and your honors—I do, body and soul—if you please, I adopt the Brigadier as my father; and my fellow human being, and tried friend, Sir John Goldencalf, here, I adopt him as my mother."

The court now formally assenting, the facts were entered of record, and my brother Downright was requested to proceed with the defence.

The counsel for the prisoner, like *Dandin*, in Racine's comedy of *les Plaideurs*, was disposed to pass over the deluge, and to plunge instantly into the core of his subject. He commenced with a review of the royal prerogatives, and with a definition of the words "to reign." Referring to the dictionary of the academy, he showed triumphantly, that to reign, was no other than to "govern as a sovereign;" while to govern, in the familiar signification, was no more than to govern in the name of a prince, or as a deputy. Having successfully established this point, he laid down the position, that the greater might contain the less, but that the less could not possibly contain the greater. That the right to reign, or to govern, in the generic signification of the term, must include all the lawful attributes of him who only governed, in the secondary signification; and that, consequently, the King not only reigned, but governed. He then proceeded to show that a memory was indispensable to him who governed, since, without one, he could neither recollect the laws, make a suitable disposition of rewards and punishments, nor, in fact, do any other intelligent or necessary act. Again, it was contended that by the law of the land the King's conscience was in the keeping of his first-cousin; now, in order that the King's conscience should be in such keeping, it was clear that he must *have* a conscience, since a nonentity could not be in keeping, or even put in commission; and, having a conscience, it followed, *ex necessitate rei*, that he must have the attributes of a conscience, of which memory formed one of the most essential features. Conscience was defined to be "the faculty by which we judge of the goodness or wickedness of our own actions." [See Johnson's Dictionary, page 163., letter C. London edition. Rivington, publisher.] Now, in what manner can one judge of the goodness or wickedness of his acts, or of those of any other person, if he knows nothing about them?—and how can he know anything of the past, unless endowed with the faculty of a memory?

Again; it was a political corollary from the institutions of Leaphigh, that the King could do no wrong——

"I beg your pardon, my brother Downright," interrupted the Chief Justice, "it is not a corollary, but a proposition—and one, too, that is held to be demonstrated. It is the paramount law of the land."

"I thank you, my Lord," continued the Brigadier, "as your Lordship's high authority makes my case so much the stronger. It is, then, settled law, gentlemonikins of the jury, that the Sovereign of this realm can do no wrong. It is also settled law, —their Lordships will correct me, if I misstate,— it is also settled law, that the Sovereign is the fountain of honor, that he can make war and peace, that he administers justice, sees the laws executed——"

"I beg your pardon, again, brother Downright," interrupted the Chief Justice. "This is not the law, but the prerogative. It is the King's prerogative to be and do all this, but it is very far from being law."

"Am I to understand, my Lord, that the court makes a distinction between that which is prerogative, and that which is law?"

"Beyond a doubt, brother Downright! If all that is prerogative, was also law, we could not get on an hour."

"Prerogative, if your Lordship pleases, or *pre rogativa*, is defined to be 'an exclusive or peculiar privilege.' [Johnson. Letter P. page 139., fifth clause from bottom. Edition as aforesaid.—Speaking slow, in order to enable Baron Longbeard to make his notes.] Now, an *exclusive privilege*, I humbly urge, must supersede all enactments, and——"

"Not at all, sir—not at all, sir," put in my Lord Chief Justice, dogmatically,—looking out of the window at the clouds, in a way to show that his mind was quite made up. "Not at all, good sir. The King has his prerogatives, beyond a question; and they are sacred;—a part of the constitution. They are, moreover, exclusive and peculiar, as stated by Johnson; but their exclusion and peculiarity are not to be construed in the vulgar acceptations. In treating of the vast interests of a state, the mind must take a wide range; and I hold, brother Longbeard, there is no principle more settled than the fact, that *prerogativa* is one thing, and *lex*, or the law, another." The Baron bowed assent. "By exclusion, in this case, is meant that the prerogative touches only his Majesty. The prerogative is exclusively his property, and he may do what he pleases with it; but the law is made for the nation, and is altogether a different matter. Again: by peculiar, is clearly meant peculiarity, or that this case is analogous to no other, and must be reasoned on by the aid of a peculiar logic. No, sir,—the King can make peace and war, it is true, under his prerogative; but then his conscience is hard and fast in the keeping of another, who alone can perform all legal acts."

"But, my Lord, justice, though administered by others, is still administered in the King's name."

"No doubt, in his name:—this is a part of the *peculiar* privilege. War is made in his Majesty's name, too,—so is peace. What is war? It is the personal conflicts between bodies of men of different nations. Does his Majesty engage in these conflicts? Certainly not. The war is maintained by taxes.—does his Majesty pay them?—No. Thus we see that while the war is constitutionally the King's, it is practically the people's. It follows, as a corollary,—since you quote corollaries, brother Downright,—that there are *two* wars—or the war of the prerogative, and the war of the fact. Now, the prerogative is a constitutional principle—a very sacred one, certainly;—but a fact is a thing that comes home to every monikin's fire-side; and, therefore, the courts have decided, ever since the reign of Timid II., or ever since they dared, that the prerogative was one thing, and the law another."

My brother Downright seemed a good deal perplexed by the distinctions of the court, and he concluded much sooner than he otherwise would have done; summing up the whole of his arguments, by showing, or attempting to show, that if the King had even these *peculiar* privileges, and nothing else, that he must be supposed to have a memory.

The court now called upon the Attorney-General to reply; but that person appeared to think his case strong enough as it was; and the matter, by agreement, was submitted to the jury, after a short charge from the bench.

"You are not to suffer your intellects to be confused, gentlemonikins, by the argument of the prisoner's counsel," concluded the Chief Justice. "He has done his duty, and it remains for you to be equally conscientious. You are, in this case, the judges of the law and the fact; but it is a part of my functions to inform you what they both are. By the law, the King is supposed to have no faculties. The inference drawn by counsel, that not being capable of erring, the King must have the highest possible moral attributes, and consequently a memory, is unsound. The constitution says his Majesty *can* do no wrong. This inability may proceed from a variety of causes. If he can do *nothing* for instance, he can do no wrong. The constitution does not say that the Sovereign *will* do no wrong—but, that he *can* do no wrong. Now, gentlemonikins, when a thing *cannot* be done, it becomes impossible; and it is, of course, beyond the reach of argument. It is of no moment whether a person has a memory, if he cannot use it, and, in such a case, the legal presumption is, that he is without a memory; for, otherwise, Nature, who is ever wise and beneficent, would be throwing away her gifts.

"Gentlemonikins, I have already said you are the judges, in this case, of both the law and the fact. The fate of the prisoner is in your hands.—God forbid that it should be, in any manner, influenced by me; but this is an offence against the King's dignity, and the security of the realm; the law is against the prisoner, the facts are all against the prisoner, and I do not doubt that your verdict will be the spontaneous decision of your own excellent judgments, and of such a nature as will prevent the necessity of our ordering a new trial."

The jurors put their tails together, and in less than a minute, their foremonikin rendered a verdict of guilty. Noah sighed, and took a fresh supply of tobacco.

The case of the Queen was immediately opened by her Majesty's Attorney-General; the prisoner having been previously arraigned, and a plea entered of not guilty.

The Queen's advocate made a bitter attack on the *animus* of the unfortunate prisoner. He described her Majesty as a paragon of excellencies; as the depository of all the monikina virtues, and the model of her sex. "If she, who was so justly celebrated for the gifts of charity, meekness, religion, justice, and submission to feminine duties, had no memory, he asked leave to demand, in the name of God, who had? Without a memory, in what manner was this illustrious personage to recall her duties to her royal consort, her duties to her royal offspring, her duties to her royal self? Memory was peculiarly a royal attribute; and without its possession no one could properly be deemed of high and ancient lineage. Memory referred to the past, and the consideration due to royalty was scarcely ever a present consideration, but a consideration connected with the past. We venerated the past. Time was divided into the past, present and future. The past was invariably a monarchical interest—the present was claimed by republicans—the future belonged to fate. If it were decided that the Queen had no memory, we should strike a blow at royalty. It was by memory, as connected with the public archives, that the King derived his title to his throne; it was to memory, which recalled the deeds of his ancestors, that he became entitled to our most profound respect."

In this manner did the Queen's Attorney-General speak for about an hour, when he gave way to the counsel for the prisoner. But, to my great surprise, for I knew that this accusation was much the gravest of the two, since the head of Noah would be the price of conviction, my brother Downright, instead of making a very ingenious reply, as I had fully anticipated, merely said a few words, in which he expressed so firm a confidence in the acquittal of his client, as to appear to think a further defence altogether unnecessary. He had no sooner seated himself, than I expressed a strong dissatisfaction with this course, and avowed an intention to make an effort in behalf of my poor friend, myself.

"Keep silence, Sir John," whispered my brother Downright; "the advocate who makes many unsuccessful applications gets to be disrespected. I charge myself with the care of the Lord High Admiral's interests; at the proper time, they shall be duly attended to."

Having the profoundest respect for the Brigadier's legal attainments, and no great confidence in my own, I was fain to submit. In the mean time the business of the court proceeded; and the jury, having received a short charge from the bench, which was quite as impartial as a positive injunction to convict could very well be, again rendered the verdict of "Guilty."

In Leaphigh, although it is deemed indecent to wear clothes, it is also esteemed exceedingly decorous for certain high functionaries to adorn their persons with suitable badges of their official rank. We have already had an account of the hierarchy of tails, and a general description of the mantle composed of tenth-hairs; but I had forgotten to say that both my Lord Chief-Justice and Baron Longbeard had tail-cases made of the skins of deceased monikins, which gave the appearance of greater development to their intellectual organs, and most probably had some influence in the way of coddling their brains, which required great care and attention on account of incessant use. They now drew over these tail-cases a sort of box-coat of a very bloodthirsty color, which, we were given to understand, was a sign that they were in earnest, and about to pronounce sentence; justice in Leaphigh being of singularly bloodthirsty habits.

"Prisoner at the bar," the Chief-Justice began, in a voice of reproof, "you have heard the decision of your peers. You have been arraigned and tried on the heinous charge of having accused the sovereign of this realm of being in possession of the faculty called "a memory," thereby endangering the peace of society, unsettling the social relations, and setting a dangerous example of insubordination and of contempt of the laws. Of this crime, after a singularly patient and impartial hearing, you have been found guilty. The law allows the court no discretion in the case. It is my duty to pass sentence forthwith; and I now solemnly ask you, if you have anything to say why sentence of decaudisation should not be pronounced against you"—Here the Chief-Justice took just time enough to gape, and then proceeded—"You are right in throwing yourself altogether on the mercy of the court, which better knows what is fittest for you, than you can possibly know for yourself. You will be taken, Noah Poke, or No. 1, sea-water-color, forthwith, to the centre of the public square, between the hours of sunrise and sunset of this day, where your *cauda* will be cut off; and after it has been divided into four parts, a part will be exposed towards each of the cardinal points of the compass; and the brush thereof being consumed by fire, the ashes will be thrown into your face, and this without benefit of clergy. And may the Lord have mercy on your soul!"

"Noah Poke, or No. 1, sea-water-color," put in Baron Longbeard, without giving the culprit breathing-time, "you have been indicted, tried, and found guilty of the enormous crime of charging the Queen-consort of this realm of being wanting in the ordinary, important, and every-day faculty of a memory. Have you anything to say why sentence should not be forthwith passed against you?—No—I am sure you are very right in throwing yourself altogether on the mercy of the court, which is quite disposed to show you all that is in its power, which happens, in this case, to be none at all. I need not dwell on the gravity of your offence. If the law should allow that the Queen has no memory other females might put in claims to the same privilege, and society would become a chaos. Marriage vows, duties, affections, and all our nearest and dearest interests would be unhinged, and this pleasant state of being would degenerate into a moral, or rather an immoral, pandemonium. Keeping in view these all-important considerations, and more especially the imperativeness of the law, which does not admit of discretion, the court sentences you to be carried hence, without delay, to the centre of the great square, where your head will be severed from your body by the public executioner, without benefit of clergy; after which, your remains are to be consigned to the public hospitals for the purposes of dissection."

The words were scarcely out of Baron Longbeard's mouth, before both the Attorneys-General started up, to move the court in behalf of the separate dignities of their respective principals. Mr. Attorney-General of the crown prayed the court so far to amend its sentence, as to give precedency to the punishment on account of the offence against the King; and Mr. Attorney-General for the Queen, to pray the court it would not be so far forgetful of her Majesty's rights and dignity, as to establish a precedent so destructive of both. I caught a glimpse of hope glancing about the eyes of my brother Downright, who, waiting just long enough to let the two advocates warm themselves over these points of law, arose and moved the court for a stay of execution, on the plea that neither sentence was legal; that delivered by my Lord Chief-Justice containing a contradiction, inasmuch as it ordered the decaudisation to take place between *the hours of sunrise and sunset*, and also *forthwith*: and that delivered by Baron Longbeard, on account of its ordering the body to be given up to dissection, contrary to the law, which merely made that provision in the case of condemned *monikins*, the prisoner at the bar being entirely of another species.

The court deemed all these objections serious, but decided on its own incompetency to take cognizance of them. It was a question for the twelve Judges, who were now on the point of assembling, and to whom they referred the whole affair on appeal. In the mean time, justice could not be stayed. The prisoner must be carried out into the square, and matters must proceed; but, should either of the points be finally determined in his favor, he could have the benefit of it, so far as circumstances would then allow. Hereupon, the court rose, and the judges, counsel and clerks, repaired in a body to the hall of the twelve Judges.

CHAPTER XXI.

Better and better—More law and more justice—Tails and heads; the importance of keeping each in its proper place

Noah was incontinently transferred to the place of execution, where I promised to meet him in time to receive his parting sigh, curiosity inducing me first to learn the issue on the appeal. The Brigadier told me in confidence, as we went to the other hall, that the affair was now getting to be one of great interest; that hitherto it had been mere boys' play, but it would in future require counsel of great reading and research to handle the arguments, and that he flattered himself there was a good occasion likely to present itself, for him to show what monikin reason really was.

The whole of the twelve wore tail-cases, and altogether they presented a formidable array of intellectual development. As the cause of Noah was admitted to be one of more than common urgency, after hearing only three or four other short applications on behalf of the crown, whose rights always have precedence on such occasions, the Attorney-General of the King was desired to open his case.

The learned counsel spoke, in anticipation, to the objections of both his adversaries, beginning with those of my brother Downright. *Forthwith,* he contended, might be at any period of the twenty-four hours, according to the actual time of using the term. Thus, *forthwith* of a morning, would mean in the morning; *forthwith* at noon, would mean at noon; and so on to the close of the legal day. Moreover, in a legal signification, *forthwith* must mean between sunrise and sunset, the statute commanding that all executions shall take place by the light of the sun, and consequently the two terms ratified and confirmed each other, instead of conveying a contradiction, or of neutralizing each other, as would most probably be contended by the opposite counsel.

To all this my brother Downright, as is usual on such occasions, objected pretty much the converse. He maintained that *all* light proceeded from the sun; and that the statute, therefore, could only mean that there should be no executions during eclipses, a period when the whole monikin race ought to be occupied in adoration. *Forthwith,* moreover, did not necessarily mean *forthwith,* for forthwith meant immediately; and "between sunrise and sunset" meant between sunrise and sunset; which might be immediately, or might not.

On this point the twelve Judges decided, firstly,

that *forthwith* did not mean *forthwith;* secondly that forthwith did mean forthwith; thirdly, that forthwith had two legal meanings; fourthly, that it was illegal to apply one of these legal meanings to a wrong legal purpose; and, fifthly, that the objection was of no avail, as respected the case of No. 1, sea-water-color. Ordered, therefore, that the criminal lose his tail *forthwith.*

The objection to the other sentence met with no better fate. Men and monikins did not differ more than some men differed from other men, or some monikins differed from other monikins. Ordered, that the sentence be confirmed with costs I thought this decision the soundest of the two; for I had often had occasion to observe, that there were very startling points of resemblance between monkeys and our own species.

The contest now commenced between the two Attorneys-General in earnest; and, as the point at issue was a question of mere rank, it excited a lively—I may say an engrossing—interest in all the hearers. It was settled, however, after a vigorous discussion, in favor of the King, whose royal dignity the twelve Judges were unanimously of opinion was entitled to precedency over that of the Queen. To my great surprise, my brother Downright volunteered an argument on this intricate point, making an exceedingly clever speech in favor of the King's dignity, as was admitted by every one who heard it. It rested chiefly on the point that the ashes of the tail were, by the sentence, to be thrown into the culprit's face. It is true this might be done physically after decapitation, but it could not be done morally. This part of the punishment was designed for a moral effect; and to produce that effect, consciousness and shame were both necessary Therefore, the moral act of throwing the ashes into the face of the criminal could only be done while he was living, and capable of being ashamed.

Meditation, Chief-Justice, delivered the opinion of the bench. It contained the usual amount of legal ingenuity and logic, was esteemed as very eloquent in that part which touched on the sacred and inviolable character of the royal prerogatives (*prerogativæ*, as he termed them,) and was so lucid in pointing out the general inferiority of the Queen-consort, that I felt happy her Majesty was not present to hear herself and sex undervalued. As might have been expected, it allowed great weight to the distinction taken by the Brigadier The decision was in the following words, viz.—"Rex et Regina versus No. 1, sea-water-color: Ordered, that the officers of justice shall proceed forthwith to decaudisate the defendant before they decapitate him; provided he has not been forthwith decapitated before he can be decaudisated."

The moment this mandamus was put into the hands of the proper officer, Brigadier Downright caught me by the knee, and led me out of the hall of justice, as if both our lives depended on our expedition. I was about to reproach him for having volunteered to aid the King's Attorney-General, when, seizing me by the root of the tail, for the want of a button-hole, he said, with evident satisfaction,—

"Affairs go on swimmingly, my dear Sir John! I do not remember to have been employed, for some years, in a more interesting litigation. Now this cause, which, no doubt, you think is drawing to a close, has just reached its pivot, or turning point; and I see every prospect of extricating our client with great credit to myself."

"How! my brother Downright!" I interrupted; "the accused is finally sentenced, if not actually executed!"

"Not so fast, my good Sir John—not so fast, by any means. Nothing is final in law, while there is a farthing to meet the costs, or the criminal can yet gasp. I hold our case to be in an excellent way; much better than I have deemed it at any time since the accused was arraigned."

Surprise left me no other power than that which was necessary to demand an explanation.

"All depends on the single fact, dear sir," continued my brother Downright, "whether the head is still on the body of the accused or not. Do you proceed, as fast as possible, to the place of execution; and, should our client still have a head, keep up his spirits by a proper religious discourse, always preparing him for the worst, for this is no more than wisdom; but, the instant his tail is separated from his body, run hither as fast as you can, to apprize me of the fact. I ask but two things of you—speed in coming with the news, and perfect certainty that the tail is not yet attached to the rest of the frame, by even a hair.—A hair often turns the scales of justice!"

"The case seems desperate—would it not be as well for me to run down to the palace, at once; demand an audience of their Majesties, throw myself on my knees before the royal pair, and implore a pardon?"

"Your project is impracticable, for three sufficient reasons: firstly, there is not time; secondly, you would not be admitted without a special appointment; thirdly, there is neither a King nor a Queen."

"No King in Leaphigh!"

"I have said it."

"Explain yourself, brother Downright, or I shall be obliged to refute what you say, by the evidence of my own senses."

"Your senses will prove to be false witnesses then. Formerly there *was* a King in Leaphigh·

and one who governed, as well as reigned. But the nobles and grandees of the country, deeming it indecent to trouble His Majesty with affairs of state any longer, took upon themselves all the trouble of governing, leaving to the sovereign the sole duty of reigning. This was done in a way to save his feelings, under the pretence of setting up a barrier to the physical force and abuses of the mass. After a time, it was found inconvenient and expensive to feed and otherwise support the royal family, and all its members were privately shipped to a distant region, which had not yet got to be so far advanced in civilization, as to know how to keep up a monarchy without a monarch."

"And does Leaphigh succeed in effecting this prodigy?"

"Wonderfully well. By means of decapitations and decaudisations enough, even greater exploits may be performed."

"But am I to understand literally, brother Downright, there is no such thing as a monarch in this country?"

"Literally."

"And the presentations?"

"Are like these trials, to maintain the monarchy."

"And the crimson curtains?—"

"Conceal empty seats."

"Why not, then, dispense with so much costly representation?"

"In what way could the grandees cry out that the throne is in danger, if there were no throne? It is one thing to have no monarch, and another to have no throne. But all this time our client is in great jeopardy. Hasten, therefore, and be particular to act as I have just instructed you."

I stopped to hear no more, but in a minute was flying towards the centre of the square. It was easy enough to perceive the tail of my friend waving over the crowd; but grief and apprehension had already rendered his countenance so rueful, that, at the first glance, I did not recognize his head. He was, however, still in the body; for, luckily for himself, and more especially for the success of his principal counsel, the gravity of his crimes had rendered unusual preparations necessary for the execution. As the mandate of the court had not yet arrived—justice being as prompt in Leaphigh as her ministers are dilatory—two blocks were prepared, and the culprit was about to get down on his hands and knees between them, just as I forced my way through the crowd to his side.

"Ah! Sir John, this is an awful predicament!" exclaimed the rebuked Noah; "a ra'ally awful situation for a human Christian to have his enemies lying athwart both bows and starn!"

"While there is life there is hope; but it is always best to be prepared for the worst—he who is thus prepared never can meet with a disagreeable surprise. Messrs. Executioners,"—for there were two, that of the King and that of the Queen, or one at each end of the unhappy criminal—"Messrs. Executioners, I pray you to give the culprit a moment to arrange his thoughts, and to communicate his last requests in behalf of his distant family and friends!"

To this reasonable petition neither of the high functionaries of the law made any objection, although both insisted if they did not forthwith bring the culprit to the last stages of preparation, they might lose their places. They did not see, however but a man might pause for a moment on the brink of the grave. It would seem that there had been a little misunderstanding between the executioners themselves on the point of precedency, which had been one cause of the delay, and which had been disposed of by an arrangement that both should operate at the same instant. Noah was now brought down to his hands and knees, "moored head and starn," as that unfeeling blackguard Bob, who was in the crowd, expressed it, between the two blocks, his neck lying on one and his tail on the other While in this edifying attitude, I was permitted to address him.

"It may be well to bethink you of your soul, my dear Captain," I said; "for, to speak truth, these axes have a very prompt and sanguinary appearance."

"I know it, Sir John, I know it; and, not to mislead you, I will own that I have been repenting with all my might, ever since that first vardict That affair of the Lord High Admiral, in particular, has given me a good deal of consarn; and I now humbly ask your pardon for being led away by such a miserable deception, which is all owing to that riptyle Dr. Reasono, who I hope will yet meet with his desarts. I forgive everybody, and hope everybody will forgive me. As for Miss Poke, it will be a hard case; for she is altogether past expecting another consort, and she must be satisfied to be a relic the rest of her days."

"Repentance, repentance, my dear Noah—repentance is the one thing needful, for a man in your extremity."

"I do—I do, Sir John, body and soul—I repent, from the bottom of my heart, ever having come on this v'y'ge,—nay, I don't know but I repent ever having come outside of Montauk Point. I might, at this moment, have been a schoolmaster or a tavern-keeper in Stunin'tun; and they are both good wholesome births, particularly the last. Lord love you! Sir John, if repentance would do any good, I should be pardoned on the spot."

Here Noah caught a glimpse of Bob grinning in the crowd, and he asked of the executioners, as a last favor, that they would have the boy brought near, that he might take an affectionate leave of him. This reasonable request was complied with, in despite of poor Bob's struggles; and the youngster had quite as good reasons for hearty repentance as the culprit himself. Just at this trying moment, the mandate for the order of the punishments arrived, and the officials seriously declared that the condemned must prepare to meet his fate.

The unflinching manner in which Captain Poke submitted to the mortal process of decaudisation, extracted plaudits from, and awakened sympathy in, every monikin present. Having satisfied myself that the tail was actually separated from the body, I ran, as fast as legs could carry me, towards the hall of the twelve Judges. My brother Downright, who was impatiently expecting my appearance, instantly arose and moved the bench to issue a mandamus for a stay of execution, in the case of—"Regina versus Noah Poke, or No. 1, sea-water-color. By the statute of the 2d of Longevity and Flirtilla, it was enacted, my Lords," put in the Brigadier, "that in no case shall a convicted felon suffer loss of life, or limb, while it can be established that he is *non compos mentis.* This is also a rule, my Lords, of common law—but being common sense and common monikinity, it has been thought prudent to enforce it by an especial enactment. I presume Mr. Attorney-General for the Queen will scarcely dispute the law of the case——"

"Not at all, my Lords—though I have some doubts as to the fact. The fact remains to be established," answered the other, taking snuff.

"The fact is certain, and will not admit of cavil In the case of Rex versus Noah Poke, the court ordered the punishment of decaudisation to take precedence of that of decapitation, in the case of Regina versus the same. Process had been issued from the bench to that effect; the culprit has, in consequence, lost his *cauda*, and with it his reason; a creature without reason has always been held to be *non compos mentis*, and by the law of the land is not liable to the punishments of life or limb."

"Your law is plausible, my brother Downright," observed my Lord Chief Justice, "but it remains for the bench to be put in possession of the facts. At the next term, you will perhaps be better prepared——"

"I pray you, my Lord, to remember that this is a case which will not admit of three months' delay."

"We can decide the principle a year hence, as well as to-day; and we have now sat longer *in banco*," looking at his watch, "than is either usual, agreeable, or expedient."

"But, my Lords, the proof is at hand. Here is a witness to establish that the *cauda* of Noah Poke, the defendant of record, has actually been separated from his body——"

"Nay—nay—my brother Downright, a barrister of your experience must know that the twelve can only take evidence on affidavit. If you had an affidavit prepared, we might possibly find time to hear it, before we adjourn,—as it is, the affair must lie over to another sitting."

I was now in a cold sweat, for I could distinctly scent the peculiar odor of the burning tail; the ashes of which being fairly thrown into Noah's face, there remained no further obstacle to the process of decapitation,—the sentence, it will be remembered, having kept his countenance on his shoulders, expressly for that object. My brother Downright, however, was not a lawyer to be defeated by so simple a stumbling-block.—Seizing a paper that was already written over in a good legal hand, which happened to be lying before him, he read it, without pause or hesitation, in the following manner:—

"Regina *versus* Noah Poke.

Kingdom of Leaphigh, Season of Nuts, this fourth day of the Moon. } Personally appeared before me, Meditation, Lord Chief Justice of the Court of King's Bench, John Goldencalf Baronet, of the Kingdom of Great Britain, who, being duly sworn, doth depose and say, viz., That he, the said deponent, was present at, and did witness the decaudisation of the defendant in this suit, and that the tail of the said Noah Poke, or No. 1, sea-water-color, hath been truly and physically separated from his body.—And further this deponent sayeth not. Signature, &c."

Having read, in the most fluent manner, the foregoing affidavit, (which existed only in his own brain,) my brother Downright desired the court to take my deposition to its truth.

"John Goldencalf, Baronet," said the Chief Justice, "you have heard what has just been read; do you swear to its truth?"

"I do."

Here, the affidavit was signed by both my Lord Chief Justice and myself, and it was duly put on file. I afterwards learned that the paper used by my brother Downright on this memorable occasion, was no other than the notes which the Chief Justice himself had taken on one of the arguments in the case in question, and, that seeing the names and title of the cause, besides finding it no easy matter to read his own writing, that high officer of the crown had, very naturally, supposed that all was right. As to the rest of the bench, they were in too great a hurry to go to dinner, to stop and read affidavits, and the case was instantly disposed of, by the following decision.

"Regina *versus* Noah Poke, &c. Ordered, That he culprit be considered *non compos mentis*, and that he be discharged, on finding security to keep the peace for the remainder of his natural life."

An officer was instantly dispatched to the great square with this reprieve, and the court rose. I delayed a little in order to enter into the necessary recognizances in behalf of Noah, taking up at the same time, the bonds given the previous nignt, for his appearance to answer to the indictments. These forms being duly complied with, my brother Downright and myself repaired to the place of execution, in order to congratulate our client,—the former justly elated with his success, which he assured me was not a little to the credit of his own education.

We found Noah surprisingly relieved by his liberation from the hands of the Philistines; nor was he at all backward in expressing his satisfaction at the unexpected turn things had taken. According to his account of the matter, he did not set a higher value on his head than another; still, it was convenient to have one; had it been necessary to part with it, he made no doubt he should have submitted to do so like a man, referring to the fortitude with which he had borne the amputation of his *cauda*, as a proof of his resolution; for his part, he should take very good care how he accused any one with having a memory, or any thing else, again, and he now saw the excellence of those wise provisions of the laws, which cut up a criminal in order to prevent the repetition of his offences; he did not intend to stay much longer on shore, believing he should be less in the way of temptation on board the Walrus than among the monikins; and, as for his own people, he was sure of soon catching them on board again, for they had now been off their pork twenty-four hours, and nuts were but poor grub for fore-mast hands, after all; philosophers might say what they pleased about governments, but, in his opinion, the only ra'al tyrant on 'arth was the belly; he did not remember ever to have had a struggle with his belly—and he had a thousand—that the belly did n't get the better; that it would be awkward to lay down the title of Lord High Admiral, but it was easier to lay down that than to lay down his head; that as for a *cauda*, though it was certainly agreeable to be in the fashion, he could do very well without one, and when he got back to Stunnin'tun, should the worst come to the worst, there was a certain saddler in the place, who could give him as good a fit as the one he had lost; that Miss Poke would have been greatly scandalized, however, had he come home after decapitation; that it might be well to sail for Leaplow, as soon as convenient, for in that country he understood bobs were in fashion, and he admitted that he should not like to cruise about Leaphigh, for any great length of time, unless he could look as other people look; for his part, he bore no one a grudge, and he freely forgave everybody but Bob, out of whom, the Lord willing, he proposed to have full satisfaction, before the ship should be twenty-four hours at sea, &c. &c. &c.

Such was the general tendency of the remarks of Captain Poke, as we proceeded towards the port, where he embarked and went on board the Walrus, with some eagerness, having learned that our rear-admirals and post-captains had, indeed, yielded to the calls of nature, and had all gone to their duty, swearing they would rather be fore-mast Jacks in a well-victualled ship, than the King of Leaphigh upon nuts.

The Captain had no sooner entered the boat, taking his head with him, than I began to make my acknowledgments to my brother Downright, for the able manner in which he had defended my fellow human being; paying, at the same time, some well-merited compliments to the ingenious and truly phi losophical distinctions of the Leaphigh system of jurisprudence

"Spare your thanks and your commendations, I beg of you, good Sir John," returned the Brigadier, as we walked back towards my lodgings. "We did as well as circumstances would allow; though our whole defence would have been upset, had not the Chief Justice very luckily been unable to read his own handwriting. As for the principles and forms of the monikin law,—for in these particulars Leaplow is very much like Leaphigh,—as you have seen them displayed in these two suits, why, they are such as we have. I do not pretend that they are faultless; on the contrary, I could point out improvements myself—but we get on with them as well as we can: no doubt, among men, you have codes that will better bear examination."

CHAPTER XXII.

A neophyte in diplomacy—diplomatic introduction—a calculation—a shipment of Opinions—how to choose an invoice, with an assortment.

I NOW began seriously to think of sailing for Leaplow; for I confess I was heartily tired of being thought the governor of his Royal Highness Prince Bob, and pined to be restored once more to my proper place in society. I was the more incited to make the change, by the representations of the Brigadier, who assured me that it was sufficient to come from foreign parts, to be esteemed a nobleman in Leaplow, and that I need not apprehend in his country, any of the ill-treatment I had received in the one in which I now was. After talking over the matter, therefore, in a familiar way, we determined to repair at once to the Leaplow legation, in order to ask for our passports, and to offer, at the same time, to carry any dispatches that Judge People's Friend might have prepared for his government,—it being the custom of the Leaplowers to trust to these God-sends in carrying on their diplomatic correspondence.

We found the Judge in undress, and a very different figure he cut, certainly, from that which he made when I saw him the previous night at court. Then he was all *queue;* now, he was all *bob*. He seemed glad to see us, however, and quite delighted when I told him of the intention to sail for Leaplow, as soon as the wind served. He instantly asked a passage for himself, with republican simplicity.

There was to be another turn of the great and little wheels, he said, and it was quite important to himself to be on the spot; for, although every thing was, beyond all question, managed with perfect republican propriety, yet, somehow, and yet he did not know exactly how, but *somehow*, those who are on the spot always get the best prizes. If I could give him a passage, therefore, he would esteem it a great personal favor; and I might depend on it, the circumstance would be well received by the party. Although I did not very well understand what he meant by this party, which was to view the act so kindly, I very cheerfully told the Judge that the apartments lately occupied by my Lord Chatterino and his friends were perfectly at his disposal. I was then asked when I intended to sail; and the answer was, the instant the wind hauled, so we could lay out of the harbour. It might be within half an hour. Hereupon Judge People's Friend begged I would have the goodness to wait until he could hunt up a chargé d'affaires. His instructions were most peremptory never to leave the legation without a chargé d'affaires; but he would just brush his bob, and run into the street, and look up one in five minutes, if I would promise to wait so long. It would have been unkind to refuse so trifling a favor and the promise was given. The Judge must have run as fast as his legs would carry him; for, in about ten minutes, he was back again, with a diplomatic recruit. He told me his heart had misgiven him sadly. The three first to whom he offered the place had plumply refused it, and, indeed, he did not know but he should have a quarrel or two on his hands; but, at last, he had luckily found one who could get nothing else to do, and he pinned him on the spot.

So far every thing had gone on swimmingly; but the new chargé had, most unfortunately, a very long *cauda*, a fashion that was inexorably proscribed by the Leaplow usages, except in cases where the representative went to court—for it seems the Leaplow political ethics, like your country buck, has two dresses; one for every-day wear, and one for Sundays. The Judge intimated to his intended substitute, that it was absolutely indispensable he should submit to an amputation, or he could not possibly confer the appointment, *queues* being proscribed at home by both public opinions, the horizontal and the perpendicular. To this the candidate objected that he very well knew the Leaplow usages on this head, but that he had seen his Excellency himself going to court with a singularly apparent brush; and he had supposed from that, and from sundry other little occurrences he did not care to particularize, that the Leaplowers were not so bigoted in their notions, but they could act on the principle of doing at Rome as is done by the Romans. To this the Judge replied, that this principle was certainly recognized in all things that were agreeable and that he knew, from experience, how hard it was to go in a bob, when all around him went in *caudæ*; but that tails were essentially anti-republican, and as such had been formally voted down in Leaplow, where even the Great Sachem did not dare to wear one, let him long for it as much as he would; and if it were known that a public chargé offended in this particular, although he might be momentarily protected by one of the public opinions, the matter would certainly be taken up by the opposition public opinion, and then the people might order a new turn of the little wheel, which heaven it knew!—occurred now a great deal oftener than was either profitable or convenient.

Hereupon the candidate deliberately undid the fastenings and removed the *queue*, showing, to our admiration, that it was false, and that he was, after all, neither more nor less than a Leaplower in masquerade; which, by the way, I afterwards learned, was very apt to be the case with a great many of that eminently original people, when they got without the limits of their own beloved land. Judge People's Friend was now perfectly delighted. He told us this was exactly what he could most have wished for. "Here is a bob," said he, "for the horizontals and perpendiculars, and there is a capital ready-made *cauda* for his Majesty and his Majesty's first-cousin! A Leaphighized Leaplower, more especially if there be a dash of caricature about him, is the very thing in our diplomacy." Finding matters so much to his mind, the Judge made out the letter of appointment on the spot, and then proceeded to give his substitute the usual instructions.

"You are on all occasions," he said, "to take the utmost care not to offend the court of Leaphigh, or the meanest of the courtiers, by advancing any of our peculiar opinions, all of which, beyond dispute, you have at your finger-ends; on this score, you are to be so particular, that you may even, in your own person, *pro tempore*, abandon republicanism—yea, sacred republicanism itself!—knowing that can easily be resumed on your return home again, you are to remember there is nothing so undiplomatic, or even vulgar, as to have an opinion on any subject, unless it should be the opinion of the persons you may happen to be in company with; and, as we have the reputation of possessing that quality in an eminent degree, everywhere but at home, take especial heed to eschew vulgarity—if you can; you will have the greatest care, also, to wear the shortest bob in all your private, and the longest tail in all your public, relations, this being one of the most important of the celebrated checks and balances of our government; our institutions being expressly formed by the mass, for the particular benefit of all, you will be excessively careful not to let the claims of any one citizen, or even any set of citizens, interfere with that harmony which it is so necessary, for the purposes of trade, to maintain with all foreign courts; which courts being accustomed themselves to consider their subjects as cattle, to be worked in the traces of the state, are singulary restive whenever they hear of any individual being made of so much importance. Should any Leaplower become troublesome on this score, give him a bad name at once; and in order to effect that object with your own single-minded and right-loving countrymen, swear that he is a disorganizer, and my life on it, both public opinions at home will sustain you; for there is nothing on which our public opinions agree so well as the absolute deference which they pay to foreign public opinions,—and this the more especially, in all matters that are likely to affect profits, by deranging commerce. You will, above all things, make it a point to be in constant relations with some of the readiest paragraph-writers of the newspapers, in order to see that facts are properly stated at home. I would advise you to look out some foreigner who has never seen Leaplow, for this employment; one that is also paid to write for the journals of Leapup, or Leapdown, or some other foreign country; by which means you will be sure to get an impartial agent, or one who can state things in your own way, who is already half paid for his services, and who will not be likely to make blunders by meddling with distinctive thought. When a person of this character is found, let him drop a line now and then in favor of your own sagacity and patriotism; and if he should say a pleasant thing occasionally about me, it will do no harm, but may help the little wheel to turn more readily. In order to conceal his origin, let your paragraph-agent use the word *our* freely; the use of this word, as you know, being the only qualification of citizenship in Leaplow. Let him begin to spell the word O–U–R, and then proceed to pronounce it, and be careful that he does not spell it H–O–U–R, which might betray his origin. Above all things, you will be patriotic and republican, avoiding the least vindication of your country and its institutions, and satisfying yourself with saying that the latter are, at least, well suited to the former; if you should say this in a way to leave the impression on your hearers, that you think the former fitted for nothing else, it will be particularly agreeable and thoroughly republican, and most eminently modest and praiseworthy. You will find the diplomatic agents of all other states, sensitive on the point of their peculiar political usages, and prompt to defend them; but this is a weakness you will rigidly abstain from imitating, for our polity being exclusively based on reason, you are to show a dignified confidence in the potency of that fundamental principle, nor in any way lessen the high character that reason already enjoys, by giving any one cause to suspect you think reason is not fully able to take care of itself. With these leading hints, and your own natural tendencies, which I am glad to see are eminently fitted for the great objects of diplomacy, being ductile, imitative, yielding, calculating, and, above all, of a foreign disposition, I think you will be able to get on very cleverly Cultivate, above all things, your foreign dispositions, for you are now on foreign duty, and your country reposes on your shoulders and eminent talents, the whole burthen of its foreign interests in this part of the world."

Here the Judge closed his address, which was oral, apparently well satisfied with himself and with his raw-hand in diplomacy. He then said,—

"That he would now go to court to present his substitute, and to take leave himself; after which he would return as fast as possible, and detain us no longer than was necessary to put his *cauda* in pepper, to protect it against the moths; for heaven knew what prize he might draw in the next turn of the little wheel!"

We promised to meet him at the port, where a messenger just then informed us, Captain Poke had landed, and was anxiously waiting our appearance. With this understanding we separated; the Judge undertaking to redeem all our promises paid in at the tavern, by giving his own in their stead.

The Brigadier and myself found Noah and the cook bargaining for some private adventures, with a Leaphigh broker or two, who, finding that the ship was about to sail in ballast, were recommending their wares to the notice of these two worthies.

"It would be a ra'al sin, Sir John," commenced

the Captain, "to neglect an occasion like this to turn a penny. The ship could carry ten thousand immigrunts, and they say there are millions of them going over to Leaplow; or it might stow half the goods in Aggregation. I'm resolved, at any rate, to use my cabin privilege; and I would advise you, as owner, to look out for suthin' to pay port-charges with, to say the least."

"The idea is not a bad one, friend Poke; but, as we are ignorant of the state of the market on the other side, it might be well to consult some inhabitant of the country about the choice of articles. Here is the Brigadier Downright, whom I have found to be a monikin of experience and judgment, and if you please, we will first hear what he has to say about it."

"I dabble very little in merchandise," returned the Brigadier; "but, as a general principle, I should say that no article of Leaphigh manufacture would command so certain a market in Leaplow as Opinions."

"Have you any of these opinions for sale?" I inquired of the broker.

"Plenty of them, sir, and of all qualities—from the very lowest to the very 'ighest prices—those that may be had for next to nothing, to those that we think a great deal of ourselves. We always keeps them ready packed for exportation, and send wast invoices of them, hannually, to Leaplow in particular. Opinions are harticles that help to sell each other; and a ship of the tonnage of yours might stow enough, provided they were properly assorted, to carry all before them for the season."

Expressing a wish to see the packages, we were immediately led into an adjoining warehouse, where, sure enough, there were goodly lots of the manufactures in question. I passed along the shelves, read ing the inscriptions of the different packages. Pointing to several bundles that had "*Opinions on Free Trade*" written on their labels, I asked the Brigadier what he thought of that article.

"Why, they would have done better, a year or two since, when we were settling a new tariff; but I should think there would be less demand for them now."

"You are quite right, sir," added the broker; "we *did* send large invoices of them to Leaplow formerly, and they were all eagerly bought up, the moment they arrived. A great many were dyed over again, and sold as of 'ome manufacture. Most of these harticles are now shipped for Leapup, with whom we have negotiations that give them a certain value."

"'*Opinions on Democracy, and on the polity of governments in general;*' I should think these would be of no use in Leaplow?"

"Why, sir, they goes pretty much hover the whole world. We sell powers on 'em on our own continent, near by, and a great many do go even to Leaplow; though what they does with 'em there, I never could say, seeing they are all government monikins in that queer country."

An inquiring look extorted a clearer answer from the Brigadier:—

"To admit the fact, we have a class among us who buy up these articles with some eagerness. I can only account for it, by supposing they think differing in their tastes from the mass, makes them more enlightened and peculiar."

"I'll take them all. An article that catches these propensities is sure of a sale. '*Opinions on Events;*' what can possibly be done with these?"

"That depends a little on their classification, returned the Brigadier. "If they relate to Leaplow events, while they have a certain value, they cannot be termed of current value; but if they refer to the events of all the rest of the earth, take them, for heaven's sake! for we trust altogether to this market for our supplies."

On this hint I ordered the whole lot, trusting to dispose of the least fashionable by aid of those that were more in vogue.

"'*Opinions on Domestic Literature.*'"

"You may buy all he has; we use no other."

"'*Opinions on Continental Literature.*'"

"Why, we know little about the goods themselves—but I think a selection might answer."

I ordered the bale cut in two, and took one half, at a venture.

"'*Opinions on Leaplow Literature*, from No. 1, up to No. 100.'"

"Ah! it is proper I should explain," put in the broker, "that we has two varieties of them 'ere harticles. One is the true harticle, as is got up by our great wits and philosophers, they says, on the most approved models; but the other is nothing but a sham harticle that is really manufactured in Leaplow, and is sent out here to get our stamp. That's all—I never deceives a customer—both sell well, I hear, on the other side, however."

I looked again at the Brigadier, who quietly nodding assent, I took the whole hundred bales.

"'*Opinions of the Institutions of Leaphigh.*'"

"Why, them 'ere is assorted, being of all sizes, forms and colors. They came coastwise, and are chiefly for domestic consumption; though I have known 'em sent to Leaplow, with success."

"The consumers of this article among us," observed the Brigadier, "are very select, and rarely take any but of the very best quality. But then hey are usually so well stocked, that I question if a new importation would pay freight. Indeed, our consumers cling very generally to the old fashions in this article, not even admitting the changes produced by time. There was an old manufacturer called Whiterock, who has a sort of Barlow-knife reputation among us, and it is not easy to get another article to compete with his. Unless they are very antiquated, I would have nothing to do with them."

"Yes, this is all true, sir. We still sends to Leaplow quantities of that 'ere manufacture; and the more hantiquated the harticle, the better it sells; but then the new fashions has a most wonderful run at 'ome."

"I'll stick to the real Barlow, through thick or thin. Hunt me up a bale of his notions; let them be as old as the flood. What have we here?—'*Opinions on the Institutions of Leaplow.*'"

"Take them," said the Brigadier, promptly.

"This 'ere gentleman has an hidear of the state of his own market," added the broker, giggling. "Wast lots of these things go across yearly—and I don't find that any on 'em ever comes back."

"'*Opinions on the State of Manners and Society in Leaplow.*'"

"I believe I'll take an interest in that article myself, Sir John, if you can give me a ton or two between decks. Have you many of this manufacture?"

"Lots on 'em, sir—and they *do* sell so!—That 'ere are a good harticle both at 'ome and abroad. My eye! how they does go off in Leaplow!"

"This appears to be also your expectation, Brigadier, by your readiness to take an interest?"

"To speak the truth, nothing sells better in our beloved country."

'Permit me to remark that I find your readiness

to purchase this and the last article, a little singular If I have rightly comprehended our previous conversations, you Leaplowers profess to have improved not only on the ancient principles of polity, but on the social condition, generally."

"We will talk of this during the passage homeward, Sir John Goldencalf; but, by your leave, I will take a share in the investment in 'Opinions on the State of Society and Manners in Leaplow,' especially if they treat at large on the deformities of the government, while they allow us to be genteel. This is the true notch—some of these goods have been condemned because the manufacturers had n't sufficient skill in dyeing."

"You shall have a share, Brigadier. Harkee, Mr. Broker; I take it these said opinions come from some very well known and approved manufactory?"

"All sorts, sir. Some good, and some good for nothing—everything sells, however. I never was in Leaplow, but we says over here, that the Leaplowers eat, and drink, and sleep on our opinions. Lord, sir, it would really do your heart good to see the stuff, in these harticles, that they does take from us without higgling!"

"I presume, Brigadier, that you use them as an amusement—as a means to pass a pleasant hour, of an evening—a sort of moral segar?"

"No, sir," put in the broker, "they does n't smoke em, my word on't, or they wouldn' buy em in such lots!"

I now thought enough had been laid in on my own account, and I turned to see what the Captain was about. He was higgling for a bale marked "Opinions on the lost condition of the monikin soul." A little curious to know why he had made this seection, I led him aside, and frankly put the question.

"Why, to own the truth, Sir John," he said

"religion is an article that sells in every market, in some shape or other. Now, we are all in the dark about the Leaplow tastes and usages, for I always suspect a native of the country to which I am bound, on such a p'int; and if the things should n't sell there, they'll at least do at Stunin'tun. Miss Poke alone would use up what there is in that there bale, in a twelvemonth. To give the woman her due, she's a desperate consumer of snuff and religion."

We had now pretty effectually cleared the shelves, and the cook, who had come ashore to dispose of his slush, had not yet been able to get anything.

"Here is a small bale as come *from* Leaplow, and a pinched little thing it is," said the broker, laughing; "it do n't take at all, here, and it might do to go 'ome again—at any rate you will get the drawback. It is filled with 'Distinctive Opinions of the Republic of Leaplow.'" The cook looked at the Brigadier, who appeared to think the speculation doubtful. Still it was Hobson's choice; and, after a good deal of grumbling, the doctor, as Noah always called his cook, consented to take the "harticle," at half the prime cost.

Judge People's Friend now came trotting down to the port, thoroughly *en républicain*, when we immediately embarked, and in half an hour, Bob was kicked to Noah's heart's content, and the Walrus was fairly under way for Leaplow.

CHAPTER XXIII.

Political boundaries—Political rights—Political selections, and political disquisitions; with political results.

THE aquatic mile-stones of the monikin seas have been already mentioned; but I believe I omitted to say, that there was a line of demarcation drawn in the water, by means of a similar invention, to point out the limits of the jurisdiction of each state. Thus, all within these water-marks, was under the laws of Leaphigh; all between them and those of some other country, was the high seas; and all within those of the other country, Leaplow for instance, was under the exclusive jurisdiction of that other country.

With a favorable wind, the Walrus could run to the water-marks in about half a day; from thence to the water-marks of Leaplow was two days' sail, and another half day was necessary to reach our haven. As we drew near the legal frontiers of Leaphigh, several small fast-sailing schooners were seen hovering just without the jurisdiction of the King, quite evidently waiting our approach. One boarded us, just as the outer end of the spanker-boom got clear of the Leaphigh sovereignty. Judge People's Friend rushed to the side of the ship, and before the crew of the boat could get on deck, he had ascertained that the usual number of prizes had been put into the little wheel.

A monikin in a bob of a most pronounced character, or which appeared to have been subjected to the second amputation, being what is called in Leaplow a bob-upon-bob, now approached, and inquired if there were any emigrants on board. He was made acquainted with our characters and objects. When he understood that our stay would most likely be short, he was evidently a little disappointed.

"Perhaps, gentlemen," he added, "you may still remain long enough to make naturalization desirable?"

"It is always agreeable to be at home in foreign countries—but are there no legal objections?"

"I see none, sir—you have no tails, I believe?"

"None but what are in our trunks. I did not know, however, but the circumstance of our being of a different species might throw some obstacles in the way."

"None in the world, sir. We act on principles much too liberal for so narrow an objection. You are but little acquainted with the institutions and policy of our beloved and most happy country, I see, sir. This is not Leaphigh, nor Leapup, nor Leapdown, nor Leapover, nor Leapthrough, nor Leapunder; but good old, hearty, liberal, free and independent, most beloved, happy, and prosperous beyond example, Leaplow. Species is of no account under our system. We would as soon naturalize one animal as another, provided it be a republican animal. I see no deficiency about any of you. All we ask is certain general principles. You go on two legs——"

"So do turkeys, sir."

"Very true—but you have no feathers."

"Neither has a donkey."

"All very right, gentlemen—you do not bray however."

"I will not answer for that," put in the captain sending his leg forward in a straight line, in a way to raise an outcry in Bob, that almost upset the Leaplower's proposition.

"At all events, gentlemen," he observed, "there is a test that will put the matter at rest, at once."

He then desired us, in turn, to pronounce the word "our"—"*Our* liberties"—"*our* country"—"*our* firesides"—"*our* altars." Whoever expressed a wish to be naturalized, and could use this word in the proper manner, and in the proper place, was entitled to be a citizen. We all did very well but the second mate, who, being a Herefordshire man, could not, for the life of him, get any nearer to the Doric, in the latter shibboleth, than "our halters." Now, it would seem, that, in carrying out a great philanthropic principle in Leaplow, halters had been proscribed; for, whenever a rogue did any thing amiss, it had been discovered that, instead of punishing him for the offence, the true way to remedy the evil was to punish the society against which he had offended. By this ingenious turn, society was naturally made to look out sharp how it permitted any one to offend it. This excellent idea is like that of certain Dutchmen, who, when they cut themselves with an axe, always apply salve and lint to the cruel steel, and leave the wound to heal as fast as possible.

To return to our examination: we all passed but the second mate, who hung in his halter, and was pronounced to be incorrigible. Certificates of naturalization were delivered on the spot, the fees were paid, and the schooner left us.

That night it blew a gale, and we had no more visiters until the following morning. As the sun rose, however, we fell in with three schooners, under the Leaplow flag, all of which seemed bound on errands of life or death. The first that reached us sent a boat on board, and a committee of six "bob-upon-bobs" hurried up our side, and lost no time in introducing themselves. I shall give their own account of their business and characters.

It would seem that they were what is called a "nominating committee" of the Horizontals, for the city of Bivouac, the port to which we were bound, where an election was about to take place for members of the great National Council. Bivouac was entitled to send seven members; and having nominated themselves, the committee were now in quest of a seventh candidate to fill the vacancy. In order to secure the naturalized interests, it had been determined to select as new a comer as possible. This would also be maintaining the principle of liberality, in the abstract. For this reason they had been cruising for a week, as near as the law would allow to the Leaphigh boundaries, and they were now ready to take any one who would serve.

To this proposition I again objected the difference of species. Here they all fairly laughed in my face, Brigadier Downright included, giving me very distinctly to understand that they thought I had very contracted notions on matters and things, to suppose so trifling an obstacle could disturb the harmony and unity of a Horizontal vote. They went for a principle, and the devil himself could not make them swerve from the pursuit of so sacred an object.

I then candidly admitted that nature had not fitted me, as admirably as it had fitted my friend the Judge, for the throwing of summersets; and I feared that when the order was given "to go to the right about," I might be found no better than a bungler. This staggered them a little; and I perceived that they looked at each other, in doubt.

"But you can, at least, turn round suddenly, at need?" one of them asked, after a pause.

"Certainly, sir," I answered, giving ocular evi dence that I was no idle boaster, making a com plete gyration on my heels, in very good time.

"Very well!—admirably well!" they all cried in a breath. "The great political essential is to be able to perform the evolutions in their essence,—the facility with which they are performed being no more than a personal merit."

"But, gentlemen, I know little more of your constitution and laws, than I have learned in a few broken discussions with my fellow-travellers."

"This is a matter of no moment, sir. Our constitution, unlike that of Leaphigh, is written down, and he who runs can read; and then we have a political fugleman in the house, who saves an immense deal of unnecessary study and reflection to the members. All you will have to do, will be to watch his movements; and, my life on it, you will go as well through the manual exercise as the oldest member there."

"How, sir, do all the members take the manœuvres from this fugleman?"

"All the Horizontals, sir—the Perpendiculars having a fugleman of their own."

"Well, gentlemen, I conceive this to be an affair in which I am no judge, and I put myself entirely in the hands of my friends."

This answer met with much commendation, and manifested, as they all protested, great political capabilities; the statesman who submitted all to his friends never failing to rise to eminence in Leaplow. The committee took my name in writing, and hastened back to their schooner, in order o get into port to promulgate the nomination. These persons were hardly off the deck, before another party came up the opposite side of the ship. They announced themselves to be a nominating committee of the Perpendiculars, on exactly the same errand as their opponents. They, too, wished to propitiate the foreign interests, and were in search of a proper candidate. Captain Poke had been an attentive listener to all that occurred during the circumstances that preceded my nomination; and he now stepped promptly forward, and declared his readiness to serve. As there was quite as little squeamishness on one side as on the other, and the Perpendicular committee, as it owned itself, was greatly pressed for time, the Horizontals having the start of them, the affair was arranged in five minutes, and the strangers departed with the name of NOAH POKE, THE TRIED PATRIOT, THE PROFOUND JURIST, AND THE HONEST MONIKIN, handsomely placarded on a large board—all but the name having been carefully prepared in advance.

When the committee was fairly out of the ship, Noah took me aside, and made his apologies for opposing me in this important election. His reasons were numerous and ingenious, and, as usual, a little discursive. They might be summed up as follows: He never had sat in a parliament, and he was curious to know how it would feel; it would increase the respect of the ship's company, to find their commander of so much account in a strange port; he had had some experience at Stunin'tun by reading the newspapers, and he didn't doubt of his abilities at all, a circumstance that rarely failed of making a good legislator; the Congressman in his part of the country was some such man as himself, and what was good for the goose was good for the gander; he knew Miss Poke would be pleased to hear he had been chosen; he wondered if he should be called the Honorable Noah Poke, and whether he should receive eight dollars a day, and mileage from the spot where the ship then was; the Perpendiculars might count on him, for his word was as good as his bond; as for the constitution, he had got on under the constitution at home, and he believed a man who could do that might get on under any constitution; he didn't intend to say a great deal in parliament, but what he did say he hoped might be recorded for the use of his children; together with a great deal more of the same sort of argumentation and apology.

The third schooner now brought us to. This vessel sent another committee, who announced themselves to be the representatives of a party that was termed the Tangents. They were not numerous, but sufficiently so to hold the balance whenever the Horizontals and the Perpendiculars crossed each other directly at right angles, as was the case at present; and they had now determined to run a single candidate of their own. They, too, wished to fortify themselves by the foreign interest, as was natural, and had come out in quest of a proper person. I suggested the first mate; but against this Noah protested, declaring that come what would, the ship must on no account be deserted. Time pressed; and, while the Captain and the subordinate were hotly disputing the propriety of permitting the latter to serve, Bob, who had already tasted the sweets of political importance, in his assumed character of Prince-Royal, stepped slyly up to the committee, and gave in his name. Noah was too much occupied to discover this well-managed movement; and by the time he had sworn to throw the mate overboard if he did not instantly relinquish all ambitious projects of this nature, he found that the Tangents were off. Supposing they had gone to some other vessel, the Captain allowed himself to be soothed, and all went on smoothly again.

From this time until we anchored in the bay of Bivouac, the tranquillity and discipline of the Walrus were undisturbed. I improved the occasion to study the constitution of Leaplow, of which the Judge had a copy, and to glean such information from my companions, as I believed might be useful in my future career. I thought how pleasant it would be for a foreigner to teach the Leaplowers their own laws, and to explain to them the application of their own principles! Little, however, was to be got from the Judge, who was just then too much occupied with some calculations concerning the chances of the little wheel, with which he had been furnished by a leading man of one of the nominating committees.

I now questioned the Brigadier touching that peculiar usage of his country which rendered Leaphigh opinions concerning the Leaplow institutions, society and manners, of so much value in the market of the latter. To this I got but an indifferent answer, except it was to say, that his countrymen having cleared the interests connected with the subjects from the rubbish of time, and set everything at work, on the philosophical basis of reason and common sense, were exceedingly desirous of knowing what other people thought of the success of the experiment.

"I expect to see a nation of sages, I can assure you, Brigadier; one in which even the very children are profoundly instructed in the great truths of your system; and, as to the monikinas, I am not without dread of bringing my theoretical ignorance in collision with their great practical knowledge of the principles of your government."

"They are early fed on political pap."

"No doubt, sir, no doubt. How different must they be from the females of other countries! Deeply imbued with the great distinctive principles of your system, devoted to the education of their children in the same sublime truths, and indefatigable in their discrimination, among the meanest of their households!"

"Hum!"

"Now, sir, even in England, a country which I trust is not the most debased on earth, you will find women, beautiful, intellectual, accomplished and patriotic, who limit their knowledge of these fundamental points to a zeal for a *clique*, and the whole of whose eloquence on great national questions is bounded by a few heartfelt wishes for the downfall of their opponents."

"It is very much so at Stunin'tun, too, if truth must be spoken," remarked Noah, who had been a listener

"Who, instead of instructing the young suckers that cling to their sides in just notions of general, social distinctions, nurture their young antipathies with pettish philippics against some luckless chief of the adverse party."

"'T is pretty much the same at Stunin'tun, as I live!"

"Who rarely study the great lessons of history in order to point out to the future statesmen and heroes of the empire the beacons of crime, the incentives for public virtue, or the charters of their liberties; but who are indefatigable in echoing the cry of the hour, however false or vulgar, and who humanize their attentive offspring by softly expressed wishes that Mr. Canning, or some other frustrator of the designs of their friends, were fairly hanged!'"

"Stunin'tun, all over!"

"Beings that are angels in form—soft, gentle, refined, and tearful as the evening with its dews, when there is a question of humanity or suffering; but who seem strangely transformed into she-tigers, whenever any but those of whom they can approve attain to power; and who, instead of entwining their soft arms around their husbands and brothers, to restrain them from the hot strife of opinions, cheer them on by their encouragement, and throw dirt with the volubility and wit of fish-women."

"Miss Poke, to the back-bone!"

"In short, sir, I expect to see an entirely different state of things at Leaplow. There, when a political adversary is bespattered with mud, your gentle monikinas, doubtless, appease anger by the mild soothings of philosophy, tempering zeal by wisdom, and regulating error by apt and unanswerable quotations from that great charter which is based on the eternal and immutable principles of right."

"Well, Sir John, if you speak in this elocutionary manner in the house," cried the delighted Noah, "I shall be shy of answering! I doubt, now, if the Brigadier himself could repeat all you have just said."

"I have forgotten to inquire, Mr. Downright, a little about your Leaplow constituency. The suffrage is, beyond question, confined to those members of society who possess a 'social stake.'"

"Certainly, Sir John. They who live and breathe."

"Surely none vote but those who possess the money, and houses, and lands of the country?"

"Sir, you are altogether in error; all vote who possess ears, and eyes, and noses, and bobs, and lives, and hopes, and wishes, and feelings, and wants. Wants we conceive to be a much truer test of political fidelity, than possessions."

"This is novel doctrine, indeed! but it is in direct hostility to the social-stake system."

"You were never more right, Sir John, as respects your own theory, or never more wrong as respects the truth. In Leaplow we contend—and contend justly—that there is no broader or bolder fallacy than to say that a representation of mere effects, whether in houses, lands, merchandise, or money, is a security for a good government. Property is affected by measures; and the more a monikin has, the greater is the bribe to induce him to consult his own interests, although it should be at the expense of those of everybody else."

"But, sir, the interest of the community is composed of the aggregate of these interests."

"Your pardon, Sir John; nothing is composed of it, but the aggregate of the interests of a class. If your government is instituted for their benefit only, your social-stake system is all well enough; but if the object be the general good, you have no choice but to trust its custody to the general keeping. Let us suppose two men—since you happen to be a man, and not a monikin—let us suppose two men perfectly equal in morals, intelligence, public virtue and patriotism, one of whom shall be rich and the other shall have nothing. A crisis arrives in the affairs of their common country, and both are called upon to exercise their franchise, on a question—as almost all great questions must—that unavoidably will have some influence on property generally. Which would give the most impartial vote—he who, of necessity, must be swayed by his personal interest, or he who has no inducement of the sort to go astray?"

"Certainly he who has nothing to influence him to go wrong.—But the question is not fairly put——"

"Your pardon, Sir John,—it is put fairly as an abstract question, and one that is to prove a principle. I am glad to hear you say that a man would be apt to decide in this manner; for it shows his identity with a monikin. We hold that all of us are apt to think most of ourselves on such occasions."

"My dear Brigadier, do not mistake sophistry for reason. Surely, if power belonged only to the poor,—and the poor, or the comparatively poor, always compose the mass,—they would exercise it in a way to strip the rich of their possessions."

"We think not, in Leaplow. Cases might exist, in which such a state of things would occur under a reaction; but reactions imply abuses, and are not to be quoted to maintain a principle. He who was drunk yesterday, may need an unnatural stimulus to-day; while he who is uniformly temperate preserves his proper tone of body without recourse to a remedy so dangerous. Such an experiment, under a strong provocation, might possibly be made; but it could scarcely be made twice among any people, and not even once among a people that submits in season to a just division of its authority, since it is obviously destructive of a leading principle of civilization. According to our monikin histories, all the attacks upon property have been produced by property's grasping at more than fairly belongs to its immunities. If you make political power a concomitant of property, both may go together, certainly; but if kept separate, the danger to the latter will never exceed the danger in which it is put daily by the arts of the money-getters, who are, in truth, the greatest foes of property, as it belongs to others."

I remembered Sir Joseph Job, and could not but admit that the Brigadier had, at least, some truth on his side.

"But do you deny that the sentiment of property elevates the mind, ennobles, and purifies?"

"Sir, I do not pretend to determine what may be the fact among men, but we hold among monikins, that 'the love of money is the root of all evil.'"

"How, sir! do you account the education which is a consequence of property, as nothing?"

"If you mean, my dear Sir John, that which pro perty is most apt to teach, we hold it to be selfishness; but if you mean that he who has money, as a rule, will also have information to guide him aright, I must answer, that experience, which is worth a thousand theories, tells us differently. We find that on questions which are purely between those who have and those who have not, the *haves* are commonly united, and we think this would be the fact if they were as unschooled as bears; but on all other questions, they certainly do great discredit to education, unless you admit that there are, in every case, *two* rights; for, with us, the most highly educated generally take the two extremes of every argument. I state this to be the fact with monikins, you will remember—doubtless, educated men agree much better."

"But, my good Brigadier, if your position about the greater impartiality and independence of the elector who is not influenced by his private interests, be true, a country would do well to submit its elections to a body of foreign umpires."

"It would indeed, Sir John, if it were certain these foreign umpires would not abuse the power to their own particular advantage, if they could have the feelings and sentiments which ennoble and purify a nation far more than money, and if it were possible they could thoroughly understand the character, habits, wants, and resources of another people. As things are, therefore, we believe it is wisest to trust our own elections to ourselves —not to a portion of ourselves—but to all of ourselves."

"Immigrun'ts included," put in the Captain.

"Why, we do carry the principle well out in the case of gentlemen like yourselves," returned the Brigadier, politely; "but liberality is a virtue. As a principle, Sir John, your idea of referring the choice of our representatives to strangers, has more merit than you probably imagine, though, certainly, impracticable, for the reasons already given. When we seek justice, we commonly look out for some impartial judge. Such a judge is unattainable, however, in the matter of the interests of a state, for the simple reason that power of this sort, permanently wielded, would be perverted on a principle which, after a most scrupulous analysis, we have been compelled to admit is incorporated with the very monikin nature—viz. selfishness. I make no manner of doubt that you men, however, are altogether superior to an influence so unworthy?"

Here I could only borrow the use of the Brigadier's "Hum!"

"Having ascertained that it would not do to submit the control of our affairs to utter strangers, or to those whose interests are not identified with our own, we set about seeing what could be done with a selection from among ourselves. Here we were again met by that same obstinate principle of selfishness; and we were finally driven to take shelter in the experiment of intrusting the interests of all, to the management of all."

"And, sir, are these the opinions of Leaphigh?"

"Very far from it. The difference between Leaphigh and Leaplow is just this: the Leaphighers, being an ancient people, with a thousand vested interests, are induced, as time improves the mind, to seek reasons for their facts; while we Leaplowers, being unshackled by any such restraints, have been able to make an effort to form our facts on our reasons."

"Why do you, then, so much prize Leaphigh opinions on Leaplow facts?"

"Why does every little monikin believe his own father and mother to be just the two wisest, best, most virtuous, and discreetest old monikins in the whole world, until time, opportunity, and experience show him his error?"

"Do you make no exceptions, then, in your franchise, but admit every citizen who, as you say, has a nose, ears, bob and wants, to the exercise of the suffrage?"

"Perhaps we are less scrupulous on this head than we ought to be, since we do not make ignorance and want of character bars to the privilege. Qualifications beyond mere birth and existence may be useful, but they are badly chosen when they are brought to the test of purely material possessions. This practice has arisen in the world from the fact that they who had property had power, and not because they ought to have it."

"My dear Brigadier, this is flying in the face of all experience."

"For the reason just given, and because all experience has hitherto commenced at the wrong end. Society should be constructed as you erect a house; not from the roof down, but from the foundation upward."

"Admitting, however, that your house has been badly constructed at first,—in repairing it, would you tear away the walls at random, at the risk of bringing all down about your ears?"

"I would first see that sufficient props were eared, and then proceed with vigor, though always with caution. Courage in such an experiment is less to be dreaded than timidity. Half the evils of life, social, personal and political, are as much the effects of moral cowardice as of fraud."

I then told the Brigadier, that as his countrymen rejected the inducements of property in the selection of the political base of their social compact, I expected to find a capital substitute in virtue.

"I have always heard that virtue is the great essential of a free people, and doubtless you Leaplowers are perfect models in this important particular?"

The Brigadier smiled, before he answered me, first looking about, to the right and left, as if to regale himself with the odor of perfection.

"Many theories have been broached on these subjects," he replied, "in which there has been some confusion between cause and effect. Virtue is no more a cause of freedom, except as it is connected with intelligence, than vice is a cause of slavery. Both may be consequences, but it is not easy to say how either is necessarily a cause. There is a homely saying among us monikins, which is quite to the point in this matter: 'Set a rogue to catch a rogue.' Now, the essence of a free government is to be found in the responsibility of its agents. He who governs without responsibility is a master, while he who discharges the duties of a functionary under a practical responsibility is a ser vant. This is the only true test of governments, let them be mistified as they may in other respects. Responsibility to the mass of the nation is the criterion of freedom. Now responsibility is the *substitute* for virtue in a politician, as discipline is the substitute for courage, in a soldier. An army of brave monikins without discipline, would be very apt to be worsted by an army of monikins of less natural spirit, with discipline. So a corps of originally virtuous politicians, without responsibility, would be very apt to do more selfish, lawless, and profligate acts, than a corps of less virtue, who were kept rigidly under the rod of responsibility. Unrestrained power is a great corrupter of virtue, of itself; while the liabilities of a restrained authority are very apt to keep it in check. At least, such is the fact with us monikins—men very possibly get along better."

"Let me tell you, Mr. Downright, you are now uttering opinions that are diametrically opposed to those of the world, which considers virtue an indispensable ingredient in a republic."

"The world—meaning always the monikin world—knows very little about real political liberty, except as a theory. We of Leaplow are, in effect, the only people who have had much to do with it, and I am now telling you what is the result of my own observation, in my own country. If monikins were purely virtuous, there would be no necessity for government at all; but, being what they are, we think it wisest to set them to watch each other."

"But yours is self-government, which implies self-restraint; and self-restraint is but another word for virtue."

"If the merit of our system depended on self government, in your signification, or on self-re straint, in any signification, it would not be worth the trouble of this argument, Sir John Goldencalf. This is one of those balmy fallacies with which ill judging moralists endeavor to stimulate monikins to good deeds. Our government is based on a directly opposite principle; that of watching and restraining each other, instead of trusting to our ability to restrain ourselves. It is the want of responsibility, and not its constant and active presence, which infers virtue and self-control. No one would willingly lay legal restraints on himself, in any thing, while all are very happy to restrain their neighbors. This refers to the positive and necessary rules of intercourse, and the establishment of rights; as to mere morality, laws do very little towards enforcing its ordinances. Morals usually come of instruction; and when all have political power, instruction is a security that all desire."

"But when all vote, all may wish to abuse their trust to their own especial advantage, and a political chaos would be the consequence."

"Such a result is impossible, except as especial advantage is identified with general advantage. A community can no more buy itself in this manner, than a monikin can eat himself, let him be as ravenous as he will. Admitting that all are rogues, necessity would compel a compromise."

"You make out a plausible theory, and I have little doubt that I shall find you the wisest, the most logical, the discreetest, and the most consistent community I have yet visited. But another word:—How is it that our friend the Judge gave such very equivocal instructions to his chargé; and why, in particular, did he lay so much stress on the employment of means, which give the lie flatly to all you have here told me?"

Brigadier Downright hereupon stroked his chin.

and observed that he thought there might possibly be a shift of wind; and he also wondered quite audibly, when we should make the land. I afterwards persuaded him to allow that a monikin was but a monikin, after all, whether he had the advantages of universal suffrage, or lived under a despot.

CHAPTER XXIV.

An arrival—An election—Architecture—A rolling-pin, and Patriotism of the most approved water.

In due time the coast of Leaplow made its appearance, close under our larboard bow. So sudden was our arrival in this novel and extraordinary country, that we were very near running on it, before we got a glimpse of its shores. The seamanship of Captain Poke, however, stood us in hand; and, by the aid of a very clever pilot, we were soon safely moored in the harbor of Bivouac. In this happy land, there was no registration, no passports, "no nothin'"—as Mr. Poke pointedly expressed it. The formalities were soon observed, although I had occasion to remark, how much easier, after all, it is to get along in this world with vice than with virtue. A bribe offered to a custom-house officer was refused; and the only trouble I had, on the occasion, arose from this awkward obtrusion of a conscience. However, the difficulty was overcome, though not quite as soon or as easily as if *douceurs* had happened to be in fashion; and we were permitted to land with all our necessary effects.

The city of Bivouac presented a singular aspect as I first put foot within its hallowed streets. The houses were all covered with large placards, which, at first, I took to be lists of the wares to be vended, for the place is notoriously commercial; but which, on examination, I soon discovered were merely electioneering handbills. The reader will figure to himself my pleasure and surprise, on reading the first that offered. It ran as follows:—

HORIZONTAL NOMINATION.

Horizontal-Systematic-Endoctrinated-Republicans, Attention!

Your sacred rights are in danger; your dearest liberties are menaced; your wives and children are on the point of dissolution; the infamous and unconstitutional position that the sun gives light by day, and the moon by night, is openly and impudently propagated, and now is the only occasion that will probably ever offer to arrest an error so pregnant with deception and domestic evils. We present to your notice a suitable defender of all these near and dear interests, in the person of

JOHN GOLDENCALF,

The known patriot, the approved legislator, the profound philosopher, the incorruptible statesman. To our adopted fellow-citizens we need not recommend Mr. Goldencalf, for he is truly one of themselves; to the native citizens we will only say, "Try him, and you will be more than satisfied."

I found this placard of great use, for it gave me the first information I had yet had of the duty I was expected to perform in the coming session of the Great Council; which was merely to demonstrate that the moon gave light by day, and that the sun gave light by night. Of course, I immediately set about, in my own mind, hunting up the proper arguments by which this grave political hypothesis was to be properly maintained. The next placard was in favor of—

NOAH POKE,

The experienced navigator, who will conduct the ship of state into the haven of prosperity—the practical astronomer who knows by frequent observations, that Lunars are not to be got in the dark.

Perpendiculars, be plumb, and lay your enemies on their backs!

After this, I fell in with—

THE HONORABLE ROBERT SMUT

Is confidently recommended to all their fellow-citizens by the nominating committee of the Anti-Approved-Sublimated-Politico-Tangents, as the real gentleman, a ripe scholar,* an enlightened politician, and a sound democrat.

But I should fill the manuscript with nothing else, were I to record a tithe of the commendations and abuse that were heaped on us all, by a community to whom, as yet, we were absolutely strangers. A single sample of the latter shall suffice

AFFIDAVIT.

Personally appeared before me, John Equity, Justice of the Peace, Peter Veracious, &c. &c., who, being duly sworn upon the Holy Evangelists, doth depose and say, viz. That he was intimately acquainted with one John Goldencalf in his native country, and that he is personally knowing to the fact that he, the said John Goldencalf, has three wives, seven illegitimate children, is moreover a bankrupt without character, and that he was obliged to emigrate in consequence of having stolen a sheep.

Sworn, &c.

(Signed,) PETER VERACIOUS.

---

* I afterwards found this was a common phrase in Leaplow, being uniformly applied to every monikin who wore spectacles.

I naturally felt a little indignant at this impudent statement, and was about to call upon the first passer-by for the address of Mr. Veracious, when the skirts of my skin were seized by one of the Horizontal nominating committee, and I was covered with congratulations on my being happily elected. Success is an admirable plaster for al wounds, and I really forgot to have the affair of the sheep and of the illegitimate children inquired into; although I still protest, that had fortune been ess propitious, the rascal who promulgated this calumny would have been made to smart for his temerity. In less than five minutes it was the turn of Captain Poke. He, too, was congratulated in due form; for, as it appeared, the "immigrunt interest," as Noah termed it, had actually carried a candidate on each of the two great opposing tickets. Thus far, all was well; for, after sharing his mess so long, I had not the smallest objection to sit in the Leaplow parliament with the worthy sealer; but our mutual surprise and, I believe I might add, indignation were a good deal excited by shortly encountering a walking notice, which contained a programme of the proceedings to be observed at the "*Reception* of the Honorable Robert Smut."

It would seem that the Horizontals and the Perpendiculars had made so many spurious and mistified ballots, in order to propitiate the Tangents, and to cheat each other, that this young blackguard actually stood at the head of the poll!—a political phenomenon, as I subsequently discovered, however, by no means of rare occurrence in the Leaplow history of the periodical selection of the wisest and best.

There was certainly an accumulation of interest on arriving in a strange land, to find oneself both extolled and vituperated on most of the corners of its capital, and to be elected to its parliament, all in the same day. Still, I did not permit myself to be either so much elated or so much depressed, as not to have all my eyes about me, in order to get as correctly as possible, and as quickly as possible, some insight into the characters, tastes, habits, wishes and wants of my constituents.

I have already declared that it is my intention to dwell chiefly on the moral excellencies and peculiarities of the people of the monikin world. Still I could not walk through the streets of Bivouac without observing a few physical usages, that I shall mention, because they have an evident connexion with the state of society, and the historical recollections of this interesting portion of the polar region.

In the first place, I remarked that all sorts of quadrupeds are just as much at home in the promenades of the town, as the inhabitants themselves, a fact that I make no doubt has some very proper connexion with that principle of equal rights, on which the institutions of the country are established In the second place, I could not but see that their dwellings are constructed on the very minimum of base, propping each other, as emblematic of the mutual support obtained by the republican system, and seeking their development in height, for the want of breadth; a singularity of customs that I did not hesitate at once to refer to a usage of living in trees, at an epocha not very remote. In the third place, I noted, instead of entering their dwellings near the ground, like men, and indeed like most other unfledged animals, that they ascend by means of external steps, to an aperture about half-way between the roof and the earth, where, having obtained admission, they go up or down within the building, as occasion requires. This usage, I made no question, was preserved from the period, and that, too, no distant one, when the savage condition of the country induced them to seek protection against the ravages of wild beasts, by having recourse to ladders, which were drawn up after the family, into the top of the tree, as the sun sunk beneath the horizon. These steps or ladders are generally made of some white material, in order that they may, even now, be found in the dark, should the danger be urgent; although I do not know that Bivouac is a more disorderly or unsafe town than another, in the present day. But habits linger in the usages of a people, and are often found to exist as fashions, long after the motive of their origin has ceased and been forgotten. As a proof of this, many of the dwellings of Bivouac have still enormous iron *chevaux-de-frise* before the doors, and near the base of the stone-ladders; a practice unquestionably taken from the original, unsophisticated, domestic defences of this wary and enterprising race. Among a great many of these *chevaux-de-frise*, I remarked certain iron images, that resemble the kings of chess-men, and which I took, at first, to be symbols of the calculating qualities of the owners of the mansions, a species of republican heraldry; but which the Brigadier told me, on inquiry, were no more than a fashion that had descended from the custom of having stuffed images before the doors, in the early days of the settlement, to frighten away the beasts at night, precisely as we station scare crows in a corn-field. Two of these well-padded sentinels, with a stick stuck up in a firelock-attitude, he assured me, had often been known to maintain a siege of a week, against a she-bear and a numerous family of hungry cubs, in the old-n times; and, now that the danger was gone, he presumed the families which had caused these iron monuments to be erected, had done so to record some marvellous risks of this nature, from which their forefathers had escaped by means of so ingenious an expedient.

Everything in Bivouac bears the impress of the sublime principle of the institutions. The houses of the private citizens, for instance, overtop the roofs of all the public edifices, to show that the public is merely a servant of the citizen. Even the churches have this peculiarity, proving that the road to heaven is not independent of the popular will. The great Hall of Justice, an edifice of which the Bivouackers are exceedingly proud, is constructed in the same recumbent style, the architect, with a view to protect himself from the imputation of believing that the firmament was within reach of his hand, having taken the precaution to run up a wooden finger-board from the centre of the building, which points to the place where, according to the notions of all other people, the ridge of the roof itself should have been raised. So very apparent was this peculiarity, Noah observed that it seemed to him as if the whole "'arth" had been rolled down by a great political rolling-pin, by way of giving the country its finishing touch.

While making these remarks, one drew near at a brisk trot, who, Mr. Downright observed, eagerly desired our acquaintance. Surprised at his pretending to know such a fact without any previous communication, I took the liberty of asking why he thought that we were the particular objects of the other's haste.

"Simply because you are fresh arrivals. This person is one of a sufficiently numerous class among us, who, devoured by a small ambition seek notoriety—which, by the way, they are near obtaining in more respects than they proba b.y desire—by obtruding themselves on every stranger who touches our shore. Theirs is not a generous and frank hospitality tnat would fain serve others, but an irritable vanity that would glorify themselves. The liberal and enlightened monikin is easily to be distinguished from all of this *clique*. He is neither ashamed of, nor bigoted in favor of any usages, simply because they are domestic. With him the criterions of merit are propriety, taste, expediency and fitness. He distinguishes, while these crave; he neither wholly rejects, nor wholly lives by, imitation, but judges for himself, and uses his experience as a respectable and useful guide; while these think that all they can attain that is beyond the reach of their neighbors, is, as a matter of course, the sole aim of life. Strangers they seek, because they have long since decreed that this country, with its usages, its people, and all it contains, being founded on popular rights, is all that is debased and vulgar, themselves and a few of their own particular friends excepted; and they are never so happy as when they are gloating on, and basking in, the secondary refinements of what we call the 'Old Region.' Their own attainments, however, being pretty much God-sends, or such as we all pick up in our daily intercourse, they know nothing of any foreign country but Leaphigh, whose language we happen to speak; and, as Leaphigh is also the very *beau idéal* of exclusion, in its usages, opinions and laws, they deem all who come from that part of the earth, as rather more entitled to their profounc homage than any other strangers."

Here Judge People's Friend, who had been vigor

ously pumping the nominating committee on the subject of the chances of the little wheel, suddenly left us, with a sneaking, self-abased air, and with his nose to the ground, like a dog who has just caught a fresh scent.

The next time we met the ex-envoy, he was in mourning for some political backsliding that I never comprehended. He had submitted to a fresh amputation of the bob, and had so thoroughly humbled the seat of reason, that it was not possible for the most envious and malignant disposition to fancy he had a particle of brains left. He had, moreover, caused every hair to be shaved off his body, which was as naked as the hand, and altogether he presented an edifying picture of penitence and self-abasement. I afterwards understood that this purification was considered perfectly satisfactory, and that he was thought to be, again, within the limits of the most Patriotic Patriots.

In the mean time the Bivouacker had approached me, and was introduced as Mr. Gilded Wriggle.

"Count Poke de Stunin'tun, my good sir," said the Brigadier, who was the master of ceremonies on this occasion, "and the Mogul Goldencalf—both noblemen of ancient lineage, admirable privileges, and of the purest water;—gentlemen, who, when they are at home, have six dinners daily, always sleep on diamonds, and whose castles are none of them less than six leagues in extent."

"My friend General Downright has taken too much pains, gentlemen," interrupted our new acquaintance, "your rank and extraction being self-evident. Welcome to Leaplow! I beg you will make free with my house, my dog, my cat, my horse, and myself. I particularly beg that your first, your last, and all the intermediate visits, wil be to me. Well, Mogul, what do you really think of us? You have now been on shore long enough to have formed a pretty accurate notion of our institutions and habits. I beg you will not judge of all of us by what you see in the streets——"

"It is not my intention, sir."

"You are cautious, I perceive!—We are in an awful condition, I confess; trampled on by the vulgar, and far—very far from being the people that, I dare say, you expected to see. I couldn't be made the assistant alderman of my ward, if I wished it, sir; too much jacobinism—the people are fools, sir; know nothing, sir; not fit to rule themselves, much less their betters, sir—here have a set of us, some hundreds in this very town, been telling them what fools they are, how unfit they are to manage their own affairs, and how fast they are going to the devil, any time these twenty years, and still we have not yet persuaded them to intrust one of us with authority! To say the truth, we are in a most miserable condition; and if anything *could* ruin this country, democracy would have ruined it, just thirty-five years ago."

Here the wailings of Mr. Wriggle were interrupted by the wailings of Count Poke de Stunin'-tun. The latter, by gazing in admiration at the speaker, had inadvertently struck his toe against one of the forty-three thousand seven hundred and sixty inequalities of the pavement, (for everything in Leaplow is exactly equal, except the streets and highways,) and fallen forward on his nose. I have already had occasion to allude to the sealer's readiness in using opprobrious epithets. This *contretems* happened in the principal street of Bivouac, or in what is called the Wide-path, an avenue of more than a league in extent; but, notwithstanding its great length, Noah took it up at one end and abused it all the way to the other, with a precision, fidelity, rapidity and point, that excited general admiration. "It was the dirtiest, worst paved, meanest, vilest street he had ever seen, and if they had it at Stunin'tun, instead of using it as a street at all, they would fence it up at each end, and turn it into a hog-lot." Here Brigadier Downright betrayed unequivocal signs of alarm. Drawing us aside, he vehemently demanded of the Captain, if he were mad, to berate in this unheard-of manner, the touchstone of Bivouac sentiment, nationality, taste and elegance! This street was never spoken of except by the use of superlatives; a usage, by the way, that Noah himself had by no means neglected. It was commonly thought to be the longest and the shortest, the widest and the narrowest, the best built and the worst built avenue in the universe. "Whatever you say or do," he continued, "whatever you think or believe, never deny the superlatives of the Wide-path. If asked if you ever saw a street so crowded, although there be room to wheel a regiment, swear it is stifling; if required to name another promenade so free from interruption, protest by your soul, that the place is a desert! Say what you will of the institutions of the country——"

"How!" I exclaimed; "of the sacred rights of monikins!"

"Bedaub them, and the mass of the monikins, too, with just as much filth as you please. Indeed, if you wish to circulate freely in genteel society, I would advise you to get a pretty free use of the words 'jacobins,' 'rabble,' 'mob,' 'agrarians,' '*canaille*,' and 'democrats;' for they recommend many to notice who possess nothing else. In our happy and independent country, it is a sure sign of lofty sentiments, a finished education, a regu lated intellect, and a genteel intercourse, to know how to bespatter all that portion of your fellow-creatures, for instance, who live in one-story edifices."

"I find all this very extraordinary, your government being professedly a government of the mass!"

"You have intuitively discovered the reason—is it not fashionable to abuse the government everywhere? Whatever you do, in genteel life, ought to be based on liberal and elevated principles; and, therefore, abuse all that is animate in Leaplow, the present company, with their relatives and quadrupeds, excepted; but do not raise your blaspheming tongues against anything that is inanimate! Respect, I entreat of you, the houses, the trees, the rivers, the mountains, and, above all, in Bivouac, respect the Wide-path! We are a people of lively sensibilities, and are tender of the reputations of even our stocks and stones. Even the Leaplow philosophers are all of a mind on this subject."

"King!"

"Can you account for this very extraordinary peculiarity, Brigadier?"

"Surely you cannot be ignorant that all which is property is sacred! We have a great respect for property, sir, and do not like to hear our wares underrated. But lay it on the mass so much the harder, and you will only be thought to be in possession of a superior and a refined intelligence."

Here we turned again to Mr. Wriggle, who was dying to be noticed once more.

"Ah! gentlemen, last from Leaphigh!"—he had been questioning one of our attendants—"How comes on that great and consistent people?"

"As usual, sir;—great and consistent."

"I think, however, we are quite their equals eh?—Chips of the same blocks?"

"No, sir,—blocks of the same chips."

Mr. Wriggle laughed, and appeared pleased with the compliment; and I wished I had even laid it on a little thicker.

"Well, Mogul, what are our great forefathers about? Still pulling to pieces that sublime fabric of a constitution, which has so long been the wonder of the world, and my especial admiration?"

"They are talking of changes, sir, although I believe they have effected no great matter. The Primate of all Leaphigh, I had occasion to remark, still has seven joints to his tail."

"Ah! they are a wonderful people, sir!" said Wriggle, looking ruefully at his own bob, which, as I afterwards understood, was a mere natural abortion. "I detest change, sir; were I a Leaphigher, I would die in my tail!"

"One for whom Nature has done so much in this way, is to be excused a little enthusiasm."

"A most miraculous people, sir—the wonder of the world—and their institutions are the greatest prodigy of the times!"

"That is well remarked, Wriggle," put in the Brigadier; "for they have been tinkering them, and altering them, any time these five hundred and fifty years, and still they remain precisely the same!"

"Very true, Brigadier, very true—the marvel of our times! But, gentlemen, what do you indeed think of us? I shall not let you off with generalities. You have now been long enough on shore to have formed some pretty distinct notions about us, and I confess I should be glad to hear them. Speak the truth with candor—are we not most miserable, forlorn, disreputable devils, after all?"

I disclaimed the ability to judge of the social condition of a people on so short an acquaintance:

but to this Mr. Wriggle would not listen. He insisted that I must have been particularly disgusted with the coarseness and want of refinement in the rabble, as he called the mass, who, by the way had already struck me as being relatively much the better part of the population, so far as I had seen things!—more than commonly decent, quiet and civil. Mr. Wriggle, also, very earnestly and piteously begged I would not judge of the whole country by such samples as I might happen to fall in with in the highways.

"I trust, Mogul, you will have charity enough to believe we are not all of us quite as bad as appearances, no doubt, make us in your polished eyes. These rude beings are spoiled by our jacobinical laws; but we have a class, sir, that *is* different. But, if you will not touch on the people, how do you like the town, sir? A poor place, no doubt, after your own ancient capitals?"

"Time will remedy all that, Mr. Wriggle."

"Do you then think we really want time!—now, that house at the corner, there, to my taste is fit for a gentleman in any country—eh?"

"No doubt, sir; fit for one."

"This is but a poor street in the eyes of you travellers, I know, this Wide-path of ours; though we think it rather sublime?"

"You do yourself injustice, Mr. Wriggle—though not equal to many of the——"

"How, sir, the Wide-path not equal to anything on earth! I know several people who have been in the old world"—so the Leaplowers call the region of Leaphigh, Leapup, Leapdown, &c.—and they swear there is not as fine a street in any part of it. I have not had the good fortune to travel, sir; but, sir, permit me, sir, to say, sir that some of them, sir, that *have* travelled, sir think, sir, the Wide-path, sir, the most magnificent public avenue, sir, that their experienced eyes ever beheld, sir—yes, sir, that their very experienced eyes ever beheld, sir."

"I have seen so little of it, as yet, Mr. Wriggle, that you will pardon me if I have spoken hastily."

"Oh! no offence—I despise the monikin who is not above local vanities and provincial admiration! You ought to have seen that, sir, for I frankly admit, sir, that no rabble can be worse than ours, and that we are all going to the devil, as fast as ever we can. No, sir, a most miserable rabble, sir.—But as for this street, and our houses, and our cats, and our dogs, and certain exceptions—you understand me, sir—it is quite a different thing. Pray, Mogul, who is the greatest personage, now, in your nation?"

"Perhaps I ought to say the Duke of Wellington, sir."

"Well, sir, allow me to ask if he lives in a better house than that before us?—I see you are delighted, eh! We are a poor, new nation of pitiful traders, sir, half savage, as everybody knows; but we *do* flatter ourselves that we know how to build a house! Will you just step in and see a new sofa that its owner bought only yesterday—I know him intimately, and nothing gives him so much pleasure as to show his new sofa."

I declined the invitation on the plea of fatigue, and by this means got rid of so troublesome an acquaintance. On leaving me, however, he begged that I would not fail to make his house my home, swore terribly at the rabble, and invited me to admire a very ordinary view that was to be obtained by looking up the Wide-path in a particular direction, but which embraced his own abode When Mr. Wriggle was fairly out of ear-shot, I demanded of the Brigadier if Bivouac, or Leap low, contained many such prodigies.

"Enough to make themselves very troublesome, and us ridiculous," returned Mr. Downright. "We are a young nation, Sir John, covering a great surface, with a comparatively small population, and, as you are aware, separated from the older parts of the monikin region by a belt of ocean. In some respects we are like people in the country, and we possess the merits and failings of those who are so situated. Perhaps no nation has a larger share of reflecting and essentially respectable inhabitants than Leaplow; but, not satisfied with being what circumstances so admirably fit them to be, there is a *clique* among us, who, influenced by the greater authority of older nations, pine to be that which neither nature, education, manners nor facilities will just yet allow them to become. In short, sir, we have the besetting sin of a young community—imitation. In our case the imitation is not always happy, either; it being necessarily an imitation that is founded on descriptions. If the evil were limited to mere social absurdities, it might be laughed at—but that inherent desire of distinction, which is the most morbid and irritable, unhappily, in the minds of those who are the least able to attain anything more than a very vulgar notoriety, is just as active here, as it is elsewhere; and some who have got wealth, and and who can never get more than what is purely dependent on wealth, affect to despise those who are not as fortunate as themselves in this particular. In their longings for pre-eminence, they turn to other states—Leaphigh more especially, which is the *beau idéal* of all nations and people, who wish to set up a caste in opposition to despotism—for rules of thought, and declaim against that very mass which is at the bottom of all their prosperity, by obstinately refusing to allow of any essential innovation on the common rights. In addition to these social pretenders, we have our political Endoctrinated."

"Endoctrinated! Will you explain the meaning of the term?"

"Sir, an Endoctrinated is one of a political school who holds to the validity of certain theories which have been made to justify a set of adventitious facts, as is eminently the case in our own great model, Leaphigh. We are peculiarly placed in this country. Here, as a rule, facts—meaning political and social facts—are greatly in advance of opinion, simply because the former are left chiefly to their own free action, and the latter is necessarily trammelled by habit and prejudice; while in the 'old-region' opinion, as a rule, and meaning the leading or better opinion, is greatly in advance of facts, because facts are restrained by usage and personal interests, and opinion is incited by study, and the necessity of change."

"Permit me to say, Brigadier, that I find your present institutions a remarkable result to follow such a state of things."

"They are a cause, rather than a consequence. Opinion, as a whole, is everywhere on the advance; and it is further advanced, even here, *as a whole*, than anywhere else. Accident has favored the foundation of the social compact; and once founded, the facts have been hastening to their consummation faster than the monikin mind has been able to keep company with them. This is a remarkable but true state of the whole region. In other monikin countries, you see opinion tugging at rooted practices, and making desperate efforts to eradicate them from their bed of vested interests, while here you see facts dragging opinion after them like a tail wriggling behind a kite.* As to our purely social imitation and social follies, absurd as they are, they are necessarily confined to a small and an immaterial class; but the *Endoctrinated* spirit is a much more serious affair. That unsettles confidence, innovates on the right, often innocently and ignorantly, and causes the vessel of state to sail like a ship with a drag towing in her wake."

"This is truly a novel condition for an enlightened monikin nation!"

"No doubt, men manage better; but of all this you will learn more in the Great Council. You may, perhaps, think it strange that our facts should preserve their ascendency in opposition to so powerful a foe as opinion; but you will remember that a great majority of our people, if not absolutely on a level with circumstances, being purely practical, are much nearer to this level, than the class termed the Endoctrinated. The last are troublesome and delusive, rather than overwhelming."

"To return to Mr. Wriggle—is his sect numerous?"

"His class flourishes most in the towns. In Leaplow we are greatly in want of a capital, where the cultivated, educated, and well-mannered can assemble, and, placed by their habits and tastes

---

* One would think that Brigadier Downright had lately paid a visit to our own happy and much enlightened land. Fifty years since, the negro was a slave in New-York, and incapable of contracting marriage with a white. Facts have, however, been progressive; and, from one privilege to another, he has at length obtained that of consulting his own tastes in this matter, and, so far as he himself is concerned, of doing as he pleases. This is the *fact;* but he who presumes to *speak* of it, has his windows broken by *opinion*, for his pains!
Note by the Editor.

above the ordinary motives and feelings of the less instructed, they might form a more healthful, independent, appropriate, and manly public sentiment than that which now pervades the country. As things are, the real *élite* of this community are so scattered, as rather to receive an impression *from* than to impart one *to* society. The Leaplow Wriggles, as you have just witnessed, are selfish and exacting as to their personal pretensions, irritably confident as to the merit of any particular excellence which limits their own experience, and furiously proscribing to those whom they fancy less fortunate than themselves."

"Good Heavens!—Brigadier—all this is excessively human!"

"Ah! it is—is it? Well, this is certainly the way with us monikins. Our Wriggles are ashamed of exactly that portion of our population of which they have most reason to be proud, viz. the mass; and they are proud of precisely that portion of which they have most reason to be ashamed, viz themselves. But plenty of opportunities will offer to look farther into this; and we will now hasten to the inn."

As the Brigadier appeared to chafe under the subject, I remained silent, following him as fast as I could, but keeping my eyes open, the reader may be very sure, as we went along. There was one peculiarity I could not but remark in this singular town. It was this:—all the houses were smeared over with some coloured earth, and then, after all this pains had been taken to cover the material, an artist was employed to make white marks around every separate particle of the fabric, (and they were in millions,) which ingenious particularity gives the dwellings a most agreeable air of detail, imparting to the architecture, in general, a sublimity that is based on the multiplication table. If to this be added the black of the *chevaux-de-frise*, the white of the entrance-ladders, and a sort of standing-collar to the whole, immediately under the eaves, of some very dazzling hue, the effect is not unlike that of a platoon of drummers, in scarlet coats, cotton lace, and cuffs and capes of white. What renders the similitude more striking, is the fact that no two of the same platoon appear to be exactly of a size, as is very apt to be the case with your votaries in military music.

CHAPTER XXV.

A fundamental principle, a fundamental law, and a fundamental error.

The people of Leaplow are remarkable for the deliberation of their acts, the moderation of their views, and the accumulation of their wisdom. As a matter of course, such a people is never in an indecent haste. Although I had now been legally naturalized, and regularly elected to the Great Council fully twenty-four hours, three entire days were allowed for the study of the institutions, and to become acquainted with the genius of a nation who, according to their own account of the matter, have no parallel in heaven or earth, or in the waters under the earth, before I was called upon to exercise my novel and important functions. I profited by the delay, and shall seize a favorable moment to make the reader acquainted with some of my acquisitions on this interesting topic.

The institutions of Leaplow are divided into two great moral categories, viz. the *legal*, and the *substitutive*. The former embraces the provisions of the great *elementary*, and the latter all the provisions of the great *alimentary* principle. The first, accordingly, is limited by the constitution, or the Great National Allegory, while the last is limited by nothing but practice; one contains the proposition, and the other its deductions; this is all hypothesis, that, all corollary. The two great political land-marks, the two public opinions, the bob-upon-bobs, the rotatory action, and the great and little wheels, are merely inferential; and I shall, therefore, say nothing about them in my present treatise which has a strict relation only to the fundamental law of the land, or to the Great and Sacred National Allegory.

It has been already stated that Leaplow was originally a scion of Leaphigh. The political separation took place in the last generation, when the Leaplowers publicly renounced Leaphigh and all it contained, just as your catechumen is made to renounce the devil and all his works. This renunciation, which is also sometimes called the *denunciation*, was much more to the liking of Leaplow than to that of Leaphigh; and a long and sanguinary war was the consequence. The Leaplowers, after a smart struggle, however, prevailed in their firm determination to have no more to do with Leaphigh. The sequel will show how far they were right.

Even preceding the struggle, so active was the sentiment of patriotism and independence, that the citizens of Leaplow, though ill-provided with the productions of their own industry, proudly resorted to the self-denial of refusing to import even a pin from the mother country, actually preferring nakedness to submission. They even solemnly voted that their venerable progenitor, instead of being, as she clearly ought to have been, a fond, protecting and indulgent parent, was, in truth, no other than a rapacious, vindictive and tyrannical step-mother. This was the opinion, it will be remembered, when the two communities were legally united, had but one head, wore clothes, and necessarily pursued a multitude of their interests in common.

By the lucky termination of the war, all this was radically changed. Leaplow pointed her thumb at Leaphigh, and declared her intention henceforth to manage her own affairs in her own way. In order to do this the more effectually, and, at the same time, to throw dirt into the countenance of her late step-mother, she determined that her own polity should run so near a parallel, and yet should be so obviously an improvement on that of Leaphigh, as to demonstrate the imperfections of the latter to the most superficial observer. That this patriotic resolution was faithfully carried out in practice, I am now about to demonstrate.

In Leaphigh, the old human principle had long prevailed, that political authority came from God; though why such a theory should ever have prevailed anywhere, as Mr. Downright once expressed it, I cannot see, the devil very evidently having a greater agency in its exercise than any other influence, or intelligence, whatever. However, the *jus divinum* was the regulator of the Leaphigh social compact, until the nobility managed to get the better of the *jus*, when the *divinum* was left to shif' for itself. It was at this epocha the present constitution found its birth. Any one may have observed that one stick placed on end will fall, as a matter of course, unless rooted in the earth. Two sticks fare no better, even with their tops united; but three sticks form a standard. This simple and beautiful idea gave rise to the polity of Leaphigh. Three moral props were erected in the midst of the community, at the foot of one of which was placed the King, to prevent it from slipping; for all the danger, under such a system, came from that of the base slipping; at the foot of the second, the nobles; and at the foot of the third, the people. On the summit of this tripod was raised the machine of state. This was found to be a capital invention in theory, though practice, as practice is very apt to do, subjected it to some essential modifications. The King, having his stick all his own way, gave a great deal of trouble to the two other sets of stick-holders; and, unwilling to disturb the theory, for that was deemed to be irrevocably settled and sacred, the nobility, who, for their own particular convenience, paid the principal workmen at the base of the people's stick to stand steady, set about the means of keeping the King's stick, also, in a more uniform and serviceable attitude. It was on this occasion that, discovering the King never could keep his end of the great social stick in the place where he had sworn to keep it, they solemnly declared that he must have forgotten where the constitutional foot-hole was, and that he had irretrievably lost his memory,—a decision that was the remote cause of the recent calamity of Captain Poke. The King was no sooner constitutionally deprived of his memory, than it was an easy matter to strip him of all his other faculties; after which it was humanely decreed, as indeed it ought to be in the case of a being so destitute, that he could do no wrong. By way of following out the idea on a humane and Christian-like principle, and in order to make one part of the practice conform to the other, it was shortly after determined that he should do nothing; his eldest first-cousin of the masculine gender being legally proclaimed his substitute. In the end, the crimson curtain was drawn before the throne. As, however, this cousin might begin to wriggle the stick in his turn, and derange the balance of the tripod, the other two sets of stick-holders next decided that, though his Majesty had an undeniable constitutional right to say who *should be* his eldest first-cousin of the masculine gender, they had an undoubted constitutional right to say who he *should not be*. The result of all this was a compromise; his Majesty, who, like other people, found the sweets of authority more palatable than the bitter, agreeing to get up on top of the tripod, where he might appear seated on the machine of state, to receive salutations, and eat and drink in peace, leaving the others to settle among themselves who should do the work at the bottom, as well as they could. In brief, such is the history, and such was the polity, of Leaphigh, when I had the honor of visiting that country.

The Leaplowers were resolute to prove that all this was radically wrong. They determined, in the first place, that there should be but one great social beam; and, in order that it should stand perfectly steady, they made it the duty of every citizen to prop its base. They liked the idea of a tripod well enough, but, instead of setting one up in the Leaphigh fashion, they just reversed its form, and stuck it on top of their beam, legs uppermost, placing a separate agent on each leg, to work their machine of state; taking care, also, to send a new one aloft periodically. They reasoned thus: If one of the Leaphigh beams slip—and they will be very apt to slip in wet weather, with the King, nobles, and people wriggling and shoving against each other—down will come the whole machine of state, or, to say the least, it will get so much awry as never to work as well as at first; and therefore we will have none of it. If, on the other hand, one of our agents makes a blunder and falls, why, he will only break his own neck. He will, moreover, fall in the midst of us, and, should he escape with life, we can either catch him and throw him back again, or we can send a better hand up in his place, to serve out the rest of his time. They also maintain that one beam, supported by all the citizens, is much less likely to slip than three beams, supported by three powers of very uncertain, not to say unequal, forces.

Such, in effect, is the substance of the respective National Allegories of Leaphigh and of Leaplow; I say Allegories, for both governments seem to rely on this ingenious form of exhibiting their great distinctive national sentiments. It would, in fact, be an improvement, were all constitutions nenceforth to be written in this manner, since they would necessarily be more explicit, intelligible, and sacred than they are by the present attempt at literality.

Having explained the governing principles of these two important states, I now crave the reader's attention, for a moment, while I go a little into the details of the *modus operandi*, in both cases.

Leaphigh acknowledged a principle, in the outset, that Leaplow totally disclaimed, viz. that of primogeniture. Being an only child myself, and having no occasion for research on this interesting subject, I never knew the basis of this peculiar right, until I came to read the great Leaphigh commentator, Whiterock, on the governing rules of the social compact. I there found that the first-born, *morally* considered, is thought to have better claims to the honors of the genealogical tree, on the father's side, than these offspring whose origin is to be referred to a later period in connubial life. On this obvious and highly discriminating principle, the crown, the rights of the nobles, and indeed all other rights, are transferred from father to son, in the direct male line, according to primogeniture.

Nothing of this is practised in Leaplow. There, the supposition of legitimacy is as much in favor of the youngest as of the oldest born, and the practice is in conformity. As there is no hereditary chief to poise on one of the legs of the great tripod, the people at the foot of the beam choose one from among themselves, periodically, who is called the Great Sachem. The same people choose another set, few in number, who occupy a common seat, on another leg. These they term the Riddles. Another set, still more numerous and popular in aspect, if not in fact, fills a large seat on the third leg. These last, from their being supposed to be supereminently popular and disinterested, are familiarly known as the Legion. They are also pleasingly nicknamed the Bobees, an appellation that took its rise in the circumstance that most of the members of their body have submitted to the second dock, and, indeed, have nearly obliterated every sign of a *cauda*. I had, most luckily, been chosen to sit in the House of Bobees, a station for which I felt myself to be well qualified, in this great essential at least; for all the anointing and forcing resorted to by Noah and myself, during our voyage out, and our residence in Leaphigh, had not produced so much as a visible sprout in either.

The Great Sachem, the Riddles, and the Legion, had conjoint duties to perform, in certain respects, and separate duties, in others. All three, as they owed their allegorical elevation to, so were they dependent on, the people at the foot of the great social stick, for approbation and reward,—that is to say, for all rewards other than those which they have it in their power to bestow on themselves. There was another authority, or agent of the public, that is equally perched on the social beam, though not quite so dependent as the three just named, upon the main prop of the people,—being also propped by a mechanical disposition of the tripod itself. These are termed the Supreme Arbitrators, and their duties are to revise the acts of the other three agents of the people, and to decide whether they are or are not in conformity with the recognized principles of the Sacred Allegory.

I was greatly delighted with my own progress in the study of the Leaplow institutions. In the first place, I soon discovered that the principal thing was to reverse the political knowledge I had acquired in Leaphigh, as one would turn a tub upside-down, when he wished to draw from its stores at a fresh end, and then I was pretty sure of being within at least the spirit of the Leaplow law. Every thing seemed simple, for all was dependent on the common prop, at the base of the great social beam.

Having got a thorough insight myself, into the governing principles of the system under which I had been chosen to serve, I went to look up my colleague, Captain Poke, in order to ascertain how he understood the great Leaplow Allegory.

I found the mind of the sealer, according to a beautiful form of speech already introduced in this narrative, "considerably exercised," on the several subjects that so naturally presented themselves to a man in his situation. In the first place, he was in a towering passion at the impudence of Bob in presuming to offer himself as a candidate for the Great Council; and having offered himself, the rage of the Captain was in no degree abated by the circumstance of the young rascal's being at the head of the poll. He most unreservedly swore "that no subordinate of his should ever sit in the same legislative body with himself; that he was a republican by birth, and knew the usages of republican go vernments quite as well as the best patriot among them; and although he admitted that all sorts of critturs were sent to Congress in his country, no man ever knew an instance of a cabin-boy's being sent there. They might elect just as much as they pleased; but coming ashore, and playing politician, were very different things from cleaning his boots, and making his coffee, and mixing his grog." The Captain had just been waited on by a committee of the Perpendiculars, (half the Leaplow community is on some committee or other,) by whom he had been elected, and they had given notice, that instructions would be sent in, forthwith, to all their representatives, to perform Gyration No. 3., as soon after the meeting of the Council as possible. He was no tumbler, and he had sent for a master of political saltation, who had just been with him, practising. According to Noah's own statement, his success was any thing but flattering. "If they would give a body room, Sir John," he said, in a complaining accent, "I should think nothing of it—but you are expected to stand shoulder to shoulder—yard-arm and yard-arm,—and throw a flap-jack as handily as an old woman would toss a johnny-cake! It's unreasonable to think of waring ship without room; but give me room, and I'll engage to get round on the other tack, and to luff into the line again, as safely as the oldest cruiser among 'em, though not quite so quick. They do go about spitefully, that 's sartain!"

Nor were the Great National Allegories without their difficulties. Noah perfectly understood the images of the two tripods, though he was disposed to think that neither was properly secured. A mast would make but bad weather, he maintained, let it be ever so well rigged and stay'd, without being also securely stepped. He saw no use in trusting the heels of the beams to anybody. Good lashings were what were wanted, and then the people might go about their private affairs, and no fear the work would fall. That the King of Leaphigh had no memory, he could testify from bitter experience; nor did he believe that he had any conscience; and, chiefly he desired to know if we, when we got up into our places on top of the three inverted beams, among the other Bobees, were to make war on the Great Sachem and the Riddles, or whether we were to consider the whole affair as a good thing, in which the wisest course would be to make fair weather of it?

To all these remarks and questions, I answered as well as my own limited experience would allow; taking care to inform my friend that he had conceived the whole matter a little too literally, as all that he had been reading about the great political beams, the tripods, and the legislative boxes, was merely an allegory.

"And pray, then, Sir John, what may an allegory be?"

"In this case, my good sir, it is a constitution."

"And what is a constitution?"

"Why, it is sometimes, as you perceive, an allegory."

"And are we not to be mast-headed, then, according to the book?"

"Figuratively, only."

"But there are actually such critturs as the Great Sachem, and the Riddles, and above all, the Bobees! --We are boney fie-diddle-di-dee elected?"

"Boney fie-diddle-di-dee."

"And may I take the liberty of asking, what it is our duty to do?"

"We are to act practically, according to the literality of the legal, implied, figurative, allegorical significations of the Great National Compact under a legitimate construction."

"I fear we shall have to work double tides, Sir John, to do so much in so short a time! Do you mean that, in honest truth, there is no beam?"

"There is, and there is not."

"No fore, main, and mizzen-tops, according to what is here written down?"

"There is not, and there is."

"Sir John, in the name of God, speak out!—Is all this about eight dollars a day, no better than a take in?"

"That, I believe, is strictly literal."

As Noah now seemed a little mollified, I seized the opportunity to tell him he must beware how he attempted to stop Bob from attending the Council. Members were privileged, going and coming; and unless he was guarded in his course, he might have some unpleasant collision with the serjeant-at-arms. Besides, it was unbecoming the dignity of a legislator to be wrangling about trifles, and he to whom was confided the great affairs of a state, ought to attach the utmost importance to a grave exterior which commonly was of more account with his constituents than any other quality. Any one could tell whether he was grave or not, but it was by no means so easy a matter to tell whether he or his constituents had the greatest cause to appear so. Noah promised to be discreet, and we parted, not to meet again until we assembled to be sworn in.

Before continuing the narrative, I will just mention that we disposed of our commercial investments that morning. All the Leaphigh opinions brought good prices; and I had occasion to see how well the Brigadier understood the market, by the eagerness with which, in particular, the opinions on the state of society in Leaplow, were bought up. But, by one of those unexpected windfalls which raise up so many of the chosen of the earth to their high places, the cook did better than any of us. It will be remembered, that he had bartered an article of merchandise that he called slush against a neglected bale of Distinctive Leaplow Opinions, which had no success at all in Leaphigh. Coming as they did from abroad, these articles had taken as a novelty in Bivouac, and he sold them all before night, at enormous advances; the cry being that something new and extraordinary had found its way into the market!

CHAPTER XXVI.

How to enact laws—Oratory, logic and eloquence, all considered in their every-day aspects.

Political oaths are very much the same sort of thing everywhere, and I shall say no more about our inauguration than simply to state it took place as usual. The two houses were duly organized, and we proceeded, without delay, to the transaction of business. I will here state that I was much rejoiced to find Brigadier Downright among the Bobees, the Captain whispering that most probably he had been mistaken for an "immigrunt," and chosen accordingly.

It was not a great while before the Great Sachem sent us a communication, which contained a *compte rendu* of the state of the nation. Like most accounts it is my good fortune to receive, I thought it particularly long. Agreeably to the opinions of this document, the people of Leaplow were, by a good deal, the happiest people in the world; they were also considerably more respected, esteemed, beloved, honored, and properly appreciated, than any other monikin community; and, in short, they were the admiration and glory of the universe. I was exceedingly glad to hear this, for some of the facts were quite new to me; a circumstance which shows one can never get correct notions of a nation except from itself.

These important facts properly digested, we all of us set about our several duties with a zeal that spoke fairly for our industry and integrity. Things commenced swimmingly, and it was not long before the Riddles sent us a resolution for concurrence, by way of opening the ball. It was conceived in the following terms:—"Resolved, that the color which has hitherto been deemed to be black, is really white."

As this was the first resolution that involved a principle on which we had been required to vote, I suggested to Noah the propriety of our going round to the Brigadier, and inquiring what might be the drift of so singular a proposition. Our colleague answered the question with great good nature, giving us to understand that the Perpendiculars and the Horizontals had long been at variance on the mere coloring property of various important questions, and the real matter involved in the resolution was not visible. The former had always maintained, (by always, he meant ever since the time they maintained the contrary,) the doctrine of the resolution, and the latter its converse. A majority of the Riddles, just at this moment, are Perpendiculars; and, as it was now seen, they had succeeded in getting a vote on their favorite principle.

"According to this account of the matter, Sir John," observed the Captain, "I shall be compelled to maintain that black is white, seeing that I am in on the Parpendic'lar interest?"

I thought with the Captain, and was pleased that my own legislative debût was not to be characterized by the promulgation of any doctrine so much at variance with my preconceived ways of thinking. Curious, however, to know his opinion, I asked the Brigadier in what light he felt disposed to view the matter himself.

"I am elected by the Tangents," he said; "and, by what I can learn, it is the intention of our friends to steer a middle course; and one of our leaders is already selected, who, at a proper stage of the affair, is to move an amendment."

"Can you refer me, my dear friend, to anything connected with the Great National Allegory, that bears on this point?"

"Why, there is a clause among the fundamental and immutable laws, which it is thought was intended to meet this very case; but, unhappily, the sages by whom our Allegory was drawn up, have not paid quite as much attention to the phraseology as the importance of the subject demanded."

Here the Brigadier laid his finger on the clause in question, and I returned to a seat to study its meaning. It was conceived as follows:—Art. IV. Clause 6: "The Great National Council shall, in no case whatever, pass any law, or resolution, declaring white to be black."

After studying this fundamental enactment to the bottom, turning it on every side, and finally considering it upside-down, I came to the conclusion that its tenor was, on the whole, rather more favorable than unfavorable to the horizontal doctrine. It struck me, a very good argument was to be made out of the constitutional question, and that it presented a very fair occasion for a new member to venture on a maiden speech. Having so settled the matter, entirely to my own satisfaction, I held myself in reserve, waiting for the proper moment to produce an effect.

It was not long before the Chairman of the Committee on the Judiciary (one of the effects of the resolution was entirely to change the coloring of all testimony throughout the vast republic of Leaplow) made his report on the subject-matter of the resolution. This person was a Tangent, who had a besetting wish to become a Riddle, although the leaning of our house was decidedly horizontal; and, as a matter of course, he took the Riddle side of this question. The report, itself, required seven hours in the reading, commencing with the subject at the epocha of the celebrated caucus that was adjourned *sine die*, by the disruption of the earth's crust, and previously to the distribution of the great monikin family into separate communities, and ending with the subject of the resolution in his hand. The reporter had set his political palette with the utmost care, having completely covered the subjec with neutral tints, before he got through with it and glazing the whole down with ultramarine, in such a way as to cause the eye to regard the matter through a fictitious atmosphere. Finally, he repeated the resolution, verbatim, and as it came from the other house.

Mr. Speaker now called upon gentlemen to deliver their sentiments. To my utter amazement, Captain Poke arose, put his tobacco back into its box, and opened the debate, without apology.

The Honorable Captain said he understood this question to be one implicating the liberties of every body. He understood the matter literally, as it wa propounded in the Allegory, and set forth in the resolution; and, as such, he intended to look at it with unprejudyced eyes. "The natur' of this proposal lay altogether in color. What is color, after all? Make the most of it, and in the most favorabl position, which, perhaps, is the cheek of a comely young woman, and it is but skin-deep. He remembered the time when a certain female in another part of the univarse, who is commonly called Miss Poke, might have out-rosed the best rose in a place called Stunin'tun; and what did it all amount to? He should n't ask Miss Poke herself, for obvious reasons—but he would ask any of the neighbors how she looked now? Quitting female natur', he would come to human natur' generally. He had often remarked that sea-water was blue, and he had frequently caused pails to be lowered, and the water brought on deck, to see if he could come at any of this blueing matter—for indigo was both scarce and dear in his part of the world, but he never could make out anything by the experiment; from which he concluded that, on the whull, there was pretty much no such thing as color, at all.

"As for the resolution before the house, it depended entirely on the meaning of words. Now, after all, what is a word? Why, some people's words are good, and other people's words are good for nothing. For his part, he liked sealed instruments—which might be because he was a sealer—but as for mere words, he set but little store by them. He once tuck a man's word for his wages; and the long and short of it was, that he lost his money. He had known a thousand instances in which words had proved to be of no value, and he did not see why some gentlemen wished to make them of so much importance here. For his part, he was for puffing up nothing, no, not even a word or a color above its desarts. The people seemed to call for a change in the color of things, and he called upon gentlemen to remember that this was a free country, and one in which the laws ruled; and therefore he trusted they would be disposed to adapt the laws to the wants of the people. What had the people asked of the house in this matter? So far as his knowledge went, they had really asked nothing in words, but he understood there was great discontent on the subject of the old colors; and he construed their silence into an expression of cor.empt for words in general. He was a Parpendic'lai, and he should always maintain parpendic'lar sentiments. Gentlemen might not agree with him, but, for one, he was not disposed to jipordyze the liberties of his constituents, and therefore he gave the rizolution just as it came from the Riddles, without altering a letter—although he did think there was one word misspelt—he meant 'really,' which he had been taught to spell 'ra'ally'—but he was ready to sacrifice even his opinions on this point to the good of the country; and therefore he went with the Riddles, even to their misprints. He hoped the rizolution would pass, with the entire unanimity so important a subject demanded."

This speech produced a very strong sensation. Up to this time, the principal orators of the house had been much in the practice of splitting hairs about some nice technicality in the Great Allegory; but Noah, with the simplicity of a truly great mind, had made a home-thrust at the root of the whole matter; laying about him with the single-heartedness of the illustrious Manchechan, when he couched his lance against the wind-mills. The points admitted, that there were no such things as colors, and that words were of no moment, this, or indeed any other resolution, might be passed with impunity. The Perpendiculars in the house were singularly satisfied, for, to say the truth, their arguments hitherto had been rather flimsy. Out of doors, the effect was greater still; for it wrought a complete change in the whole tenor of the Perpendicular argument. Monikins who the day before had strenuously affirmed that their strength lay in the phraseology of the Great Allegory, now suddenly had their eyes opened, clearly perceiving that words had no just value. The argument had certainly undergone some modifications: but, luckily, the deduction was undisturbed. The Brigadier noticed this apparent anomaly; explaining, however, that it was quite common in Leaplow, more especially in all matters affecting politics; though he felt persuaded men must be more consistent.

No great time is required to put a well-organized political corps to the right-about, when proper attention has been paid to the preparatory drills. Although several of the best speakers among the Perpendiculars had appeared in their places, with ample notes, and otherwise in readiness to show that the phraseology of the resolution was altogether in favor of their views of the question, every monikin of them promptly rejected his previous argument, for the simple and more conclusive views of Captain Poke. On the other hand, the Horizontals were so completely taken by surprise, that not an orator among them all had a word to say for himself. So far from replying, they actually permitted one of their antagonists to rise and to follow up the blow of the Captain; a pretty certain sign that they were bothered.

The new speaker was a very prominent leader of the Perpendiculars. He was one of those politicians who are only the more dexterous from having been of all sides, knowing by experience the weak and the strong points of each, and being familiar with every subdivision of political sentiment that had ever existed in the country. This ingenious orator took up the subject with spirit, treating it throughout on the principle of the honorable member who had last spoken. According to his views of the question, the *gist* of a resolution, or a law, was to be found in things and not in words. Words were so many false lights to mislead, and—he need not tell this house a fact that was familiar to all who heard him—words would be, and were, daily moulded to suit the convenience of all sorts of per sons. It was a capital error in political life to be lavish of words, for the time might come when the garrulous and voluble would have cause to repent of having used them. He asked the house if the *thing* proposed were necessary—did the public interests require it—was the public mind prepared for it; if so, he begged gentlemen to do their duties to themselves, their characters, their consciences, their religion, their property, and, lastly, their constituents.

This orator had endeavored to destroy words by words, and I thought the house regarded his effort rather favorably. I now determined to make a rally in favor of the fundamental law, which evidently had as yet been but little regarded in the discussion. I caught the Speaker's eye, accordingly, and was on my feet in a moment.

I commenced by paying elaborate compliments to the talents and motives of those who had preceded me; and made some proper allusions to the known intelligence, patriotism, virtue, and legal attainments of the house. All this was so well received, that taking courage, I determined to come down upon my adversaries, at once, with the text of the written law. Prefacing the blow with an eulogium on the admirable nature of those institutions which were universally admitted to be the wonder of the world, and which were commonly pronounced to be the second perfection of monikin reason, those of Leaphigh being invariably deemed the first, I made a few apposite remarks on the necessity of respecting the vital ordinances of the body politic, and asked the attention of my hearers while I read to them a particular clause, which it had struck me had some allusion to the very point now in consideration. Having thus cleared the way, I had not the folly to defeat the objects of so much preparation, by an indiscreet precipitancy. So far from it, previously to reading the extract from the constitution, I waited until the attention of every member present was attracted more forcibly by the dignity, deliberation, and gravity of my manner, than by the substance of what had yet been said. In the midst of this deep silence and expectation I read aloud, in a voice that reached every cranny of the hall—

"The Great Council shall, in no case whatever pass any law, or resolution, declaring white to be black."

If I had been calm in the presentation of this authority, I was equally self-possessed in waiting for its effect. Looking about me, I saw surprise, perplexity, doubt, wonder and uncertainty, in every countenance, if I did not find conviction. One fact embarrassed even me. Our friends the Horizontals were evidently quite as much at fault as our opponents the Perpendiculars, instead of being, as I had good reason to hope, in an ecstasy of pleasure on hearing their cause sustained by an authority so weighty.

"Will the honorable member have the goodness to explain from what author he has quoted?" one of the leading Perpendiculars at length ventured to inquire.

"The language you have just heard, Mr. Speaker," I resumed, believing that now was the favorable instant to follow up the matter, "is language that must find an echo in every heart—it is language that can never be used in vain in this venerable hall, language that carries with it conviction and command"—I observed that the members were now fairly gaping at each other with wonder—"Sir, I am asked to name the author from whom I have quoted these sententious and explicit words—Sir, what you have just heard is to be found in the Article IV Clause 6. of the Great National Allegory——"

"Order—Order—Order!" shouted a hundred raven throats.

I stood aghast, even more amazed than the house itself had been only the instant before.

"Order—Order—Order—Order—Order!" continued to be yelled, as if a million of demons were screeching in the hall.

"The honorable member will please to recollect," said the bland, and ex-officio impartial Speaker who, by the way, was a Perpendicular, elected by fraud, "that it is out of order to use personalities."

"Personalities! I do not understand, sir——"

"The instrument to which the honorable member has alluded, his own good sense will tell him, was never written by itself—so far from this, the very members of the convention by which it was drawn up, are at this instant members of this house, and most of them supporters of the resolution now before the house; and it will be deemed personal to throw into their faces former official acts, in this unheard-of manner. I am sorry it is my duty to say, that the honorable member is entirely out of order."

"But, sir, the Sacred National——"

"Sacred, sir, beyond a doubt—but in a sense different from what you imagine—much too sacred, sir, ever to be alluded to here. There are the works of the commentators, the books of constructions, and especially the writings of various foreign and perfectly disinterested statesmen,—need I name Ekrub in particular!—that are at the command of members; but so long as I am honored with a seat in this chair, I shall peremptorily decide against all personalities."

I was dumb-founded. The idea that the authority itself would be refused never crossed my mind, though I had anticipated a sharp struggle on its construction. The constitution only required that no law should be passed declaring black to be white, whereas the resolution merely ordered that henceforth white should be black. Here was matter for discussion, nor was I at all sanguine as to the result; but to be thus knocked on the head by a club, in the outset, was too much for the modesty of a maiden speech. I took my seat in confusion: and I plainly saw that the Perpendiculars, by their sneers, now expected to carry everything triumphantly their own way. This, most probably, would have been the case, had not one of the Tangents immediately got the floor, to move the amendment.

To the vast indignation of Captain Poke, and, in some degree, to my own mortification, this duty was intrusted to the Hon. Robert Smut. Mr. Smut commenced with entreating members not to be led away by the sophistry of the first speaker. That honorable member, no doubt, felt himself called upon to defend the position taken by his friends; but those that knew him well, as it had been his fate to know him, must be persuaded that his sentiments had, at least, undergone a sudden and miraculous change. That honorable member denied the existence of color, at all! He would ask that honorable member if he had never been instrumental himself in producing what is generally called "black and blue color?" he should like to know if that honorable member placed as little value, at present, on blows as he now seemed to set on words—he begged pardon of the house, but this was a matter of great interest to himself—he knew that there never had been a greater manufacturer of "black and blue color" than that honorable member, and he wondered at his now so pertinaciously denying the existence of colors, and at his wish to underrate their value. For his part, he trusted he understood the importance of words, and the value of hues; and while he did not exactly see the necessity of deeming black so inviolable as some gentlemen appeared to think it, he was not by any means prepared to go as far as those who had introduced this resolution. He did not believe that public opinion was satisfied with maintaining that black was black, but he thought it was not yet disposed to affirm that black was white. He did not say that such a day might not arrive; he only maintained that it had not yet arrived, and with a view to meet that which he believed was the public sentiment, he should move, by way of amendment, to strike out the whole of the resolution after the word "really," and insert that which would cause the whole resolution to read as follows, viz.

"Resolved, that the color which has hitherto been deemed to be black, is really *lead-color*."

Hereupon, the Honorable Mr. Smut took his seat, leaving the house to its own ruminations. The leaders of the Perpendiculars, foreseeing that if they got half-way this session, they might effect the rest of their object the next, determined to accept the compromise; and the resolution, as amended, passed by a handsome majority. So this important point was finally decided for the moment, leaving great hopes among the Perpendiculars of being able to lay the Horizontals even flatter on their backs than they were just then.

The next question that presented itself was of far less interest, exciting no great attention. To understand it, however, it will be necessary to refer a little to history. The government of Leapthrough had, about sixty-three years before, caused one hundred and twenty-six Leaplow ships to be burned on the high seas, or otherwise destroyed. The pretence was, that they incommoded Leapthrough. Leaplow was much too great a nation to submit to so heinous an outrage, while, at the same time, she was much too magnanimous and wise a nation to resent it in an every-day and vulgar manner. Instead of getting in a passion and loading her cannon, she summoned all her logic and began to reason. After reasoning the matter with Leapthrough for fifty-two years, or until all the parties who had been wronged were dead, and could no longer be benefited by her logic, she determined to abate two-thirds of her pretensions in a pecuniary sense, and all her pretensions in an honorary sense, and to compromise the affair by accepting a certain insignificant sum of money as a salve to the whole wrong. Leapthrough conditioned to pay this money, in the most solemn and satisfactory manner; and everybody was delighted with the amicable termination of a very vexatious and a seemingly interminable discussion. Leapthrough was quite as glad to get rid of the matter as Leaplow, and very naturally, under all the circumstances, thought the whole thing at length was done with, when she conditioned to pay the money. The Great Sachem of Leaplow, most unfortunately, however, had a "will of iron," or, in other words, he thought the money ought to be paid as well as conditioned to be paid. This despotic construction of the bargain had given rise to unheard-of dissatisfaction in Leapthrough, as indeed might have been expected; but it was, oddly enough, condemned with some heat even in Leaplow itself, where it was stoutly maintained by certain ingenious logicians, that the only true way to settle a bargain to pay money, was to make a new one for a less sum, whenever the amount fell due; a plan that, with a proper moderation and patience, would be certain, in time, to extinguish the whole debt.

Several very elaborate patriots had taken this matter in hand, and it was now about to be presented to the house, under four different categories

Category No. 1, had the merit of simplicity and precision. It proposed merely that Leaplow should pay the money itself, and take up the bond, using its own funds. Category No. 2, embraced a recommendation of the Great Sachem for Leaplow to pay itself, using, however, certain funds of Leapthrough. Category 3d, was a proposal to offer ten millions to Leapthrough to say no more about the transaction at all. Category 4th, was to commence the negotiating or abating system mentioned, without delay, in order to extinguish the claim by instalments as soon as possible.

The question came up on the consideration of the different projects connected with these four leading principles. My limits will not admit of a detailed history of the debate. All I can do, is merely to give an outline of the logic that these various propositions set in motion, of the legislative ingenuity of which they were the parents, and of the multitude of legitimate conclusions that so naturally followed.

In favor of Category No. 1, it was urged that, by adopting its leading idea, the affair would be altogether in our own hands, and might consequently be settled with greater attention to purely Leaplow interests; that further delay could only proceed from our own negligence; that no other project was so likely to get rid of this protracted negotiation in so short a time; that by paying the debt with the Leaplow funds, we should be sure of receiving its amount in the good legal currency of the republic; that it would be singularly economical, as the agent who paid might also be authorized to receive, whereby there would be a saving in salary; and, finally, that, under this category, the whole affair might be brought within the limits of a nut-shell, and the compass of any one's understanding.

In favor of Category No. 2, little more than very equivocal sophisms, which savored strongly of common-place opinions, were presented. It was pretended, for instance, that he who signed a bond was in equity bound to pay it; that, if he refused, the other party had the natural and legal remedy of compulsion; that it might not always be convenient for a creditor to pay all the obligations of other people which he might happen to hold; that if his transactions were extensive, money might be wanting to carry out such a principle; and that, as a precedent, it would comport much more with Leaplow prudence and discretion to maintain the old and tried notions of probity and justice, than to enter on the unknown ocean of uncertainty that was connected with the new opinions, by admitting which, we could never know when we were fairly out of debt.

Category No. 3, was discussed on an entirely new system of logic, which appeared to have great favor with that class of the members who were of the more refined school of ethics. These orators referred the whole matter to a sentiment of honor. They commenced by drawing vivid pictures of the outrages in which the original wrongs had been committed. They spoke of ruined families, plundered mariners, and blasted hopes. They presented minute arithmetical calculations to show that just forty times as much wrong had, in fact, been done, as this bond assumed; and that, as the case actually stood, Leaplow ought, in strict justice, to receive exactly forty times the amount of the money that was actually included in the instrument. Turning from these interesting details, they next presented the question of honor. Leapthrough, by attacking the Leaplow flag, and invading Leaplow rights, had made it principally a question of honor, and, in disposing of it, the principle of honor ought never to be lost sight of. It was honorable to *pay* one's debts—this no one could dispute; but it was not so clear, by any means, that there was any honor in *receiving* one's dues. The national honor was concerned; and they called on members, as they cherished the sacred sentiment, to come forward and sustain it by their votes. As the matter stood, Leaplow had the best of it. In compounding with her creditor, as had been done in the treaty, Leapthrough lost some honor—in refusing to pay the bond, she lost still more; and now, if we should send her the ten millions proposed, and she should have the weakness to accept it, we should fairly get our foot upon her neck, and she could never look us in the face again!

The Category No. 4, brought up a member who had made political economy his chief study. This person presented the following case:—According to his calculations, the wrong had been committed precisely sixty-three years, and twenty-six days, and two-thirds of a day, ago. For the whole of that long period Leaplow had been troubled with this vexatious question, which had hung like a cloud over the otherwise unimpaired brightness of her political landscape. It was time to get rid of it. The sum stipulated was just twenty-five millions, to be paid in twenty-five annual instalments, of a million each. Now, he proposed to reduce the instalments to one half the number, but in no way to change the sum. That point ought to be considered as irrevocably settled. This would diminish the debt one half. Before the first instalment should become due, he would effect a postponement, by diminishing the instalments again to six, referring the time to the latest periods named in the last treaty, and always most sacredly keeping the sums precisely the same. It would be impossible to touch he sums, which, he repeated, ought to be considered as sacred. Before the expiration of the first seven years, a new arrangement might reduce the instalments to two, or even to one—always respecting the sum; and finally, at the proper moment, a treaty could be concluded, declaring that there should be no instalment at all, reserving the point, that if there *had* been an instalment, Leaplow could never have consented to reduce it below one million. The result would be, that in about five-and-twenty years the country would be fairly rid of the matter, and the national character, which it was agreed on all hands was even now as high as it well could be, would probably be raised many degrees higher. The negotiation had commenced in a spirit of compromise; and our character for consistency required that this spirit of compromise should continue to govern our conduct as long as a single farthing remained unpaid.

This idea took wonderfully; and I do believe it would have passed by a handsome majority, had not a new proposition been presented, by an orator of singularly pathetic powers.

The new speaker objected to all four of the categories. He said that each and every one of them would lead to war. Leapthrough was a chivalrous and high-minded nation, as was apparent by the present aspect of things. Should we presume to take up the bond, using our own funds, it would mortally offend her pride, and she would fight us; did we presume to take up the bond, using her funds, it would offend her financial system, and she would fight us; did we presume to offer her ten millions to say no more about the matter, it would offend her dignity by intimating that she was to be bought off from her rights, and she would fight us; did we presume to adopt the system of new negotiations, it would mortally offend her honor, by intimating that she would not respect her old negotiations, and she would fight us. He saw war in all four of the categories. He was for a peace category, and he thought he had in his hand a proposition, that by proper management, using the most tender delicacy, and otherwise respecting the sensibilities of the high and honorable nation in question, we might possibly get out of this embarrassing dilemma without actually coming to blows—he said to blows, for he wished to impress on honorable members the penalties of war. He invited gentlemen to recollect that a conflict between two great nations was a serious affair. If Leapthrough were a little nation, it would be a different matter, and the contest might be conducted in a corner; our honor was intimately connected with all we did with great nations. What was war? Did gentlemen know?—He would tell them.

Here the orator drew a picture of war that caused suffering monikinity to shudder. He viewed it in its four leading points: its religious, its pecuniary, its political, and its domestic penalties. He described war to be the demon-state of the monikin mind; as opposed to worship, to charity, brotherly love, and all the virtues. On its pecuniary penalties, he touched by exhibiting a tax-sheet. Buttons which cost six-pence a gross, he assured the house would shortly cost seven-pence a gross.—Here he was reminded that monikins no longer wore buttons.—No matter, they bought and sold buttons, and the effects on trade were just the same. The political penalties of war he fairly showed to be frightful; but when he came to speak of the domestic penalties, there was not a dry eye in the house. Captain Poke blubbered so loud that I was in an agony lest he should be called to order.

"Regard that pure spirit," he cried, "crushed as t has been in the whirlwind of war. Behold her standing over the sod that covers the hero of his country, the husband of her virgin affections. In vain the orphan at her side turns its tearful eye upward, and asks for the plumes that so lately pleased its infant fancy; in vain its gentle voice inquires when he is to return, when he is to gladden their hearts with his presence"—But I can write no more. Sobs interrupted the speaker, and he took his seat in an ecstasy of godliness and benevolence.

I hurried across the house, to beg the Brigadier would introduce me to this just monikin without a moment's delay. I felt as if I could take him to my heart at once, and swear an eternal friendship with a spirit so benevolent. The Brigadier was too much agitated, at first, to attend to me; but, after wiping his eyes at least a hundred times, he finally succeeded in arresting the torrents, and looked upward with a bland smile.

"Is he not a wonderful monikin?"

"Wonderful indeed! How completely he puts us all to shame!—Such a monikin can only be influenced by the purest love for the species."

"Yes, he is of a class that we call the third monikinity. Nothing excites our zeal like the principles of the class of which he is a member!"

"How! Have you more than one class of the humane?"

"Certainly—the Original, the Representative and the Speculative.'

"I am devoured by the desire to understand the distinctions, my dear Brigadier."

"The Original is an every-day class, that feels under the natural impulses. The Representative is a more intellectual division, that feels chiefly by proxy The Speculatives are those whose sympathies are excited by positive interests, like the last speaker. This person has lately bought a farm by the acre, which he is about to sell, in village lots, by the foot, and war will knock the whole thing in the head. It is this which stimulates his benevolence in so lively a manner."

"Why, this is no more than a development of the social-stake system——"

I was interrupted by the Speaker, who called the house to order. The vote on the resolution of the last orator was to be taken. It read as follows:—

"Resolved, that it is altogether unbecoming the dignity and character of Leapthrough, for Leaplow to legislate on the subject of so petty a consideration as a certain pitiful treaty between the two countries."

"Unanimity—unanimity!" was shouted by fifty voices. Unanimity there was; and then the whole house set to work, shaking hands and hugging each other, in pure joy at the success of the honorable and ingenious manner in which it had got rid of this embarrassing and impertinent question.

CHAPTER XXVII.

An effect of logarithms on morals—An obscuration, a dissertation, and a calculation.

The house had not long adjourned before Captain Poke and myself were favored with a visit from our colleague Mr. Downright, who came on an affair of absorbing interest. He carried in his hand a small pamphlet; and the usual salutations were scarcely over, before he directed our attention to a portion of its contents. It would seem that Leaplow was on the eve of experiencing a great moral eclipse. The periods and dates of the phenomenon (if that can be called a phenomenon which was of too frequent occurrence) had been calculated, with surprising accuracy, by the academy of Leaphigh, and sent, through its minister, as an especial favor, to our beloved country, in order that we should not be taken by surprise. The account of the affair read as follows:—

"On the third day of the season of nuts, there will be the commencement of a great moral eclipse, in that portion of the monikin region which lies immediately about the pole. The property in eclipse will be the great moral postulate usually designated by the term Principle; and the intervening body will be the great immoral postulate, usually known as Interest. The frequent occurrence of the conjunction of these two important postulates has caused our moral mathematicians to be rather negligent of their calculations on this subject, of late years; but, to atone for this inexcusable indifference to one of the most important concerns of life, the calculating committee was instructed to pay unusual attention to all the obscurations of the present year and this phenomenon, one of the most decided of our age, has been calculated with the utmost nicety and care. We give the results.

"The eclipse will commence by a motive of monikin vanity coming in contact with the sub-postulate of charity, at 1 A. M. The postulate in question will be totally hid from view, in the course of 6 h. 17 m. from the moment of contact. The passage of a political intrigue will instantly follow, when the several sub-postulates of truth, honesty, disinterestedness and patriotism, will all be obscured in succession, beginning with the lower limb of the first, and ending with all the limbs of the whole of them, in 3 h. 42 m. from the moment of contact The shadow of vanity and political intrigue will first be deepened by the approach of prosperity, and this will be soon succeeded by the contact of a great pecuniary interest, at 10 h. 2 m. 1 s.; and in exactly 2 s. and 3-7 s., the whole of the grea moral postulate of Principle will be totally hid from view. In consequence of this early passage of the darkest shadow that is ever cast by Interest, the passages of the respective shadows of ambition, hatred, jealousy, and all the other minor satellites of Interest, will be invisible.

"The country principally affected by this eclipse will be the republic of Leaplow, a community whose known intelligence and virtues are perhaps better qualified to resist its influence than any other. The time of occultation will be 9 y. 7 m. 26 d. 4 h. 16 m. 2 s. Principle will begin to reappear to the moral eye at the end of this period, first by the approach of Misfortune, whose atmosphere being much less dense than that of Interest, will allow of imperfect views of the obscured postulate; but the radiance of the latter will not be completely restored until the arrival of Misery, whose chastening colors invariably permit all truths to be discernible although through a sombre medium. To resume:—

'Beginning of eclipse, 1 A. M.
Ecliptic opposition, in 4 y. 6 m. 12 d. 9 h. from beginning of eclipse.
Middle, in 4 y. 9 m. 0 d. 7. h. 9 m. from beginning of eclipse
End of eclipse, 9 y. 11 m. 20 d. 3 h. 2 m. from beginning.
Period of occultation, 9 y. 7 m. 26 d. 4 h. 16 m. 2 s."

I gazed at the Brigadier in admiration and awe. There was nothing remarkable in the eclipse itself, which was quite an every-day affair; but the precision with which it had been calculated added to its other phenomena the terrible circumstance of obtaining a glimpse into the future. I now began to perceive the immense difference between living consciously under a moral shadow, and living under it unconsciously. The latter was evidently a trifle compared to the former. Providence had most kindly provided for our happiness in denying the ability to see beyond the present moment.

Noah took the affair even more at heart than myself. He told me, with a rueful and prognosticating countenance, that we were fast drawing near to the autumnal equinox, when we should reach the commencement of a natural night of six months' duration; and although the benevolent substitute of steam might certainly in some degree lessen the evil, that it was a furious evil, after all, to exist for a period so weary without enjoying the light of the sun. He found the eternal glare of day bad enough, but he did not believe he should be able to endure its total absence. Natur' had made him a 'watch and watch' crittur'. As for the twilight of which so much was said, it was worse than nothin', being neither one thing nor the other. For his part, he liked things 'made out of whole cloth.' Then he had sent the ship round to a distant roadstead, in order that there might be no more post-captains and rear-admirals among the people; and here had he been as much as four days on nothing but nuts. Nuts might do for the philosophy of a monkey, but he found, on trial, that it played the devil with the philosophy of a man. Things were bad enough as they were. He pined for a little pork—he cared not who knew it; it might not be very sentimental, he knew, but it was capital sea-food; his natur' was pretty much pork; he believed most men had, in some way or other, more or less pork in their human natur's; nuts might do for monikin natur', but human natur' loved meat; if monikins did not like it, monikins need not eat it; there would be so much the more for those that did like it—he pined for his natural aliment, and as for living nine years in an eclipse, it was quite out of the question. The longest Stunin'tun eclipses seldom went over three hours—he once knew Deacon Spiteful pray quite through one, from *apogee* to *perigee*. He therefore proposed that Sir John and he should resign their seats without delay, and that they should try to get the Walrus to the north'ard as quick as possible, lest they should be caught in the polar night. As for the Hon. Robert Smut, he wished him no better luck than to remain where he was all his life, and to receive his eight dollars a day in acorns.

Although it was impossible not to hear, and having heard, not to record the sentiments of Noah, still my attention was much more strongly attracted by the demeanor of the Brigadier, than by the jeremiad of the sealer. To an anxious inquiry if he were not well, our worthy colleague answered plaintively, that he mourned over the misfortune of his country.

"I have often witnessed the passage of the passions, and of the minor motives, across the disk of the great moral postulate, Principle; but an occultation of its light by a Pecuniary Interest, and for so long a period, is fearful! Heaven only knows what will become of us!"

"Are not these eclipses, after all; so many mere illustrations of the social-stake system? I confess this occultation, of which you seem to have so much dread, is not so formidable a thing, on reflection, as it at first appeared to be."

"You are quite right, Sir John, as to the character of the eclipse itself, which, as a matter of course, must depend on the character of the intervening body. But the wisest and best of our philosophers hold that the entire system of which we are but insignificant parts, is based on certain immutable truths of a divine origin. The premises, or postulates, of all these truths, are so many moral guides in the management of monikin affairs; and, the moment they are lost sight of, as will be the case during these frightful nine years that are to come, we shall be abandoned entirely to selfishness. Now. selfishness is only too formidable when restrained by Principle; but, left to its own grasping desires and audacious sophisms, to me the moral perspective is terrible. We are only too much addicted to turn our eyes from Principle, when it is shining in heavenly radiance, and in full glory, before us; it is not difficult, therefore, to foresee the nature of the consequences which are to follow its total and protracted obscuration."

"You then conceive there is a rule superior to interest, which ought to be respected in the control of monikin affairs?"

"Beyond a doubt; else in what should we differ from the beasts of prey?"

"I do not exactly see whether this does, or does not, accord with the notions of the political economists of the social-stake system."

"As you say, Sir John, it does, and it does not. Your social-stake system supposes that he who has what is termed a distinct and prominent interest in society, will be the most likely to conduct its affairs wisely, justly, and disinterestedly. This would be true, if those great principles which lie at the root of all happiness were respected; but unluckily, the stake in question, instead of being a stake in jus tice and virtue, is usually reduced to be merely a stake in property. Now, all experience shows that the great property-incentives are to increase property, protect property, and to buy with property those advantages which ought to be independent of property, viz. honors, dignities, power and immunities. I cannot say how it is with men, but our histories are eloquent on this head. We have had the property-principle carried out thoroughly in our practice, and the result has shown that its chief operation is to render property as intact as possible, and the bones, and sinews, and marrow of all who do not possess it, its slaves. In short, the time has been, when the rich were even exempt from contributing to the ordinary exigencies of the state. But it is quite useless to theorize on this subject, for, by that cry in the streets, the lower limb of the great postulate is beginning to be obscured, and, alas! we shall soon have too much practical information."

The Brigadier was right. On referring to the clocks, it was found that, in truth, the eclipse had commenced some time before, and that we were on the verge of an absolute occultation of Principle, by the basest and most sordid of all motives, Pecuniary Interest.

The first proof that was given of the true state of things, was in the language of the people. The word interest was in every monikin's mouth, while the word principle, as indeed was no more than suitable, seemed to be quite blotted out of the Leaplow vocabulary. To render a local term into English, half of the vernacular of the country appeared to be compressed into the single word "dollar." "Dollar—dollar—dollar"—nothing but "dollar!" "Fifty thousand dollars—twenty thousand dollars—a hundred thousand dollars"—met one at every turn. The words rang at the corners—in the public ways—at the exchange—in the drawing-rooms—ay, even in the churches. If a temple had been reared for the worship of the Creator, the first question was, how much did it cost?—If an artist submitted the fruits of his labors to the taste of his fellow-citizens, conjectures were whispered among the spectators, touching its value in the current coin of the republic.—If an author presented the offspring of his genius to the same arbiters, its merits were settled by a similar standard; and one divine, who had made a strenuous, but an ill-timed appeal to the charity of his countrymen, by setting forth the beauties as well as the rewards of the god-like property, was fairly put down by a demonstration that his proposition involved a considerable outlay, while it did not clearly show much was to be gained by going to heaven!

Brigadier Downright had good reasons for his sombre anticipations, for all the acquirements, knowledge, and experience, obtained in many years of travel, were now found to be worse than useless. If my honorable colleague and co-voyager ventured a remark on the subject of foreign policy, a portion of politics to which he had given considerable attention, it was answered by a quotation from the stock-market; an observation on a matter of taste was certain to draw forth a nice distinction between the tastes of certain liquors, together with a shrewd investigation of their several prices; and once, when the worthy monikin undertook to show, from what struck me to be singularly good data, that the foreign relations of the country were in a condition to require great firmness, a proper prudence, and much foresight, he was completely silenced by an antagonist showing, from the last sales, the high value of lots up-town!

In short, there was no dealing with any subject that could not resolve itself into dollars, by means of the customary exchanges. The infatuation spread from father to son; from husband to wife; from brother to sister, and from one collateral to another, until it pretty effectually assailed the whole of what is usually termed "society." Noah swore bitterly at this antagonist state of things. He affirmed that he could not even crack a walnut in a corner, but every monikin that passed appeared to grudge him the satisfaction, small as it was; and that Stunin'tun, though a scramble-penny place as any he knew, was paradise to Leaplow, in the present state of things.

It was melancholy to remark how the lustre of the ordinary virtues grew dim, as the period of occultation continued, and the eye gradually got to be accustomed to the atmosphere cast by the shadow of Pecuniary Interest. I involuntarily shuddered at the open and undisguised manner in which individuals, who might otherwise pass for respectable monikins, spoke of the means that they habitually employed in effecting their objects, and laid bare their utter forgetfulness of the great postulate that was hid. One coolly vaunted how much cleverer he was than the law; another proved to demonstration that he had outwitted his neighbor; while a third, more daring or more expert, applied the same grounds of exultation to the entire neighborhood. This had the merit of cunning; that of dissimulation; another of deception, and all of success!

The shadow cast its malign influence on every interest connected with monikin life. Temples were raised to God on speculation; the government was perverted to a money-investment, in which profit and not justice and security, was the object; holy wedlock fast took the aspect of buying and selling, and few prayed who did not identify spiritual benefits with gold and silver.

The besetting propensity of my ancestor soon began to appear in Leaplow. Many of these pure and unsophisticated republicans shouted "Property is in danger!" as stoutly as it was ever roared by Sir Joseph Job, and dark allusions were made to "revolutions" and "bayonets." But certain proof of the prevalence of the eclipse, and that the shadow of Pecuniary Interest lay dark on the land, was to be found in the language of what are called the "few." They began to throw dirt at all opposed to them, like so many fish-women; a sure symptom that the spirit of selfishness was thoroughly awakened. From much experience, I hold this sign to be infallible that the sentiment of aristocracy is active and vigilant. I never yet visited a country in which a minority got into its head the crotchet it was alone fit to dictate to the rest of its fellow-creatures, that it did not, without delay, set about proving its position, by reviling and calling names. In this particular "the few" are like women, who, conscious of their weakness, seldom fail to make up for the want of vigor in their limbs, by having recourse to the vigor of the tongue. The "one" hangs; the "many" command by the dignity of force; the "few" vituperate and scold. This is, I believe, the case all over the world, except in those peculiar instances, in which the "few" happen also to enjoy the privilege of hanging.

It is worthy of remark that the terms "rabble," "disorganizers," "jacobins," and "agrarians"* were

* It is scarcely necessary to tell the intelligent reader there is no proof that any political community was ever so bent on self-destruction as to enact agrarian laws, in the vulgar sense in which it has suited the arts of narrow-minded politicians to represent them ever since the revival of letters. The celebrated agrarian laws of Rome did not essentially differ from the distribution of our own military lands, or perhaps the similitude is greater to the modern Russian military colonies. Those who feel an interest in this subject would do well to consult Niebuhr.—*Note by the Editor.*

bandied from one to the other, in Leaplow, under this malign influence, with precisely the same justice, discrimination and taste, as they had been used by my ancestor in London, a few years before. Like causes notoriously produce like effects; and there is no one thing so much like an Englishman under the property-fever, as a Leaplow monikin suffering under the same malady.

The effect produced on the state of parties by the passage of the shadow of Pecuniary Interest, was so singular as to deserve our notice. Patriots who had long been known for an indomitable resolution to support their friends, openly abandoned their claims on the rewards of the little wheel, and went over to the enemy; and this, too, without recourse to the mysteries of the "flap-jack." Judge People's Friend was completely annihilated for the moment—so much so, indeed, as to think seriously of taking another mission—for, during these eclipses, long service, public virtue, calculated amenity, and all the other bland qualities of your patriot, pass for nothing, when weighed in the scale against profit and loss. It was fortunate the Leapthrough question was, in its essence, so well disposed of, though the uneasiness of those who bought and sold land by the inch, pushed even that interest before the public again by insisting that a few millions should be expended in destroying the munitions of war, lest the nation might improvidently be tempted to make use of them in the natural way. The cruisers were accordingly hauled into the stream and converted into tide-mills, the gun-barrels were transformed into gas-pipes, and the forts were converted, as fast as possible, into warehouses and tea-gardens. After this, it was much the fashion to affirm that the advanced state of civilization had rendered all future wars quite out of the question. Indeed, the impetus that was given, by the effects of the shadow, in this way, to humanity in gross, was quite as remarkable as were its contrary tendencies on humanity in detail.

Public opinion was not backward in showing how completely it was acting under the influence of the shadow. Virtue began to be estimated by rent-rolls. The affluent, without hesitation, or, indeed, opposition, appropriated to themselves the sole use of the word respectable, while taste, judgment, honesty, and wisdom, dropped like so many heir-looms quietly into the possession of those who had money. The Leaplowers are a people of great acuteness, and of singular knowledge of details. Every considerable man in Bivouac soon had his social station assigned him, the whole community being divided into classes, of "hundred-thousand-dollar monikins"—"fifty-thousand-dollar monikins"—"twenty-thousand-dollar monikins." Great conciseness in language was a consequence of this state of feeling. The old questions of 'is he honest?' 'is he capable?' 'is he enlightened?' 'is he wise?' 'is he good?' being all comprehended in the single interrogatory of 'is he rich?'

There was one effect of this very unusual state of things, that I had not anticipated. All the money-getting classes, without exception, showed a singular predilection in favor of what is commonly called a strong government; and Leaplow being not only a republic, but virtually a democracy, I found that much the larger portion of this highly respectable class of citizens, was not at all backward in expressing its wish for a change.

"How is this?" I demanded of the Brigadier, whom I rarely quitted; for his advice and opinions were of great moment to me, just at this particular crisis—'how is this, my good friend?—I have always been led to think that trade is especially favorable to liberty; and here are all your commercial interests the loudest in their declamations against the institutions."

The Brigadier smiled; it was but a melancholy smile, after all; for his spirits appeared to have quite deserted him.

"There are three great divisions among politicians," he said;—"they who do not like liberty at all—they who like it, as low down as their own particular class—and they who like it, for the sake of their fellow-creatures. The first are not numerous, but powerful by means of combinations; the second is a very irregular corps, including, as a matter of course, nearly every body, but is wanting, of necessity, in concert and discipline, since no one descends below his own level; the third are but few, alas, how few! and are composed of those who look beyond their own selfishness. Now, your merchants, dwelling in towns, and possessing concert, means, and identity of interests, have been able to make themselves remarkable for contending with despotic power, a fact which has obtained for them a cheap reputation for liberality of opinion; but, so far as monikin experience goes—men may have proved to be better disposed—no government that is essentially influenced by commerce has ever been otherwise than exclusive, or aristocratic."

I bethought me of Venice, Genoa, Pisa, the Hanse Towns, and all the other remarkable places of this character in Europe, and I felt the justice of my friend's distinction, at the same time I could not but observe how much more the minds of men are under the influence of names and abstractions than under the influence of positive things. To this opinion the Brigadier very readily assented, remarking, at the same time, that a well-wrough theory had generally more effect on opinion than fifty facts; a result that he attributed to the circumstance of monikins having a besetting predisposition to save themselves the trouble of thinking.

I was, in particular, struck with the effect of the occultation of Principle on motives. I had often remarked that it was by no means safe to depend on one's own motives, for two sufficient reasons; first, that we did not always know what our own motives were; and secondly, admitting that we did, it was quite unreasonable to suppose that our friends would believe them what we thought them to be ourselves. In the present instance, every monikin seemed perfectly aware of the difficulty; and, instead of waiting for his acquaintances to attribute some moral enormity as his governing reason, he prudently adopted a moderately selfish inducement for his acts, which he proclaimed with a simplicity and frankness that generally obtained credit. Indeed, the fact once conceded that the motive was not offensively disinterested and just, no one was indisposed to listen to the projects of his friend, who usually rose in estimation, as he was found to be ingenious, calculating and shrewd. The effect of all this was to render society singularly sincere and plain-spoken; and one unaccustomed to so much ingenuousness, or who was ignorant of the cause, might, plausibly enough, suppose, at times, that accident had thrown him into an extraordinary association with so many *artistes* who, as it is commonly expressed, live by their wits I will avow that, had it been the fashion to wear pockets at Leaplow, I should often have been concerned for their contents; for sentiments so purely unsophisticated, were so openly advanced under the influence of the shadow, that one was inevitably led, oftener than was pleasant to think of the relations between *meum* and *tuum*, as well as of the unexpected causes by which they were sometimes disturbed.

A vacancy occurred, the second day of the eclipse, among the representatives of Bivouac, and the candidate of the Horizontals would certainly have been chosen to fill it, but for a *contre-tems* connected with this affair of motives. The individual in question had lately performed that which, in most other countries, and under other circumstances, would have passed for an act of creditable national feeling; but which, quite as a matter of course, was eagerly presented to the electors, by his opponents, as a proof of his utter unfitness to be intrusted with their interests. The friends of the candidate took the alarm, and indignantly denied the charges of the Perpendiculars, affirming that their monikin had been well paid for what he had done. In an evil hour, the candidate undertook to explain, by means of a handbill, in which he stated that he had been influenced by no other motive than a desire to do that which he believed to be right. Such a person was deemed to be wanting in natural abilities, and, as a matter of course, he was defeated; for your Leaplow elector was not such an ass as to confide the care of his interests to one who knew so little how to take care of his own.

About this time, too, a celebrated dramatist produced a piece in which the hero performed prodigies under the excitement of patriotism, and the labor of his pen was incontinently damned for his pains; both pit and boxes—the galleries dissenting—deciding that it was out of all nature to represent a monikin incurring danger, in this unheard-of manner, without a motive. The unhappy wight altered the last scene, by causing his hero to be rewarded by a good, round sum of money, when the piece had a very respectable run for the rest of the season, though I question if it ever were as popular as it would have been, had this precaution been taken before it was first acted.

CHAPTER XXVIII.

The importance of motives to a legislator—Moral consecutiveness, comets, kites, and a convoy; with some every-day legislation; together with cause and effect.

Legislation, during the occultation of the great moral postulate Principle by the passage of Pecuniary Interest, is, at the best, but a melancholy affair. It proved to be peculiarly so with us just at that moment, for the radiance of the divine property had been a good deal obscured, in the houses, for a long time previously, by the interference of various minor satellites. In nothing, therefore, did the deplorable state of things which existed make itself more apparent, than in our proceedings.

As Captain Poke and myself, notwithstanding our having taken different stands in politics, still continued to live together, I had better opportunities to note the workings of the obscuration on the ingenuous mind of my colleague than on that of most other persons. He early began to keep a diary of his expenses, regularly deducting the amount at night from the sum of eight dollars, and regarding the balance as so much clear gain. His conversation, too, soon betrayed a leaning to his personal interests, instead of being of that pure and elevated cast which should characterize the language of a statesman. He laid down the position, pretty dogmatically, that legislation, after all, was work; that "the laborer was worthy of his hire;" and that, for his part, he felt no great disposition to go through the vexation and trouble of helping to make laws, unless he could see, with a reasonable certainty, that something was to be got by it. He thought Leaplow had quite laws enough as it was—more than she respected or enforced—and if she wanted any more, all she had to do was to pay for them. He should take an early occasion to propose that all our wages—or, at any rate, his own; others might do as they pleased—should be raised, at the very least, two dollars a day, and this while he merely sat in the house; for he wished to engage me to move, by way of amendment, that as much more should be given to the committees. He did not think it was fair to exact of a member to be a committee-man for nothin', although most of them were committee-men for nothin'; and if we were called on to keep two watches, in this manner, the least that could be done would be to give us *two pays.* He said, considering it in the most favorable point of view, that there was great wear and tear of brain in legislation, and he should never be the man he was before he engaged in the trade; he assured me that his idees, sometimes, were so complicated that he did not know where to find the one he wanted, and that he had wished for a *cauda*, a thousand times, since he had been in the house, for, by keeping the end of it in his hand, like the bight of a rope, he might always have suthin' tangible to cling to. He told me, as a great secret, that he was fairly tired of rummaging among his thoughts for the knowledge necessary to understand what was going on, and that he had finally concluded to put himself, for the rest of the session. under the convoy of a God-like. He had been looking out for a fit fugleman of this sort, and he had pretty much determined to follow the signals of the great God-like of the Parpendic'lars, like the rest of them, for it would occasion less confusion in the ranks, and enable him to save himself a vast deal of trouble, in making up his mind. He did n't know, on the whole, but eight dollars a day might give a living profit, provided he could throw all the thinking on his God-like, and turn his attention to suthin' else; he thought of writing his v'y'ges, for he understood that anything from foreign parts took like wild-fire in Leaplow; and if they did n't take, he could always project charts for a living.

Perhaps it will be necessary to explain what Noah meant by saying that he thought of engaging a God-like. The reader has had some insight into the nature of one set of political leaders in Leaplow, who are known by the name of the Most Patriotic Patriots. These persons, it is scarcely necessary to say, are always with the majority, or in a situation to avail themselves of the evolutions of the little wheel. Their great rotatory principle keeps them pretty constantly in motion, it is true; but while there is a centrifugal force to maintain this action, great care has been had to provide a centripetal counterpoise, in order to prevent them from bolting out of the political orbit. It is supposed to be owing to this peculiarity in their party organizations, that your Leaplow patriot is so very remarkable for going round and round a subject, without ever touching it.

As an off-set to this party arrangement, the Perpendiculars have taken refuge in the God-likes. A God-like, in Leaplow politics, in some respects resembles a saint in the Catholic calendar; that is to say, he is canonized, after passing through a certain amount of temptation and vice with a whole skin after having his cause pleaded for a certain number of years before the high authorities of his party; and, usually, after having had a pretty good taste of purgatory. Canonization attained, however, all gets to be plain sailing with him. He is spared, singular as it may appear, even a large portion of his former "wear and tear" of brains, as Noah had termed it, for nothing puts one so much at liberty in this respect, as to have full powers to do all the thinking. Thinking in company, like travelling in company, requires that we should have some respect to the movements, wishes and opinions of others; but he who gets a *carte blanche* for his sentiments, resembles the uncaged bird, and may fly in whatever direction most pleases himself, and feel confident, as he goes, that his ears will be saluted with the usual traveller's signal of "all's right." I can best compare the operation of your God-like and his votaries, to the action of a locomotive with its rail-road train. As that goes, this follows; faster or slower, the movement is certain to be accompanied; when the steam is up they fly, when the fire is out they crawl, and that, too, with a very uneasy sort of motion; and when a bolt is broken, they who have just been riding without the smallest trouble to themselves, are compelled to get out and push the load ahead as well as they can, frequently with very rueful faces, and in very dirty ways The cars whisk about, precisely as the locomotive whisks about, all the turn-outs are necessarily imitated, and, in short, one goes after the other very much as it is reasonable to suppose will happen when two bodies are chained together, and the entire moving power is given to only one of them. A God-like in Leaplow, moreover, is usually a Riddle. It was the object of Noah to hitch on to one of these moral steam-tugs, in order that he too might be dragged through his duties without effort to himself; an expedient, as the old sealer expressed it, that would, in some degree, remedy his natural want of a *cauda*, by rendering him nothing but tail.

"I expect, Sir John," he said, for he had a practice of expecting by way of conjecture, "I expect this is the reason why the Leaplowers dock themselves. They find it more convenient to give up the management of their affairs to some one of these God-likes, and fall into his wake like the tail of a comet, which makes it quite unnecessary to have any other *cauda*."

"I understand you; they amputate to prevent tautology."

Noah rarely spoke of any project until his mind was fairly made up; and the execution usually soon followed the proposition. The next thing I heard of him, therefore, he was fairly under the convoy, as he called it, of one of the most prominent of the Riddles. Curious to know how he liked the experiment, after a week's practice, I called his attention to the subject, by a pretty direct inquiry.

He told me it was altogether the pleasantest mode of legislating that had ever been devised. He was now perfectly master of his own time, and in fact, he was making out a set of charts for the Leaplow marine, a task that was likely to bring him in a good round sum, as pumpkins were cheap, and in the polar seas he merely copied the monikin authorities, and out of it he had things pretty much his own way. As for the Great Allegory, when he wanted a hint about it, or, indeed, about any other point at issue, all he had to do was to inquire what his God-like thought about it, and to vote accordingly. Then he saved himself a great deal of breath in the way of argument out of doors for he and the rest of the *clientelle* of this Riddle, having officially invested their patron with all their own parts, the result had been such an accumulation of knowledge in this one individual, as enabled them ordinarily to floor any antagonist by the simple quotation of his authority. Such or such is the opinion of God-like this or of God-like that, was commonly sufficient; and then there was no lack of material, for he had taken care to provide himself with a Riddle who, he really believed, had given an opinion, at some time or other, on every side of every subject that had ever been mooted in Leaplow. He could nullify, or mollify, or qualify, with the best of them; and these, which he termed the three *fies*, he believed were the great requisites of a Leaplow legislator. He admitted, however, that some show of independence was necessary, in order to give value to the opinions of even a God-like, for monikin nature revolted at anything like total mental dependence; and that he had pretty much made up his mind to think for himself on a question that was to be decided that very day.

The case to which the Captain alluded was this. The city of Bivouac was divided into three pretty nearly equal parts, which were separated from each other by two branches of a marsh; one part of the town being on a sort of island, and the other two parts on the respective margins of the low land. It was very desirable to connect these different portions of the capital by causeways, and a law to that effect had been introduced in the house. Everybody, in or out of the house, was in favor of the project, for the causeways had become, in some measure, indispensable. The only disputed point was the length of the works in question. One who is but little acquainted with legislation, and who has never witnessed the effects of an occultation of the great moral postulate Principle, by the orb of Pecuniary Interest, would very plausibly suppose that the whole affair lay in a nut-shell, and that all we had to do was to pass a law ordering the causeways to extend just as far as the public convenience rendered it necessary. But these are mere tyros in the affairs of monikins. The fact was that there were just as many different opinions and interests at work to regulate the length of the causeways, as there were owners of land along their line of route. The great object was to start in what was called the business quarter of the town, and then to proceed with the work as far as circumstances would allow. We had propositions before us in favor of from one hundred feet as far as up to ten thousand. Every inch was fought for with as much obstinacy as if it were an important breach that was defended; and combinations and conspiracies were as rife as if we were in the midst of a revolution. It was the general idea that by filling in with dirt, a new town might be built wherever the causeway terminated, and fortunes made by an act of parliament. The inhabitants of the island rallied *en masse* against the causeway leading one inch *from* their quarter, after it had fairly reached it; and, so throughout the entire line, monikins battled for what they called their interests, with an obstinacy worthy of heroes.

On this great question, for it had, in truth, become of the last importance by dragging into its consideration most of the leading measures of the day, as well as six or seven of the principal ordinances of the Great National Allegory, the respective partisans logically contending that, for the time being nothing should advance a foot in Leapiow that did not travel along that causeway, Noah determined to take an independent stand. This resolution was not lightly formed, for he remained rather undecided, until, by waiting a sufficient time, he felt quite persuaded that nothing was to be got by following any other course. His God-like luckily was in the same predicament, and everything promised a speedy occasion to show the world what it was to act on principle; and this, too, in the middle of a moral eclipse.

When the question came to be discussed, the landholders along the first line of the causeway were soon reasoned down by the superior interests of those who lived on the island. The rub was the point of permitting the work to go any further. The islanders manifested great liberality, according to their account of themselves; for they even consented that the causeway should be constructed on the other marsh to precisely such a distance as would enable any one to go as near as possible to the hostile quarter, without absolutely entering it. To admit the latter, they proved to demonstration, would be changing the character of their own island from that of an *entrepôt* to that of a mere thoroughfare. No reasonable monikin could expect it of them.

As the Horizontals, by some calculation that I never understood, had satisfied themselves it might better answer their purposes to construct the entire work, than to stop anywhere between the two extremes, my duty was luckily, on this occasion, in exact accordance with my opinions; and, as a matter of course, I voted, this time, in a way of which I could approve. Noah, finding himself a free agent, now made his push for character, and took sides with us. Very fortunately we prevailed, all the beaten interests joining themselves, at the last moment, to the weakest side, or, in other words, to that which was right; and Leaplow presented the singular spectacle of having a just enactment passed during the occultation of the great moral postulate, so often named. I ought to mention that I have termed principle a postulate, throughout this narrative, simply because it is usually in the dilemma of a disputed proposition.

No sooner was the result known, than my worthy colleague came round to the Horizontal side of the house, to express his satisfaction with himself for the course he had just taken. He said it was certainly very convenient and very labor-saving to obey a God-like, and that he got on much better with his charts now he was at liberty to give his whole mind to the subject; but there was suthin'—he did n't know what—but "a sort of Stunin'tun feeling" in doing what one thought right, after all, that caused him to be glad that he had voted for the whole causeway. He did not own any land in Leaplow, and, therefore, he concluded that what he had done, he had done for the best; at any rate, if he had got nothin' by it, he had lost nothin' by it, and he hoped all would come right in the end. The people of the island, it is true, had talked pretty fair about what they would do for those who should sustain their interests, but he had got sick of a currency in promises; and fair words, at his time of life, did n't go for much; and so, on the whole, he had pretty much concluded to do as he had done. He thought no one could call in question his vote, for he was just as poor and as badly off now he had voted, as he was while he was making up his mind. For his part, he should n't be ashamed, hereafter, to look both Deacon Snort and the Parson in the face, when he got home, or even Miss Poke. He knew what it was to have a clean conscience, as well as any man; for none so well knew what it was to be without anything, as they who had felt by experience its want. His God-like was a very labor-saving God-like; but he had found, on inquiry that he came from another part of the island, and that he did n't care a straw which way his kite-tail (Noah's manner of pronouncing *clientelle*) voted. In short, he defied any one say aught ag'in him this time, and he was not sorry the occasion had offered to show his independence, for his enemies had not been backward in remarking that, for some days, he had been little better than a speaking-trumpet to roar out anything his God-like might wish to have proclaimed. He concluded by stating that he could not hold out much longer without meat of some sort or other, and by begging that I would second a resolution he thought of offering, by which regular substantial rations were to be dealt out to all the human part of the house. The inhumans might live upon nuts still, if they liked them.

I remonstrated against the project of the rations made a strong appeal to his pride, by demonstrating that we should be deemed little better than brutes if we were seen eating flesh, and advised him to cause some of his nuts to be roasted, by way of variety. After a good deal of persuasion, he promised further abstinence, although he went away with a singularly carnivorous look about the mouth, and an eye that spoke *pork* in every glance.

I was at home the next day, busy with my friend the Brigadier, in looking over the Great National Allegory, with a view to prevent falling, unwittingly, into any more offences of quoting its opinions, when Noah burst into the room, as rabid as a wolf that had been bitten by a whole pack of hounds. Such, indeed, was, in some measure, his situation; for, according to his statement, he had been baited that morning, in the public streets even, by every monikin, monikina, monikino, brat and beggar, that he had seen. Astonished to hear that my colleague had fallen into this disfavor with his constituents, I was not slow in asking an explanation.

The Captain affirmed that the matter was beyond the reach of any explanation it was in his power to give. He had voted in the affair of the causeway, in strict conformity with the dictates of his conscience, and yet here was the whole population accusing him of bribery—nay, even the journals had openly flouted at him for what they called his barefaced and flagrant corruption. Here the Captain laid before us six or seven of the leading journals of Bivouac, in all of which his late vote was treated with quite as little ceremony as if it had been an unequivocal act of sheep-stealing.

I looked at my friend the Brigadier for an explanation. After running his eye over the articles in the journals, the latter smiled, and cast a look of commiseration at our colleague.

"You have certainly committed a grave fault here, my friend," he said, "and one that is seldom forgiven in Leaplow—perhaps I might say never, during the occultation of the great moral postulate, as happens to be the case at present."

"Tell me my sins at once, Brigadier," cried Noah, with the look of a martyr, "and put me out of pain."

'You have forgotten to display a *motive* for your stand during the late hot discussion; and, as a matter of course, the community ascribes the wors that monikin ingenuity can devise. Such an oversight would ruin even a God-like!"

"But, my dear Mr. Downright," I kindly interposed, "our colleague, in this instance, is supposed o have acted on principle."

The Brigadier looked up, turning nis nose into

the air, like a pup that has not yet opened its eyes, and then intimated that he could not see the quality I had named, it being obscured by the passage of the orb of Pecuniary Interest before its disk. I now began to comprehend the case, which really was much more grave than, at first, I could have believed possible. Noah himse f seemed staggered; for, I believe, he had fallen on the simple and natural expedient of inquiring what he himself would have thought of the conduct of a colleague who had given a vote on a subject so weighty, without exposing a motive.

"Had the Captain owned but a foot square of earth, at the end of the causeway," observed the Brigadier, mournfully, "the matter might be cleared up; but as things are, it is, beyond dispute, a most unfortunate occurrence."

"But Sir John voted with me, and he is no more a freeholder in Leaplow, than I am myself."

"True: but Sir John voted with the bulk of his political friends."

"All the Horizontals were not in the majority; for at least twenty went, on this occasion, with the minority."

"Undeniable—yet every monikin of them had a visible *motive*. This owned a lot by the way-side; that had houses on the island, and another was the heir of a great proprietor at the same point of the road. Each and all had their distinct and positive interests at stake, and not one of them was guilty of so great a weakness as to leave his cause to be defended by the extravagant pretension of mere Principle!"

"My God-like, the greatest of all the Riddles, absented himself, and did not vote at all."

"Simply because he had no good ground to justify any course he might take. No public monikin can expect to escape censure, if he fail to put his friends in the way of citing some plausible and intelligible motive for his conduct."

"How, sir! cannot a man, once in his life, do an act without being bought like a horse or a dog and escape with an inch of character?"

"I shall not take upon myself to say what *men* can do," returned the Brigadier; "no doubt they manage this affair better than it is managed here; but, so far as monikins are concerned, there is no course more certain to involve a total loss of character—I may say so destructive to reputation even for intellect—as to act without a good, apparent and substantial *motive*."

"In the name of God, what is to be done, Brigadier?"

"I see no other course than to resign. Your constituents must very naturally have lost all confidence in you; for one who so very obviously neglects his own interests, it cannot be supposed will be very tenacious about protecting the interests of others. If you would escape with the little character that is left, you will forthwith resign. I do not perceive the smallest chance for you by going through Gyration No. 4, both public opinions uniformly condemning the monikin who acts without a pretty obvious, as well as a pretty weighty, motive."

Noah made a merit of necessity; and, after some further deliberation between us, he signed his name to the following letter to the Speaker, which was drawn up on the spot, by the Brigadier.

Mr. Speaker:—The state of my health obliges me to return the high political trust which has been confided to me by the citizens of Bivouac, into the hands from which it was received. In tendering my resignation, I wish to express the great regret with which I part from colleagues so every way worthy of profound respect and esteem, and I beg you to assure them, that wherever fate may hereafter lead me, I shall ever retain the deepest regard for every honorable member with whom it has been my good fortune to serve. The emigrant interest, in particular, will ever be the nearest and dearest to my heart.

Signed, NOAH POKE.

The Captain did not affix his name to this letter without many heavy sighs, and divers throes of ambition; for even a mistaken politician yields to necessity with regret. Having changed the word emigrant to that of "immigrunt," however, he put as good a face as possible on the matter, and wrote the fatal signature. He then left the house, declaring that he did n't so much begrudge his successor the pay, as nothing but nuts were to be had with the money; and that, as for himself, he felt as sneaking as he believed was the case with Nebuchadnezzar, when he was compelled to get down on all-fours, and eat grass.

CHAPTER XXIX.

Some explanations—A human appetite—A dinner, and a *bonne bouche.*

THE Brigadier and myself remained behind to discuss the general bearings of this unexpected event.

"Your rigid demand for motives, my good sir," I remarked, "reduces the Leaplow political morality very much, after all, to the level of the social-stake system of our part of the world."

"They both depend on the crutch of personal

interests, it is true; though there is, between them the difference of the interests of a part and of the interests of the whole."

"And could a part act less commendably than the whole appear to have acted in this instance?"

"You forget that Leaplow, just at this moment, is under a moral eclipse. I shall not say that these eclipses do not occur often, but they occur quite as frequently in other parts of the region, as they occur here. We have three great modes of controlling monikin affairs, viz. the one, the few, and the many——"

"Precisely the same classification exists among men!" I interrupted.

"Some of our improvements are reflected backwards; twilight following as well as preceding the passage of the sun," quite coolly returned the Brigadier. "We think that the many come nearest to balancing the evil, although we are far from believing even them to be immaculate. Admitting that the tendencies to wrong are equal in the three systems, (which we do not, however, for we think our own has the least,) it is contended that the many escape one great source of oppression and injustice, by escaping the onerous provisions which physical weakness is compelled to make, in order to protect itself against physical strength."

"This is reversing a very prevalent opinion among men, sir, who usually maintain that the tyranny of the many is the worst sort of all tyrannies."

"This opinion has got abroad simply because the lion has not been permitted to draw his own picture. As cruelty is commonly the concomitant of cowardice, so is oppression nine times out of ten the result of weakness. It is natural for the few to dread the many, while it is not natural for the many to dread the few. Then, under institutions in which the many rule, certain great principles that are founded on natural justice, as a matter of course, are openly recognized; and it is rare, indeed, that they do not, more or less, influence the public acts. On the other hand, the control of a few requires that these same truths should be either mistified or entirely smothered; and the consequence is injustice."

"But, admitting all your maxims, Brigadier, as regards the few and the many, you must yourself allow that here, in your beloved Leaplow itself, monikins consult their own interests; and this, after all, is acting on the fundamental principle of the great European social-stake system."

"Meaning that the goods of the world ought to be the test of political power. By the sad confusion which exists among us, at this moment, Sir John, you must perceive that we are not exactly under the most salutary of all possible influences. I take it that the great desideratum of society is to be governed by certain great moral truths. The inferences and corollaries of these truths are principles, which come of heaven. Now, agreeably to the monikin dogmas, the love of money is 'of the earth earthy;' and, at the first blush, it would not seem to be quite safe to receive such an inducement as the governing motive of one monikin, and, by a pretty fair induction, it would seem to be equally unwise to admit it for a good many. You will remember, also, that when none but the rich have authority, they control not only their own property, but that of others who have less. Your principle supposes, that in taking care of his own, the elector of wealth must take care of what belongs to the rest of the community; but our experience shows that a monikin can be particularly careful of himself, and singularly negligent of his neighbor. There fore do we hold that money is a bad foundation for power."

"You unsettle everything, Brigadier, without finding a substitute."

"Simply because it is easy to unsettle everything, and very difficult to find substitutes. But, as respects the base of society, I merely doubt the wisdom of setting up a qualification that we all know depends on an unsound principle. I much fear, Sir John, that, so long as monikins are monikins, we shall never be quite perfect; and as to your social-stake system, I am of opinion that as society is composed of all, it may be well to hear what all have to say about its management."

"Many men, and, I dare say, many monikins, are not to be trusted even with the management of their own concerns."

"Very true; but it does not follow that other men, or other monikins, will lose sight of their own interests on this account, if vested with the right to act as their substitutes. You have been long enough a legislator, now, to have got some idea how difficult it is to make even a direct and responsible representative respect entirely the interests and wishes of his constituents; and the fact will show you how little he will be likely to think of others, who believes that he acts as their master and not as their servant."

"The amount of all this, Brigadier, is that you have little faith in monikin disinterestedness, in any shape; that you believe he who is intrusted with power will abuse it; and therefore you choose to divide the trust, in order to divide the abuses; that the love of money is an 'earthy' quality, and not to be confided in as the controlling power of a state; and, finally, that the social-stake system is radically wrong, inasmuch as it is no more than carrying out a principle that is in itself defective?"

My companion gaped, like one content to leave the matter there. I wished him a good morning, and walked up stairs in quest of Noah, whose carnivorous looks had given me considerable uneasiness. The Captain was out; and, after searching for him in the streets, for an hour or two, I returned to our abode fatigued and hungry.

At no great distance from our own door, I met Judge People's Friend, shorn and dejected, and I stopped to say a kind word, before going up the ladder. It was quite impossible to see a gentleman, whom one had met in good society and in better fortunes, with every hair shaved from his body, his apology for a tail still sore from its recent amputation, and his entire mien expressive of republican humility, without a desire to condole with him. I expressed my regrets, therefore, as succinctly as possible, encouraging him with the hope of seeing a new covering of down before long, but delicately abstaining from any allusion to the *cauda*, whose loss I knew was irretrievable. To my great surprise, however, the Judge answered cheerfully; discarding, for the moment, every appearance of self-abasement and mortification.

"How is this?" I cried; "you are not then miserable!"

"Very far from it, Sir John—I never was in better spirits, or had better prospects, in my life."

I remembered the extraordinary manner in which the Brigadier had saved Noah's head, and was fully resolved not to be astonished at any manifestation of monikin ingenuity. Still I could not forbear demanding an explanation.

"Why, it may seem odd to you, Sir John, to find a politician, who is apparently in the depths of des pair, really on the eve of a glorious preferment. Such, however, is in fact my case. In Leaplow, humility is everything. The monikin who will take care and repeat sufficiently often that he is just the poorest devil going, that he is absolutely unfit for even the meanest employment in the land, and in other respects ought to be hooted out of society, may very safely consider himself in a fair way to be elevated to some of the dignities he declares himself the least fitted to fill."

"In such a case, all he will have to do, then, will be to make his choice, and denounce himself loudest touching his especial disqualifications for that very station?"

"You are apt, Sir John, and would succeed, if you would only consent to remain among us!" said the Judge, winking.

"I begin to see into your management—after all, you are neither miserable nor ashamed?"

"Not the least in the world. It is of more importance for monikins of my calibre to seem to be anything than to be it. My fellow-citizens are usually satisfied with this sacrifice; and, now Principle is eclipsed, nothing is easier."

"But how happens it, Judge, that one of your surprising dexterity and agility should be caught tripping? I had thought you particularly expert, and infallible in all the gyrations. Perhaps the little affair of the *cauda* has leaked out?"

The Judge laughed in my face.

"I see you know little of us, after all, Sir John. Here have we proscribed *caudæ*, as anti-republican, both public opinions setting their faces against them; and yet a monikin may wear one abroad a mile long with impunity, if he will just submit to a new dock when he comes home, and swear that he is the most miserable wretch going. If he can throw in a favorable word, too, touching the Leaplow cats and dogs—Lord bless you, sir! they would pardon treason!"

"I begin to comprehend your policy, Judge, if not your polity Leaplow being a popular government, it becomes necessary that its public agents should be popular too. Now, as monikins naturally delight in their own excellencies, nothing so disposes them to give credit to another, as his professions that he is worse than themselves."

The Judge nodded and grinned.

"But another word, dear sir—as you feel yourself constrained to commend the cats and dogs of Leaplow, do you belong to that school of philocats, who take their revenge for their amenity to the quadrupeds, by berating their fellow-creatures?"

The Judge started, and glanced about him as if he dreaded a thief-taker. Then earnestly imploring me to respect his situation, he added in a whisper, that the subject of the people was sacred with him, that he rarely spoke of them without a reverence, and that his favorable sentiments in relation to the cats and dogs were not dependent on any particular merits of the animals themselves, but merely because they were the people's cats and dogs. Fearful that I might say something still more disagreeable, the Judge hastened to take his leave, and I never saw him afterwards. I make no doubt, however, that in good time his hair grew as he grew again into favor, and that he found the means to exhibit the proper length of tail on all suitable occasions.

A crowd in the street now caught my attention. On approaching it, a colleague who was there was kind enough to explain its cause.

It would seem that certain Leaphighers had been

travelling in Leaplow; and, not satisfied with this liberty, they had actually written books concerning things that they had seen, and things that they had not seen. As respects the latter, neither of the public opinions was very sensitive, although many of them reflected severely on the Great National Allegory and the sacred rights of monikins; but as respects the former, there was a very lively excitement. These writers had the audacity to say that the Leaplowers had cut off all their *caudæ*, and the whole community was convulsed at an outrage so unprecedented. It was one thing to take such a step, and another to have it proclaimed to the world in books. If the Leaplowers had no tails, it was clearly their own fault. Nature had formed them with tails. They had bobbed themselves on a republican principle; and no one's principles ought to be thrown into his face, in this rude manner, more especially during a moral eclipse.

The dispensers of the essence of lopped tails threatened vengeance; caricaturists were put in requisition; some grinned, some menaced, some swore, and all read!

I left the crowd, taking the direction of my door again, pondering on this singular state of society, in which a peculiarity that had been deliberately and publicly adopted, should give rise to a sensitiveness of a character so unusual. I very well knew that men are commonly more ashamed of natural imperfections than of those which, in a great measure, depend on themselves; but then men are, in their own estimation at least, placed by nature at the head of creation, and in that capacity it is reasonable to suppose they will be jealous of their natural privileges. The present case was rather Leaplow than generic; and I could only account for it, by supposing that Nature had placed certain nerves in the wrong part of the Leaplow anatomy.

On entering the house, a strong smell of roasted meat saluted my nostrils, causing a very unphilosophical pleasure to the olfactory nerves, a pleasure which acted very directly, too, on the gastric juices of the stomach. In plain English, I had very sensible evidence that it was not enough to transport a man to the monikin region, send him to parliament and keep him on nuts for a week, to render him exclusively ethereal. I found it was vain "to kick against the pricks." The odor of roasted meat was stronger than all the facts just named, and I was fain to abandon philosophy, and surrender to the belly. I descended incontinently to the kitchen, guided by a sense no more spiritual than that which directs the hound in the chase.

On opening the door of our refectory, such a delicious perfume greeted the nose, that I melted like a romantic girl at the murmur of a waterfall, and, losing sight of all the sublime truths so lately acquired, I was guilty of the particular human weakness which is usually described as having the "mouth water."

The sealer had quite taken leave of his monikin forbearance, and was enjoying himself in a peculiarly human manner. A dish of roasted meat was lying before him, and his eyes fairly glared as he turned them from me to the viand, in a way to render it a little doubtful whether I was a welcome visiter. But that honest old principle of seamen which never refuses to share equally with an ancien messmate, got the better even of his voracity.

"Sit down, Sir John," the Captain cried, without ceasing to masticate, "and make no bones of it. To own the fact, the latter are almost as good as the flesh. I never tasted a sweeter morsel!"

I did not wait for a second invitation, the reade may be sure; and in less than ten minutes the dish was as clear as a table that had been swept by harpies. As this work is intended for one in which truth is rigidly respected, I shall avow that I do not remember any cultivation of sentiment which gave me half so much satisfaction as that short and hurried repast. I look back to it, even now, as to the very *beau idéal* of a dinner! Its fault was in the quantity, and not in quality.

I gazed greedily about for more. Just then, I caught a glimpse of a face that seemed looking at me with melancholy reproach. The truth flashed upon me in a flood of horrible remorse. Rushing upon Noah like a tiger, I seized him by the throat, nd cried, in a voice of despair:—

"Cannibal! what hast thou done?"

"Loosen your gripe, Sir John—we do not relish these hugs at Stunin'tun."

"Wretch! thou hast made me the participator of thy crime! We have eaten Brigadier Downright!"

"Loosen, Sir John, or human natur' will rebel."

"Monster! give up thy unholy repast—dost not see a million reproaches in the eyes of the innocent victim of thy insatiable appetites?"

"Cast off, Sir John, cast off, while we are friends. I care not if I have swallowed all the Brigadiers in Leaplow—off hands!"

"Never, monster! until thou disgorgest thy unholy meal!"

Noah could endure no more; but, seizing me by the throat, on the retaliating principle, I soon had some such sensations as one would be apt to feel if his gullet were in a vice. I shall not attempt to describe very minutely the miracle that followed. Hanging ought to be an effectual remedy for many delusions; for, in my case, the bow-string I was under certainly did wonders in a very short time. Gradually the whole scene changed. First came a mist, then a vertigo; and finally, as the Captain relaxed his hold, objects appeared in new forms, and instead of being in our lodgings in Bivouac, I found myself in my old apartment in the Rue de Rivoli, Paris.

"King!" exclaimed Noah, who stood before me, red in the face with exertion; "this is no boy's play, and if it's to be repeated, I shall use a lashing! Where would be the harm, Sir John, if a man had eaten a monkey?"

Astonishment kept me mute. Every object, just as I had left it the morning we started for London, on our way to Leaphigh, was there. A table, in the centre of the room, was covered with sheets of paper closely written over, which, on examination, I found contained this manuscript as far as the last chapter. Both the Captain and myself were attired as usual; I à la Parisienne, and he à la Stunin'tun. A small ship, very ingeniously made, and very accurately rigged, lay on the floor, with "Walrus" written on her stern. As my bewildered eye caught a glimpse of this vessel, Noah informed me that, having nothing to do except to look after my welfare, (a polite way of characterizing his ward over my person, as I afterwards found,) he had employed his leisure in constructing the toy.

All was inexplicable. There was really the smell of meat. I had also that peculiar sensation of fullness which is apt to succeed a dinner, and a dish well filled with bones was in plain view. I took up one of the latter, in order to ascertain its *genus*. The Captain kindly informed me that it was the remains of a pig, which it had cost him a great deal of trouble to obtain, as the French viewed the act of eating a pig but very little less heinous than the act of eating a child. Suspicions began to trouble me, and I now turned to look for the head and reproachful eye of the Brigadier.

The head was where I had just before seen it, visible over the top of a trunk; but it was so far raised as to enable me to see that it was still planted on its shoulders. A second look, enabled me to distinguish the meditative, philosophical countenance of Dr. Reasono, who was still in the hussar-jacket and petticoat, though, being in the house, he had very properly laid aside the Spanish hat with bedraggled feathers.

A movement followed in the ante-chamber, and a hurried conversation, in a low earnest tone, succeeded. The Captain disappeared, and joined the speakers. I listened intently, but could not catch any of the intonations of a dialect founded on the decimal principle. Presently the door opened, and Dr. Etherington stood before me!

The good divine regarded me long and earnestly. Tears filled his eyes, and, stretching out both hands towards me, he asked:—

"Do you know me, Jack?"

"Know you, dear sir!—Why should I not?"

"And do you forgive me, dear boy?"

"For what, sir?—I am sure, I have most reason to demand your pardon for a thousand follies."

"Ah! the letter—the unkind—the inconsiderate letter!"

"I have not had a letter from you, sir, in a twelvemonth: the last was anything but unkind."

"Though Anna wrote, it was at my dictation"

I passed a hand over my brow, and had dawnings of the truth.

"Anna?"

"Is here—in Paris,—and miserable—most miserable!—on your account."

Every particle of monikinity that was left in my system instantly gave way to a flood of human sensations.

"Let me fly to her, dear sir—a moment is an age!"

"Not just yet, my boy. We have much to say to each other, nor is she in this hotel. To-morrow, when both are better prepared; you shall meet."

"Add, never to separate, sir, and I will be patient as a lamb."

"Never to separate, I believe it will be better to say."

I hugged my venerable guardian, and found a delicious relief from a most oppressive burthen of sensations, in a flow of tears.

Dr. Etherington soon led me into a calmer tone of mind. In the course of the day, many matters were discussed and settled. I was told that Captain Poke had been a good nurse, though in a sealing fashion; and that the least I could do was to send him back to Stunin'tun, free of cost. This was agreed to, and the worthy but dogmatical mariner was promised the means of fitting out a new "Debby and Dolly."

"These philosophers had better be presented to some academy," observed the Doctor, smiling, as he pointed to the family of amiable strangers, "being already F. U. D. G. E's and H. O. A. X's. Mr. Reasono, in particular, is unfit for ordinary society."

"Do with them as you please, my more than father. Let the poor animals, however, be kept from physical suffering."

"Attention shall be paid to all their wants, both physical and moral."

"And in a day or two, we shall proceed to the rectory?"

"The day after to-morrow, if you have strength.

"And to-morrow?

"Anna will see you."

"And the next day?"

"Nay, not quite so soon, Jack; but the moment we think you perfectly restored, she shall share your fortunes for the remainder of your common probation."

CHAPTER XXX.

Explanations—A leave-taking—Love—Confessions, but no penitence.

A NIGHT of sweet repose left me refreshed, and with a pulse that denoted less agitation than on the preceding day. I awoke early, had a bath, and sent for Captain Poke to take his coffee with me, before we parted; for it had been settled, the previous evening, that he was to proceed towards Stunin'tun, forthwith. My old messmate, colleague, co-adventurer, and fellow-traveller, was not slow in obeying the summons. I confess his presence was a comfort to me, for I did not like looking at objects that had been so inexplicably replaced before my eyes, unsupported by the countenance of one who had gone through so many grave scenes in my company.

"This has been a very extraordinary voyage of ours, Captain Poke," I remarked, after the worthy sealer had swallowed sixteen eggs, an omelette, seven *cotelettes*, and divers accessaries. "Do you think of publishing your private journal?"

"Why, in my opinion, Sir John, the less that either of us says of the v'y'ge the better."

"And why so? We have had the discoveries of Columbus, Cook, Vancouver and Hudson—why not those of Captain Poke?"

"To own the truth, we sealers do not like to speak of our cruising grounds—and, as for these monikins, after all, what are they good for? A thousand of them would n't make a quart of 'ile, and by all accounts their fur is worth next to nothin'."

"Do you account their philosophy for nothing? and their jurisprudence?—you, who were so near losing your head, and who did actually lose your tail, by the axe of the executioner?"

Noah placed a hand behind him, fumbling about the seat of reason, with evident uneasiness. Satisfied that no harm had been done, he very co y placed half a muffin in what he called his ' ovision-hatchway."

"You will give me this pretty model of our good old Walrus, Captain?"

"Take it, o' Heaven's sake, Sir John, and good luck to you with it. You, who give me a full-grown schooner, will be but poorly paid with a toy."

"It's as like the dear old craft, as one pea is like another!"

"I dare say it may be. I never knew a model that had n't suthin' of the original in it."

"Well, my good shipmate, we must part You know I am to go and see the lady who is soon to be my wife, and the *diligence* will be ready to take you to Havre, before I return."

"God bless you! Sir John, God bless you!" Noah blew his nose till it rung like a French horn. I thought his little coals of eyes were glittering, too, more than common, most probably with moisture. "You're a droll navigator, and make no more of the ice than a colt makes of a rail. But though the man at the wheel is not always awake, the heart seldom sleeps."

"When the Debby and Dolly is fairly in the

water, you will do me the pleasure of letting me know it."

"Count on me, Sir John. Before we part, I have, however, a small favor to ask."

"Name it."

Here Noah drew out of his pocket a sort of *basso relievo* carved in pine. It represented Neptune armed with a harpoon instead of a trident; the Captain always contending that the god of the seas should never carry the latter, but that, in its place, he should be armed either with the weapon he had given him, or with a boat-hook. On the right of Neptune was an English gentleman holding out a bag of guineas. On the other was a female who I was told, represented the goddess of Liberty, while it was secretly a rather flattering likeness of Miss Poke. The face of Neptune was supposed to have some similitude to that of her husband. The Captain, with the modesty which is invariably the companion of merit in the arts, asked permission to have a copy of this design placed on the schooner's stern. It would have been churlish to refuse such a compliment; and I now offered Noah my hand, as the time for parting had arrived. The sealer grasped me rather tightly, and seemed disposed to say more than adieu.

"You are going to see an angel, Sir John."

"How!—Do you know anything of Miss Etherington?"

"I should be as blind as an old bum-boat else. During our late v'y'ge, I saw her often."

"This is strange!—But there is evidently something on your mind, my friend: speak freely."

"Well, then, Sir John, talk of anything but of our v'y'ge, to the dear crittur. I do not think she is quite prepared yet to hear of all the wonders we saw."

I promised to be prudent; and the Captain, shaking me cordially by the hand, finally wished me farewell. There were some rude touches of feeling in his manner, which reacted on certain chords in my own system; and he had been gone several minutes before I recollected that it was time to go to the Hotel de Castile. Too impatient to wait for the carriage, I flew along the streets on foot, believing that my own fiery speed would outstrip the zig-zag movement of a *fiacre* or a *cabriolet de place*.

Dr. Etherington met me at the door of his *appartement*, and led me to an inner room without speaking. Here he stood gazing, for some time, in my face, with parental concern.

"She expects you, Jack, and believes that you rang the bell."

"So much the better, dear sir. Let us not lose a moment; let me fly and throw myself at her feet, and implore her pardon."

"For what, my good boy?"

"For believing that any social-stake can equal that which a man feels in the nearest, dearest, ties of earth!"

The excellent rector smiled, but he wished to curb my impatience.

"You have already every stake in society, Sir John Goldencalf," he answered, assuming the air which human beings have, by a general convention, settled shall be dignified, "that any reasonable man can desire. The large fortune left by your late father, raises you, in this respect, to the height of the richest in the land; and now that you are a baronet, no one will dispute your claim to participate in the councils of the nation. It would perhaps be better, did your creation date a century or two nearer the commencement of the monarchy; but, in this age of innovations, we must take things as they are, and not as we might wish to have them."

I rubbed my forehead, for the Doctor had incidentally thrown out an embarrassing idea.

"On your principle, my dear sir, society would be obliged to begin with its great-grandfathers to qualify itself for its own government."

"Pardon me, Jack, if I have said anything disagreeable—no doubt all will come right in Heaven. Anna will be uneasy at our delay."

This suggestion drove all recollection of the good rector's social-stake system, which was exactly the converse of the social-stake system of my late ancestor, quite out of my head. Springing forward, I gave him reason to see that he would have no farther trouble in changing the subject. When we had passed an ante-chamber, he pointed to a door, and admonishing me to be prudent, withdrew.

My hand trembled as it touched the door-knob, but the lock yielded. Anna was standing in the middle of the room, (she had heard my footstep,) an image of womanly loveliness, womanly faith, and womanly feeling. By a desperate effort she was, however, mistress of her emotions. Though her pure soul seemed willing to fly to meet me, she obviously restrained the impulse, in order to spare my nerves.

"Dear Jack!"—and both her soft, white, pretty little hands met me, as I eagerly approached.

"Anna!—dearest Anna!"—I covered the rosy fingers with kisses.

"Let us be tranquil, Jack, and, if possible, endeavor to be reasonable, too."

"If I thought this could really cost one habitually discreet as you an effort, Anna!"

"One habitually discreet as I, is as likely to feel strongly on meeting an old friend, as another."

"I think it would make me perfectly happy, could I see thee weep."

As if waiting only for this hint, Anna burst into a flood of tears. I was frightened, for her sobs became hysterical and convulsed. Those precious sentiments which had been so long imprisoned in her gentle bosom, obtained the mastery, and I was well paid for my selfishness, by experiencing an alarm little less violent than her own outpouring of feeling.

Touching the incidents, emotions, and language of the next half-hour, it is not my intention to be very communicative. Anna was ingenuous, unreserved, and, if I might judge by the rosy blushes that suffused her sweet face, and the manner in which she extricated herself from my protecting arms, I believe I must add she deemed herself indiscreet in that she had been so unreserved and ingenuous.

"We can now converse more calmly, Jack," the dear creature resumed, after she had erased the signs of emotion from her cheeks—"more calmly, if not more sensibly."

"The wisdom of Solomon is not half so precious as the words I have just heard—and as for the music of the spheres——"

"It is a melody that angels only enjoy."

"And art not thou an angel!"

"No, Jack, only a poor, confiding girl; one instinct with the affections and weaknesses of her sex, and one whom it must be your part to sustain and direct. If we begin by calling each other by these superhuman epithets, we may awake from the delusion sooner than if we commence with believing ourselves to be no other than what we really are. I love you for your kind, excellent and generous heart, Jack; and as for these poetical beings, they are rather proverbial, I believe, for having no hearts at all."

As Anna mildly checked my exaggeration of language—after ten years of marriage I am unwilling to admit there was any exaggeration of idea—she placed her little velvet hand in mine again, smiling away all the severity of the reproof.

"Of one thing, I think you may rest perfectly assured, dear girl," I resumed after a moment's reflection. "All my old opinions concerning expansion and contraction are radically changed. I have carried out the principle of the social-stake system in the extreme, and cannot say that I have been at all satisfied with its success. At this moment I am the proprietor of vested interests which are scattered over half the world. So far from finding that I love my kind any more for all these social stakes, I am compelled to see that the wish to protect one, is constantly driving me into acts of injustice against all the others. There is something wrong, depend on it, Anna, in the old dogmas of the political economists!"

"I know little of these things, Sir John, but to one ignorant as myself, it would appear that the most certain security for the righteous exercise of power is to be found in just principles."

"If available, beyond a question. They who contend that the debased and ignorant are unfit to express their opinions concerning the public weal, are obliged to own that they can only be restrained by force. Now, as knowledge is power, their first precaution is to keep them ignorant; and then they quote this very ignorance, with all its debasing consequences, as an argument against their participation in authority with themselves. I believe there can be no safe medium between a frank admission of the whole principle——"

"You should remember, dear Goldencalf, that this is a subject on which I know but little. It ought to be sufficient for us that we find things as they are; if change is actually necessary, we should endeavor to effect it with prudence and a proper regard to justice."

Anna, while kindly leading me back from my speculations, looked both anxious and pained.

"True—true"—I hurriedly rejoined, for a world would not tempt me to prolong her suffering for a moment. "I am foolish and forgetful, to be talking thus, at such a moment; but I have endured too much to be altogether unmindful of ancient theories. I thought it might be grateful to you, at least, to know, Anna, that I have ceased to look for happiness in my affections for all, and am only so much the better disposed to turn in search of it to one."

"To love our neighbor as ourself, is the latest and highest of the divine commands," the dear girl answered, looking a thousand times more lovely than ever, for my conclusion was very far from being displeasing to her. "I do not know that this object is to be attained by centering in our persons as many of the goods of life as possible; but I do think, Jack, that the heart which loves one truly, will be so much the better disposed to entertain kind feelings towards all others."

I kissed the hand she had given me, and we now began to talk a little more like people of the world, concerning our movements. The interview lasted an hour longer, when the good Doctor interposed and sent me home, to prepare for our return to England.

In a week we were again in the old island. Anna

and her father proceeded to the rectory, while I was left in town, busied with lawyers, and looking after the results of my numerous investments.

Contrary to what many people will be apt to suppose, most of them had been successful. On the whole, I was richer for the adventures; and with such prospects accompanying the risks, I had little difficulty in disposing of them to advantage. The proceeds, together with a large balance of dividends that had accrued during my absence, was lodged with my banker, and I advertised for further landed property.

Knowing the taste of Anna, I purchased one of those town residences which look out on St. James's Park, where the sight of fragrant shrubbery and verdant fields will be constantly before her serene eyes, during the period of what is called a London winter,—or from the Easter holidays to midsummer.

I had a long and friendly interview with my Lord Pledge, who was not a man to abandon a ministry, but who continued in place just as active, as respectable, as logical and as useful as ever. Indeed, so conspicuous was he for the third of these qualities, that I caught myself peeping, once or twice, to see if he were actually destitute of a *cauda*. He gave me the comfortable assurance that all had gone on well in parliament during my absence, politely intimating, at the same time, that he did not believe I had been missed. We settled certain preliminaries together, which will be explained in the next chapter; when I hurried, on the wings of love, alias, in a post-chaise and four, towards the rectory, and to the sweetest, kindest, gentlest, truest girl in an island which has so many of the sweet, the kind, the gentle and the true.

CHAPTER XXXI.

Bliss—The best investment in society—The result of much experience, and The End.

THAT day two months found me at the rectory of Tenthpig, the happiest man in England. The season had advanced to the middle of July, and the shrubbery near the bow-window of my excellent father-in-law's library, was in full verdure. The plant, in particular, whose flowers had so well emulated the bloom of Anna's cheek, was rioting in the luxuriance of renewed fertility, its odors stealing gently over the senses of my young wife and myself, as we sat alone, enjoying the holy calm of a fine summer morning, and that delicious happiness which is apt to render the bliss of the first months of a well-assorted union almost palpable.

Anna was seated so near the window that the tints of the rose-bush suffused her spotless robe, rendering her whole figure a perfect picture of that attractive creature the poets have so often sung—a blushing bride. The quiet light had to traverse a wilderness of sweets before it fell on her bland features, every polished lineament of which was eloquent of felicity, and yet, if it be not a contradiction, I would also add, not entirely without the shadows of thought. She was never more lovely, and I had never known her so subdued and tender, as within the last half-hour. We had been speaking, without reserve, of the past, and Anna had just faithfully described the extreme suffering with which she had complied with the command of the good rector, in writing the letter that had so completely unmanned me.

"I ought to have known you better, love, than to

suspect you of the act," I rejoined to one of her earnest protestations of regret, and gazing fondly into those eyes which have so much of the serenity, as they have the hues, of heaven. "You never yet were so unkind to one who was offensive; much less could you willingly have plotted this cruelty to one you regard!"

Anna could no longer control herself, but her cheeks were wetted with the usual signs of feeling in her sex. Then smiling in the midst of this little outbreaking of womanly sensibility, her countenance became playful and radiant.

"That letter ought not to be altogether proscribed, neither, Jack. Had it not been written, you would never have visited Leaphigh, nor Leaplow, nor have seen any of those wonderful spectacles which are here recorded."

The dear creature laid her hand on a roll of manuscript which she had just returned to me, after its perusal. At the same time, her face flushed, as vivid and transient feelings are reflected from the features of the innocent and ingenuous, and she made a faint effort to laugh.

I passed a hand over my brow, for whenever this subject is alluded to between us, I invariably feel that there is a species of mistiness, in and about the region of thought. I was not displeased, however, for I knew that a heart which loved so truly would not willingly cause me pain, nor would one habitually so gentle and considerate, utter a syllable that she might have reason to think would seriously displease.

"Hadst thou been with me, love, that journey would always be remembered as one of the pleasantest events of my life; for, while it had its perils and its disagreeables, it had also its moments of extreme satisfaction."

"You will never be an adept in political saltation, John!"

"Perhaps not—but here is a document that will render it less necessary than formerly."

I threw her a packet which had been received that morning from town, by a special messenger but of whose contents I had not yet spoken. Anna was too young a wife to open it without an approving look from my fond eye. On glancing over its contents, she perceived that I was raised to the House of Peers by the title of Viscount Householder. The purchase of three more boroughs, and the influence of my old friend Lord Pledge, had done it all.

The sweet girl looked pleased, for I believe it is in female nature to like to be a Viscountess; but, throwing herself into my arms, she protested that her joy was at my elevation and not at her own.

"I owed you this effort, Anna, as some acknowledgment for your faith and disinterestedness in the affair of Lord M'Dee."

"And yet, Jack, he had neither high cheek-bones, nor red hair; and his accent was such as might please a girl less capricious than myself!"

This was said playfully and coquettishly, but in a way to make me feel how near folly would have been to depriving me of a treasure, had the heart I so much prized been less ingenuous and pure. I drew the dear creature to my bosom, as if afraid my rival might yet rob me of her possession. Anna looked up, smiling through her tears; and, making an effort to be calm, she said, in a voice so smothered as to prove how delicate she felt the subject to be:—

"We will speak seldom of this journey, dear John, and try to think of the long and dark journey which is yet before us. We will speak of it, how ever, for there should be nothing totally concealed between us."

I kissed her serene and humid eyes, and repeated what she had just said, syllable for syllable. Anna has not been unmindful of her words; for rarely, indeed, has she touched on the past, and then oftener in allusion to her own sorrows, than in reference to my impressions.

But, while the subject of my voyage to the monikin region is, in a measure, forbidden between me and my wife, there exists no such restraint as between me and other people. The reader may like to know, therefore, what effect this extraordinary adventure has left on my mind, after an interval of ten years.

There have been moments when the whole has appeared a dream; but, on looking back, and comparing it with other scenes in which I have been an actor, I cannot perceive that this is not quite as indelibly stamped on my memory as those. The facts themselves, moreover, are so very like what I see daily in the course of occurrence around me, that I have come to the conclusion, I did go to Leaphigh in the way related, and that I must have been brought back during the temporary insanity of a fever. I believe, therefore, that there are such countries as Leaphigh and Leaplow; and after much thought, I am of opinion that great justice has here been done to the monikin character in general.

The result of much meditation on what I witnessed, has been to produce sundry material change in my former opinions, and to unsettle even many of the notions in which I may be said to have been born and bred. In order to consume as little of the reader's time as possible, I shall set down a summary of my conclusions, and then take my leave of him, with many thanks for his politeness in reading what I have written. Before completing my task in this way, however, it will be well to add a word on the subject of one or two of my fellow-travellers.

I never could make up my mind relating to the fact whether we did or did not actually eat Brigadier Downright. The flesh was so savory, and it tasted so delicious after a week of philosophical meditation on nuts, and the recollection of its pleasures is so very vivid, that I am inclined to think nothing but a good material dinner could have left behind it impressions so lively. I have had many melancholy thoughts on this subject, especially in November; but observing that men are constantly devouring each other, in one shape or another, I endeavor to make the best of it, and to persuade myself that a slight difference in species may exonerate me from the imputation of cannibalism.

I often get letters from Captain Poke. He is not very explicit on the subject of our voyage, it is true; but, on the whole, I have decided that the little ship he constructed was built on the model of, and named after, our own Walrus, instead of our own Walrus being built on the model of, and named after, the little ship constructed by Captain Poke. I keep the latter, therefore, to show my friends as a proof of what I tell them, knowing the importance of visible testimony with ordinary minds.

As for Bob and the mates, I never heard any more of them. The former most probably continued a "*kickee*," until years and experience enabled him to turn the tables on humanity, when, as is usually the case with Christians, he would be very likely to take up the business of a "kicker" with so much the greater zeal, on account of his early sufferings.

To conclude, my own adventures and observations lead to the following inferences, viz.—

That every man loves liberty for his own sake and very few for the sake of other people.

That moral saltation is very necessary to political success at Leaplow, and quite probably in many other places.

That civilization is very arbitrary, meaning one thing in France, another thing at Leaphigh, and still a third in Dorsetshire.

That there is no sensible difference between motives in the polar region and motives anywhere else.

That truth is a comparative and local property, being much influenced by circumstances; particularly by climate and by different public opinions.

That there is no portion of human wisdom so select and faultless that it does not contain the seeds of its own refutation.

That of all the 'ocracies, (aristocracy and democracy included) hypocrisy is the most flourishing.

That he who is in the clutches of the law may think himself lucky if he escape with the loss of his tail.

That liberty is a convertible term, which means exclusive privileges in one country, no privileges in another, and *inclusive* privileges in all.

That religion is a paradox, in which self-denial and humility are proposed as tenets, in direct contradiction to every man's senses.

That *phrenology* and *caudology* are sister sciences, one being quite as demonstrable as the other, and more too.

That philosophy, sound principles, and virtue, are really delightful; but, after all, that they are no more than so many slaves of the belly; a man usually preferring to eat his best friend to starving.

That a little wheel and a great wheel are as necessary to the motion of a commonwealth, as to the motion of a stage-coach, and that what this gains in periphery that makes up in activity, on the rotatory principle.

That it is one thing to have a king, another to have a throne, and another to have neither.

That the reasoning which is drawn from particular abuses, is no reasoning for general uses.

That, in England, if we did not use blinkers, our cattle would break our necks; whereas, in Germany we travel at a good pace, allowing the horse the use of his eyes; and in Naples we fly, without even a bit!

That the converse of what has just been said of horses is true of men, in the three countries named.

That occultations of truth are just as certain as the aurora borealis, and quite as easily accounted for.

That men who will not shrink from the danger and toil of penetrating the polar basin, will shrink from the trouble of doing their own thinking, and put themselves, like Captain Poke, under the convoy of a God-like.

That all our wisdom is insufficient to protect us from frauds, one outwitting us by gyrations and flapjacks, and another by adding new joints to the *cauda*.

That men are not very scrupulous touching the humility due to God, but are so tenacious of their own privileges in this particular, they will confide in plausible rogues rather than in plain-dealing honesty

That they who rightly appreciate the foregoing facts, are People's Friends, and become the salt of the earth—yea, even the Most Patriotic Patriots!

That it is fortunate "all will come right in Hea

CPSIA information can be obtained
at www.ICGtesting.com
Printed in the USA
LVHW040719020323
740708LV00002B/70

9 783382 114152